TALES OF TH

TALES
of
THE SAMURAI

Stories of Old Japan
BOOK 1

By

Roald Knutsen

RENAISSANCE BOOKS

TALES OF THE SAMURAI
STORIES OF OLD JAPAN:
Book 1
by Roald Knutsen

First published 2012 by
RENAISSANCE BOOKS
PO Box 219
Folkestone
Kent CT20 2WP

Renaissance Books is an imprint of Global Books Ltd

ISBN 978-1-898823-02-5

British Library Cataloguing in Publication Data

A CIP catalogue entry for this book is available from the British Library

Set in Bembo11 on 11.5 by Dataworks, Chennai, India
Printed in the EU by Scandinavian Book

For Pat and Susan

Life is a lying dream,
he only wakes
Who casts the World aside.
Seami (Fourteenth Century)

CONTENTS

PREFACE

Whilst all these idle tales are to be regarded as fiction – although who can really tell? – they are presented in the hope that they will help give what is now the distant medieval past of a remote culture some warmth and vitality. All the tales are from the pen of a swordsman who has immersed himself in these warrior traditions for well over half-a-century; the initial inspiration deriving from the presentation of *'Yamato-damashii'*, the 'Spirit of Old Japan' contained in the enthusiastic translations and writings about the samurai by a number of late-nineteenth century scholars. However, those accounts, although very good and of great interest to many, seemed to romanticize the past rather than present it as it truly was; in other words they often lacked a certain realism or, as the Japanese might put it, a feeling of *'jidai-geki'*. The author also acknowledges a enduring debt to the insights to warrior life expressed cinematically by Kurosawa Akira. The occasional violent encounters described in these pages must be viewed as inevitable in such a warlike society as that of the samurai, but it should also be remembered that many of these warriors governed their lives by strict moral codes and, for some, a total belief in the powers of the female war deity, Marishi-ten. It was from the latter and her 'messengers', the *tengu*, that they derived their martial skills. The pieces presented here, some quite short and others rather longer, are set across the best part of a thousand years, ending during the final upheavals of the mid-sixteenth century. They have no real substance, despite the occasional textual claims to the contrary, and are, at best, quasi-historical records; like darting dragonflies playing over a placid lily pond, they may divert the reader with a few moments of pleasure by providing a window on times now long past.

Roald Knutsen
Summer, 2011

1

HOLDING THE PASS

'Torii Masamori!'

'My lord?'

'You have served me devotedly through many years of adversity.'

'It was my duty.'

The Prince permitted a slight smile to play around his mouth.

'It was also the duty of others, yet few haven't hesitated to change sides when it suited them to do so. Why did you not do the same? There have been many opportunities.'

'Should I answer that question, my lord?'

The August Prince of the Great Pagoda gave him a shrewd look and sighed.

'I have asked you to remain after the council to request a last service. As you know, matters are now serious and I must withdraw from these mountains with all haste . . .'

The Prince hesitated in talking for so long that Masanori said: 'Sir, please ask what you will.'

'At the Hour of the Rat I intend to lead our forces away from this stronghold. It is important that we have as much time as possible to distance ourselves from pursuit in order to reach the southern capital. You understand my meaning?'

'I understand, my lord. Please march at midnight. You will not be followed before the beginning of the Hour of the Horse.'

'Your loyalty will be remembered,' said the Honourable Prince with tears in his eyes. 'If I live, I shall offer prayers to the Buddha on your behalf.' He took up a small gourd of fine ō-sake and a delicate cup from four on a whitewood tray to offer Masamori a parting drink, a signal honour.

And so it was that the August Prince slipped out of that fortress in Yoshino accompanied by four-hundred-and-fifty brave warriors. It was at midnight in the warm spring of that year. Torii Masanori and just five of his faithful housemen remained behind watching their lord ride forth and brushing away the salt tears for they all knew that they would not see him again in this Middle World.

About the middle watch of the night His Highness reached the billowing waters of the Kinogawa and in fording the stream looked back through the break between the swelling mountains to behold flames rising from the distant heights.

'Can it be that the fortress has already been taken; overwhelmed by the enemy hordes?'

One of the boldest of his escort, the brave Kidera Sagami, stood up in his wide stirrups and said: 'If that is our stronghold in flames then it was not by the hand of the enemy but by torches set to the timbers by Torii Shimotsuke-no-jō.'

'Sir, my father would not fall so easily!' The speaker was Morichiyō, the young son of Masamori, who had been forbidden to remain behind by his father and on that last evening had been adopted by Kidera Sagami.

'Yet the flames are fierce.'

Kidera spoke up harshly.

'How regrettable it is that His Highness should even think of subduing the provinces with such a weak spirit! The Deputy Governor of Southern Shimotsuke has said that he will bar the way after us for many hours. That he will do so, I have no doubt! Yet His Highness cannot think of using the opportunity properly!'

Morichiyō turned his horse and shouted out in a clear voice, for he was not yet twelve: 'This way leads to Nara and our friends; that way leads to Hell and defeat!'

'This child is right! His father will succeed!'

The Prince pulled at the striped reins and the troop continued on its way northwards without another glance at the sad pyre far behind them.

Almost as soon as the August Prince had passed out through the small postern gate to wend his way down the tortuous path into the gorge, Torii Masamori had begun his preparations for the defensive battle. Together, his five strong followers and he set about tearing up the fine tatami mats, brocade-edged with the finest gold thread; piling them against the unhung shōji partitions in that once beautiful mansion. If the enemy had launched themselves to an assault at that moment they would have found only straw figures clad in armour to oppose them; ghosts of the valiant defenders standing frozen still beneath their banners tied to bushes and trees!

In the course of one short hour the Torii *kerai* had, with heavy spirits, wreaked untold damage to the fine mansion. It presented a forlorn sight, stripped and ravaged from its former elegance, but at last Masamori was satisfied that all was prepared. He and his followers were not the only ones to destroy the tranquillity of that well-proportioned yashiki for in some places the enemy assaults had sent arrows even to the very centre of the spacious rooms, their barbed tips splintering cedarwood pillars and leaving their broken shafts still embedded where they struck.

'Saburō-sama, are the enemy moving?'

'No movement . . . no, none at all, sir,' came the reply.

For the two previous days the Yamashirō Lay Monk had sent his men up the precipitous slopes to battle for this gateway, but each time they were forced to withdraw in haste under the withering arrows of the defenders. Many a brave warrior, hoping to secure praise and advancement, had died below these smoke-blackened timbers, their pale swollen corpses lit up by the flaring braziers Saburō had kindled as darkness fell.

The two bushi peered down the mountainside at the campfires that flickered and glowed just two or three bowshots distant.

'So close, yet so far!'

'That is true, my lord; but it takes a resolute man to climb that path against our bows!'

'Not any more! If only they knew that they could walk up here and the yashiki would be theirs for nothing! Time we were going, Saburō-sama; there is one last trick to mislead their general.'

'My lord?'

Masamori laughed. 'I have something in mind. Follow me.'

When they reached the main hall, Torii Masamori ordered that the body of one of the warriors who had fallen only that afternoon should be brought to the eastern high place and stripped of armour. His men looked one at the other.

'This is no dishonour, my friends. The soul of this valorous bushi is doubtless waiting at the gates of the other world to accompany and serve his still living lord when at last he deigns to depart this Middle World. How happy his spirit will feel when he knows that his now discarded corpse will still be able to render service to His Highness?' He turned to Saburō: 'Tie this *waidate* to the body.' He handed a fine gold-encrusted piece of body armour to the surprised retainer.

'But it is part of the August Commander's armour, sir . . ?'

'That is so!'

'An honour, indeed!' growled Saburō, as he secured the green printed leather shoulder straps.

'Now remove his head!'

'Uh?'

'Cut off his head . . . this must not be found!'

The headless man was carefully positioned kneeling on a round mat with the right hand grasping a fine dagger, the blade of which had gashed the white belly. Fresh blood was splashed about. The body was allowed to sink forwards and lay on its right shoulder, exactly as if the samurai had committed suicide as a final act of defiance. By this strategm Masamori hoped that when the Yamashirō Lay Monk was informed of the discovery, he might be misled to thinking that this was indeed the corpse of His Highness.

When the other bodies had been similarly prepared, Masamori ordered: 'Put torches all around and burn the yashiki! They must think that we are on our way to the other world.'

Like so many wraiths, the six warriors slipped out of the little postern gateway leaving behind them the coiling smoke from the fires that would soon reduce the fort to worthless ash. Out of respect for the unknown warrior who posthumously served the Honourable Prince, his head was borne with them in a headbox and would be buried with due honour if the opportunity arose.

Torii Shimotsuke-no-jō Masamori pulled at the striped reins of his horse and the animal leapt and lurched up the steep bank of the Yoshinogawa. He waited for the rest of his small band to follow. Under the setting moon the men looked grim enough, but pitifully few for the task they had been set.

'It is here,' announced Masamori, 'that we commence our defence. Fell three trees and drag their branches to this bank. Saburō, please bring those four wooden shields from the pack horse . . .'

As the pale moonlight faded behind the nearby ridge the first of the makeshift barricades was already in place; two of the kerai anchoring them firmly with roughly hewn stakes driven hard into the ground using the heavy wooden war-mallet carried by one of the men, a giant of a fellow named Denzaemon.

Every man in the band knew that he had reached the very last page in his life and each exhalted that he had been favoured to serve his master's lord in a manner that would bring lasting honour to their name and to their descendants. As it is said: for the bushi there was one way only; to face death unflinchingly.

With the last of the wooden shields positioned, Saburō stood forward and knelt on the hard ground.

'My lord, my family have received countless valuable favours from your line and have been quite unable to repay them as is right and proper. I hold in my hand this strong Kantō bow and my right arm aches to draw its string back to my ear and loose my arrows at your enemies. I request that I should be selected to remain here at this place.'

'Ah, Saburō-dono, your petition is granted, though my heart is heavy to leave you here alone. I had hoped that we would be able to fight our last battle shoulder to shoulder. But, know, the name of Ichikawa Saburō will live forever!'

The warrior bowed his head in deep respect.

'Although you will go on, master, I shall resist the enemy like a rock amidst breaking waves. It will be a long time before the tide sweeps over me!'

As they departed, Ichikawa Saburō had undone two spare bundles of sharp-pointed arrows and set them conveniently upright before him in the ground. Masamori knew that his redoubtable follower, who had served him well through many wars, was not a man to give in easily, nor was he one who would foolishly seek vainglory in an arrow exchange trying to transfix only the enemy general with his hawk-fletched shaft. His unerring aim would send many a careless warrior to the abyss of eternity before he decided that it was time to go, too.

Beyond the river the way was narrow and strewn with fallen boulders, recently dislodged from the soaring heights above by the earthquake deity. With the night skies in the east paling before the coming dawn, the bushi picked their way to a place where they knew that the mountain road climbed steeply to a humped bridge that spanned a water-cut cleft. It was here that Masamori proposed to make his last stand, knowing that their enemies either had to force a passage or face a long detour if they wished to continue the pursuit.

Seemingly a long way off in the direction they had travelled the burning yashiki still lit up the heights; they could no longer see the actual flames because of the intervening mountainside; only Ichikawa Saburō, waiting alone by the river below, would have a clear view that would soon fade as the dawn light strengthened.

The sun was halfway to its full height when the first calls of the enemy conchshell horns echoed through the valley.

'It seems that our ruse has been discovered! They are gathering!'

'Ichikawa-sama is readying himself, master. See, he is stringing his bow.'

Sure enough, the brave man had waxed a fresh bowstring and was bending back the powerful bow across his braced left thigh.

'Ah, he has seen something!'

Masamori grunted and nodded. He had recognized a further call from the horagai.

'They are on their way, that's true. Ichikawa will put on his helmet in a minute or two!'

Their position beyond the bridge gave them a clear view upstream to the lone warrior standing by the ford. He was a little less than a quarter-of-a-mle away but in the pure air his every movement was easily seen.

'Time to remove the ties from these foot timbers.'

'All is ready, my lord,' reported Akihide Hyōsuke, whose brother, Koichirō, was another member of the little group.

'See, Ichikawa-sama dons his *kabutō*!' Kataoka called down from his vantage point by the lone camphor tree above the track.

'Make your preparations, my friends, for the moment has come.' Masamori took a short drink from the dipper of water offered him by his youngest follower, Matsuo Shinzaemon. The pure water tasted like nectar.

'You are a young man, Shinzaemon; a mere youth. Last night you stepped forward to request to remain with me on this duty. Your life has hardly begun yet you would discard it lightly?'

'My lord, it is impossible for me to foretell what may happen in the future. By not knowing, I have no regrets in remaining to fight here for I cannot tell if my life will be good or bad. But this I do know, I must fight here because you have need of me and it is the duty of the warrior to follow his lord.'

'Bravely said!'

The five men completed checking their armour cords and securing their strong helmets of rivetted iron around their chins. With care all five recrossed the loosened timbers of the small bridge and took up their positions amongst the jumbled rocks where the road finished climbing at the top of the steep incline.

Ichikawa Saburō stood resolute behind the larger of his breastwork shields. He had arranged the three *tate* so that his front and left side were protected by the upright ones, but he placed the third on the right on its side. Long before the enemy appeared he could hear the drum of their horses' hooves. Methodically, he nocked a bulbous signal arrow. The first white banners appeared beyond the rocks and coarse scrub bushes. Round the bend in the stony track swept the vanguard of the Yamashirō Lay-Monk's force.

Almost at once they were aware that the ford ahead was defended and men and horses pulled up in some confusion. As order was restored they realized that only one man barred their passage. Those at the rear hooted with laughter at the discomforture of their fellows.

'Who will be the first who dares cross these shallow waters and fall before the emblem of the brave Kusunoki?' Thus shouted Ichikawa. He referred, of course, to the crest of the famed general who had remained so faithful a supporter of His Highness the Prince. A flower floating on the billowing waves . . .

An officer wearing a vermillion-laced harness rode forwards and shouted: 'Who is the man that speaks?'

'I am Ichikawa Saburō, one of the *roto* of my lord, Torii Shimotsuke-no-jō Masamori; the descendant of many brave generations of Genji!'

'I, too, am of the Genji line; Mitaka Hanzaemon, son of the Ise Intendant. I shall kill you and present your head as a gift to my lord!'

Mitaka Hanzaemon clapped his heavy stirrups into his horse's flanks and as the animal leapt forwards, drew forth his bright-forged blade. But hardly had he reached the steep bank when he fell backwards from his saddle as the singing arrow pierced him full through his mouth.

A groan went up from the watching squadron, followed at once by a shout of anger. Two more men pushed forward out of the milling throng and galloped towards the ford, each bravely loosing arrows as they sped along.

'It is not enough,' shouted Ichikawa, and in rapid succession he sent feathered shafts into the throats of the horses, each barbed point sinking deep into the animals' vitals so that they took a few steps and stumbled to their knees. One after the other the two thrown riders came to their feet only to be pierced by the well-aimed shots from the warrior's black bound Kantō bow.

'Shoot the impudent fellow down immediately!' ordered the angry Yamashirō Lay Monk, his round face empurpled with rage at being held up by a single stubborn foe. As if in reply his sleeve was suddenly transfixed by one of Saburō's shafts and the general decided that he had best retire a short way, not without a disapproving smile or two from his already jaded followers for they could see in that retreat none of the authority they might have expected.

'Kill him . . . Destroy him!' blustered the commander. 'Is one man to hold up the advance of the Imperial army?'

But there was a certain reluctance on the part of his men, and seeing this, Ichikawa Saburō threw back his head and bellowed with mocking laughter.

'What, has the Honourable Commander lost his nerve? Has he not enough power to overwhelm the mighty enemy force that awaits him across the raging waters of this wide river?'

His taunting peals of bitter mirth echoed around the valley sides and could clearly be heard by the watching Masamori and his companions.

Stung by the barbed words that implied cowardice and realizing that he was in danger of losing his prestige, the general renewed his grip upon his bow and drew out two shafts from his deekskin quiver that was embellished with a golden dragonfly. Fitting one shaft to his waxed bowstring, he shouted: 'You are a bushi of the Torii clan? You are hardly worthy of my attack!'

'Not worthy? You forfeited worthiness, my lord, when you sought shelter just a moment ago! Either you must overcome Ichikawa Saburō or your brave followers will melt away like the spring snows!'

The Yamashirō Lay Monk knew that this was true for the long reverses his army had suffered during the protracted siege had caused many warriors to return to their homes sensing that there was little glory to be found in these mountain wastes. There would be few rewards, too, even if they were victorious. He pulled back his bowstring to his right ear, but before his elegantly gloved fingers could open, his horse, alarmed by something, threw down its head and lashed out. The arrow, prematurely released, struck the surface of the river and glanced away harmlessly far to Saburō's left side.

O, inauspicious! The general regained control and kicked his animal forward. Realizing that something positive must be done, two of his retinue joined him.

Saburō loosed his second arrow and it lodged deep in the Lay Monk's shoulder. Laying down his bow, he caught up his formidable halberd.

'Remember the name of Ichikawa Saburō,' he roared out, 'and fear the bushi of Shimotsuke province!'

Whirling his heavy weapon about his head he stood awaiting the charge.

Nor was he disappointed. With the general in the lead the three bushi reached the shallow Yoshinogawa and plunged into the foaming waters. Awaiting them, beside his shieldworks, stood the lone warrior. Now, the river swung round in a tight bend at this fording place, the sole safe crossing for some distance. At first the waters were shallow but when the general's horse came to the final seven or eight paces the bottom shelved away, scoured by the force of the leaping mountain torrent, and there was a sharp climb up the bank that was now guarded by the resolute samurai.

The trenchant naginata spun like a waterwheel and as the Yamashirō Lay Monk attempted to struggle up the blade cut upwards to pass easily through his outstretched left leg, slicing open the animal's belly beneath the tigerskin blanket and up to sever the general's great artery in his left groin. With a dreadful shriek of anguish the unfortunate commander fell out of his blood-soaked saddle into the cold waters of the river and his horse, entrails spilling out, leapt upwards and crashed back onto him in a foam of reddened spray. The following bushi, their mounts confused by the dramatic action, were unable to stop and they, too, paid the penalty when they gave up their lives to that demonic halberd.

Something had to be done to force a crossing and several men had run down to the river shallows behind the horsemen. Recalling accounts of the renowned Saitō Musashi-bō Benkei who likewise held a river crossing for almost a whole day although he was, in fact, stone dead, they determined to shoot their arrows into this Kantō bushi and finish the affair without further delay.

With many shafts lodged in his harness, Saburō threw himself behind his shield catching up his bow and began to shoot from kneeling. He loosed with a deadly accuracy just as if he were showing his prowess at a shrine or in his lord's practice butts. Yet he knew that there could be but one outcome to such an unequal contest. In a final rage a solid pack of at least ten samurai swept forwards across the waters. Taking one last shot into the closed ranks, Ishikawa Saburō drew out his fine tachi and placing the point in his mouth, fell onto his sword and died before the first man reached the bank, the keen blade driven through his head to lodge beneath his helmet bowl.

'Make every arrow tell,' ordered Masamori. 'We shall fight as the men who faced the barbarian Mongols learned and not in the traditional manner of our ancestors!'

'Lord,' cried out Akihide Koichirō, 'what are we to do when our arrows are spent?'

'Follow the example shown by Ishikawa Saburō! That will please his fierce spirit who even now stands beside us and waits to accompany you to hell!'

Someone chuckled. 'That road will be crowded this day . . ! I hope that Emma-ō has made it wide enough!'

'Oh, he is sure to have worked hard once he realized that it was us here in these mountains!'

They all joined in the grim laughter. Below them the whole enemy force had crossed the ford past the corpse of their brave friend. The vanguard must now be just below the turn in the track that would bring them both into sight and, more importantly, just into bowshot of the waiting Torii.

The youthful Matsuo Shinzaemon called out: 'Torii-sama, someone comes from the north.'

'You hear something?'

'It is a horseman, sir.'

'Just one?' said the bushi, surprised.

'That is so . . . at least, I think I am right.'

'Then it must be a friend! I will hazard a guess. It will be the incomparable Kidera Sagami!'

There was no time to wait to see if he was correct. The leading enemy warriors had already rounded the corner and were swarming up the steep track. Those in the lead realized that the heights were defended but were unable to stop through the pressure of those behind. The first Torii shafts flashed downwards venomously and men began to fall.

'Shinzaemon-san! Run back to the bridge and warn Kidera Sagami-sama of the loose timbers. Hurry!'

The lad dashed off and reached the nearside bank just as Kidera jumped from his sweating mount.

'Sir, my master welcomes you . . . for he realized who was coming. Please take . . .'

'Take care, lad? Oh, I know very well what my comrade will have done!'

Kidera stretched out his long bow for the youth to steady him and lightly stepped across the moving planks.

'Come on, boy; we have work to do!'

Despite taking seemingly limitless losses, the enemy forced their way further and further up the track. They had sent down for Ishikawa's arrow-riddled shields and when these arrived some of their bravest scrambled upwards a foot or a yard at a time, advancing the breastworks; the others following on as best they could.

With the Torii arrows nearly exhausted, these Imperial bushi would soon realize that they were not being shot at as often as at first; then they would gather themselves for a final assault. Judging that the time had come, Masamori raised his long-handled war fan as a signal to Akihide Denzaemon and he and his *rōtō* began to fall back towards the bridge.

'What, retreat, Torii-sama?' growled Kidera in surprise.

'Retreat, yes! Give up, no!' came the reply. The war fan swept down. High above them the Akihide brothers threw themselves at some piled boulders.

'So that's your plan, eh?'

'Come, Kidera-sama; we're hardly finished yet!'

Already the straining sinews of Denzaemon was unbalancing the largest rock. Both brothers heaved with all their might and the rock moved slightly. Hyōsuke leapt out from behind and slid round to the base where he began to prize out some smaller stones with his dirk. Four or five arrows from below bounced off the cliff beside him but three others found their marks . . . The boulder lurched and rolled over crushing the warrior's foot before bouncing out into space and smashing down into the awestruck men below, With frantic, almost superhuman, effort, Denzaemon heaved down rock after rock before he shouted out: 'See how the Torii can die! I am Denzaemon Koichirō and I follow my brother, Hyōsuke . . .'

His deep-throated shout was lost in the roar of the enemy thrown again into confusion and disarray by the missiles and the sword-brandishing warrior who hurtled into them from the cliffs above.

One after another, the retreating Torii tore up the second half of the bridge timbers. They left in place the ones on the enemy side. Hardly had the last footplank been cast down into the deep ravine that their pursuers spilled out onto the narrow approach. The four survivors shot their last arrows before retiring to the shelter of three gnarled and ancient pine trees that somehow managed to cling to life in that wind-torn spot.

'I shall defend first,' declared Kataoka Ichiemon in a resolute voice, but they could all see that he had been severely wounded several times and that his green and white laced *dō-maru* armour was heavily stained with blood.

'Kataoka-dono . . .' began Masamori, 'you cannot . . .'

'Foregive my rudeness, your lordship, but I not only can, but I will!'

Drawing out his long sword, Ichiemon stepped onto the left hand support of the bridge and shouted out that he was waiting. An arrow streaked across the abyss but fell at his feet, broken in two by his ready blade. Another followed but he took no notice for it was ill-aimed. Five or six more came together and his whirling sword seemed to brush them aside . . . but he was, at last, trasfixed through the left forearm and forced to use his tachi with only his right hand. Seeing that this was the final moment, he stepped onto the loose timbers and lightly jumped to the further side . . . More arrows, aimed now at a target that no one could miss, pierced him and he slowly crumpled to his knees. A samurai ran forwards to take his head but with one last effort, Ichiemon struck upwards and the tempered blade cut open his attacker's belly from groin to hip. Together, both men's spirits departed this life.

The enemy troops, perhaps gathering courage, pushed forward and the first man stepped out onto the bridge. This time they found themselves facing the youthful Matsu Shinzaemon.

'So we only have boys to deal with now?' they shouted, rudely.

'It is true that I have only just received my adult name, but none will forget Matsu Shinzaemon!'

He rushed forwards into their midst, a move that took them completely by surprise, and siezed three men by their armour cords, flinging his weight to the right. The struggling quartet hardly moved for a moment but one of those behind stepped in to assist his comrades. Two planks up-ended with a sharp crack and all five plunged off the side and hurtled to the rocks waiting below.

'The August Prince has gained safety?' asked Masamori.

'He will soon be amongst friends at the Tōdaiji,' replied Kidera Sagami.

'In that case we have succeeded in this mission.'

'You have something else in mind?'

Torii Masamori laughed.

'I have in mind that we have by no means inflicted enough losses on these dogs of rebels for our armies to be remembered! Farewell, old comrade! Now we shall show just how a bushi should fight for his cause!'

Shoulder to shoulder they stepped forth from behind the gnarled pine trees and shouted their names. Masamori grasped a long-handled halberd with red and brown stripes down the haft; Sagami was armed with his tachi.

'Face us with your forged blades,' shouted Masamori, 'for now is the testing time!'

'How can we come to grips with you?' called the enemy commander. 'You have destroyed the bridge.'

'Is that all? A mere trifle for a warrior!'

'It is a wide and dangerous gulf. We are afraid that many will be killed by you in attempting to cross over!'

'You have two of the poisons that a warrior must overcome! Fear and doubt.' The taunt went straight to their opponent's heart.

'Your master will lose,' called the opposing commander.

'Perhaps you are right, but doubtless it will be through duplicity. Stand back,' shouted Masamori, 'we intend to come to you!'

The two warriors walked firmly across the curved supporting timbers just as if the bridge had been complete; neither man feared death on the jagged rocks below or the sharp blades of the enemy. The samurai fell back in awe for these men seemed almost superhuman in what they had achieved that day.

'Join us, Torii-dono, and my master will surely reward you,' urged Shiba Yoshitsuna.

Masamori laughed aloud at the proposal.

'You may recall a poem by the illustrious Minamoto-no-Sanetomo? It sums up what we stand for here:

Mountains may split,
And the seas grow shallow;
But I will never
Show two faces
To my Emperor.

'That is your last word?' asked Yoshitsuna,

'It is!'

'Then there is no other course but battle!'

With a fierce shout the two warriors brandished their weapons and rushed, slashing and cutting at all who stood before them, until at last the forged steel broke in pieces. Kidera Sagami flung the stump of his sword at the nearest opponent and leapt into the mêlée flourishing his dirk. He soon vanished amidst his armoured adversaries.

Torii Masamori, in the meantime, cut a bloody swathe through the enemy ranks, sending a number over the side of the ravine as he leapt about with the swiftness of an angry tiger. All his days since he was a small child he had trained with the halberd; wielded by his powerful arms it was a formidable weapon indeed. At last he cut his way to confront the successor to the Yamashirō Lay Monk.

'Face me now, Shiba-dono, for you are a man worthy of my rank.'

The general accepted the challenge, certain that the outcome would be with him. He drew out his long sword and saw Masamori throw aside the damaged *nagamaki* and do the same. Not one of his warriors dared to intervene; custom dictated that this should be so.

Masamori had sustained a number of wounds, none of which were serious in themselves, but taken together they resulted in the loss of a great deal of blood. He knew that he only had a short space of time left and resolved that he would take the second enemy captain with him to the realms of death. Hardly had their swords clashed when he succeeded in cutting away Yoshitsuna's left shoulder guard. Angry that this had happened before his men, the general rushed upon the tiring Masamori who stood calmly awaiting the onslaught with his tachi blade horizontal at his right hip. Yoshitsuna slashed obliquely at his left neck, aiming at the narrow space between helmet and the neck flanges, but at that instant Masamori bent his knees and thrust his sword forward with a snap. As his arm reached full stretch, so the sharp tip entered beneath his enemy's arm and, with the man's impetus, passed up through his throat to emerge from the back of his neck.

The dying bushi pitched over him, wrenching the impaling weapon from his grasp. Immediately, Torii Masamori grasped the reeling man by his wide helmet guard and, using him as a shield from the arrows of his foes, he stepped backwards to the lip of the chasm.

'This is how a warrior should leave this world,' he shouted, and both men were gone forever.

2

TREACHERY

The fluctuating fortunes of the Torii family had never diminished their zeal to study military philosophy at a level that was warranted by their rank. Not that this was really enthusiasm as other people, for example, embraced such pursuits as *go*, linking verse in *renga*, or the performing skills of *Noh*; it was the necessity of life that warriors of their high position must thoroughly understand the arts of war, sure in the knowledge that there was but one clear fate that followed in the wake of defeat.

From early youth Torii Munemori had shown a precocious grasp of swordsmanship and the use of the spear. Fortunate indeed, in those years of continuous erosion of the old *bushi* values when many men saw in the weakening power of the Rokuhara a chance to advance their own material ambitions. Perhaps his father, the Constable of western Kōzuke province, had sensed that the power of the older warrior families was about to dramatically decline as the unprecedented incidence of warfare increased throughout the land. It was even like this in distant provinces, so remote that many people would regard them almost as foreign lands; warfare caused by treachery and usurpation, by naked ambition that flew in the face of the traditional and long-tested bonds of blood and true loyalties . . .

Torii Takamori, the Honourable Constable, enjoyed sufficient prestige and rice lands to attract to his banner three truly expert *shugyosha* at his Kusatsu *yashiki* to give instruction in their particular skills. One of these was a master of *tō-sō-jutsu*, a grandson of that Kabusetoki who gave the youthful Iisasa Chōisai at Katori his grounding in the art of spearmanship.When, in that year of ill-omen, 1488, the famous founder of this branch of the Shintō-ryu tradition passed away at the age of one-hundred-and-one; the grandson of Kabusetoki was only thirty-four. Another of the formidable trio was a pupil of the fifth head of the Oda-ryū who resided at Miki-jō under Tsukuba's sacred twin peaks. The third, an *umajirushi* rōnin from Dewa province in the north, was an expert with the halberd, a man of whom it was said that he could, with the greatest ease, cut the wing from a striking hawk while the bird was in full flight.

It was at Kusatsu in the old fashioned mansion so beloved of his forebears, that the children of Takamori were brought up. It was a safe place deep in the high mountains, cooled in the heat of summer by its high altitude, and warmed amidst the deep winter snows by the many hot springs that bubbled up in its valleys, The main Torii fortress was some miles to the east guarding the highway that came through the Three Province Pass and descended to the Kantō plain; lands where the laws of the Ashikaga government were largely ignored and the turmoil of warfare rose and fell like surf boiling on a rock-girt coast.

One spring, as the snows receded, two vassals of the Nagao gathered their men and attacked the lord of Minowa a few miles northeast of the Torii domain. It was far from a large affair; only a few hundred men were involved, but the result was the almost total destruction at the edge of the sword of Osumi Kage-ie, his family, and his chief retainers. The fighting surged back and forth across the Osumi lands and destruction was widespread. Many of his peasants fled for their lives into the mountains and some pitiful survivors tried to cross the closed borders to the protection of Torii Takamori, or went north into the Uesugi domains in Echigo. There was nothing remarkable in this event except that one of the refugees was the younger son of Kage-ie, a lad about the same age as Munemori. The fact that he had survived the bloody aftermath of the taking of his family mansion and that he had been closely pursued to the border by a strong group of enemy samurai, indicated that the two rebel generals were fearful that if he survived he would sooner or later seek his revenge. Therefore, according to the ethic of those days, Torii Takamori realized that by sheltering the young man he could confidently expect assassins would follow in his wake and that these secret agents would stop at nothing to achieve their ends.

The neighbouring war dragged on sporadically and destroyed by fire three more of the Osumi forts and quite soon it was reported by agents that another powerful landowner, Yamashirō Saemon, an Ashikaga adherent, was about to throw his men into battle in an attempt to wrest power from the two usurpers now that they were weakened in their successful war. An emissary from Saemon had presented himself to Torii Takamori with a proposal that the two lords become allies to their mutual advantage in dividing the rich rice lands held by the dead Osumi. He even proposed that his son might be considered a suitable match for Takamori's daughter, Hana-o. On the surface these secret proposals were attractive, but they carried the veiled threat that Osumi Kagemitsu, the youth who was now protected by Takamori, should cease to pose a problem to the future of the alliance and, further, the implication that the marriage would provide Saemon with a valuable hostage should the agreement wear thin. The latter provision was all too common in those turbulent days of mistrust and double-dealing. The messenger added that, of course, no one would expect Takamori to go back on his word over Osumi Kagemitsu; an excellent solution would be if the lad transferred to the safekeeping of his own master thereby relieving the Torii of an unsolicited commitment and at the same time ensuring that the surviving Osumi vassals would tacitly accept the land division and the new overlordship.

Torii Takamori gave no firm answer to the first messenger since he could see clearly that Yamashirō Saemon might also be seeking to combine with the two usurpers and attack him at the moment that he was weakest. He gave the emissary gifts and sent him back to his master with the promise of a reply before the coming new moon.

Hardly had the dust settled from his departure than Takamori secretly sent out the war-arrow to raise all his vassals and dependants from the valleys radiating from the fast-flowing Kusatsu river. Rumours of impending action, whether a ceremonial escort for a wedding or a full blown war, spread far and wide, attracting masterless men in their dozens until the small garrison town of Nakanojo seethed and swelled; what with the Torii kerai and the sometimes desperate rōnin, who were hoping to find employment, the population doubled, though some thought it actually trebled. Some of these drifters came with little more than their ragged clothing and weapons, singly or in gangs, but others had horses and were accompanied, on occasion, by several lower-ranking followers.

Even with the most stringent checks on the eastern borders these dangerous men managed to get through. Some were successful and were employed by the Torii but many were turned away. Others simply hung about in case hostilities should break out, knowing that then they might be welcomed into the armies, and these gathered in the poorest makeshift inns that had been set up by the even larger numbers of itinerant innkeepers and whoremasters who saw in any military adventure the chance of unchecked profit.

It was at this stage that one rōnin in particular began to attract attention. He was a big man, powerfully built, named Makino Ryūji, who claimed that he was from Hitachi province. Two days after he was first noted, word reached Takamori's brother, the chief kerai, that this Makino boasted to know both the late-Lord Osumi and of the untrustworthiness of Yamashirō Saemon. The councillor sent two of his immediate followers to locate this rōnin and sound him out. The following day the man was summoned to the Nakanojo fortress at the invitation of the Chief Councillor, Torii Hidetaka.

The audience was conducted in the second tower so as to arouse no suspicions since it was a place that would normally be under the command of a man of Hidetaka's rank, but behind a loose panelled wall sat both Takamori and the youthful Osumi Kagemitsu in order that they could hear all that was said.

Hidetaka asked many searching questions to probe Makino's background and his motives before he finally relaxed a little and laughed out loud.

'You know, Makino-sama, I think I believe you! One cannot be too careful these days . . . I shall report all that you have said to my lord; in the meantime we cannot permit a man of your qualities to remain uncomfortable in an overcrowded *ryokan*. Doubtless you would prefer to have proper quarters within our palisaded walls?'

'Torii-dono,' Makino replied, bowing low to the floor, 'my services will be of great value to the Honourable Constable, your brother. As this invitation must be with the approval of the Lord Constable, I accept.'

'Excellent!' Hidetaka smiled. 'Looking at your clothes I will have some new apparel sent to you . . . Oh, and some other – er – comforts to make your stay pleasant!'

He clapped his hands loudly and issued a string of orders to the two young samurai who came to the *shoji*. He escorted the rōnin personally to the guest quarters on the further side of the second bailey.

For three days and nights, Makino was entertained exactly as if he had been a man of *hatamoto* rank. Two young servant girls were specially brought in from one of the favoured *onsen* springs to look after his every want and nothing was overlooked that might arouse his suspicion. During the days he met with Hidetaka from time to time for more discussions, his proposal was of real interest and intrigued the clan councillors; at the same time he was secretly observed day and night for the bushi were always suspicious.

At length he was given an audience with Torii Takamori, himself, and came to the council chamber in the company of Hidetaka. For the first time the Torii lord was able to see him close to, and he liked what he saw.

'I heard that you were once favoured by the late-Lord Osumi? What services did you render him?'

'My lord, I gave instruction in field tactics.'

'Is that so?' Takamori looked across at his brother. 'Hidetaka-dono, you didn't mention this the other day when our guest arrived.'

'I failed to ask him then about this matter; but it is interesting, is it not?'

'Yet Osumi Kageie was killed by his enemies,' remarked Takamori. 'Your tactics were not much help to him.'

'The enemy attacked by stealth, my lord; the late-lord had no warning. He did not, apparently, heed my admonitions that a wise leader's eyes are his agents; they must be everywhere.'

'I heard that at the time of Lord Osumi's death you were in the Yamashirō domain. Is this true?'

'You are correct, my lord. I had been despatched there to request Lord Yamashirō Saemon's help because my late-lord suspected that sooner or later Councillor Naganuma or the other vassals might act treacherously.'

'Why did he think that?'

Makino wrinkled up his nose.

'Because. my lord, he had refused to permit Sadamasa, Councillor Naganuma's ally, to cross through his domains in any strength for fear of trouble. He would only do so on express instructions from Lord Nagao, himself.'

'What was your opinion of that?'

'My opinion, your lordship? Why, I considered it a prudent decision.'

Takamori regarded him for five or six seconds then nodded his head slowly.

'And what was the result of your message to Saemon?'

'He agreed to help my master, but . . .'

'But what?'

'I couldn't help noticing two familiar faces amongst his rear vassals. These men I recognized as belonging to Naganuma Yoshimitsu.'

'You were certain of this?'

'Oh, yes, my lord; I was quite certain.'

'And how did you know?'

'These men had also been rōnin and were swordsmen lately come up from Miyakō after the fighting there ten years ago. I had observed them once at a match between two samurai at Kawagoe.'

'So you mistrusted Lord Saemon? You thought that he was plotting to double-cross your master?'

'That is so, my lord . . . and I think he intends to do the same towards you.'

Takamori looked closely at the ronin.

'I am told that the secret message from Lord Saemon was not well kept. Is that why you came?'

'After Lord Osumi was killed with all his family, I realized that Yamashirō Saemon would move soon . . . I simply remained to closely observe events.'

'Did you know that Lord Osumi's son escaped the sword?'

This time it was Makino Ryūji's turn to appear surprised.

'But he was killed at the fall of Minowa yashiki!'

'Fortunately not!'

'. . . My Lord, I thought that he was dead . . . His body was said to have been found afterwards floating in the moat . . .'

Takamori shook his head.

'You think that I should ally myself to Yamashirō and when all is prepared, I should ensure that his army crosses the borders of the Osumi lands first? What then?'

'My lord, allow him to engage the enemy at Mōji village and then strike at his flank without warning. In this way you will crush both Yamashirō and Naganuma. I advise that Sadamasa Hideo will withdraw in haste and not bother you again. You will be master of broad lands!'

'What do you think of this plan, brother?'

Hidetaka drew in his breath. He scratched his chin.

'The plan would work, my lord; I have no doubt of that.'

'But it would be against proper respect, would it not?'

'Certainly it could be described as expedient, but it would have an excellent result for our house.'

'Can you justify that?'

'Certainly, honoured brother. The true treachery would be in Yamashirō's double-dealing, if what Makino-sama says is correct.'

Takamori narrowed his eyes and nodded in agreement.

'True . . . The audience is ended, Makino-dono. I shall consider all you have said and decide tomorrow.'

Later that evening, Torii Takamori sat in his private quarters on the upper floor of the main *tenshaku*. He was attended by his son, Munemori, his brother, Hidetaka, and the Osumi heir, Kagemitsu.

'Kagemitsu-sama, are you sure that this man, Makino Ryūji, did indeed serve your father at Minowa?'

'I am sure, sir. I saw him there often.'

'There is something about him that bothers me,' said Takamori, 'but I can't quite think what it is?'

Hidetaka scratched the side of his stubbly chin.

'Was it likely that he would be asked to go as an emissary to Yamashirō Saemon? Would your father entrust such a mission to a man of his rank?'

'My father was a shrewd man,' replied the young man, 'but I think he always acted in good faith. While he might have entrusted Makino-san I feel he would surely have despatched one of our senior rōtō.'

'A good answer for so young a man! That is exactly what I would think, too . . . We must take care!'

'What will you tell him, honoured brother?'

'I shall not meet him. You, Hidetaka, will inform him that I think his plan is a sound one. However, nothing will be done yet. Tell him, too, that I have already sent word to Saemon agreeing to the union of our two families. After that, we shall watch this man closely.'

Munemori had sat quietly through all of this listening carefully.

'But, father;' he burst out, 'he is not to be trusted! He is an agent!'

'My son, I know that! Dissemblence is the nature of warfare. We shall watch and wait!'

Munemori was deeply concerned by all that he had heard. He had formed the opinion based on his intuitive understanding of swordsmanship, that it had been a grave error to permit an unknown agent to come into the castle and be allowed such freedom. Already the man was treated with respect by the senior samurai because it seemed to them that his father and the councillors trusted the fellow. As the meeting ended and Munemori descended to his room next to the Inner Gateway, he resolved to keep close guard on his new friend, Osumi Kagemitsu, fearing within himself that some deeper treachery was afoot.

Preparations for the union between the two families went ahead in the customary way until the day arrived when Yamashirō Saemon was to exchange gifts and receive the Lady Hana-o as bride for his son, Norimasa. Throughout the proceedings Torii Takamori had carefully evaded the question of the young refugee in his safekeeping and no mention was made concerning him. Munemori's sister, Hana-o, was to ride to the border in a beautifully decorated *kago* palanquin with an escort of two-hundred fully armed men. She would be met at the Mōjō Myōjin temple by Saemon's embassy and the initial ceremonies would be conducted there and completed later at Saemon's yashiki. The temple lay just over three miles from Nakanojo to the south where the ground rose to some low hills covered by the vestiges of a once extensive forest. The debatable lands formerly ruled by Osumi Kageie were to the east and Saemon's domain further to the south on the topmost edge of the flat Kantō plain around the town of Hirai.

As the Lady Hana-o's procession was nearly formed up under her uncle's direction, the skies darkened and thunder rolled around the mountain valleys. He had already raised his leather war fan to signal the escort to move off when there came the loudest detonation from the heavens and a bolt of lightning struck the left roof of the Heron Gate tower. Down showered tiles and some timber beams throwing several men and horses into confusion. Despite this inauspicious omen order was at last restored and eventually the procession began its journey; but there were those who saw in this incident a prophesy of ill to follow.

At the start, the samurai and foot soldiers marched beneath the shelter of oiled umbrellas but after that single burst of noise the storm muttered off towards the Chichibu mountains and the bright rays of the sun began to shaft down through the breaks in the clouds. Soon the curling banners dried out and waved bravely over the helmeted heads of the escort and the bride's kago carried by near naked porters glistened richly. To the casual observer this was just another warrior's wedding procession, escorted, perhaps, with some show of martial strength prudent with warfare flaring in the nearby fief; a happy ceremonial, nonetheless.

At the head of the column behind the two tall Torii banners and twenty spearmen, rode the resplendent *ō-karō*, Torii Hidetaka, accompanied by the young Munemori and several high-ranking members of the rōtō, men who for generations had held their rice lands under the protection of the Genji. Behind the officers on their vermillion tasselled horses came the Lady Hana-o with her attendants. Further back were more spearmen escorting boxes containing her dowry gifts to her new husband-to-be, Yamashirō Norimasa. Bringing up the rear was a large contingent of ashigaru on foot and a rearguard of fifty mounted samurai, all in their armour.

Hidetaka looked calm and impassive as his horse paced slowly along. He watched the two *yari-mochi*, who bore the tall *ke-yari* symbols of the Torii clan aloft, twist and turn the feathered spear scabbards with every dancing step. At his back fluttered his white *sashimono* emblazoned with the black crest of the Torii, the simple form of the gateway to the great Kashima shrine of Takamikadzouchi-no-kami, the powerful deity who guarded over warriors and swordsmen. He betrayed no sign whatsoever of his heightened awareness of impending trouble so clearly forewarned by the bolt that damaged the Heron-mon a short while before; yet he was acutely aware that he was escorting his niece into great danger and this day was intended as a decoy to find out the real intentions of the Yamashirō clan. But he also knew that during the hours of darkness, his brother, Lord Takamori, had ridden out secretly with another five-hundred troops from the Western Fort, intending to take up positions near to the Myōjin-ji – just in case there was trouble.

'Uncle,' said Munemori, joining the ō-karō. 'does father intend to go ahead with this union?'

The Chief Councillor turned his helmeted head and pulled back his mouth into a smile beneath the vermillion cords.

'Contain your impatience, young man, and be ready.'

'Ready? For formal duties, or what?'

'You will see all in due time . . . meanwhile, I suggest you first tighten your helmet strings!'

When he heard his uncle's words, Munemori knew that his fears were justified.

'I shall go back to my position,' he said, and drew aside to allow some officers to pass by before rejoining the column beside the Hitachi samurai, Makino Ryūji. He was now determined that come what may he would not allow this rōnin to pass from his sight.

Torii Takamori and his three captains stood under the cover of a thick grove of bamboo where they had a clear view down onto the thatched roofs of the temple and the countryside immediately about. Their men were hidden in the fields behind, no banners flying.

'See, there . . !' exclaimed Chikuma Mitsushige, pointing: 'There are the flags of Saemon-dono!'

Brushing aside a whining mosquito, Takamori nodded his head.

'They will arrive early! Excellent!'

'Hidetaka-sama carries out his task well!' remarked another of the officers.

'Yes! I can see the tall banners,' Takamori pointed with his riding cane. 'Now we shall see what happens . . . Over there, who are those men?'

A short distance to the east of the cluster of roofs they glimpsed several tell-tale flashes of reflected light . . . Spears . . ?

Takamori uttered a grim laugh.

'I am disappointed! I would have thought that Sadamasa Hideo would have ensured against discovery by dulling his yari blades!'

'You were right to think they might attack, my lord,' said Mitsushige.

'I didn't expect they *might* attack; I knew that they *would* do so!'

Below them they watched the Yamashirō escort reach the temple's approach avenue, their banners appearing and disappearing from view beneath the maple and cypress trees. It was like the unfolding of a play as from the east came strangers who were clearly in some strength and held military formation. Closer and closer came the two groups until at last the observers thought they must surely see each other

'General Hidetaka's banners advance on the village!'

By a quirk of the deep-scored river course, the Lady Hana-o's procession had swung westwards beneath the steep hillside on which her concealed father stood. It was just at this time that the figures from the east began to flow together into tighter groups. Even without hearing the watching bushi knew what orders were being issued. On the gentle southern airs came floating the mournful calls of horagai; the notes rose and fell and became more insistent! Time to prepare themselves for action. Both the eastern and southern groups had seen each other. It was strange to see the tiny figures move in distracted turmoil like a disturbed ant's nest.

'Yamashirō-sama is being attacked!' cried out one of the Torii *hatamoto*.

'Why, so he is!' remarked Takamori. 'Interesting!'

Chikuma Mitsushige was surprised.

'Surely Sadamasa has made an error?'

The Torii lord merely said: 'Wait just a little.'

Without doubt, the nearest figures were locked in combat but almost as it had begun the blaring horns drew the two sides apart.

'Chikuma-sama, order the men to mount!' ordered Takamori.

He saw that in a few minutes Hidetaka and his wedding column would reach the side gate of the Myōjin-ji.

The whole force was in silent readiness, but would they be needed? Would Saemon show his suspected duplicity?

The answer followed swiftly!

Figures from Saemon's procession and their erstwhile attackers separated to their respective groups and almost immediately both turned and rushed into the temple grounds. Takamori waited a few moments more to be quite sure, then he abruptly raised his white tasselled baton and shouted out: 'Follow me!'

Surging out of the bamboo grove at the foot of the hill, they swept through the thinly forested slopes, weapons at the ready . . .

Hearing the first blare of the warhorns, Hidetaka gathered his men; he knew that his brother's fears were justified and Yamashirō Saemon would try to seize his niece, the Lady Hana-o, by force and thereby provoke a war that might lead to the destruction of the Torii house. His column had just entered the Western Gate when he ordered his warriors to take up defensive positions, Some of the ashigaru tore down a number of wooden partitions and in haste stood these on their long edges, firmly secured to uprights of pointed bamboo uprooted and trimmed from the grove beside the gate. More sharpened bamboo was set at an angle to deter charging horsemen but there was little time for more as the enemy were just a long bowshot away. Without delay, the palanquin was placed in the comparative shelter of the gate railings and one of the half-rotten doors forced from its rusted hinges formed a substantial barricade.

A group of bowmen ran into view from the corner of the Sutra Hall with bows ready and shot an opening flight of arrows at the gateway. Munemori, given command of twenty archers and ready for his first experience of battle, immediately replied, driving the enemy back to shelter. Not one of his men was struck but two of their attackers were certainly wounded and only reached safety with difficulty.

The horagai sounded again and Hidetaka gave a broad smile.

'They will attack very soon,' he announced calmly.

Issuing a string of orders, he positioned his spearmen in front of the makeshift palisades and Munemori's archers on the right. Makino Ryūji also joined this group, a very long black bow held ready in his powerful hands.

'Torii Munemori,' he called out in a loud voice, 'now you will see how the warriors of Hitachi Mitō fight!'

Somehow the boast struck the wrong note in Munemori's young heart. It did not accord with his concept of how a bushi should behave, but he kept council and replied: 'You may have the name of "Dragon" but I am sure that the Torii *kerai* will match you arrow for arrow.' By 'Dragon' he referred to Makino's personal name.

Round the corner swept a close-packed mass of horsemen, all shouting as if they were wild devils; they swerved towards the gate and broke into a full charge, their animal's nostrils flaring with terror and excitement. The Torii archers loosed flight after flight of blue tipped feathered arrows into men and beasts, sending many stumbling headlong under the hooves of the rest, but the enemy banners didn't waver until, like surf breaking on a rocky shore, they met the levelled hedge of long yari of Hidetaka's determined spearmen and the sharp pointed bamboo stakes so hastily lashed into position. Swords flashed and yari gored, men and horses screamed in anger, pain, and blind fear . . . It may have been Munemori's first battlefield but he had no time to think as he drew his bow with all the skill that his masters had drilled into him as he grew to manhood.

The survivors of that brave charge wheeled and galloped away only to be succeeded by a wave of ashigaru carrying wooden shields that they intended to position as cover. Hidetada watched Munemori's men bring down several of the enemy and while they were confused and in some disarray he ordered his own spearmen to counterattack.

'Come, Makino-sama; let's see how you fight at close quarters!' yelled Munemori, throwing down his bow and rushing forwards with a long-bladed *omi-yari*.

Their attack succeeded and many of the enemy skirmishers were cut down in that impetuous rush across the wide compound already littered with the dead and maimed animals and men from the first assault. There was no chance for the youthful Munemori to seek out some ranking opponent and try to take his head after an honourable fight; this was a bloody mêlée, a free-for-all to capture a few splintered wooden and bamboo shields.

Behind them, one of the Torii captains had found a temple drum and the signal to withdraw beat out urgently. Munemori looked about him and realized that he was the last man stepping backwards across the bloody rammed earth and flagstones. Makino Ryūji was nowhere to be seen.

Again, the enemy appeared and the Torii spearmen were still several yards in front of their prepared positions. Had Hidetaka made an error in sending his men into that attack? An arrow narrowly missed Munemori's sleeve; a second plucked at his right *sode*, the shaft lodging fast in his braided armour.

Three of his yari-mochi dashed to aid their young lord and in a moment he was sheltered by two light wooden *tate* as the small group fell carefully back.

'Uncle, have you seen Makino-san?'

Hidetaka frowned. 'He was with your platoon, wasn't he?'

'So he was until we drove off those ashigaru and *sanpei* lackeys!'

'Did he fall?'

'We lost no one, sir.'

But the warhorns blared and put an end to further discussion. More shields appeared behind the enemy corpses.

'They are both Yamashirō banners and those of Sadamasa,' observed Munemori.

His uncle ground out: 'Your father anticipated this treachery!'

Next to them one of the samurai was struck full in the face by an arrow and grunted with the shock. Blood welled from the wound and Munemori saw that the wide blade had pierced to the neck below the unfortunate fellow's left ear and a dark ooze began to roll from his nostrils as his throat filled. Choking and retching, the man staggered back.

'Take what cover you can and use your bows,' ordered Hidetaka. He knew that the infamous Saemon would seek to kill from a distance and as they grew fewer so he would advance his shield wall until at last the range would be point blank. The final assault would follow without delay.

Makino re-appeared.

'That was close!' he exclaimed, seeing Munemori look at him with a questioning frown. 'My charge took me into the hall over here and I found myself cut off! I managed to get back in the confusion when they attacked this time!'

'You were beside me . . ?'

'If it wasn't for the bravery of one of your junior samurai who was cut off with me and urged me back under the cover of a broken shield, I wouldn't have made it!'

'You have taken a head?'

'Just one of the enemy I sent to Hell.'

Munemori kept silent, unconvinced. Makino Ryūji gave a sardonic laugh as he crouched behind a large tate from the searching arrows.

'How many have you defeated, my brave young friend?'

'Only two of Sadamasa's ashigaru.'

'Just two, eh? The time will come when you will take many more heads!'

The young bushi was troubled by Makino's brief disappearance. It was time enough to pass on a message . . . Easy enough, too, to take a head from a dead man and pass it off as a battle trophy. He had heard that sort of thing happened very often and would be a perfect cover for when he returned . . . He was about to say something more when a messenger ran up, doubled low to avoid the dangerous sharpshooters across the compound.

'The Honourable Lord is at hand, sir! His flags have been seen to the right!'

Hidetaka was relieved since they were already hard pressed and the enemy had managed to advance his shieldwall several paces. A second group was now forming up on the left and he realized that it was good fortune that the Outer Gateway behind them lay close against the river's deep cut ravine making a flanking attack to his rear almost impossible. Encirclement from that direction would surely spell doom. The thought crossed his mind that thus far he had only seen one or two Naganuma banners and he wondered why this should be so? There was little time for speculation at that moment.

A second wave of mixed Yamashirō Saemon and Sadamasa horsemen were forming up behind the advancing bowmen and preparing for another charge. In fact, their first line had already started to trot forward when confusion broke out behind and it seemed that the whole area beyond the corner of the Sutra Hall had become a seething mass of struggling horsemen and flashing swords. Amidst the black double-sashimono banners of the Yamashirō and the leather plantain emblems of Sadamasa's men, the tall narrow white flags of Torii Takimori's force could be seen and very soon it became evident that the latter were becoming increasingly dominant.

Torii Munemori leapt to his feet.

'We must attack, uncle! We must aid my father!' he shouted in excitement.

'Remain where you are!' he was curtly ordered. 'You must learn to watch and wait,' cautioned Hidetaka.

He had hardly uttered this sage advice when an arrow glanced off Munemori's rivetted helmet and a second clipped the edge of his upright wooden shield, striking off a large yellow splinter.

His uncle said: 'That's better! Bravery is one thing; foolishness in the face of the enemy quite another. We shall attack when the moment is right and then the enemy will be utterly defeated!'

'It is as I predicted,' said Makino Ryūji; 'Sadamasa and Saemon have determined to destroy your family!'

'Your understanding of the situation was indeed accurate,' remarked Hidetaka, but before the other could reply the captain gave the signal for the centre and right divisions to rise and charge at the confederate ashigaru who were now shooting very erratically as they became confused and unsure with the intense fighting to their rear.

'Here is your chance, Munemori-sama!'

The young man leapt up and bellowed out: 'Cut them down . . .' This time he was determined to take a suitable head and so demonstrate that Kōzuke bravery was every bit equal to that of Hitachi! It was then that he realized that Makino had vanished again. He turned and looked back, just in time to glimpse someone pass back through the gateway and to know that the figure was wearing armour that looked very much the same as that worn by the arrogant rōnin.

Something was badly wrong; he felt it deep inside.

'Uncle, that rōnin has gone again! He left through the Western Gate as we launched the attack . . !'

'You have always suspected him, haven't you, Munemori?' exclaimed Hidetaka. 'Follow him! You have my permission to leave!'

Munemori bowed and hastened back to the upturned barricades, calling three of his personal kerai to accompany him. As he crossed through the arrow-studded debris he looked at his sister's palanquin and the four terrified women attendants.

'Sister,' he called out, 'are you alright? It will soon be finished!'

The sliding door was a little open but something made him stop and peer inside . . . There was no one there! Suddenly he realized that the procession had been an elaborate ruse; his cunning father had arranged everything to find out Yamashirō Saemon's true colours . . . and he had not known . . ! But where was his sister? Still at Nakanojo? There would only be a comparatively few men there . . . That was it! Of course . . ! Makino Ryūji had been sent to worm his way into their trust and then to murder Osumi Kagemitsu . . . and he might well succeed in this and take and kill Hana-o before anyone was aware of the danger or could disengage themselves from the battle.

But even when he reached these conclusions, Munemori had only guessed part of the truth!

The small group cut loose their horses and set off at a brisk pace along the Nakanojo track. Matters took a more serious turn when after hardly a mile some red and white striped banners were observed in the valley ahead.

'Torii-sama,' shouted out the leading kerai, pulling up his horse with some difficulty, the mettlesome animal dancing and turning on the stony road; 'we must be cautious!'

'What is it?'

'There are strange flags ahead!'

All four riders came together and Munemori stood up in his wide stirrups for a keen look through the gaps in the trees. He could easily pick out the sunlit tiles of the distant yashiki and his own family banners grouped by the inner gateway. It was some moving flags that had caught the sharp-eyed retainer's attention.

'I can hardly believe what I see,' he said, dismayed. 'Ōarai-san . . . surely those are the banners of Naganuma Yoshimitsu? I must be mistaken?'

Despite his horse dancing beneath him, Ōarai also stood in his *abume*, steadying himself with his yari butt.

'Without any doubt they are the emblems of Naganuma, my lord,' he agreed.

'My father has been doubly betrayed!'

There was anger in the young man's voice.

'What shall you do, master?' asked Ōarai.

Munemori brought his horse under control as it tossed its head.

'How many men are normally at the Agatsuma fort?'

The Agatsuma *toride*?' Ōarai thought for a moment. 'If the Honourable Lord did not withdraw any, there may be about fifty there, sir.'

Munemori looked back along the road. They had already come about halfway from the temple to the main yashiki and delay might have serious consequences.

'Sadaji-san; you ride back to my uncle and inform him of the situation. Tell him that I intend to take all the men from the small Western Fort and attack Naganuma without delay from the direction of Kusatsu. Be clear on that . . .'

'Lord, I will not forget!'

'Go!'

He pulled his horse's head round and with Ōarai and the third kerai galloped of down the slope amidst a small shower of stones. Just beyond three tumbled cottages deserted by their owners for fear of the sounds of nearby conflict, the path divided and the samurai swung onto the western track and continued their headlong dash. Quite soon they came down to the level rice lands and in sight of the knoll on which stood the Agatsuma stockade. With sashimono flapping and snapping, they galloped along the winding path between the flooded paddies to the accompanyment of a surging chorus of croaking frogs.

Those inside the fort, seeing the samurai in their precipitate ride, sounded the alarm and a number of yari-mochi spilled out of the heavy-posted gateway. Behind them walked in a more leisurely manner the armoured figure of Ōno Shigeyemon, one of the four Torii Councillors and ranking just below Torii Hidetaka in the clan structure.

He took one look and recognized Munemori instantly. Barking out an order, he strode through the double line of spearmen.

Munemori leapt from his foaming horse and gave the reins to one of the ashigaru who ran forward to assist. He greeted Shigeyemon with a courteous bow and quickly told him what had occurred and the situation at the Nakanojo yashiki.

'If we are to save the Torii house we must act swiftly!' agreed Shigeyemon. 'Is there time to send word to your Honourable Father?'

'I have already done this . . . or at least to my uncle.'

'There are thirty-two samurai here besides these twenty-five ashigaru.'

'We cannot delay, Ōno-sama, and we may have to take risks that might seem imprudent . . . Send men to find every banner they can. Put up an additional three or four inside the fort and make certain, too, that the cooking fires are replenished so that some smoke rises clearly over the different ramparts . . .'

Ōno Shigeyemon gave the necessary orders to several of the senior warriors who were now in full armour.

'Make ready all the horses,' he added. Turning back to Munemori, he said: 'Anything else, young lord?'

Munemori smiled.

'You will follow me despite my age and the risk in abandoning this toride?'

'Of course! There is no alternative that I can think of!'

'None whatsoever!' Munemori looked grim. 'Leave three men under one responsible samurai. They are to move the banners on occasion and be seen on the arrow platforms walking about!'

Shigeyemon looked at the youth and felt deep pride that the Torii had produced so promising a young man.

'It looks as if Tojiri-sama managed to close the Outer Gate in time. Fortunate indeed!' observed Shigeyemon.

'How many men do you estimate are with Naganuma?'

'It is difficult to judge that, young master, but looking at the position of his flags and if that is his headquarters down there . . . I would say no more than two-hundred men.'

'So he has opted for a quick victory based on surprise when our clan should have been weak.' Munemori calmed his restless horse with his free right hand. He gazed at the scene below and along the slopes where they stood.

Only a quarter-of-a-mile away they could easily see the enemy gathered in three groups before the Heron Gate; a short distance behind these troops smoke and flames were rising above some of the buildings in the little town. Even as they watched, Naganuma's men came together and charged at the storm-damaged entrance and the few defenders on the inside ran to resist the oncoming assault. But what interested Munemori and Ōno Shigeyemon was the place where Naganuma had placed his Command Post. It was only a short way south of where they stood and about two hundred feet further down the hillside.

As the fighting recommenced outside the gateway, heavy clouds that had been gathering hid the sun and in a few minutes it began to rain heavily. The young warrior saw his chance.

Meanwhile, at the temple, Torii Takamori's headlong charge had smashed into the rear ofYamashirō Saemon's troops and in the ensuing battle they had been rolled up on themselves, creating wild confusion compounded by the sudden surprise. The main part of Saemon's force had already been forced out of their intended position by the mistaken attack by Sadamasa's men but both sides had realized their error and soon rallied to turn on the Torii marriage procession. For several minutes after Takamori galloped into the southern end of the temple compound the battle raged all about although the advantage lay in the hands of the Torii, but the turning point came when Hidetaka launched his counterattack and in a very few moments a dreadful slaughter ensued that left the treacherous confederates completely defeated and many of their men slain.

Munemori's messenger, Sadaji, flung himself from his horse at the Western Gate and ran through the victorious Torii troops to deliver his nephew's urgent warning to Torii Hidetaka. Inside the temple compounds all was crimson carnage.

He found Hidetaka sitting in the company of his brother, Lord Takamori, with Chikuma Mitsushige and two other leading hatamoto, while the heads of a number of the enemy slain were brought before them. As Sadaji arrived so they were gazing into the sightless eyes of Sadamasa Hideo who had fallen to one of Hidetaka's followers just before the end.

'My lord! I bring an urgent message from the Honourable Young Lord.'

'Munemori? He was with you, Hidetaka-san?'

'He was, but I permitted him to go back to Nakanojo,' said his brother. 'He believed some treachery was about to happen.'

'Youthful imagination, perhaps? Well, what is your message?'

'The Honourable Young Lord has seen the banners of Naganuma Yoshimitsu advanced to outside the main yashiki. He has decided to take all the men from the western fort and intends to attack Naganuma from the direction of Kusatsu!'

There was a complete silence for some seconds as this surprising news sank in.

'He has gone to the Agatsuma tōride?' repeated Takamori. 'That is commanded by Ōno Shigeyemon . . . Will he leave the fort empty at the wishes of my son?'

'That is a difficult decision for him to make!' commented Hidetaka.

Takamori grunted. It was a mistake that could easily cost the hatamoto his life.

Three samurai dragged a fourth man forward.

'Your lordship, we have found Lord Saemon and his son!'

The bound man was Yamashirō Narimasa.

'Where is Saemon-dono?'

'Dead, my lord! He ripped his belly in the monks' quarters!'

'Are you certain?'

One of the samurai came forward and knelt on one knee.

'Here is his head, my lord . . He is dead alright!'

'Yamashirō Narimasa! Look on your father's face and know of his consuming greed and duplicity!

Hidetaka leant forwards and turned the severed head with the butt of his spear.

'Do you have anything to say?'

The captive 'bridegroom' simply stared straight ahead and replied not a word.

'We have no time,' said Torii Takamori, 'behead him!'

A sword lifted high and flashed down with a slight pull back at the end of the cut. The head was deftly cut free from the small piece of skin still connecting it to the top of the blood-spurting trunk, and it was placed alongside the others. Already a secretary was brushing the names of the dead men on long strips of paper to be attacked to their topknots.

Narimasa's corpse had scarcely stopped twitching before the main party of warriors ran to gather their horses and prepare to ride back to Nakanojo.

'I would like to request your advice, Ōno-sama,' said Munemori. 'Do you think we can ride down that hillside?'

'Minamoto-no-Yoshitsune did it at Ichi-no-tani! Years ago I saw that precipice and would have thought the feat impossible, but, nonetheless he managed it with all his men. We could try!'

'But you think that it would be better on foot? Is that it?'

'It will be as my young lord wishes!'

'I am younger than Lord Yoshitsune . . . We shall descend on foot!'

Ōno Shigeyemon had always thought that his lord's son promised well; now he knew it was the truth. A wise head on young shoulders.

'What do you want done with the banners we brought?' he asked.

'Ah, yes! As soon as we attack the headquarters, all these flags are to be displayed along these thickets and some of the men are to run to and fro with the longer ones. The enemy will see them and be deceived into thinking that the whole Torii army is forming up here!'

Shigeyemon issued the necessary orders as quickly and clearly as he was able to make sure they were understood by all his men.

'You think that this ruse will work?'

'If it doesn't then my father will lose Nakanojo!'

'He will also lose his son!'

'That is unimportant! We shall succeed, never doubt it!'

The attack was made with just fifteen men; the rest were needed to create confusion and diversion with the banners. Leaving their horses in the thick bamboo groves, Munemori led his small force down through the heavy undergrowth. It was indeed fortunate that not only was it teeming with rain but also the assault on the Heron Gate had clearly reached a critical stage with a few of Naganuma's men already across the small moat.

They dropped the last thirty feet in an undignified headlong slide but, without a warning shout, reached the black and white striped curtains unseen. Inside, oblivious of the fate decreed by the deities, sat Naganuma Yoshimitsu with six of his leading Councillors. Just beyond the open front that gave the commander a clear view of the proceedings at the yashiki, a protecting contingent of yari-mochi also gazed at the fighting. Clearly, not one of them gave a single passing thought to the steep hillside behind them.

Five razor-edged *omi-no-yari* sliced down the *maku* curtains and the avenging warriors rushed through in a solid mass. The seated samurai hardly had time to turn and rise, overturning in all directions their folding camp stools, when their souls left their bodies. The powerful spears thrust them through and through; all but one . . .

Munemori ran towards the enemy general and demanded that he strip off his armour and prepare to cut his belly. He was now lost and it was time to close his account for his temerity in attacking the Torii clan.

'Who requests such a thing?' demanded Yoshimitsu.

'I do; Torii Munemori, the son of Torii Takamori, lord of this domain!'

Naganuma Yoshimitsu knew that he had indeed lost when he glanced up and saw many white Torii banners along the skyline of the mountain above. Calmly he sat down once more on his lacquered seat.

'It was a rash move to agreee to Yamashirō Saemon's greedy plan,' he remarked, starting to undo his armour cords. 'I thought then that it might cost us dearly!'

'You were right in that opinion!'

'Saemon was ambitious! He wanted both your lands, the destruction of your clan, and to have overall control of the Osumi domain!'

As he waited for Yoshimitsu to complete his final preparations, Munemori asked: 'How did he think he would achieve this ambition?'

'How?' Yoshimitsu gave a bitter laugh. 'I don't know why I'm telling you this but maybe it is because I think you will act in some way to avenge my death! In our councils long before we attacked the Osumi we were presented with a ingenious plan by one of Osumi Kageie's treacherous followers . . . It was a plan that Yamashirō Saemon wholeheartedly approved . . .'

'Was this man a certain samurai from Hitachi Province, by chance?'

'You are well informed for one lacking in years.'

'A man named Makino Ryūji?'

'As I said, you have excellent spies!'

'No, Naganuma-dono; we simply follow the precept that all warfare is based on deception. Personally, I suspected this rōnin for his glibness right from the start.'

'Torii Munemori-sama, I do not hold my death against you. It is according to custom that I should pay with my life. Please pardon my offence to your family and I would request you to seek out and destroy this man, Makino, the cause of so much trouble; thus, my wandering soul will find rest.'

Naganuma waited until the young bushi nodded his head in the affirmative before he plunged his keen dagger into his bared left side and slowly drew it across to the right and slightly upwards. A fleeting shadow crossed his lined face as the blood gushed forth.

Ōno Shigeyemon's tachi struck down from Naganuma's side and it was finished.

Ōarai ran up with the news that several of Naganuma's soldiers had escaped the attack and even now had reached the main body fighting at the gateway. The attackers at the fort must have seen the Torii banners moving down the wooded slopes and the knowledge that their headquarters had been stormed and captured could only mean that their general was dead . . . What would they do?

'Fetch the horses!' ordered Munemori. 'We shall ride into Nakanojo at once!'

'It will be too dangerous, Young Lord;' remonstrated a dismayed Shigeyemon, 'Naganuma's men are everywhere!'

'We must be bold! They will be unaware of how many men are behind us.'

Without waiting, the moment the horses arrived Torii Munemori climbed nimbly into his saddle and struck the horse's flanks with his cane. The samurai had no choice but to exalt in the spirit of their youthful master and to follow . . .

'Storm the gate immediately!' shouted Makino Ryūji angrily. 'The men are not showing enough spirit!'

'But the enemy are on that hillside, sir!' protested one of Naganuma's officers.

'It is a transparent ruse . . . a decoying move! If we take the yashiki, the battle is won and the victory will assuredly be ours!'

'The enemy are inside our headquarters; our leaders are killed!'

'What defeatest talk is that? How can you possibly know if that is true? You . . . blow the signal for the final assault!'

The young aide with the conch horagai stood undecided whether or not to carry out the menacing rōnin's command, well-knowing how close the man was to the War Council. He looked across at his officer for confirmation . . .

Within the Heron Gate, Tojiri Hachinosuke had also seen the banners moving along and beneath the wooded crest and knew at once that they were all from the Agatsuma tōride, and he shrewdly guessed who was responsible. The crossed bars on some of the flags were immediately recognizable. Through one of the arrow embrasures in the *yagura* tower he watched as the enemy prepared for another assault and, intuitively, he realized that the treacherous Makino was attempting to take over command. He could pick him out quite clearly from his distinctive green and red laced *dō-maru* which had been loaned to the rōnin when preparing to ride out with Lord Hidetaka that morning.

'Quick, man,' he said to the yumi-mochi at his side, 'hand me your bow and a signal arrow!'

Nocking the arrow, he raised the long bow high and took careful aim. Without delay, the arrow sang away from the string through the triangular loop . . . and struck full on the mouthpiece of the warhorn just as the signaller was about sound the '*Attack*'!

The shock sprang the speckled shell from the man's nerveless fingers leaving him limp from astonishment and fright. The officer at his side was also speechless.

'Attack!' screamed Makino, beside himself with thwarted fury.

As he uttered the words Munemori swept into the wreckage littered street and galloped headlong towards the enemy, his sashimono flying; behind him came the first of his men, or so thought the enemy, not knowing that they were just the merest handful.

'Naganuma Yoshimitsu is dead,' yelled Munemori; 'Yoshimitsu-*taisho* is killed and I have taken his head!'

'Shoot him down; he is almost alone!' Makino seized a black rattan-bound bow. 'It is Torii Munemori . . . kill him and you will have the victory!'

Munemori galloped on, regardless of the keen arrow being drawn against him; his mount was forced to veer a little to avoid corpses in the roadway and Makino's arrow shaft flashed harmlessly past. He swung his right arm back and with all the power that he could summon hurled forward the bloody trophy that he grasped so tightly in this headlong rush . . .

The head of Naganuma Yoshimitsu bounced and rolled to the feet of the officer who stood by the rōnin's side, and those nearest groaned aloud when they realized that Munemori's words were true.

Makino Ryūji stood with lowered bow, staring into the dust clouded eyes of that grisly trophy. He threw down the bow and drew his long sword.

'Munemori, you young whelp; you have thwarted me from killing Osumi Kagemitsu and gaining control of all these lands! I shall kill you rather than let you succeed!'

Munemori only laughed as he wheeled his excited horse.

'Traitor! You are unworthy of my blade . . . Your fate will be decided!'

But the fate determined by the deities was unexpected. High on the Heron Gate, Tojiri Hachinosuke drew another arrow in the ashigaru's bow, thinking that his young master was in deadly danger. The tiny leaf-shaped blade struck the helmetless Makino Ryūji at the base of his skull where his head met his neck and the shaft drove fully through so that the blade came out more than a hand's span from his mouth, for all the world like a serpent's tongue. A thin stream of blood spurted out between his teeth showing through his tight drawn lips, but before he could take more than a couple of steps a thicker flow filled his mouth and coursed down his chin. He fell into a muddy puddle at the roadside where his jerking limbs pitched him sideways down the bank into the rice paddy.

As the shock passed and Munemori's men joined him, the Naganuma soldiers threw down their weapons in the hope of saving their lives. Rough hands dragged the perfidious Makino up, all bemired and stinking of nightsoil.

'Execute him and place his head on a bamboo spear,' ordered the young warrior. 'It is not fitting that my father should see his head presented with honour!'

Truly, it was written by the great Sonshi that 'when those experienced in war move they make no mistakes; when they act, their resources are limitless'.

3

SNOW

It was one severe winter long years past, when Torii-no-Munetaka was still a youthful warrior as yet untried in war and before he became the Constable of Kōzuke; a time when he was fond of trudging the hard paths of the yamabushi. He had followed the Shugen ways since he was just eighteen but now, aged twenty-seven, he had already achieved the rank of *dai-sendatsu* having entered the mountains more than twenty times, seven of them in the depths of winter.

On this particular day, according to the brief early annals of the Torii-ke, there was a heavy snowfall as Munetaka, wearing his wide woven bamboo snow shoes, slowly climbed the winding track that led to some caves sacred to that fierce Guardian revered by both the Shingon-shu and the initiates of the Shugendō. Up he went, warm in body despite the bitter cold, often thrusting his staff deep down into the drifts in order to feel his steps on a path that often threatened to pitch him far down to the snow clad bamboo groves far below.

Eventually he reached a sort of shoulder of the mountainside, marked by a small but crude torii fashioned from two modest upright posts linked by a simple bar of two bamboo poles secured by coarse plaited rice-straw ropes. Taking large steps across the powdery surface he reached the dark opening of a wide cavern before which was a natural pool of spring water, unfrozen despite the penetrating cold, steam coiling up from its surface. From the dark recesses of the cave glared the fierce face of the dread Fudō Myō-ō; He who defended Buddha's Law and commanded total obedience from those who followed the Shugen creed.

After telling his beads and reciting a prayer, Munetaka turned and sought the *mizugori* cistern, also ice free, that was fed by the same pure spring that poured directly from the living rock. Swiftly he took off his clothes until his nakedness was only covered by his loincloth. Blowing three long blasts on his *horagai*, he set it down and slowly descended the five steps into the water tank reciting in a loud voice part of the Heart Sutra before as slowly emerging. Not once did he do this but thirty times, fully immersing himself in the icy waters. Amazingly, he appeared warm, heated somehow by the power of his devotions.

An hour later, in the gathering bleak winter dusk, Munetaka descended the steep winding path and was aware, along a side track, of the looming bulk of a temple gateway with its heavy upper floor and sweeping thatched roof. The snow was falling again, great soft flakes that promised to add a foot or more if it continued at this rate through the night. His breath hung white in the still crisp air as he paused on a small humped bridge across the burbling stream and stared at the gateway. He reached a decision and decided that he would shelter the night here from the coming storm so, taking a firmer hold on his stout staff, he turned and trudged towards the Ōmote-mon.

Shaking off the snow from his straw cape and removing his woven shoes, he tied on his straw *waraji* and carefully ascended the steep black staircase that led to the upper floor. Everything was pitch dark since the chamber was fast shuttered but, undeterred, Munetake felt his way along the walls and found the expected little raised platform where he settled himself for the night, oblivious of the cold, simply chewing on some soused radish and a rice cake that he carried in his wallet.

When the dawn light filtered through into the darkened room, Munetaka knew that the snowstorm had ceased. He shook himself as he sat up, legs folded, and began to tell his rosary while he recited in a low voice parts of the Heart Sutra. As he did so he became aware that he was not alone in the upper storey. The rising sun, clearing the gap in the mountains down the valley, sent its rays directly at the gateway so that they filtered through the shutter slats. In the faintly roseate light he could just make out, on the further side of the chamber, a huddled figure kneeling beside some longish object and swaying back and forth. As the light strengthened he realized that it was an old crone with unbound white hair and that at her feet lay a corpse.

The apparition fumbled about and lit a lantern glim that enabled Munetaka to see that the body was that of a young woman. The crone began to tease out to its full length the corpse's hair, at first very slowly as if she were brushing it, but gradually increasing her movements until it seemed that she intended tearing the tresses out by their roots.

Just then, they heard raised voices and the curious muffled crunch of many feet crossing deep snow. Both the crone and he stopped to listen.

'That robber has somehow escaped!' someone shouted excitedly, his voice clear in the crisp stillness of the morning air.

'We will easily track him in this snow!'

A moment later another called out: 'He's stolen the young master! And he's armed, at that!'

The group ran off towards the temple and silence descended again but not for long.

A distant voice hollered out.

'There he is! He's heading for the gatehouse . . . Summon the rest . . .'

Below them the lower sliding door crashed open.

'Get up those stairs or it will be the worse for you!' a rough voice growled and a moment later a small boy was thrust into the upper chamber closely followed by a man who must be the bandit. He dragged the child by the collar across the floor and sat down heavily with the lad between his crossed legs. Munetake saw at once that the desperado was armed with a long dirk which he held close to the boy's belly.

The robber glared about him but missed seeing Munetaka in the gloom, instead catching sight of the bizarre old hag who had resumed tearing the hair from the dead girl.

'What are you,' he yelled, 'a ghost or a demon?'

He waved his dagger threateningly.

The crone crouched down.

'Don't kill me, sir! I'm only looking after my mistress . . . I mean you no harm . . .'

'Uh?' muttered the incredulous thief. 'Your mistress looks dead to me, you stupid old witch; surely you can see that?'

'I'm only taking her hair to sell to a wigmaker, master; if she's dead she won't have need of it now . . . and I've spent years carefully brushing and combing it . . .'

'By the gods . . !'

A sudden commotion below told of the arrival of armed men, one or two of the braver already on the stairs.

' 'E's up there!'

'Careful . . !'

'Inform the master . . !'

There was a pause. 'Here he comes now . . !'

'Sir . . . he's taken the young master up there!' someone shouted.

'Don't you come up or I'll kill yer child!' called out the robber in a shaky voice.

'No, no; don't do that!'

'Burn him out . . !'

'Shut your mouth, idiot,' blurted another. 'The young master would die!'

A cautious step on the stair preceeded the appearance of a worried looking face.

'Great Buddha! Don't do anything to hurt him . . .'

The face disappeared only to be replaced a few seconds later by another. It was the child's father and from his tone and choice of words, Munetaka knew him to be a warrior.

'Get back, sir!' shouted the thief. 'Get back down . . .One more step an' I'll plunge this dagger into yer boy's belly . . . just one step . . !'

Munetaka felt it was time to stop this play acting.

'You are the boy's father?' he asked in a matter-of-fact voice.

Both the man at the stairhead and the robber started round in surprise before catching sight of him in the gloom.

'By the gods, I didn't see you'se was 'ere, but don't you move, either . . .'

The father scrambled back down the ladder for fear of being the cause of his son's death and ordered his men to stand guard. He wrung his hands not knowing what to do. The old hag, meanwhile, simply cackled harshly and tore more hair from her dead mistress's scalp.

'You took that child as a hostage or was it to save your miserable life?' demanded Munetaka. 'Tell me this instant!'

His voice was firm and commanding.

'They were going to kill me, master . . . I was sore afraid of death . . . I saw this lad and thought that he might be the means of saving me . . !' His voice cracked and clearly terrified he whispered: 'What will 'appen now, sir?'

'You climbed up here to this place of death,' said Munetaka, 'I can see little future for you.'

The robber was weeping tears of self-pity now.

'You must know 'ow to save me, sir priest; ye're a clever man . . .'

'If you let the child go this instant and throw down that knife, I may be able to do something. I will pray to the Lord Fudō!'

In a firm voice Munetaka began to intone an invocation from the Peacock Sutra, clicking his beads as he did so. The robber glared about him wildly but gradually calmed down.

'Let the boy come to me,' said Munetaka.

Meekly the man set the lad loose and the child ran across to the priest.

'You have obeyed me and I can see that you are a poor man. Your poverty was the cause of your crime, was it not? I will therefore take the lad down to his father and plead for your life.'

Munetaka took up his staff and came to his feet, the child clasped to his chest, then descended the stairs. Gently putting the child down, he watched as the boy ran straight to his sire.

'Thank you, sir priest; that felon is still up there?'

'Of course!'

'We will kill him for what he has done!'

'No, don't do that! He was desperate and on the point of starving which is why he attempted to steal some food. He took the child in the hope that it might save his miserable life. Also he obeyed my command to release your son. In such a case, you should show mercy, thus pleasing the Lord Buddha and earning merit! When he descends, give him an old horse and some provisions, then let him go. Others may not be so lenient but you will have done a noble deed!'

The yamabushi stooped and tied on his snowshoes.

A little later, the old crone crept gingerly down from the upper story, carrying a bundle of hair on her arm. Seeing the priest and the warrior backed by several fierce halberd-bearing soldiers, she grovelled low, muttering what must have been apologies.

'Let her go,' said the warrior-priest. 'She was only sheltering with her dead mistress . . .' The surrounding men gaped open mouthed. 'Go, old woman; we shall see to a proper burial!'

The crone hitched up her kimono, pulled her hooded cape closer about her head and unsteadily tottered down the steps.

'Just one moment, old woman, before you leave . . . What is that robber doing, eh? Please tell us.'

She pulled back her lips in what must have been a toothless smile, looking more hag-like than ever.

'He's preparing to come down, master . . . Like a good fellow . . .'

The crone turned and took a couple of steps out into the snow. Without any warning, Munetaka drew out his longsword and with a single stroke struck off the head of the ancient servant. Her corpse fell to the ground and her dark blood spattered across the white snow.

Aghast, the warrior and his followers backed away from the yamabushi. Swallowing hard, the father at last managed to stutter: 'But, why, sir; why . . ?'

Munetaka carefully wiped clean his swordblade and returned it to his scabbard.

'I made an error, sir!' he replied at length.

'An error? I don't quite understand? You pleaded for mercy for the kidnapper . . . but this old woman . . . What had she done . . ?'

'It was a mistake.' Munetaka repeated, bowing deeply then, smiling at the lad, he turned and trudged off through the trampled snow.

The warrior was as dumbfounded as his men, staring first at the fresh corpse and then at the figure of the priest.

'Get rid of that hag!' he ordered, brave enough now.

Two of the lackeys ran forward and turned over the corpse, another picking up the severed head.

'Why . . . it's the robber!'

In awe, they gazed at the now distant figure of Torii Munetaka.

4

A WINDOW ON THE PAST

Although no one nowadays can tell the truth of these ancient accounts for certain, or if they have already passed from the active memory of men who heard the original from one who was present, now fast fading to mere legend, embellished by half-truths and embroidery, nonetheless in the Torii annals is another story of that familiar ancestor, the warrior Torii-no-Munetaka.

When Munetaka was a young man, he had served the family of Taira-no-Munetsune, the redoubtable Lieutenant of the Left division of the Outer Palace Guards and son of that famous archer, Taira-no-Muneyori. Now, at that time, Taira-no-Munetaka was in the service of his overlord, Fujiwara Yorimichi,* the Lord of Uji, and son of the very powerful Fujiwara Michinaga, residing in Lord Yorimichi's grand mansion in Miyako. Of course, there is a well-known story told of the following incident in the 'Tales of Times Now Past', but this only hints at the truth; the account in the Torii annals fills in the gaps, or purports to do so. Who can tell at this distance of time?

---

* Fujiwara-no-Torimichi, 992–1074.

Many powerful personages waited upon the Fujiwara because of their huge influence in the Imperial Court. Patronage is often sought by some as the only means to preferment and wealth, feeding and bolstering the natural arrogance of many to the detriment of their future progress towards Buddhahood. Amongst those who were invited (or invited themselves) to Fujiwara Yorimichi's palatial mansion was the High Priest of the Onjō-ji temple at Otsu, an establishment known to many as the Miidera, one Myōzon, a man famed for his powers of healing through the efficacy of prayer. Of course, the Onjō-ji was a temple of the Jimon branch of the Tendai-shu, the esoteric sect of Buddhism lately finding great favour amongst the aristocratic families of the capital who saw in these withdrawn – but accessible – monks a certain appeal that promised those who bestowed generous patronage assurity of protection in life and advancement after death. However, be that as it may, High Priest Myōzon received word late one evening that it was, for whatever reason, imperative that he return to the Onjō-ji that night, the Lord of Uji also stipulating, obliquely of course, that Myōzon must return to his presence before dawn in order to continue his healing duties. Naturally, Myōzon realized that the future prosperity of his temple may depend on him accomplishing this rapid double journey, but also that it would be difficult. This worried him accordingly.

It happened, too, that this prelate of the Onjō-ji was a stiff and pedantic man who, even in the rarefied stiltified customs and lifestyle of the court nobility, was totally lacking in humour. In short, he was far from being the ideal guest in any household since his views and attitude on any subject were opinionated, unbending and above all boring. When he spoke on any matter affecting the Holy Scriptures he expressed thoughts that would brook no argument; on medicine, never a precise science, he would recite all the specifics and their appropriate ritual formulae invoking the proper divinities to bestow their divine help; nay, not inviting but ordering such aid. The Lord of Uji, Fujiwara Yorimichi, on the other hand, did possess a sense of humour and whilst generally observing the proper decorum of an aristocrat of exalted rank, was not adverse to enjoying his family life as a foil to the protocols of the Court.

It was he who, tiring one day of Myōzon's pettifogging lectures, determined to play a trick on his guest. Perhaps trick is not quite what he had in mind, rather to set the High Priest a riddle that he would not be able to understand by way of logic. Accordingly, he summoned Taira-no-Munetsune to his private quarters about noon on this particular day and told him what he proposed regarding the High Priest's precipitate journey that night but not his reasons, of course; that would not be appropriate.

Taira-no-Munetsune was unusual amongst the officers of the Outer Palace Guards in that he approached his duties with some gravity and performed them as any warrior should, unlike many of his contemporaries to whom their position was a sinecure obtained for them through the influence of friends or pure nepotism. On the other hand, his mind, though fully attuned to his warrior duties, was unimaginative, and when given his orders by Lord Yorimichi, was unsure what to do that would satisfy his master's requirements.

Munetsune had earned a reputation for stinginess from his fellow captains because, unlike these indolent scions of wealthy families, he had only the one attendant with him in the capital, Torii-no-Munetaka. Just one retainer, think of it! But Munetaka was exceptional; a resourceful young man brought up in the remote mountain-bound province of Kōzuke where he had soon learned, as a growing boy, to hunt, fish, and study the military arts under the tutelage of his father's followers. He listened carefully as the Lieutenant, Munetsune, told him of the Lord of Uji's commission and the fact, freely admitted, that his master wasn't sure how to proceed with any sort of subtlety that would fulfil the secret part of Fujiwara Yorimichi's plan.

'Permit me, master, to think about what must be done,' said Munetaka. 'I am sure that I shall be able to advise you correctly.'

'It seems a difficult problem, though, doesn't it?'

'That is true, master, but so too are the problems we must face in war where nothing is ever certain. There is one clear thing that I can discern and that is that my Lord of Uji requires Lord Myōzon to be adequately escorted to the Miidera temple by you.'

'Yes, that is correct! I must provide a proper escort for his safety and according to his station.'

'Sir, I request that I have your leave of absence for the remainder of the afternoon.'

'That is a highly irregular request, Torii-san, but in the circumstances I shall grant it. Do you return by the time of my departure.'

'I shall do that, master, do not fear. You will see me here one hour before sunset.'

Torii-no-Munetaka, regarded by the officers of the Outer Palace Guard as a base-born servant because he came of the despised provincial warrior stock, no one even thinking that his family were wealthy landowners in Kōzuke but, of course, without Court rank, duly bowed to his master when he returned at the agreed time.

'Sir, I have given your problem considerable thought and recommend that you follow the following plan, if it should please you to do so.'

Taira-no-Munetsune laughed wryly.

'I have little choice, do I? At this point of time my mind is still a complete blank. Tell me, what do I do?'

'Lord Yorimichi will summon you just after sundown, will he not?'

'Yes.'

'Then, master, you must report to him and Lord Myōzon dressed in your body armour, carrying your bow and a full quiver of arrows, but wearing your newest gauze *eboshi* without your helmet. Oh, please wear your straw *waraji* sandals. Needless to say, you will have one horse only and that will be fully caparisoned with a chair saddle for the lord High Priest.'

'Only one horse?' frowned Munetsune in surprise. 'But there are two of us?'

'Exactly, master! Your own horse will be ready, I assure you.'

'But . . !'

'Do not fear, master; simply tell the lord High Priest that you are fleet of foot and will naturally run by his side. It is for him to make haste!'

Munetsune shrugged his shoulders, totally mystified.

'Very well! I have no idea of what you plan but I will do as you suggest.'

'Oh, master, there will be one more small thing . . .'

'I thought there might well be more. What is it?'

'The journey to Otsu will be halted a number of times, I think. Please sir, do not show the slightest alarm but remain calm and simply reassure the Lord Myōzon of your guarantee of his safety.'

Taira-no-Munetsune shook his head doubtfully, resigning himself to his difficult task and preparing to be assisted in donning his finest armour.

The sun had long set and darkness was closing in when the order came for Myōzon to depart. The Lord of Uji had provided four torch bearers to light the way ahead and as Taira-no-Munetsune appeared leading the one splendidly caparisoned horse with its red tassels, Myōzon did indeed think that he had an escort of only one man and him on foot! Fujiwara Yorimichi, personally attending to bid his guest a safe journey, merely contented himself by saying that the Lieutenant was a fierce and bold warrior and so there was naught to fear.

Myōzon was already mystified since all this was highly irregular and such an expedition, while not that great a distance, was at night and normally would be provided, as befitted his rank, with a numerous escort. But he said nothing, contenting himself with a glare of disapproval at Munetsune's straw *waraji*, and settled himself on his cushioned seat while his single armed escort took hold of the leading rein and started off out of the compound into the evening gloom outside. It would be a dark night since it was close to a new moon.

Of course, the story of what happened after they rode forth is well-known but maybe there are those who are not familiar with the details so for their benefit it shall related here. Myōzon and his foot escort had hardly left the mansion's outer gate and proceeded no more than four or five hundred yards when two armed men could be seen in the flaring torchlight of their servants. Despite leading three horses, both armoured men sank to their knees and made deep bows in the roadway.

Nervously, the High Priest clutched at the wooden arms of his saddle-chair, but Munetsune urged him to remain calm.

'Who . . . who are these men?'

'We are your escort, my lord, and we have brought an extra horse for the honourable Lieutenant of the Outer Palace Guard.'

While Myōzon could not tell the colour of the horses, he could see the glister of their rich tassels and buckles.

'Sir, we have your *kutsu* riding boots,' added one of the newcomers.

Surprised, Munetsune slipped on the bear-fur boots over his waraji and remounted.

A few hundred yards further on, it now being almost pitch dark except for the bright stars, the same thing happened again and they were joined by two more mounted bowmen who made every sign of deep respect. This happened all the way to the heights over the Kiyomizu temple, by which time the cavalcade numbered at least fifteen men.

The distance from Miyakō to Otsu is not great, some ten kilometres, but it does require climbing over the hills to the east of the city where there was, even in those calm days, a risk of encountering disaffected criminals, but as the troupe left the last habitations behind them and began their descent so the escort had swelled to more than twenty strong fighting men.

Business concluded at the Miidera, the escorting warriors reappeared at the temple's imposing Outer Gate and, in close formation, escorted the prelate back to the capital. Myōzon said nothing when, on reaching the Kamo River the escort had shrunk to just eight men and, as they approached the Lord of Uji's outer entrance gate, there were just two men left beside Taira-no-Munetsune. They halted in the avenue where Munetsune removed his riding boots and handed them back, with his horse, to the last remaining escort. Without a word but with the deepest marks of respect, the two men vanished into the darkness. Munetsune caught hold of the lord High Priest's leading rein and ran at his side to the gateway, loudly calling out the name of his mounted master. Coming to the inner courtyard just as the first streak of dawn began to appear in the eastern sky, they were greeted by Torii-no-Munetaka who waited with a number of torchbearers.

According to 'Tales of Times now Past', the prelate, Myōzon, was by now quite astonished by these uncanny, nay, ghostly events, although maybe ghostly warriors riding phantom horses would not make any sound, and he resolved to request an explanation from Lord Fujiwara as the opportunity arose. Indeed, he was ushered to His Highness' presence in order to report on his duties regarding the Onjō-ji at Otsu and was able to comment that 'Taira-no-Munetsune, the Lieutenant of the Left Division, certainly conducted his duties in a strange way.'

'Is that so?' replied Yorimichi. 'Not to your satisfaction, then, reverend sir?'

'Oh, no! That was not what I meant! I was escorted by no less than thirty fully armed horsemen, my lord, and there was no doubt that he has splendid followers; only, and this is quite beyond my comprehension, why did these fellows join the cavalcade at intervals before we had crossed out of the eastern suburbs?'

'My revered High Priest,' said Fujiwara Yorimichi, when he had listened to Myōzon's account, 'you must have been confused by the darkness of the moonless night. The Lieutenant of the Guard is commonly reported to be a mean fellow, although a brave and redoubtable bowman. He is well-known to have only one servant, a warrior from the desolate outer province of Kōzuke and of no real account. He certainly cannot call on the services of that number of armed men and not in the depths of the night such as the one now past!'

Myōzon contemplated this puzzle all the ensuing day but could reach no resolution. Far be it from him to deign to enquire an explanation from a menial samurai such as Torii-no-Munetaka who, in any case, had not accompanied his master but remained in his quarters.

But the explanation was quite simple for Munetaka had employed his hours of freedom taking advantage of his father's generosity and foresight in sending to the capital some fifteen of his inner retainers, or *rōtō*, in order that they might remain close to his son and heir during the three years of his service with the Lieutenant of the Outer Palace Guard. He might be a benighted provincial bushi, having no influence or patronage at Court – though he performed a number of services for the Lord of Uji in protecting his interests on his Kantō estates – but he was far from a penniless yokel as many courtiers might believe. With these *rōtō* travelled a trusted Torii agent who saw to it that not only his young lord wanted for nothing but neither did his followers. At the same time this agent, an astute merchant, wisely bought and sold in the capital's market places, thereby greatly increasing his lord's wealth.

When Taira-no-Munetsune had received the Lord of Uji's commission to escort Myōzon to the Miidera and back but at the same time create an insoluble puzzle, Torii-no-Munetaka had at once gone to seek out Gunbei, the agent, who in turn arranged all that transpired. Each of the *rōtō* had recruited a friend to ride with him and so thirty men were easily raised.

Later, Taira-no-Munetsune was told the whole truth of this affair when, in the course of time, he succeeded to his father's estates in the Kantō, estates bordering on those of the Torii. He never forgot the debt that he owed and nor did his descendants to the seventh generation as they joined with the Kantō Genji in the great wars that shook the land after the death of Taira-no-Kiyomori. But this was all in the future and quite another story. Neither Fujiwara Yorimichi nor the High Priest of the Miidera ever knew the truth but their side of the event became widely known and eventually nearly a hundred years later on was written down in that anthology of bizarre tales of times now past, but, as we know, here is the truth, an account of a resourceful warrior of the Torii-ke.

5

TENGU

Time out of mind, many people firmly believe that those mischievious mountain and forest creatures, who are reputed to play their games with humans and especially the more gullible priests, actually lived. While the Buddhist clergy have long attempted to demonize these beings, the warrior level of society, and particularly that important and influential group, the masters of the *bugei*, have kept their beliefs pure and untainted, never permitting *their* tengu to be subsumed into mere folk superstition or made into comic figures to scare naughty children who won't go to their nightly rest.

It is said that today's famous incident soon fades from reality as those who witnessed or experienced the event reach their dotage and pass to the next world; as endeavours dim so the original event changes to one of legend, the details blur, and in many cases attract other stories, true or false. With the slow passage of the centuries these legends, too, metamorphose into myths, vaguely remembered and woven into the peoples' collective memory, misunderstood, dramatized, and often falsely elevated to become the deeds of the gods, themselves. Not so, the tengu, who first appeared in their, apparently, minor role and were at once associated with those strange solitary priests who later became the Shugendō yamabushi, and have maintained this image, virtually unchanged, for well over an entire millennium.

Amongst the bushi and the samurai, the tengu and the yamabushi are almost indivisible, it is true, but they also pre-date the fomalization of the Shugendō sects by several hundred years. In general, the tengu are divided into two groups, both surprisingly uniform, the superior level being the *dai-tengu*, reputedly intellectual, clever, erudite, and usually portrayed with long noses on human-like faces, also often hirsute; the second and lower level comprising the *sho-tengu* are characterized by their usually hawk-like feathered heads, wings, and boundless martial skills. Sometimes, according to those who know about these things, both classes of tengu, leaders or their minions, have bird-clawed feet, but all are agreed that in general appearance the yamabushi and the tengu costume is indistinguishable, thus giving rise to a multiplicity of legends as the years have rolled by.

The Torii records, remarkably well-preserved despite the vicissitudes of war and the passage of centuries, while not unique nonetheless provide any number of windows on the past, of down-to-earth explanations of many otherwise confused, even semi-mythical, events. Naturally, reading with some difficulty the fragmentary documents that have survived from the early-Heian, we are not presented with a cohesive history as such, but hints – fleeting or, at times, detailed – of ancestors whose names may hang in the air without substance or support, or are linked to events, usually minor, but almost invariably without proper context from the point of view of ones taking place today. Such is the nature of history, as we have already said, but we should be grateful that some nameless person did take the trouble to brush these accounts down and that others, more careful and sensitive than most, placed them in a safe place where the violence of the many war-torn years left them intact . . .

The ancestors of the Torii-ke, not so named until the middle years of the Heian, the eleventh century, have always been held to have served the later Yamato kings and emperors as fighting men in some specialized but ill-defined role. Tradition amongst the later Torii, descendants of *hatamoto* rank and therefore of substance, firmly asserts that these earliest ancestors were 'horse-leading' warriors – *umajirushi* – not mere ostlers or horse wranglers but men who led their precious mounts to battle and only mounted in order to fight. These *umajirushi*, or the standard bearers of their lords, according to these oral traditions, originated in the ancient Kingdoms of

Paekche or Kaya but may have reached there from the vast spaces of the Mongolian steppe. Not only were they horse-warriors but they also had great skills in incantation and communing with the deities, especially the goddess of war. Who now can tell the truth but so the lore has been passed down through countless generations and who are we, with so little further knowledge, to cast serious doubt?

One leaf of paper in these annals, written in small but beautiful Chinese characters, tells how one of the early ancestors, one Takihiko-maru, if that be the correct reading, was employed by the local chieftain who governed what is now the southern part of Buzen province in north-eastern Kyūshū. He was a military expert and often requested by his lord to carry out inspections of the garrisons that guarded this region and to abjure the deities to bestow their benign aid onto the chieftain and his aspirations to extend his hegemony. These religious duties appeared to entail long rituals of empowerment performed before the 'house of the deities', and sometimes at simple sacred places marked by a standing stone and a tall pole or spear surmounted by a white streaming banner set at the foot of the mountain where resided the particular god. In those unsophisticated days there were few shrine structures such as we know them but a host of such wild sites, often nearby some chieftain's mansion, thought to be places of great power. But we digress from what was so carefully brushed on this single part of what may once have been a longer scroll.

> In the tenth year of the Empress Suiko, Winter in the eleventh month, Takehiko-maru was ordered to inspect the soldiers stationed on the border near to Hidehiko-yama and who protected the roads from the north. He was commanded to enquire of the deities what offerings they demanded for their continued goodwill and the prosperity of Lord Ue-no-muraji's rice-lands.

Thus begins, with due formality, the oral tradition passed down to more recent ancestors telling that this Takehiko-maru, after enquiring into the organization and supply of the fighting men, heard that several bands of men had frequently vanished into these wild mountains known as Hidehiko-yama. Whilst folk avowed that these strangers offered no threat, they posed a question in the mind of Takehiko-maru and he felt that he must see for himself. Accordingly, on the tenth day of the month he left his escort billeted in a small village near the northern part of these jumbled heights and accompanied by one servant, a stalwart young man of undoubted strength, he prayed at the marker stone to the yama-no-kami and strode towards the thickly forested slopes.

People are still deeply wary of venturing into these wild places and will only ascend the heights in the company of many fellows in the mistaken belief that numbers will somehow ward off the anger of any malevolent deities. This may, of course, be so but in those long forgotten days when Takehiko-maru and Jirō, his servant, made their 'entry' these were truly fearsome wastes of thick virgin forest, dense undergrowth, soaring rocky heights, wild torrents, and hardly a single man-made trace of a track. These fastnesses were the home of the fierce *inoshishi* wild boars, of foxes, snakes, monkeys, and black-furred *kuma* bears. Besides all these beasts, the deep valleys and rearing mountains were the resort of angry deities and their attendant demons who deeply resented any human intrusion and would call on nature to resist and deter all such trespassers.

None of these threats bothered Takehiko-maru or Jirō as they threaded their way following a narrow brook into the first valley before being forced, at last, to clamber up amongst the soaring *sugi* in order to skirt the dense bamboo groves that clogged the ravines. It soon became clear that even woodcutters only ventured a short distance into these regions and after a warm two hours, they passed the last pile of cut saplings, neatly bundled and staked across the mountain slope to season and dry.

Reaching a shoulder of rock at the head of the first valley, they realized that they had already achieved a considerable height. In the cold winter air they could see, far in the distance, the blue smoke of cooking fires rising languidly from where Takehiko-maru estimated the Mazendō stockade would lie, but apart from that there was not the slightest sign of civilization.

'Master,' Jirō ventured in a low voice, 'we are not alone.'

The warrior smiled.

'I know that,' he replied.

Far from crestfallen, Jirō grinned. 'There are at least four personages, though I am unsure if they are human or spirits.'

'Correct! I also counted four!'

'Shall I shout fiercely and scare them away?' said Jirō, grasping his spear resolutely.

'No, Jirō; we are here to inspect so we shall wait and see what transpires.'

Picking a spot where they might easily defend themselves in case of an attack, the two men sat and ate rice cakes and drank water from a tiny spring that issued from the rockface. Thus fortified, they prepared to resume their climb towards the looming heights but stood still when confronted with the sudden appearance of a diminutive figure wearing a fantastic costume. The fellow, if indeed it was a man, was clad in a black robe that terminated in wide unbleached trousers secured to each leg just below the knee by a drawstring. This left his feet exposed and the two warriors saw that these each appeared to be three-clawed. Under his glittering black eyes was a sharp hawk's beak and his head was covered with feathers. This much they could see but then the apparition uttered a series of high-pitched cries that sounded just like the mews of the great red hawk as it circled above the forests in search of its prey, and began to leap up and down with raised arms. It looked as if it had wings and would fly off . . .

Jirō didn't hesitate but stood forward with his spear levelled.

'Who or what are you who dances before my master?' he challenged.

The figure jumped back several paces, still calling out its strange cries.

Takehiko-maru frowned.

'I don't think it intends harm, Master Jirō, but seems to want us to follow.'

'Take care, my lord; it may be a trap.'

Reluctantly, Jirō put up his spear but still regarded the stranger warily.

'My master wants to know if you wish us to follow you?'

At once the birdman capered about excitedly and produced from inside the breast of his outer garment what appeared to be a feathered fan. He raised it high above his head and then brought it down suddenly. In a moment two more similarly robed birdmen appeared and came hopping over to the two warriors.

'Careful, Jirō; we'll go with them but don't offer any threat, you understand?'

The first birdman led the way into the forest following what may just have been a faint track that climbed through the trees towards a cliff face that overhung the valley. As they clambered up the slopes the air was filled with a whole series of strange calls that echoed back and forth amongst the cliffs and through the trees, some being made from high up in the dense canopy. It was a long hard walk that took most of that bright but chill afternoon, but as dusk was drawing in they reached a wide clearing free from trailing roots and creepers that constantly threatened an unwary step.

Stepping into the open space they saw on one side a large boulder ringed just above its largest girth by a rope-tasseled *shimenawa*.[2] A little beyond this stood a small building roofed by heavy thatched up-curving eaves leading the eyes to a ridge pole surmounted by

---

[2] *Shimenawa*: A length of rice straw cord having folded 'tassels' of white paper, used to mark a sacred area or object.

wooden *chigi*.[3] On their approach, heralded by a cacophony of bird-like twittering, sliding doors opened and there emerged two more birdmen flanking a much taller figure with long flowing unkempt white hair. The attendants produced a folding stool which they carefully placed for their elderly leader to seat himself.

'Honourable Takehiko-maru, welcome to our mountains!'

For the first time the warrior noticed that the old man had a straight and somewhat prominent nose . . . He bowed deeply, remembering his manners, and motioned slightly to Jirō, who stood a little to his rear, to do the same. His retainer dropped to his left knee and extended his free right hand to knuckle the ground.

'You know who I am, sir?'

'You were sent to enquire who lives in these fastnesses. Is that not so?'

'My lord, the Intendant Governor, did indeed order this.'

'And do you know who we are?'

Takehiko-maru looked about him.

'Not yet, but is this the proper place for us to converse, honoured sir?'

The old man gazed intently at him from under his bushy white eyebrows then rapped smartly twice with his staff on the boards of the verandah apron.

'Set a round mat for my guest and then begone!' he ordered.

At once this was effected with amazing alacrity and the birdmen disappeared in every direction into the cover of the forest. Glancing about to see if he had been completely obeyed, the long-nosed man, who looked somewhat priest-like to the warrior's mind, repeated his question.

'Honoured sir; I may think one thing at this early stage only to find out that I was wrong later. This may colour my thinking when I make my report. I request you to inform me so that there can be no error in the course of time.'

The older man laughed.

'A good answer, warrior! I shall indeed tell you all that you wish to know but there is one difficulty.'

'A difficulty, sir?'

'One that will prove difficult to surmount, I fancy.'

Takehiko-maru frowned at these words.

'How is that, sir? Please explain.'

'While I will tell you and your brave follower every detail, I shall only do so on condition that neither of you shall ever divulge

---

[3] *Chigi:* Ornamental finials fashioned by prolonging and crossing the gable rafters, especially of important buildings.

anything of what you hear, see, or learn whilst in my domain. Do I have you solemn word on this?'

Takehiko-maru, not taking his gaze from the face of the old man, asked Jirō what he thought about this.

'Lord, I will do whatever you decide. I would never run contrary to your wishes!'

'Sir, you heard my retainer, but first: what if we do not so swear?'

'You have seen little enough. Tomorrow morning we shall escort you to where you entered our domain and that will be the last of the matter.'

Takehiko-maru grunted, his mind now made up.

'In that case, honoured sir, I give you my solemn word that nothing of what passes between us or we witness in these mountains will be divulged and that this covenant between us shall bind our descendants for a fifty generations!'

'Spoken well, O warrior! It is as I expected of you when I knew that you would start out on this quest. However, according to our custom you shall agree to seal this oath in the presence of our deity, the Lady of the Coming dawn, She of the Seven All-powerful Stars in the Constellation of the Bear. Our great deity demands this of all who enter her service without exception.'

'We shall agree.'

'Good! I shall recall one of my attendants!'

The white-haired old man again struck the boards a single blow and one of the birdmen darted down from behind the bowl of a cypress tree of mighty girth. A brusque order was given and in a trice a small six-legged whitewood table was placed before them and what appeared to be a scroll box set on the surface.

Bowing deeply, the bird-headed attendant opened the lacquered lid then scurried back to his *sugi* without further delay. Out from the chest was taken a small scroll, an inkstone, and the paraphernalia for writing. Picking up the scroll and unwinding the narrow blue ribbon that secured it, the white-haired man began to unroll it horizontally, reciting what was written in a sonorous voice. It was apparently a long invocation that seemed somehow familiar to Takehiko-maru and yet in some foreign language . . .

'This is the oath that both of you are bound to obey! Signify that you both agree!' When they had bowed low, he then continued: 'Come, warriors, you are both required to sign this document and this shall be in your blood drawn freshly from your left hand centre finger!'

Taking up a small tightly bound bundle of bamboo slivers, the old man beckoned Takehiko-maru to come forward and kneel before him and, laying the scroll open and facing the warrior, he took hold of his left hand and firmly jabbed the tiny bundle against the centre fingertip. As the blood welled out, Takehiko-maru wetted the brush and carefully wrote the characters of his name on the paper where the old man pointed. Then it was Jirō's turn to do the same. The strange long-nosed priest turned towards the building and holding the open scroll up before his head with both hands, intoned another formula to the mysterious female Deity of the Seven Stars. Finishing his chant, he turned again and carefully rolled close the document which he obviously held in considerable regard, and retied it with its ribbon. Everything was replaced in the box and the feathered retainer summoned to remove both box and whitewood table.

'Now, my friends, we have concluded the ceremonial and I can tell you of matters that shall remain hidden for "fifty generations to come" as you so aptly put it.

'Many years ago, in the days when the Sun-King, Hōmuda-wake-no-mikoto, reigned over the Yamato, my people were invited here to serve the high chieftains. Our skills were very ancient and were the arts of war given to us in dream-visions by our special deity. We were men who, from long ages past, were able to offer protection to rulers and guard their frontiers from malevolent deities. In the lands surrounding our territory far away in the sacred mountains where once lived the "defenders of gold", our fame spread wide although it took many forms depending on the interpretations placed on our powers by those chieftains and kings who heard of our services.

'Hōmuda-wake remembered us and sent emmisaries through his elder-brother, the ruler in Kaya, to travel far to the lands vacated by the Yama-e, thence to the mountains of the "Guardians", and we answered his call. Here, in the "Lands of the Reed-plains", we were told of many powerful beings whose tribal lands lay in the wild mountains, barbarous chieftains that were called by our new masters "evil and malignant earth-deities". The task enjoined on my people, and remember, there were very few of us since our powers did not require numbers, was to counter the sorcery of the "earth-deities" and thus give protection to the Yamato rulers. To accomplish this, small groups of our people made frequent forays into the mountain wastes abjuring these recalcitrant tribal leaders to become peaceful and submit to the Yamato rule, or using our special warrior skills to destroy those who would persist with their pitiful attempts at malevolent magic.

'As the line of rulers following the Lord Ōjin, as he was named after he joined his ancestors, established their rule, so their power increased and they decided that our small, but free, bands of men they liked to call the "Yama-be" – for it suited their arrogance to think of all those not of their blood as servitors under their direct control – were no longer of value. After all, we had cleansed many stretches of mountains of future threats from rapine and murderous incursions except in those areas where the Yamatai rulers thought they could do better.

'Our high-leaders were summoned to the Court and told of this decision and that we were free to return to our ancestral lands where none had ever seen the rolling sea-wastes, but we petitioned to remain in these islands, agreeing to retire permanently into the mountain fastnesses where we would continue to subdue such evil deities as remained and carry out rites of protection to the benefit of the peaceful rulers of these lands ruled over by the Paramount King and his chieftains. We swore sacred oaths that we would offer no threat to our former benefactors. In short, we wanted no land and would remain without great numbers that might create a threat to the princes.

'This, the Court agreed, and so we carried out our rôle to control the wild demons of the forests and the mountains, to protect such travellers or wise men who might venture into our many domains, and to perform our rituals in honour of the benign deities who, in their turn, brought increase to the farmers' fields.

'No longer do we call ourselves the Yama-be, for that name we left behind us; we are now known as "Those who lie down in the Mountains" and the two characters for this read "Yama-bushi", not "mountain-warrior" although this is how those few who know of our presence think of us, I suspect.'

Takehiko-maru had said nothing whilst he and his companion listened to this long speech. For what could they say when they knew little of these matters?

The white-haired master paused and looked shrewdly at his guests.

'You have heard that there might be men in these wild heights which is why you have come here, honoured friend, but you should know that our small groups may also be found throughout the mountainous provinces; in fact, wherever there are heights held sacred by the ancient peoples as homes to their old "earth-deities". Here on Hidehiko-yama we live as you now know; but also in the rearing peaks of Kumano and Ōmine-san where we protect the peoples of the Yamato plains and beyond; and in the bleak northern wastes where our stronghold lies in the Dewa-sanzan surrounded by many barbarian tribes to this day. In all these places we quell demons, give praise to benign beings, but above all, we remain invisible except to those few souls who are forced to eke out their miserable lives in these remote places. These people we strive to help and, in their turn, they maintain our few needs.'

Realizing that the old man had finished, Takehiko-maru bowed his head very low before venturing to ask:

'Honoured master, who, then, are your attendants for they seem so different from you?'

'That is a perceptive question, warrior,' said the old man, tugging at his long beard. 'The invitation brought by the agents of the emisaries of Hōmuda-wake was placed before our ancient Council and considered by our elders. These men were at that time still known only by their exalted rank as "Keri-bu" from their ancient task of welcoming the new dawn Sun-Deity and calling on his protection for each new day. When the elders agreed just ten Masters were appointed and when these men eventually reached these shores, at the end of a journey taking two years, they brought with them our sacred totem of the Sky deity, the mighty Tengri, and secret scrolls containing much ancient lore, scrolls received from the hand of the Great Deity, herself . . .' The sage paused, then said: 'Ah, but you will be tired; I will answer your questions tomorrow after we have welcomed the dawn.'

The following morning, after the dawn ceremony, Takehiko-maru asked: 'Honoured master, you were about to tell us about your attendants . . .'

'Is that so?' The old man pulled at his long beard for some moments before replying.

'Yes, I suppose you are right to ask . . . Now, where did I reach last night?'

'Master, you told us how your ten "Master Keri-bu" were dispatched to serve Hōmuda-wake.'

'Ah, yes; of course! They brought with them the sacred symbol of our Powerful Lady . . . Do you know what that symbol is, my friend?'

Takehiko-maru frowned, then shook his head.

'A crow, master?'

'It is now; you are quite right But at that time it was the fierce griffin, the mighty creatures who used to inhabit our mountains beyond the roof of the world . . . Alas, we found no memory of these winged beasts in these islands, animals that are the very incarnation of what a brave and resourceful warrior should be both in war and the chase. Try as we might, in those turbulent days it was only those strong fighting men who achieved true insight through our teachings who ever adopted this griffin as their token of protection and real martial power; others, subverted by the Chin, only saw in our symbol a reflection of the dragon-protector of their kingdoms and thought the griffin the same, the subtleties completely wasted on them . . . Yet, all was not lost for the Lady of the Seven Stars revealed a solution that easily adapted to these shores, that of the boar, the red hawk, and the crow!'

'There were only ten "masters"; where, then did the birdmen come from?'

'Each of the ten brought with them their families and followers. This was no small migration but meant that within the first twenty years more than five hundred people crossed to serve whichever chief wished for our special skills. But these are not really birdmen, and yet, again, they are. They wear a special costume whenever they participate in ritual and, sometimes, even for their warlike practices. They are not of the blood of the Keri-bu but are sprung from two small tribes who lived to the north of our homeland, an area of dark and desolate forests, winding marshy rivers, boundless in all directions but to the south. Long ages past, these diminutive men have served us for their gods were subservient to Tengri and their skill in communing with these deities nearly equal with ours, excelling us in one thing only.'

When the old man paused, Takehiko-maru couldn't help asking what that was.

'They know the secret art of speaking to certain gods through their sacred drums. It is this art that they offered to provide to my people forever!'

'I have heard, master, that this drumming has been known here since the Age of the Gods. Is this the same?'

'It is and it isn't. Perhaps some day I shall explain; but to continue. When we finally crossed to here from Kaya, we brought with us numbers of these faithful servants. In accordance with our mysteries, for nothing should be made easy for an enemy to find, we abandoned our former languages and made it our business to learn that of the peoples we now live amongst. We learnt to speak in the way that the Kayan chieftains converse whilst these "birdmen" learnt the language of the mountainfolk, of woodcutters, hunters and the like, hardly ever venturing to be seen other than in the narrow valleys or half-hidden in the forests.

'We were known to the great chieftains as the "Yama-be" because it pleased them to call us so, and the masters were the "*Dai-tengu*", a name applied in ignorance, I think, and a corruption from our word for "One who speaks with the Sky Deity" – the Yamato added "Great" for they love to have high-flown titles for anyone in authority. In time we, ourselves, called the birdmen "*Sho-tengu*".'

Jirō bowed his head and asked: 'Honoured master, I would like to ask something, if it is permitted?'

'You have also been inducted, Jirō-san; of course you may speak.'

'Lord, the honoured master said that these "birdmen" servants originally came from two different tribes in their homeland . . .'

'Yes?'

'Is this why I have glimpsed some with their bird masks but some with long noses and hairy faces? Is this a difference between them?'

'Maybe, Jirō-sama; maybe!' nodded the old master. 'Those that sometimes wear the bird masks are of one tribe and are adepts in the basic arts of using weapons, but those with the hairy faces . . . they are given great inner knowledge. If you face them you will need to be on your mettle for they have skills far beyond the normal. I congratulate you on your observation!'

Jirō bowed low at this praise, his humble heart singing with pleasure.

'Tomorrow we shall begin for by then you will have rested well!'

A drum beat loudly in the frosty pre-dawn air, deep and intense, echoing eerily around the darkened valleys.

BOOM – BOOM – BOOM --- Bom . . . Bom . . . Bom . . Bom . Bom . Bom --- BOOM – BOOM – BOOM . . . Thrice its rich voice reverberated through the forested slopes and soon the night air was filled with the curious chirping sounds of the sho-tengu who homed in on the mountainside clearing in what must have been large numbers.

As Takehiko-maru and Jirō emerged from the quarters allocated to them in a small rustic hut built just within the lower forest, they saw that a number of flaring torches had been set to illuminate the clearing. In front of the small building an altar had been contructed, guarded on either side by a sho-tengu of the second type whose eyes glittered through their bushy facial hair. Of the rest of the gathering there was not the slightest sign but the followers of the old dai-tengu were undoubtedly close by to judge from the faint rustling amongst the trees.

The white-haired dai-tengu appeared without warning just behind the two warriors as they gazed about the torchlit scene.

'Greetings on this auspicious new day!'

'Greetings, my lord,' both replied with deferential bows.

There followed a short ceremony kneeling before the small altar on which were set out a number of weapons and a feathered helmet that somehow looked 'foreign' to Takehiko-maru's discerning eye. The dai-tengu knelt down and intoned a series of invocations in a sing-song voice then arose and performed a ritual dance making use of his large feathered fan and a short arrowless bow. It dawned on the warriors that this stylized dance was directed at the four cardinal points, commencing towards the east. When the dance was completed, marked by another series of drum beats, the warriors became aware that behind them were ranged two long ranks of sho-tengu, all bowing low to the ground and that some appeared to wear white-laced body armour.

A shrill shout dispersed all but two of the sho-tengu to the sides of the open clearing where they stood in complete silence. The armoured pair stood at the further end of the open space, legs wide spaced, grasping staves a little over their height in length.

'You may wish to arm yourselves similarly, my friends,' suggested the dai-tengu. 'We allow no live weapons in our dawn encounters!'

Takehiko grunted and, nodding to Jirō, both removed their slung swords and placed them together with the hunting spear at the side of the altar.

At once, a single drum beat signalled the start and the two sho-tengu dashed forwards before one went to the left and the other to the right. Whirling, they tumbled and bounced up like the Chinese acrobats the warriors had seen in the marketplaces, but in this case there was the added menace of the flailing staves . . . They were here, there, and everywhere; trying to confuse the two warriors by the rapidity of their movements.

Wisely, Takehiko-maru warned Jirō to guard his back while he defended the front. He lashed out at the legs of one of their bouncing adversaries but missed and just ducked a crack aimed at his head. Jirō, on the other hand, was more fortunate, sweeping his stave upwards and flicking his attacker's shaft so well that it bowled the feathered 'enemy' head over heels to crash to the ground at the feet of the Master. Without delay, two more of the fallen birdman's friends leapt down into the arena so that the two warriors faced three adversaries instead of one.

'Attack when I give the word,' breathed Takehiko-maru, 'or we'll not survive . . .'

The three tengu evidently consulted with each other before beginning to circle their 'victims', slowly at first, then faster. Suddenly they all yelled as one and rushed forwards.

'Now!' shouted Takehiko-maru, diving left while Jirō went right.

The tengu, leaping as they were, could not immediately change direction and, perforce, passed between the two fightingmen

'Thwack . . . Thwack!'

Their two staves struck upwards, connected, and two of the tengu lay winded and helpless on the ground. The third, realizing his danger, was about to seek his escape when he, too, was bowled over by Jirō's pole and, like his predecessor, ended at the dai-tengu's feet.

The drum beat out twice.

'Enough!' called out the old man.

Takehiko-maru glanced at Jirō in surprise. Surely that couldn't be all?

'Genki-bō! Ren-bō! You and two others – attack now!'

Four shrieking figures hurled themselves down from the heights whilst the watching sho-tengu leapt up and down frenziedly amongst the trees. Takehiko-maru laid about him manfully but was soon struck a glancing blow to his left shoulder, Jirō, not so fortunate, was almost winded by a thrust but recovered to sweep the legs from under his attacker before bringing a second assailant crashing down in mid-leap.

Now, the two surviving sho-tengu, withdrew, pointing inwards with their stave ends. One sidled forwards with a fierce yell, on each right step thumping the 'blade' end of his shaft hard down onto the ground and shouting a high-pitched call . . .

'Careful, master,' cautioned Jirō, watching the tengu intently.

Suddenly, his master leapt high in the air just as his opponent delivered a low atack. As he landed, he bent his knees so that he crouched to only half his height, the tengu's following attack, aimed at his head, completely missing its target, and thrust the tip of his bladeless 'spear' up under his adversary's jaw so that any further move would have been fatal had a blade been present.

The drum thumped out twice more and at that moment the first ray of the rising sun flashed onto the altar from the east.

The white-haired Master stood at his full height, his feathered fan open and pointing forwards from his raised left hand.

'You have good skill, you warriors of the plains,' he remarked; 'you lack polish, but you certainly have spirit and understand how to act as one!'

Jirō, with his forthright character, bowed slightly, then demanded: 'Why don't you admit that my master comprehensively defeated your followers?'

The old man smiled slightly.

'Oh, I do admit it, impetuous one! But they are mainly inexperienced novices. Didn't you realize that?' As he spoke he slowly moved across the uneven space, folding his feathered fan with some care, and joined the two whilst leaning heavily on his short staff. 'They have, in most cases, only been training for around ten or twelve years. How long have you followed the "Path of the Sword", Jirō-san?'

'I have served my master for twenty years, my lord.'

'And you, Takehiko-maru; how long have you trained?'

The warrior grimaced.

'About twenty-five years, given that I first received instruction as a boy of ten . . . but why do you ask, master?'

'Because, my friends, you have permitted me to stand close by your side without a single thought of what I may be about. First I was over there by the altar of Our Lady of Light, now I am here . . . Did you really see me approach? If I had meant you harm you would now be defeated without a blow being struck!'

The two men looked one to the other then sank to their knees and bowed deeply.

'Will you still deign to teach us, master?' requested Takehiko-maru.

'I can only do so provided you give up and abandon your false warrior's pride and sense of superiority!'

Again, Takehiko-maru bowed.

'You have a degree of skill but it lies mainly on the surface. You must remain here for a long time and train with rigour. Is this what you want?'

The warrior thought for a moment, wondering about his escort down in the nearby village and his obligation to his lord.

'Oh, they have been taken care of,' said the dai-tengu. 'Already they return home bearing news of your delay.'

Surprised, Takehiko-maru looked up.

'But how did you know I would agree to stay, master?'

'You have been here two whole weeks and still you have questions and yet more questions!'

'Two weeks . . . but . . ?'

The dai-tengu clapped his hands, dismissing all his attendants.

'Come, my friends, we must discuss the future . . .'

Takehiko-maru despatched reports to his chieftain, appointed to govern the region by the Imperial Court, but did not reappear from the mountains for a period of seven years. It is said by many that after this he became famous for his miraculous mastery of the military arts, skilled with sword, spear and bow.

The record in the Torii annals does not provide us with any more details, but it was a later descendant of the Torii-ke who also followd the yamabushi paths, perhaps in the middle of the Heian era of peace, who was able to brush down two old stories still told about the formidable Takehiko-maru and his famous follower, Jirō, an ancestor of the Miki-ke.

Who now can tell the truth of these things?

6

THE SHRINE

'That boar must have passed this way, Miki-san.'

'True, my lord; see, here is some fresh bright blood smeared on the back of this cypress tree.'

The samurai put his finger on the dark patch and showed the trace to his master.

'Perhaps you wounded it more than you first thought?'

'Maybe, my lord, but such an animal as that will now be doubly dangerous, particularly as we know the sow and her litter is somewhere up there.'

'I think it is time to take a rest. This *inoshishi* is cunning and will lay an ambush somewhere up towards the shrine, if I make no mistake. If we delay the pursuit perhaps we can fool it so that it relaxes its guard. What do you think?'

'Six times we have hunted this old boar and each time it has eluded us. Such a thing has rarely if ever happened before, certainly not around these parts.'

His lord laughed silently.

'Miki-sama, you are giving this boar special qualities! You are making it out that it is an expert in the arts of warfare and the next thing you will be saying is that it is a messenger of Marishi-ten, herself!'

'It is possible, my lord, isn't it? There seems little doubt that this particular inoshishi has a clear idea of deception and invisibility.'

'Let's seat ourselves down and cool off a little, then we can debate the divine qualities of our foe!'

The two samurai made themselves comfortable against a tussocked bank next to a burbling mountain stream that tumbled and foamed down its rock strewn course from the heights above. A stone's throw downstream, where lay a shallow pool before the burn spilled over a ledge to continue on its merry way, a sudden blue flash betrayed the presence of a kingfisher hunting for minnows in the clear water. Somewhere up the densely forested mountain the two men could hear woodpeckers tapping away in search of grubs hiding in the fissured bark of the towering cypress trees.

Torii Tora-no-suke, the senior ranking of the pair, was the brother of the Deputy Constable who governed the whole of southern Kōzuke. He was a fine looking fellow, now at the height of his powers, a skilful warrior who had experienced and survived a number of wars in his thirty-six years. He wore a plain blue-laced *dō-maru* without a helmet. Tied about his head to keep in check his long unbound hair was a *hachimaki* folded lengthways, sewn on the part which crossed his forehead were five small lacquered iron plates neatly joined together with chainmail, sufficient to give protection from all but the most violent sword blow. He carried, in addition to his sword, a powerful rattan-bound Kantō bow and a full quiver of twenty-four arrows secured to his right hip.

Miki Heihachirō, his retainer, also wore a dō-maru that closed up the back, of a type that was popular amongst samurai perhaps a hundred years before. It was laced with both pale and dark green braid. An observer, had one been present, could have told from the quality of this armour that here was also a man of some substance and, in fact, he was the head of one of the chief *hatamoto* clans who had served the Torii time out of mind. Heihachirō was the same age as his lord and they had been friends since early childhood, together learning the complexities of using all kinds of weapons, riding, tactics and strategy from a number of master tacticians retained by the Torii-ke. He carried his favourite yari, a relatively short-shafted straight spear no more than eight feet in length. While his lord had elected to hunt with a bow, Heihachirō favoured the possibility of facing an angry boar with his yari which was furnished with a fine iron *hadome* parrying bar positioned about two feet down from the triangular sectioned blade. He, too, eschewed a helmet and wore, like his master, a tight folded hachimaki reinforced with a single fretted iron plate. Both men's shoulders were protected by flexible *sode* guards, Tora-no-suke's the smaller modern sort but Heihachirō's larger with gold filigree work on the top flange.

The sunshine sparkled and shimmered from the rock pools and rushing waters below them as they resumed the chase, carefully climbing the very steep and precipitous path that wound upwards into the dark forest. From a great distance away they heard the sound of a horagai but knew at once that it was not a war signal but that of a single wandering yamabushi probably communing with the gods high up in the peaks.

After half-an-hour's stiff scramble over the rough hewn steps and dangerous exposed tree roots, the slope eased somewhat and the trees thinned giving the hunters better vision. Now they could glimpse a part of the ancient shrine that was their goal; it remained a long way above them, but they also realized that their quarry was still somewhere close by. Now was not the time to relax their guard.

The shrine had been constructed, long centuries ago, on two partially levelled 'platforms' across a rugged shoulder of the mountain; the lower part, which the two hunters approached by way of the narrow westerly path would bring them first to a crude torii that was the entrance to a subsidiary shrine dedicated to deities associated with the main gods, above: the prayer hall and *shinden* were in the upper area, again reached by a flight of steep steps.

Weapons ready, the two hunters carefully mounted to the gate, every nerve tautened in case the inoshishi lay concealed for an ambuscade, but there was no sign of the cunning beast. A faint snuffling and grunts came from ahead of them where the forest closed in just before the second flight of steps.

'That's the sow, Torii-sama,' warned Heihachirō.

Tora-no-suke nodded his assent. He pointed to a slight movement in the trees. It was one of the boar's litter rooting at the edge of the undergrowth.

'Take care! That youngster will not be alone . . .'

On the opposite side of the level clearing stood two small delapidated shrines with their heavy miniature thatched roofs thick with green moss. That on the left was dedicated to a male deity whilst the one on the right, almost identical in its size and shape, to a female deity, perhaps the former's consort like Izanagi and Izanami. Both men knew this to be the case as the *chigi* roof finials of the former were cut off vertically, while those of the right were cut horizontally. Just behind these miniature buildings lay a dark hole in the mountainside, likewise distinguished by a small crude pole torii.

'Looks like an entrance to the underworld,' muttered Heihachirō.

'What, another one? The whole place must be well ventillated!'

Just then, with a short squeal, the sow briefly appeared, saw the samurai and shrilled a warning to her brood. Tails standing stiffly, the animals vanished . . . but almost before they were aware of the danger the boar, itself, hurtled out beneath the left-hand shrine and charged the few yards of open ground straight at them!

It crossed the space in just three short seconds, leaving both men just enough time to fling themselves aside as it barged between them and vanished into the lower forest.

Ruefully, both warriors picked themselves up from the dusty ground.

'My lord, that boar applied excellent generalship to the situation! First he lulled us into a false sense of well-being, then gently distracted us before unleashing his attack from our left!'

'Heihachirō-san, that might be so, but might it also have been a feint attack, as well? I would have thought Marishi-ten would have been more subtle, wouldn't you?'

'Um!'

The sound of the horagai floated in the air once more, closer this time, and answered shortly by another horn. On the upper 'platform' the inoshishi appeared again, snorting as it stared down at its pursuers, before trotting off after his sow.

'We mustn't lose them again . . .'

'Careful, my lord; that boar is clever . . . it could double back.'

'Come on, Heihachirō-san! Forget that nonsense . . . we shall have him soon!'

They moved silently across the open space to the foot of the second span of steps and Tora-no-suke tapped his retainer's arm for him to go to the right whilst he slipped between the prayer hall and the shinden. As he ducked under the steep wooden steps that connected the hall to the high verandah sacred to the deity a sudden scraping nearby warned him that the wild boar had indeed circled round and was now at his rear . . . Clever animal! It had him completely at a disadvantage and he must move very fast if he was to save himself. He heard the beast snort, reached up and swung himself onto the log steps.

'Heihachirō! The boar . . !'

Looking down from his perch clinging to the balustrade, he saw the inoshishi vanish round the side of the hall but Heihachirō had understood the danger and rushed round the other way, burst through the wicket gates and climbed to join his master.

'That was close,' He caught his breath, his scarred face running with sweat. 'I hope the kami won't be displeased!' He bowed his head slightly towards the inner sanctum.

'You know, I am changing my mind about what you said earlier!'

'You are, my lord?'

'I have a feeling that he didn't intend to attack us then but to drive us up here! We are no longer the hunters, Heihachirō-san, but the hunted!'

Heihachirō rubbed the long scar that ran diagonally down his face from his right forehead to his left cheek, the momento of a desperate mêlée against a gang of brigands the Torii had destroyed some years before. (He had been lucky that the enemy blade had only slit his skin and not blinded him.)

'Umm! We'll see about that!'

But as if to reinforce what Torii Tora-no-suke had said, the wild boar thrust his snout round the corner below them, one small eye glinting as he stared knowingly upwards at the pair. He grunted and withrew. Just as Heihachirō was about to say something, a jet of urine sprayed the ground beside the hall corner!

'So that's what he thinks, is it?'

They both laughed.

Now the hours passed slowly for the two bushi but they had little choice but to remain on the verandah. From where they sat they could see out over the lower trees to the south-west where the serried ranks of the high peaks of Kai province rose to the azure skies. They could even make out in the clear air the distant snow-clad peak of Fuji-san which must lie over seventy miles away. The afternoon sun sank to the horizon and, as the brazen colours faded, they again heard the horagai which made Heihachirō knit his brows.

'My lord, that yamabushi call . . . you don't think it is military rather than calling the gods?'

Tora-no-suke looked at his follower.

'You are thinking the same as me?'

'It sounded vaguely familiar, my lord; but then, I can't quite place the call.'

'Hmmm . . . You remember when we both trod the priest's road when we were younger and we saw some strange things? Apart from the four mass "entries" into the mountains, some of these yamabushi go around in strong groups . . .'

'Can we get into this inner shinden, my lord?'

'The priests can, only here they have locked the doors.'

'I'll see what I can do . . .' said Heihachirō, examining the lock mechanism. 'I think we need to hurry as shortly we shall have some unwelcome company!'

The bolts soon gave way despite the fact that it was clear that no one had served this shrine for a good long time, and the pair carefully stepped inside, sliding the shōji shut behind them. Neither felt the kind of awe that peasants might have had for the sacred house of the kami. Their eyes becoming accustomed to the thick gloom, they made themselves as comfortable as they could to await the following dawn. Meanwhile, immediately below them the inoshishi family also made themselves beds for the night.

Heihachirō opened his eyes but without a movement to ease his position. In his subconscious he had heard some noises outside and knew that they weren't made by the wild boars, though he did wonder why they hadn't grunted or squealed . . .

'Lord,' he whispered, 'our company has arrived.'

Tora-no-suke placed his eye to the gap between two panels but it was still too dark to see anything. He leant back.

'We must keep very still until we can take stock,' he murmured.

There was silence for a considerable time until they became aware of a strange intoning that seemed at first a monotone but gradually they recognized some slight inflections. There must be a number of people to judge from the density of the chant. This went on for some time but died down just as the first streaks of light appeared in the skies. Quite unexpectedly, several conches were blown in unison and someone beat slowly and without strength on a drum. This time the chanting was recognizable as part of the *Heart Sutra* . . .

One firmer drumbeat brought a change.

'Now we have the *Peacock Sutra*,' breathed Heihachirō, 'and that proves they *are* yamabushi . . .'

The chanting continued while the dawn light grew in strength and through the chinks in the cladding the two warriors could view parts of the two courtyards clearly. At the same time, they were aware that the inoshishi had not fled during the night; on the contrary, the huge boar was unconcernedly wandering in and out of their field of vision which could only mean that he felt no threat from these strangers. About an hour after sunrise, a sudden shouting drew their attention to the lower yard where they saw a number of the rough-looking yamabushi gathered. An order was shouted and the priests set about a vigorous *bō-jutsu* practise with their *bonden* staves, presided over by an enormous *sendatsu* who sported bristling sideburns that gave him the fiercest look imaginable.

'They are very good with those staves,' muttered the hatamoto appreciatively.

As the practice came to an end, two more of the mountain priests emerged into view dragging a bound man between them. They threw their prisoner roughly to the ground in the centre of the yard immediately opposite the two miniature shrines, leaving him to struggle up to a sitting position.

Below, in the open-sided prayer hall, the drum began to be beaten rhythmically with a long series of low blows increasing gradually in tempo, ending with three slow but harder ones.

'There's the boar again . . .' Tora-no-suke commented in a whisper.

Sure enough, the great beast had come into view and paced purposely towards the bound man where it thrust close its snout embellished with a pair of wicked up-curved tusks and sniffed all around. With a couple of final grunts, the boar turned away and balefully – deliberately – stared up at their hiding place in the shinden.

The drum beat out again and with a wild yelling several of the yamabushi ran across and began to rain savage blows on their helpless victim until at last he fell over, curling up in an attempt to save his head. A last beat halted the punishment and the mountain men retired out of sight.

'That boar is dangerous in more ways than one,' muttered Tora-no-suke. 'We need to find a deeper hiding place, Heihachirō-san. What do you think?'

Down below, the yamabushi leader shouted out a string of orders and his men noisily ran out to their bound prisoner; now was the time for them to move if they could. The small chamber, residence of the 'calm' spirit of the deity, measured roughly fifteen feet square and was partitioned further on the western side by the high seat of the deity, screened from profane eyes so that only the high priest may enter the august presence and even then the deity would be on his right, not facing him. This sacred alcove was itself roofed beneath the main timbers of the steeply pitched outer roof. It was here the warriors silently clambered to seek sanctuary, first stripping off their armour. Heihachirō pulled himself up first and his lord passed their equipment and weapons up before carefully effacing any traces on the main floor. They settled down to wait.

The sun had hardly cleared the mountain tops to warm the shrine roofs when they became aware of further chanting and a creaking of the steep flight of wooden steps leading up to the shinden accompanied by the beating of the great drum and mournful blasts of the horagai. The doors of the shinden were slid back and Tora-no-suke glimpsed the broad back of the huge sendatsu as he knelt just outside intoning a formula to the enshrined deity. When he finished his incantation the stairs creaked again, more loudly than before, and the samurai thought that something bulky had been placed outside on the verandah. The sendatsu then bowed deeply and withdrew carefully backwards down the log stairs.

The drum beat out again and, amazingly, the yamabushi sounded as if they were moving off and leaving the shrine. In the silence that ensued the two bushi didn't stir just in case watchers had been left behind but all they could hear were snuffles and grunting from the foraging inoshishi . . . and muffled groans that told them it was the beaten prisoner who lay outside.

A good hour passed before Tora-no-suke stirred.

'Time for action, Heihachirō-sama; we now shall move!'

The retainer's scarred face creased into a ready smile.

'Shall I climb down first, my lord?'

'No; I shall go first and you pass down the armour and the rest.'

Fifteen minutes later, they were fully equipped with limbs eased, ready for anything. Their first action after cautiously peering out from they vantage place, was to drag in the trussed and gagged man and cut him free from the thick ropes which bound him. He glared about him defiantly but, realizing that they were friends and not enemies, softened his gaze and muttered words of gratitude. Gradually, with much chafing, the blood began to return to his arms and legs and they realized that despite the apparent ferocity of the beating, most of the blows had fallen on his bonds rather than his body so that, apart from some stiffness, he was relatively uninjured.

'Who are you, priest?' demanded Tora-no-suke.

'A yamabushi!'

'We can see that! What is your name?'

'I am Gotembō! I am from Kumano.'

'Who were the others, eh? Did you know them?'

'Oh, yes! I know them alright, samurai!' Gotembō shrugged his shoulders. 'They are a bad lot; a gang of near-brigands, who think they have the sole right to levy dues from the poor villages in Shinano and Echizen, to the exclusion and good name of wandering yamabushi like myself!'

Heihachirō laughed sardonically.

'I thought that was what you Shugendō priests did all the time with your mumbo-jumbo and evil spells! So how are you any different, tell us?'

Gotembō looked at him for four or five seconds then replied: 'Samurai! You look to me to be a true bushi and you follow the "Sword's Path", don't you? Unless I miss my guess, both you and your lord, here, have also tramped the hard byways of the yamabushi. Is it not the truth?'

Heihachirō glanced at his lord and Tora-no-suke nodded.

'It is so!'

'In that case,' Gotembō snorted, 'you know by instinct that I am not like any of those scum but one of you. Isn't that so, samurai?' The yamabushi pulled back his full sleeves and thrust out his wrists. 'Look, samurai-dono; look at these and you will understand!'

Heihachirō narrowed his eyes and leant forwards in the gloom the better to see. Sure enough, both the priest's wrists were thickened and at first glance appeared to be the circumference of his middle forearms with fingers on the end. Such powerful wrist development could only be the result of swinging heavy bokutō since early youth . . . and many a hard blow received on the painfully bruised lower arms. Only *kenshi* had such distinctive wrists.

He bowed in acknowledgement and Tora-no-suke visibly softened as he, too, recognized the quality of the late captive.

'Do you know where that gang have gone, Gotembō-sama?'

'They will have gone to the "Rock of Sins", my lord. Two of their number have not confessed past iniquities satisfactorily and will be punished.'

'Punished? What do you mean by that?'

'They will be trussed up and pushed over the cliff to dangle above the abyss. Every time that sadistic *sendatsu*, Renzō-bō, thinks they are lying to save their miserable skins, the ropes are released so that without warning they drop a further foot or two, much to their great terror for they know the cords are only rice straw and not very strong. Below them jut out the jagged rocks of the cliff past which they will hurtle to their deaths!'

The hatamoto pulled a face.

'What about the wild boar, Gotembō-sama?'

'Boar? What boar is that?' The yamabushi seemed surprised at the question.

'You saw no boar?'

'I don't follow you, my friend; I know nothing of any boar, well, except that the great Marishi-ten is held to ride on the back of such a beast, though only on our *honzon*,[4] I think.'

---

[4] *Honzon*: A drawn votive image of the deity or symbol venerated by the faithful.

'We have chased such a boar to this shrine, Gotembō-sama, and even now he wanders below, waiting for us to descend!'

'Eh? That sounds unusual!' The yamabushi looked serious. 'You saw the animal but I didn't, and nor did the gang . . . How can this be, I wonder?'

'You didn't see the inoshishi and yet it came across and smelt you as you knelt before those two small shrines? You saw or felt nothing?'

'Nothing! I sat there praying to the gods in front of the entrance to the Land of Yōmi, the Underworld of the Lord Emma. I saw nothing!' Gotembō was plainly mystified.

A horagai was blown nearby. There was now little time to give thought to something which seemed, on the surface, as supernatural, yet both the warriors had clearly seen the huge boar wandering unconcernedly amongst the yamabushi gang. This was surely a strange mystery, indeed.

'They are back!' said Tora-no-suke.

'What do you intend to do, Lord Torii?'

'Do? Why give battle, of course! You can fight, can you not?'

'Against that mob! Of course!'

'Can you use a bow?'

The yamabushi grinned.

'Then we shall attack them when they least expect it and so reduce their numbers before we come to quarters hand-to-hand. You, Gotembō, will make every keen arrow count . . . not two shafts to kill a man but only one to disable him. When they are down to ten or twelve we shall charge in and destroy them.'

'Always remember the boar, my lord. Gotembō-sama may not have seen him but we did . . !'

As they made ready, Gotembō methodically tested the bowstring and heavy Kantō bow. He clearly had practised hands. The two bushi flexed and stretched their muscles. They had purposely left the shinden doors open, just as the yamabushi leader had left them, and concealed themselves on either side in readiness.

The first gang members to appear immediately saw that Gotembō had vanished and shouted out to Renzō-bō to come and see for himself. He brusquely shouldered his way through the excited throng.

'What is all this, eh?' he bawled angrily. 'Who has taken him . . . He certainly can't have untied those ropes by himself!'

There was a silence at this then Heihachirō had a brainwave. He cupped his hands about his mouth and roared out in his fiercest voice: 'I, Susa-nō-ō, took him, priest!'

As the three peered through the chinks in the wall planking they saw that the result was devastating. Every single yamabushi crowded below them, with the single exception of the burly leader, was thunderstruck for a second or two before dropping to their knees down to the floor, bowing and grovelling as low as possible. The thick-set Renzō-bō let his jaw drop open then closed it like a trap and bowed his body but still standing.

'My lord accepts the offering?' he shouted.

'No!' bellowed Heihachirō, 'It is not enough!'

Gotembō, awaiting this chance, stepped forward and sent an arrow deep into the small of one of the kneeling men's back. A second shaft pierced his neighbour as he looked up in alarm; the bowman was out of sight and no one knew from where the arrows came. The second man clawed wildly at the arrow and fell sideways. Consternation ensued . . . Renzō-bō roared out orders but for several seconds all was chaos.

'Get back!' the gang leader shouted, 'This is no god but that wretch we had captive . . . somehow he has found a bow!'

A third arrow, loosed from deep inside the shinden, buried itself deep in the back of a third victim as he scrabbled to get over the balustrade to cover. Three down, just seventeen or eighteen to go!

'Every arrow to count, Gotembō,' hissed Tora-no-suke. 'They don't know there are three of us as yet!'

By now, the gang had all concealed themselves out of sight at the further end of the prayer hall by the entrance steps.

Gotembō shouted out: 'You gave me a beating and left me to die! This is my revenge, you coward, Renzō-bō!'

'We will do more than beat you when you run out of arrows, you'll see!' the sendatsu fiercely rejoined. 'We shall tear you apart limb from limb!'

'I can't wait, you cowards!'

One of the yamabushi crowding the front of the hall, lost his grip on the side rails and tumbled out into the yard. He made a dash for the trees but it was too easy a target and he, too, fell on his face, impaled through the base of his skull.

'Fifteen!' muttered Heihachirō in admiration; Gotembō was indeed a formidable bowman.

A further hour passed in relative silence as Renzō-bō decided what was to be done. The waiting bushi, putting themselves in the sendatsu's place, decided that his only course of action was to risk a couple of casualties and rush their tormentor. While he might just have time to loose two shafts, they would overwhelm him in a trice . . . and vengeance would surely follow!

'They have no bows, Torii-sama,' signed Gotembō.

All three knew that they needed to reduce the odds still further but it was the bowman who acted. He nocked an arrow then darted out through the open shōji to the right side of the apron verandah. From there he could see into the corner of the hall and some of the tight packed yamabushi. Dropping to his right knee he sent an arrow into the crowd and a second one before they had scrambled away to the sheltered side.

'Charge him!' bawled the sendatsu, and brandishing his paper decorated bonden, laid about him to drive several of the angry men up the steep steps to catch Gotembō before he could do more damage. But now the gang had to stumble up the steps in the face of Gotembō's arrows and two more fell immediately and a third followed as the leaders, shouting wildly, reached the verandah and turned to rush their deadly adversary. Three of them passed the open shōji when Heihachirō's yari took the next man in the side, hoicking him screaming over the side of the steps to smash down the rotten screen below. He struck a second man in the side of the jaw, felling him, when Tora-no-suke cut down two of those who had run past to engage Gotembō.

In the greatest fear, the remainder tumbled back down the stairway, two on their backsides, whilst Renzō-bō, beside himself with rage, abjured them to resume the attack. They had had enough; even fear of the sendatsu's cruel venom or the ordeals that they knew he was capable of devising, would not drive them back and their cowardice was compounded when Gotembō winged another one of the survivors with an arrow painfully driven through his shoulder.

'We'll burn them out!' snarled Renzō-bō.

'You can't do that, master' remonstrated one of the gang. 'Think of the vengeance of Lord Susa-nō-ō . . .'

The leader hit him violently across the mouth sending him reeling. His face was an evil mask . . . He had already lost about twelve men and it was all due to that black-hearted yamabushi from Yoshino . . . how could it happen? They should have beaten him to death . . !

'Break down those shōji,' he rasped; 'break them up quickly!'

Soon he had a pile of matchwood which two of the scared *shingyaku* novices pushed towards the stairs with their bonden, fearful of a searching arrow if they showed so much as an inch of flesh. He took out some fine shavings tinder and a live charcoal that such men keep ready to hand and soon had an improvised torch flaring.

'Toss that on the pile, Myō-bō,' he ordered, but the young yamabushi rolled his eyes, looking to be in mortal fear. 'Gōki-san! Beat the disobedient dog!'

A shrivelled up little man sidled out of the group, little more than a dwarf, and viciously swung a cudgel that felled Myō-bō to the floor whereupon Gōki rained a succession of merciless blows about his head and shoulders . . . No one saw that Gotembō had descended the staircase and levelled his bow.

The wild-haired yamabushi loosed the bowstring and the feathered shaft sank deep into Gōki's back so that the blue steel blade burst from the front of his chest. The dwarf pitched over his victim, drowning in his own blood. Renzō-bō started back and clutched for the hilt of his low-slung tachi, for he was the only one of the gang to wear a longsword. Facing the now demoralized mob were the three vengeance-seeking men. At the sight of the two bushi as well as their erstwhile victim, now nocking yet another deadly shaft into his bowstring, four of the remaining yamabushi took to their heels and dived for the forest, so much in fear of their lives that three of them simply threw away their bonden . . .

There was a sudden shrill squeal and the absent inoshishi materialized, charging up the step and across the prayer hall, running full pelt between Renzō-bō's wide-planted legs, up-ending the sendatsu across his back. Regaining his balance with a desperate twist, he strikingly resembled those images of Marishi-ten dressed in yamabushi garb, riding on the back of a boar. The flaring torch that he grasped in his hand flew to one side and rolled harmlessly to the ground, but giving the apparition a momentary nimbus of flame.

Heihachirō and Gotembō, in what may have seemed a simultaneous movement, prepared to meet their foes, the warrior firmly jamming his spear butt against the lower step, the yamabushi loosing a final arrow. The boar hurled its weight onto the yari, the whole blade and head of the shaft piercing deep into its throat and chest, whilst the arrow impaled Renzō-bō's neck just below his chin . . . The boar's weight carried it down the shaft until the iron crossbar struck its chest, the sudden arrested motion flinging the wounded sendatsu forwards so that he flew between Heihachirō and Tora-no-suke, breaking his neck as he hit the log ladder. In what seemed like slowed action, Heihachirō saw his yari shaft bend to a marked curve then snap in two, but the boar was already dead before it hit the ground at their feet.

'Hmm! Now I see your boar!' remarked Gotembō.

The two bushi and their new follower, the yamabushi, found themselves a safe rock shelter far down the valley in order to spend the night. They made a small fire in the lee of a great out-jutting boulder where no reflections of the flames could be observed from beyond.

'That was what I call an "interesting" hunt,' remarked Torii Tora-no-suke, 'I'm not really certain if I really enjoyed it or not. What do you think, Heihachirō-san?'

The hatamoto laughed. 'Oh, I enjoyed parts of it, my lord, though I regret the breaking of my yari.'

'And you, Gotembō-san?'

'I had a splendid time ... no doubt about it! First I was trussed up, then licked by an invisible wild boar, beaten with staves; well, you know it all! An adventurous day that will long be remembered!'

Heihachirō looked up. All the stars had vanished from the late evening sky and there was a leaden heaviness in the air. He sniffed and smelt rain coming from the western mountain ranges.

'May I suggest we sit inside our shelter, my lord? I think we are about to have a heavy rainstorm.'

As if to underscore his words, there came a distant roll of thunder from the heights up the valley. A second roll followed immediately.

Gotembō grinned hugely as he kicked dirt onto the flames.

'You did tempt fate chasing that strange inoshishi, you know, and the more so by offending Susa-nō-ō in his sacred house!'

'Interesting, what you said just now, Gotembō-san,' said Tora-no-suke as they sat and watched the teeming downpour; 'I wonder which deity was upset the more – the Storm kami, Susa-nō-ō, for our temerity, or Marishi-ten, for killing her messenger? How about you asking them?'

'Who, me? Not I, my lord: I am far too lowly in rank to take any such risk!'

'Oh, I don't know, Master Yamabushi; I was considering the possibility of offering you a position amongst my retainers, if such a proposal would be of interest to a wanderer like yourself?'

'Might this offer mean a promotion, my lord?'

'I think it might, yes.'

'Then there is a risk that at some point you might still order me to find out what those deities think? I shall have to consider the matter seriously!'

Heihachirō chuckled. 'There is only one of them that Lord Torii may wish you to have dealings with and, remember, it was I who killed the boar!'

'In that case, my lord, I accept your offer.' Gotembō bowed low.

In high good humour, they made themselves comfortable for the night.

7

THE SETTLERS

According to the Tellers, who from their early childhood commit to memory all those things that our people hold sacred and which would otherwise be lost with the passing years, our race came to these shores twenty generations ago. They were led by our Great Ancestor, Bright Spear, himself, a man held by some to have stood almost twice the height of the tallest amongst us to-day. So tall, in fact, that his head was level with the carved line around the 'Spear Stone' hard by the sacred grove where only the wise men may venture. These Tellers can name, in their proper order and with all their rolling titles, those who ruled our village down the years to our present defender's father, the all-powerful Shining Deer whose memory inspires us all. They recite the legends of when we embarked on the billowing waves, praying to those terrible beings who could raise violent storms that they would permit our frail oars to take us across the waters away from that land where slavery prevailed, a land of soaring peaks where the sun set to the distant land of rising clouds and the home of the coming day, no one knew what lay in store; of our reaching this welcoming shore where we found a place of great beauty, a thousand islands, a place where the deities had raised many towering and verdant mountains, providing rich flat valleys between them and the blue waters teeming with succulent fish; valleys promising overflowing yields of rice. After carefully performing the rites and dances to those then unknown deities who ruled over these fecund places, of ensuring that our labours to clear and plant our new fields would be fruitful, to the evident enjoyment of our womenfolk and the increase of our race, we awaited the abundance that was to come, ekeing out our sustenance by fowling and hunting our surroundings but taking care not to encroach into those nearby heights where others, dark hairy men, resided but who never came near us by day. There was room for all, it seemed, though we did hear tell of malevolent demons further to the west who caused hurt to the sacred places of our kinsmen and broke down the banks between those settlers' fields. But all that was just hearsay and may have happened long years before, no one could really say for sure.

All this is common knowledge and told and re-told whenever men gathered with the elders around the evening fire in the centre of our village. It is a scene repeated, I am quite sure, at hearthsides in every direction. We were, at that time, quite content with our lot and memories of that land far to the west where violence and death once stalked everywhere had faded to just dark tales voiced to quieten unruly children . . . We were happy and well-fed; sickness and hunger, once dark spectres, were banished forever; our protecting ancestors benign and farseeing . . . Huhh! All this halcyon life withered and vanished just one warm and magnificient day in the springtime of the eleventh year of Shining Deer, the day we gathered to celebrate the White Dog and the first planting of his sacred rice. Listen carefully and I will tell you of what happened just over there where you can see that double peak across the rippling waters . . .

'Old man! Stop this maudlin prattle! We haven't been molested these twelve years or more and well you know it!'

'Maybe not, Lame Badger, but all the more reason that our young men shouldn't forget the past!'

'The masters won't like it!' someone chipped in.

'That's right! You know very well they have told us to ignore what has happened long ago and only think about work . . .'

'Work just for them, eh? By our ancestors, we slave away in the fields and give them everything . . . All we get in return is poor millet, a few tares, and what we can catch in the rivers . . .'

One of the young men seated cross-legged with his friends, shouted out: 'Let Priest Pheasant say his piece. We all heard the story when we were small but most have forgotten. I, for one, want to hear it again now!'

His friends all agreed and the older villagers sat back reluctantly, mumbling and clicking their teeth. 'No good would come of it', more than one muttered aloud.

Pheasant, our narrator, indeed filled the position of the village priest and healer. To him, because he was gifted with the ability to talk with the unseen deities, fell the tasks of preparing the gift-tribute to the gods and the daily round of visiting the countless places in and around the village and its fields where the spirits were held to reside. Every single field, for example, was once in the care of such a spirit and each and every one of these was descended from the kin of the White Dog. It was an old hairy man clad in a skin cloak, who had met their ancestors long long ago as Bright Spear had first stepped ashore, and told them that they may have these reeded watermeadows provided they showed proper reverence to this great spirit. No one had questioned how it was that Bright Spear had been able to converse with this fierce old man but it had happened and they were content. In the third descendant's time, the grizzled ancient, himself, had taken up residence in the sacred grove and prayers were offered for his continued benificence even though already memories of him had faded. Now, both he and Bright Spear together presided as their defenders.

The priest came stiffly to his feet and adjusted his woven coat that was trimmed with fringes of brown and black *kiji* feathers. He leant on his staff of office that was carved with sacred barred lines near to its head, and gazed about him for several seconds before taking a deep breath and sighing. He began to speak, at first in little more than a sibilant whisper that even those closest to him had to strain to catch at his words, but gradually increasing the power of his voice until those women gathered at the back in the flickering light and shadow could hear.

'Shining Deer had just celebrated his confirmation as our blood chief at the ceremony of the Sacred Spear when the skies darkened and the white clad warriors came!' He paused and glared around him. Many of those sitting by that fire carefully averted their eyes lest they look into his at that moment for he had the power of sight and assuredly could gaze into their inner-most souls. 'It was my father who conducted that rite; it was he who had brought to the "Pen of Rites" beside the sacred grove the eleven sleek animals from who Great Shining Deer, himself, would select the sacrifice.'

A groan rose from the gathering and some who had at first demurred to hearing the story raised their hands before their faces and clapped their palms together twice in case they should have then angered their ancestors.

'My father, Sharp-eyed Pheasant, knelt on the ground before the dais of our chief, and made obeisance, his hands outstretched before his lowered head. "Great master!" he petitioned, "Which of these eleven spears must I use?" A distant roll of thunder came from the nearby mountains and Shining Deer, who was already on his feet and reaching out to the line of planted spears, turned his head momentarily, his hand wavering. When he turned back, he had caught up the tenth shaft . . . not the eleventh! My father, who didn't see this happen, waited, head still bowed, until he was told to rise. Only the grandfather of our Teller witnessed the error . . . and knew that no good would ensue.

'Nor did it. Sharp-eyed Pheasant seized the proffered spear and whirled around towards the sacred deer pen, casting the "arm of the gods" in a single movement. The sanctified spear flew from his grasp high up and plunged down into those brown-mottled animals . . . and missed any mark!

'Lamentations and shrill keening welled up to the darkening skies for this was an ill-portent. The ceremony could not be repeated; the deities would not permit such a thing. All that could be done was to pray that no real ill would follow and Sharp-eyed Pheasant sprinkled pure water over all present, albeit in some haste, to absolve them from future hurt.

'It was later that the Teller told him which spear had been grasped by the Lord Chief and when he went, alone, to retrieve the feather-bladed weapon, he found, to his consternation, that its tip was buckled and the very end snapped off.

'That evening, the same day, a dreadful storm broke across the valley and the river partly overflowed its banks, flooding the new-planted sacred rice field and washing away half the young plants. Hardly had this been found by the elders than three black-tarred long boats were seen heading for our shores.

'Fearful of what this meant, his head full of worries concerning the ceremony that had gone awry, my father summoned a young man, fleet of foot, and ordered him to run as fast as his feet would carry him, to the village of our chieftain's cousin, a man descended from the senior line of rulers, there to request that he should not delay but come here. He added, further, that his spear of office should be brought, too. It was a heavy message indeed.

'The strangers' boats were very large; bigger by far than any that we had then seen, and they carried a multitude of men. After the night's storm, the day had dawned calm and clear as is often the case in these lands, though amongst the distant hills two or three clouds were rising into the heavens. At first, the strangers brought their mighty vessels to a stop in the bay and we saw them drop overboard the heavy stones they used as anchors. It was a curious thing that my father told me long afterwards when I was nine years old and had already memorized many sacred *norito* prayers . . . He must have considered me ready for such knowledge, I reckon, but it was weighty at the time. On the right side of our bay, and you can see it over there scarce hidden by the tumbling headland, is the Island of Cats. Usually clouds of noisy "sea-cats"[5] wheel and dive whenever our men come in with their night's catch, but on this day not a single bird flew in the skies and those on the island remained silent. It was by reason of this black day that our people do not hold the sea-cat sacred nor raise stones where they might be worshipped . . .

'But I nearly omitted to tell you that while we were largely gathered on that pebble strand, some hairy men who took wood from the forests behind the rock-bound cliffs, had made a sudden and unexpected descent into our collection of outlying small farms that lay towards Hira. Maybe these were men from another mountain people and not from those who we considered friendly, if aloof, and whose ancestor was revered by us alongside our own? Who could tell just then?

'The first report that something was amiss came when an old man and the second of his young wives reached our gathering that noon. At first they were hardly noticed because it was just at the time that one of the black boats hauled up its stone and began to be rowed slowly towards the shore. While we gazed at the boat and saw many banners flying from the two stout masts that stood behind a sort of house towards its stern, the first cries of alarm alerted Shining Deer that all was not well at the back of the crowd. One of the senior elders and a lower ranking novice-priest were sent to find out the reason for the commotion but soon returned with a distraught woman tearing at her hair and scratching her naked breasts beside the corpse of her husband . . . his bloody body showing ghastly wounds, the cause of his untimely death, no doubt.

'When the woman calmed herself a little, she related how she had been in her field planting the young rice together with her two daughters and three girls born of the principle wife, when two *Emishi* hairy mountain men had come down out of the nearby forest carrying an *inoshishi* they had killed. While the women continued to plant, her husband and an uncle respectfully greeted the men and it seemed to her that they were talking about bartering something in

[4] *Sea-cats*: seagulls.

exchange for the wild pig. One of the Emishi had pointed towards the women, his gesture causing their uncle to look, too.

' "Uncle wishes us to go over, I think," said one of the girls.

'The junior wife hadn't seen, but said: "Young Heron, you go and see if that is the case; you are nearest the field dyke. The rest of you, get on with your planting for we have much more to do."

'It was nearly time for their beforenoon rest and after bedding four more bundles of the young plants, the younger wife straightened up her aching back and saw that two more of the hairy Emishi were sauntering along the further dyke. At that moment, one of the others grabbed at the girl who began to struggle and protest. The two newcomers broke into a fast loping run and without any warning, raised their hard wooden clubs and struck at the younger man, felling him instantly. The husband began to protest but he, too, was struck and fell back into the muddy paddy. As he scrabbled to his feet he was struck again with one of the flatter clubs and gored with the short boarspear that was borne by the leader. Wounded and dazed as he was, he managed to drag himself away. By now, the women had splashed to the bank but the younger wife ran back to help her husband.

' "Run fast to the farms and raise the alarm," she screamed out, and the girls needed little urging.

'The four hairy Emishi together with their struggling captive were already entering the forest trees and vanished from sight. The younger wife dragged her husband from the clinging mud but had the presence of mind to aid him, bloody and gashed as he was, straight to our gathering not half a mile away.

'Lord Shining Deer was perplexed as to what he should do. Here he was together with the elders, all dressed in their finest feathered regalia to show honour to the strangers from the deep, and on the pebbles lay a blood-streaked corpse and an agitated woman, close kinsfolk, of course, violently attacked within his territory . . .

'So matters stood; but decisions had to be made as the newcomers again anchored their vessel both fore and aft not a half bowshot from the shore. As the heavy stones fell with great splashes into the wavelets so a row of woven shields were hung from the nearer bulwarks so that most of the strangers could not be seen from the strand. In the bows there appeared an imposing man clad in some white costume who wore a flashing golden disc in some way attached to his forehead. In his hand he flourished what all could see was a long sword. This sword must have been nearly four feet in length and had, even at this distance, a bulbous end to its hilt.

'In a great and powerful voice this lord, for such he must have been as none like him any of Shining Deer's people had ever encountered before, called out in a strange tongue that seemed somehow familiar but no one could understand. Well, not quite all for the Teller approached his lord and, crouching down before him, said that the "divine lord" from the sea spoke in a language once used by their forefathers when they, themselves, first reached these shores. He turned to my father with a sideways glance, saying that he, too, must know many words as they were contained in the *norito*.

' "Well, Sharp-eyed Pheasant, is this so?"

'Frowning, my father nodded his head.

' "Then reply to this 'Divine' Sea-Lord for I can see his growing impatience!"

'Sharp-eyed Kiji descended to the water's edge together with the Teller, and in a halting fashion they found the words to shout across the vessel that they were welcome to land here. Some baskets of fresh fruit and fish were also brought down and displayed with many a friendly gesture. Our intentions were clearly understood and soon the big boat came to the gently lapping wavelets at the water's edge and grounded. Eight grim-faced armed men jumped out and stood in a menacing line before us.

'Wisely, Shining Deer, ordered a wide space to be cleared so that the thronging onlookers, for we numbered more than sixty souls, stood well back, and as the Sea-Lord, his hair dressed in plaited coils at each side of his head with the golden head disk above, descended to the dry strand across the backs of four servants, our chief signalled that all should kneel down with extended arms as is our custom when displaying due honour to the mighty.

'Only Shining Deer stood as he considered himself an equal to this stranger chief. My father later told me that he thought that our master had at that moment committed a grave error of judgement since he saw a shadow pass across the stranger's brow, but a second big man, similarly dressed and armed, had followed the other and stood at his shoulder.

' "We are the Lords of the Sacred Armies, Commanders of Myriad Hosts, Rulers of Boundless Plains, and we have come to claim all these lands for the Great Divinities of the Skies!"

'Away to the south, as if in answer, came a mutter of thunder. All at once, vast numbers of the sea-cats rose screaming into the air over the Island of Cats making it difficult to hear anything that might be said.

'The first "Divine" Sea-Lord frowned fiercely and waved his naked sword above his head. At once, a mournful call came from a man bearing a huge conch and in response the two vessels out in the bay raised their anchors and began to row closer. It was at this point that the second of these armed men noticed the bloody corpse of the old farmer and his weeping bare-breasted wife, now slumped down beside her dead husband. Of a sudden, these important beings looked aghast and fell into talk amongst themselves.

'My father realized that it was the sight of all-polluting blood that offended these personages and that whatever their plans, they had been set at naught by the presence of the slain man. As the stranger chiefs came together to confer about the situation, my father drew himself up and, haltingly, began to say that the sea strand was hardly a fitting place for such honoured visitors to meet with his ruler and, therefore, he suggested that they should retire to the chieftain's own residence where they could be properly entertained. Naturally, it would be fitting for the great lords to bring with them a suitable retinue of, perhaps, ten or fifteen men. A further glance at the dead man and the two strangers agreed, while in the meantime Sharp-eyed Pheasant explained the situation to Shining Deer and the elders.

'It was clear that either these personages agreed to go inland the half-mile to Shining Deer's compound or that they would have to withdraw to their vessels. Clearly, too, the latter course was not acceptable. Additionally, the skies had by now clouded over and a heavy storm threatened, falling curtains of rain were already to be seen beyond the southern headland.

'As they reached Shining Deer's house the heavens indeed opened, heralded by intense and deafening thunder, and the whole party crammed under the shelter of the thatched roofs; there was scarce enough room for thirty men but somehow they all got in with just enough space clear about the leading chieftains for decency. This clearly didn't meet with approval but with the thunderstorm raging and great bolts of lightning flashing from the angry clouds, what could anybody do?

' "We demand to meet your high ruler!" the leader of the "divine" sea-lords shouted out during a slight lull in the cacophony outside.

'The Teller and Sharp-eyed Pheasant translated what was said to Shining Deer and thought that their chief looked undecided, even nervous.

' "Tell them that a messenger has been sent to our chieftain's mansion. We expect that he will come here soon in response."

' "This place is not satisfactory . . !" bawled the second "divinity", glowering at the throng of farmers. "Clear these out of here at once! It is not meet that we should be treated thus! These are common riff-raff!"

'My father looked at the teeming rain outside the rickety hurdle doors; already there were deep pools of water gathering in the earthen yard, threatening soon to flood down onto the pit floor. He could see a row of dejected faces where other of their kinsmen were squatting in such shelter as they could find against the clay plastered outer wall.

' "My lord," he ventured to Shining Deer, "our guests feel threatened by so many people. They request that all should leave except the Elders and yourself. Can you agree to this?"

'Just at that moment a bedraggled figure burst in out of the downpour and looking about him in surprise at the great crowd in the hall, flung himself at the feet of Shining Deer. "Master! Hino farm has been attacked! It is all on fire despite the rain . . . The kin of Master Hawk are distraught and calling for aid . . ."

' "Who has done this thing?" questioned the old chief. He already had to contend with the disgruntled strangers here, that was difficult enough, and also the murdered farmer's body on the beach; what else could there possibly be? Now came tidings of an attack . . ! He turned to the Elders. "What's to be done? What do you make of all this?" And he rung his hands and made loud lamentations.

'That didn't solve his quandary; nothing would but firm action, my father knew that. He bowed low and suggested that his lord should consult with the gods without further delay.

' "But the deities are angry, O Priest! They are in no mood to heed my prayers, are they?"

' "They might if you offer them a suitable sacrifice, lord!"

'A fresh commotion outside further distracted the chief and angered his unwelcome guests. Sharp-eyed Kiji closed his eyes and grimaced to himself. "What fresh calamity could there be?" he thought, but he was soon to find out. Almost together, some of the younger farmers rushed into the compound shouting out that they were attacked by the hairy tribesmen; at the same moment, a knot of armed men from the boat hammered at the gates and hurled themselves into the hall where they quickly gathered about the sea-lords, mingling with their bodyguards. There was no let up to the fury outside and the gods were truly ill-tempered, of that Sharp-eyed Kiji was certain.

'In the chaos that ensued, the strangers began to drive everyone out of the hall, kicking and shouting at those reluctant to leave, beating them about with their spear shafts, and finally barred the wicket doors. Wet through by the rain that still fell so heavily that only the nearest hillside could be seen, the Elders and their chieftain commandeered the largest of the cluster of huts nearby while the rest found any shelter they could.

'Meanwhile, the widowed junior wife stood a forlorn and bedraggled figure in the centre of the coutyard, weeping and wringing her hands in despair. Taking pity on her, Sharp-eyed Kiji beckoned across his boy-assistant and whispered into his ear. The lad appeared to shudder before running off through the downpour, soon returning with Kiji's wife, my formidable mother . . .'

Pheasant's listeners glanced apprehensively at each other for the woman's fame was fearful to contemplate as she was remembered as a great sorceress who was able to bring the most powerful spirits to subjection.

'When all was explained, Pheasant's consort uttered a piercing unearthly scream and shook her clenched fists up at the angry skies, calling for her "deity horse" and other sacred items to be brought. While this was being done she seated herself before Shining Deer's shelter, plainly oblivious of all around her whilst she muttered a long incantation. My father later affirmed that at this moment the storm god departed and the rain simply ceased. Not a single drop had fallen on her head! Not one . . !

'Her "horse" was, of course, the sacred drum fashioned from the hide of a backwards-flayed piebald horse, a dread instrument that only my father and the acolyte were permitted to touch, and then only with unwashed new-woven cloth. No, not even our chief, himself. The black contents of her leathern wallet were too fearful to describe for they were protected by the outlined image of a sacred splayed frog . . . The witch-wife caught up her drumstick which was fashioned from a human birthcord drawn over a sacred wood that ended in a flattened "paddle". She began to strike the stretched drumhead.

Pheasant fell silent, apparently lost in his thoughts, then glared wild-eyed about him. Whatever it was that passed at that moment before his mind's eye must have been so powerful as to bring a froth of spittle to the corners of his drawn back lips . . . The onlookers palpably felt through the strength of his pent-up emotion something of what was in his mind . . . 'This Kuna was not of our people,' he rasped at last, his voice strangled by the admission. 'She came from that strange nation who live beyond the Hairy People in Kikushi, the Dog-faced Hayatō! Only my father knew this; he told me this truth as he sweated on his death couch, my mother having long since vanished.'

' "Woman, approach!" my mother shouted suddenly at the junior wife, the widow of the murdered man: "Kuna of the White-Grey Horse commands that you dance the Dance of the Slain!" At once the tempo of her drumbeats changed; sometimes surging to a crescendo, sometimes slowing and softening, but always accompanied by a wailing, unearthly chant, the shaman's voice almost unrecognizable . . .

Sea of milk's three spirits,
Creatures of moon and sun;
The drum-mare speaks –

Listen and protect:
Armour of my head!

'The poor young woman moved about the rain-soaked space, tears streaming down her face. Her torn tunic rent open to the waist so that her full breasts (for she had only recently borne a girl child) beginning to bounce with her steps . . .

Life soul-spirit
Twice sixty feet wing
Spirit of my soul,
White grey horse . . .

'The acolyte *shingyaku* ran across with that peculiar bowed gait used in such ceremonies and thrust a small branch torn from a sacred lance tree into her hands. In a moment, her face became serene, her eyes closed, and she, too, started to chant but using words from some tongue that no one there but the Teller and my father could understand, at the same time waving the leafy branch to the north, the east, the south and the west.

Tell, mighty spirit;
Hear my words!
Welcome the drum-horse
That beckons the fifteen
To thy feasting . . .

'Of a sudden, she fell to the ground, writhing with her breath coming in great gasps . . . and her voice changed dramatically from that of a woman to the rougher, harsher intonation of a man, one in the grip of passionate anger at that!

' "*You have summoned me, O my people! For why? Your impertinence has disturbed the creators of this land! I hear only wheedling, pitiful pleas that do nothing for my honour and my high rank!*"

'The drum beat out imperiously, the tone of Kuna's chanting changing to a higher pitch until she practically screamed foul invective at the possessed half-naked woman, mud-caked on the ground . . . "*Ask now* . . . demand of the ancestor what should be done!" she shrilled . . .'

' "***Kill! Destroy them all! Delay, and my people are lost** . . !*" came the deafening reply, and it was immediately followed by a violent detonation in the skies above such a fire-mountain might make when it spews out its white hot destruction

'Our chieftain made his decision, leaping to his feet and brandishing his wreathed spear of authority.

' "Run! Run for your weapons; fetch your bows and sharpened arrows, catch up your spears and shields . . ."

'Something must have warned the strangers in the hall that danger was imminent for my father told me that the doors of that mighty hut burst open, the sea-warriors rushed out with their leaders in their midst, and with great noise ran off in the direction of the beach . . . You shall hear what then occured from the Teller, himself.'

'I am the grandson of Kimi-no-bito, Teller to Lord Shining Deer, and I will tell you the truth as the words were handed on to me!' The Teller was a man of about thirty-five summers, standing tall but with a sallow, cavernous face whereon his cheekbones stood out like two ridges. 'It was as Sharp-eyed Kiji related to his son, Pheasant, here standing beside me . . . As the sea-warriors strode forth, the ancestor of our All-Powerful Ruler, He-who-Governs-all-under-Heaven, the terrible Storm God, himself, raised an even greater tempest than that we had just witnessed.

'The sea-warriors hesitated then, exhorted by their gold-crowned leaders, and dashed away towards the ocean only to be confronted by a dark mass of armed men who barred their way in the narrow path to the beach. Through the skeins of driving rain and with the darkened skies rent with lightning bolts, we could only just witness the battle that ensued. Terrible, it was, as the weapon-storm vied with the elements. Each flash of wrath from the Deity lit a scene of slaughter where it seemed, in the rare glimpses we were afforded, the slain were piled up in mountains. In awed silence we stood, fearful lest we do aught to break the Divine Ancestor's battle fury . . .

'At length, all fell silent and the night closed in for the day was spent, only darkness remained. Bedraggled and soaked, we stood there as if we had taken root. For how long, we are not told . . . in some matters the accounts always vary . . . but it was Sharp-eyed Kiji and my ancestor, Kimi-no-bito, who, protected by the still fierce insistence of Kuna-no-Hayatō's "horse", strode forward with their tokens of power held aloft, to witness the truth.'

Pheasant stood forward and renewed his account:

'That truth was stranger still, my kinsmen; far stranger that anything else! The sea-warriors were gone; the dark shape of their vessel already receding out to join their fellows on the rain-pocked oily swell. Where the fierce battle had been joined not one of those strangers' bodies was to be found, only some fifteen slain Hairy Men. When the storm abated and spluttering torches were brought, the earth was dark-stained by their barbarous blood. When the Elders examined those barbarians more carefully, the all-wise Kiji avowed that "there was exaltation in our hearts and on our lips . . ."

'Daylight dawned and strengthened; the young widow had recovered sufficiently to come, supported by others, to view the corpses and at once recognized the two mountain men who had slain her husband. She screamed out and horribly stabbed the two bodies with a dagger she had hidden in her torn tunic but Sharp-eyed Kiji let no one interfere as it was her right to vent such anger.'

Pheasant sighed a deep sigh and muttered some exhortation to the spirits. No one in his audience dared breathe a word for some of the older listeners in their dotage had lived through this event and the younger amongst them sensed that herein lay deep mysteries.

'Shining Deer ordered that the slain be gathered up and carried to the sacred grove. There they were secured with leather thongs, one to each tree; the two recognized as the killers of his kinsman were beheaded and the heads placed on the Spear Stone as an offering to our Guardian Ancestors. Kuna exhorted these powerful spirits to witness the retribution and our deep gratitude . . . but always at the back of my mind I recalled the failed ceremonial rite and the casting of the tenth spear . . . a black portent, indeed . . .

'When we returned to the village, we were greeted by the son of the Great Kinsman, himself, and a feast was prepared in celebration of the battle. There was much discussion about the strangers: who they were, where they had come from, and why had they appeared from the deeps at all? The hours passed until night fell and all sought sleep for they had each eaten and drunk his fill . . . We thought our trials were all passed.

'At dawn, lo, on our beach sat the three great vessels and to our consternation we faced not twenty but a hundred fierce warriors and their two golden-crowned leaders!

'Shining Deer and the son of our "Ruler of Wide Fields", for his father was abroad bringing retribution to the Mountain Dwellers, stepped forwards concealing their surprise, but the tall "Divine" Sea-Lord, himself, raised up his sword on high and stopped them in their tracks. Without a pause, this stranger lifted a bronze mirror before him and sent a brilliant reflection of the rising sun directly into our chief's face. Momentarily blinded by the rays, Shining Deer fell back a pace and somehow entangled his feet in his Spear of Office, tripping himself over . . . The shaft snapped and he pitched onto the upright blade. Pierced through his vitals he hung for a moment in a backwards arch, the patterned bronze bursting out from his belly . . . Whatever it was that the "Divine" Sea-Lord said at that moment was lost in a great cry of anguish from the assembled crowd and when we all turned our shocked gaze back we saw these two leaders seated cross-legged on the pebbles, the hilts of their naked swords driven into the ground before them, points upright . . .'

Pheasant turned to the Teller at his side, his shoulders drooping as if he carried a great load across his back.

'What happened after this has been told many times by you, good friend. All I can add is that I think, in my deepest heart, that we fared rather better than our more distant kin. At least we still have the grandson of our "*Great-Ruler-over-Wide-Lands*", as he is now styled, to be chieftain in his splendid palace at Kamōsu; aye, and we still have all our sacred gods. No one has taken those away from us. And for what reason this good fortune remains despite the demands of foreign tax-gatherers? I shall tell you all lest you should ever forget. It was the sacrifice of the old farmer and the fierce retribution called down by his young wife that spilled blood on our shores. It was a powerful magic of pollution that the Men who came from the Land to the West, as we now know, were not able to dispel despite their overwhelming skills of sorcery.

'My story is now told and is the lasting truth. Keep it in your memory for ever!'

8

TWO HUNTERS

Many an old family, from generation to generation, maintain chronicles of varying quality. The Torii-ke were no exception. Some of the records comprised plain unembellished accounts of wars and battlefield exploits performed by some noted ancestor, others were more mundane and simply list those who served this lord or that; but the monk, Enshin, in reading through many of the preserved documents, found one bizarre tale of a minor, but strange event, that occurred early in the Kamakura period three hundred years before. Even after considering what was written, verified as a true account of the event by no less than two of the Torii lords, Enshin could only shake his head and marvel. Who was he to doubt the words of these exalted ancestors, but he decided in the end to place the facts before posterity and let others decide?[6]

[5] Many of Torii Enshin's adventures are told in *Stories of Old Japan – Book 2: Tales of Enshin, the Reluctant Samurai.*

As a reward for his meritorious services rendered to the Minamoto clan during the recent Gempei War, Torii-no-Masachiyō was appointed the Deputy Governor of a considerable part of Kōzuke province. The Torii clan were based, since the early Heian period, in and around Kusatsu where there were many hot springs high in the tortuous mountain valleys and along the tracks that led to Echigo and the narrow plain bordering the sea coast. This was hunting country and it goes without saying that the younger Torii and their kin were great hunters.

Two of these cousins, Torii Tarōemon and Ei-no-Kuranosuke, one day rode out of the Iwagu yashiki that lay near the Mitsukuni-no-toge Pass as an important part of the border defences, intent on spending three or four days hunting a reputedly dangerous and large wild boar.

This inoshishi had recently attacked and killed two farmers but it was said that his unpredictable temper may have been caused by an old but galling wound. The cousins, brave bushi as they were, set out on this expedition on foot, intending to face and kill such a powerful beast since this feat would greatly add to their reputations.

For just two men to chase their quarry across these steep and rugged heights, without their personal retainers, would have been foolhardy in the extreme and neither man was driven simply to seek fame; this hunt's main objective was to kill the offending inoshishi and so free the farmers from their very real fears. Accordingly, they adopted the strategy of lying in wait for the beast at a point where they considered he might eventually appear.

To do this they found a place where the boar's trail led between some pine trees. As the evening drew on they agreed to settle themselves on either side of the path in adjoining trees, their powerful bows and arrow quivers beside them, and waited for the rising full moon to illuminate the forest and track.

They remained sitting on their makeshift platforms in the branches until the moon had risen to quite a height and was just about to disappear behind the towering southern mountain when Tarōemon thought he noticed a movement further up the slope and took up his bow in readiness. At the same time, Kuranosuke heard a twig snap and he, too, prepared for action . . .

Something caught tight hold of Tarōemon's *motodori* . . . perhaps a twig . . . and began to pull him upwards . . . What could it be; what sort of thing, or being, would do such a thing? The painful tugging lifted him almost to his feet in the crotch of the branch . . . It could only be a demon . . .

Feeling upwards with his arrow hand he touched some sort of clawed fist that had him fast in its grip. Abandoning all thought of the boar he called out to Kuranosuke and told him what was happening. What should he do?

'If it is a supernatural being, I hear that forked arrows are effective in such cases,' offered his friend. 'What would you have me do?'

'I think you should shoot your arrow above where you hear my voice . . . This will drive off the demon!'

'But I might pierce you, cousin? It is too dangerous!'

'I am already half-dead and in danger of losing my soul to be eaten by the devil! Take aim, Kuranosuke, despite the darkness; take aim and kill whatever it is that is doing this!'

Ei-no-Kuranosuke eased his position, drew out the longest of his three turnip-headed arrows, and fitted it to his bowstring.

'Talk, cousin; talk so that I shall know where you are.'

He drew back the string bending the powerful red-lacquered bow to its fullest curve, closed his eyes, and aimed the whistling arrow above his friend's voice . . .

The arrow flew from the bow and at once Tarōemon dropped back to his perch, sore headed but alive. He reached up in relief, running with sweat, and found a severed clawed hand still grasping his top-knot. In the darkness it felt strangely human with its wrinkled skin and long irregular nails. The wide-forked *o-karimata* blade, with its razor edges, had neatly severed it from its owner.

'You struck the *oni*,' called out the warrior, 'I have its hand!'

Kuranosuke grunted. 'With all this noise, we may as well forget our plans. The boar is hardly likely to appear to-night!'

They climbed down from their trees and checked their weapons. The arrow was lost but perhaps could be recovered by a search party in a day or two's time. Wrapping the hand in a cloth, Torii-no-Tarōemon carefully tied it to his *uwa-obi* and they started back down the faint track to the yashiki.

They were greeted with some surprise by the senior officers on night guard as they were hardly expected for at least another day or so, but apart from saying that they had called off the hunt for a while, they retired to clean up and for some refreshments in their appartment. Hardly had they sat down prior to removing their body armour, when a woman attendant, wearing a worried look, came to the sliding *shōji* doors and urgently begged Tarōemon to attend his mother without delay.

The cousins were taken aback with this unexpected summons.

'What ails her?'

'Master, she will not say but seems to be furious, raging all about her rooms . . . I . . . we are terrified as each time we try to calm her she flies at us with anything to hand . . . Master, her maids are in terror . . . all are tearful with despair . . .'

The two warriors exchanged looks and hurried after the woman to find out what was the matter.

They were greeted by the sight of three sobbing women crouching down together on the outer verandah. From behind the fast-closed shōji came shrieks and uncouth roaring. No one dared to enter for a moment, not even the cousins.

'Send for the old yamabushi priest who stays in the temple,' ordered Tarōemon. 'He will know what to do.'

When the Shugen-ja came, wearing his full costume, he at once directed that *hinoki* wood be brought and built a small *gōma* bonfire in the paved central courtyard around which the ladies' quarters were built. He caused a white curtain screen to be placed about the fire and himself then set about chanting invocations in an increasingly powerful voice directed at exorcising the evil spirit that he avowed had possessed the old mistress. As he progressed in his offices, brushing powerful *dharani* spells on slivers of hinoki and casting them successively into the flames, each to be consumed in an instant and rise as scented smoke to the nostrils of the gods, the howls and screams from inside diminished until, as he concluded his final spell, a great stillness descended on the appartments. With a final flourish of his drawn sword towards the cardinal points in order to drive away other curious demons, the yamabushi sheathed his blade with a snap and pronounced that the wild spirit had departed.

Tarōemon and Kuranosuke cautiously entered the appartment and found the old lady lying dead, evidently of an apoplexy, and she was soon buried. The stone marking her grave, moss-covered and weathered, still stands but, curiously, outside the confines of the family graveyard hard by the Jōjō-ji temple. Of course, in those distant days many country folk, particularly in Kōzuke province, believed that very old women often fell prey to possession by ōni, even to attacking and eating their offspring, but that is a story for the ignorant; only the Lord Buddha can know the truth.

It was a somewhat mystified Enshin who carefully rolled up this short scroll to return it to its box when he noticed a scrap of paper pasted on the outside a short distance from the beginning of the scroll. It had detached itself as he had untied the decayed silk securing cord. Picking it up, he saw at once that it was only a line or two brushed by Torii-no-Tarōemon, himself, together with a date. It tersely noted that when he and his cousin entered his mother's room they found it all besplattered with blood. The Honourable Lady's right hand was missing, cleanly severed at the wrist.

9

YAMABUSHI

The tall yamabushi was an imposing man, remarkable in a number of ways and not only for his height, for he was at least a head taller than most other men, even head and shoulders. His eyes in particular were a striking feature, sometimes soft and kindly, at others keen and piercing; furthermore and unusually, he had a bristling black beard. While he was undoubtedly a wandering Shugendō priest, he only wore some of the usual garments of these strange mountain men; the white *sashinuki-bakama* trousers drawn by cords together at the bottoms and tucked into his *kyahan* shin wrappings for all the world like rather bulky 'plus-fours' or the voluminous trousers soon to become popular amongst sophisticated samurai introduced by the fashionable Dutch. His kimono was black and white checkered but over this he wore no stole or apron. Despite the lack of the other parts of the characteristic 'uniform', Denki-bō, for such was his priestly name, was armed with a formidable plain-mounted longsword, a long tantō dirk, and an eight-sided staff which stood about his height. There was no doubt that he was an experienced initiate of this secretive sect, his tanned skin clearly testifying to his years exposed to the elements throughout the changing seasons.

On this particular day in the early spring of the ninth year of *Tembun*,[7] he had decided to commune with Nature on the ocean shore where the foaming waves dashed themselves against the rocks close to the great Udō Shrine on the south-eastern coast of Kyūshū. He had no particular purpose in mind other than to use this desolate spot in order to practise a whole series of movements that he had devised with his staff as though it were a naginata and others with his straight bokutō fashioned from a length of beautifully figured rosewood. After two hours of hard practice, cutting his invisible opponents with ferocious lightning blows, he sat down and rested his sweating body on a rock, observing a fisherman sculling his boat through the breakers. It occurred to Denki-bō that the man was in some sort of trouble but, nonetheless, he managed to approach near to the shore waving one arm vigorously to attract the priest's attention. The closer the frail craft came to the beach the higher the curling breakers, but Denki-bō, setting aside his weapons, waded out into the surf and seized hold of the craft's long prow to help steady it to the strand.

'I thank you, priest, for that help,' said the fisherman, once they had safely hauled the boat beyond the hungry waves.

'Are you injured?' The priest had noticed how the rescued man hardly used his left arm.

'I struck my shoulder a severe blow, master.'

'Then, perhaps I can help you?'

While Denki-bō felt the injured shoulder the man told him that he had found a strange craft on the further side of a small island that he pointed to not a mile or so down the coast. This vessel was very large with black timbers and once had many sails.

'Once, you say? How was that?'

'It had been cast onto a reef and wrecked in last night's storm, master. It was all broken up and the masts were fallen to lie in a tangled wrack beside the broken hull.'

'And what of the men who sailed her?'

'All dead, master; drowned and lying amongst the rocks . . . Only one man survived . . . See . . . I have him lying in the bottom of my craft!'

Denki-bō frowned when he saw the castaway lying inert on the pile of nets and fish. Here was one belonging to a race he had never seen before; a man having dark deep-set eyes and, surprisingly, a small pointed beard and drooping moustaches.

---

[7] Tembun 9: 1541.

The great sea cavern prayer hall of the Udō Myōjin shrine was a strange place, unique amongst the haunts frequented by the wild yamabushi. In those turbulent years it was rarely visited by anyone for pilgrims feared the fierce bandit gangs who preyed on travellers who threaded their fearful way through this remote province. Only the occasional swordsman came here for it was a famous place for severe ascesis such as these men underwent in order to hone their formidable skills.

The injured fisherman had helped Denki-bō to bring the strange seafarer ashore and to hide amongst the rocks out of reach of the tide varous items that he had rescued from the wreck. With the assistance of a young priest, they had carried the stranger down into the cavern and the yamabushi set about treating their injuries. He reset the fisherman's dislocated shoulder and securely strapped it in place with a soft obi sash, but the seafarer was different and clearly very ill.

At first Denki-bō prayed before the carved image of Fudō Myō-ō, reciting his formulae and clicking his beads, then he brought water from the rock pool that was often sprayed by the breaking waves in the cavern's mouth. Bathing the stranger's stripped body with the cold sea water gradually brought him back to consciousness and soon the yamabushi was aware that the man's dark eyes followed his every move though he had apparently lost the power of speech. For three days he ministered to the sailor, cooked some simple food and fed him; generally seeing to his every need.

Denki-bō sat before Fudō Myō-ō deep in concentration, praying to the fierce *bodhisattva* to take him further along the difficult path to enlightenment, and maybe to give him some encouraging sign? On this night, he could see the hanging orb of the rising moon reflected from the now calm surface of the sea when, from the other side of the cave a voice called out. Bowing deeply to the deity, he rose and crossed the floor. It was the stranger who had shouted out something in his strange tongue.

The yamabushi shook his head but the man was insistent. He tried again but without luck. The sailor sank back, his eyes staring at the rocky roof then he pointed at Denki-bō's staff . . . He wanted the staff . . . With difficulty he pulled himself up so that he leant against the living stone and lifted the staff, holding it under his right arm . . . He looked at Denki-bō then shouted out a violent yell! Three times he did this, always pointing with the pole but at last he stroked the stave and looked at the disconsolate fisherman, to himself and finally to the sea.

'What does he mean, do you think?'

The yamabushi shook his head, frowning, but suddenly he had an idea.

'We carried several things to those rocks and one of them was a long bag, wasn't it?'

'Why, yes; so it was! Maybe he is worrying about it?'

Denki-bō took up his stave from the hands of the sick man, putting it to his shoulder just as he had seen. Clearly this wasn't right. He pointed to the stave and then to the seafarer. No, that wasn't it, either. Putting down the pole, he made the same motion without it, again pointing at the sick man and the sea. The fellow nodded and tried to smile.

'You are right; he wants his things brought here.'

Denki-bō smiled broadly and signed that he would go at sunrise and fetch the items. This time it was clear that he was understood.

The seafarer was bathed in a lather of sweat when Denki-bō returned as the shafts of early sunlight lit up the mouth of the cavern, the only time of day when this occurred. The man was fevered and weak but rallied when the yamabushi placed his belongings beside him and sat down cross-legged to watch.

Eventually, with some assistance the long leather bag was opened at one end and the stranger drew out an oiled cloth that, when unwrapped, exposed a long black iron rod furnished with wood and an odd-shaped handle. He smiled wanly at Denki-bō and pointed. It was indeed a strange object and the yamabushi saw at once that the tube was hollow. It was at least three-and-a-half *shaku* long but for the life of him he couldn't fathom what it was for. He raised it to his shoulder like the staff had been lifted and was pleased to see the bearded stranger's approving nod.

The seafarer closed his eyes for some moments then recovered and pulled the wallet towards him. Opening it, he drew out a number of small items and slowly set about a series of actions, constantly making sure that Denki-bō watched closely all that he did. He then made the yamabushi repeat everything until, after a tediously slow hour, he was satisfied and leant back almost asleep. Rallying, he opened a smaller bag which contained three smaller ones each filled with strange powders; one yellow, one pale and whitish, and one black. For another hour, the seaman gestured and mimed various actions with these powders until he was certain that his 'student' understood. At last he opened the last larger bag which the yamabushi saw was lined with silk cloth and as dry as a bleached bone left out in the summer sun. The contents was another blackish powder. He did more things with the iron tube and a short length of smouldering cord lit from the small cooking fire which, again, he made Denki-bō perform again and again . . . Finally, he sank down and fell asleep, apparently satisfied.

An hour later he awakened, dripping with perspiration, and gestured to Denki-bō to send away the fisherman, watching until the man had gone. Then he pointed to his iron tube and appeared happy when the yamabushi picked it up. He pointed across the cavern's mouth. Denki-bō was mystified and frowned. The sick man grinned and pointed again, curling his right forefinger. The yamabushi shrugged his broad shoulders and casually crooked his finger in the same way.

There was a tremendous, earsplitting detonation and he nearly fell backwards as the wooden handle of the 'rod' leapt back with a kick like a young horse. At that instant Denki-bō knew that Fudo-Myō-ō had indeed answered his prayer.

Deafened, coughing as the cavern was filled with white smoke, he almost dropped the heavy tube and stared down at the foreigner . . . what, in the name of a thousand devils, had happened? He had pointed the tube at a small rock balanced on another larger boulder and ran over to take a look. The rock had gone but he soon saw many sharp fragments lying about the cave floor. From the upper entrance he heard loud voices.

'Keep out of here!' he bawled lustily.

'But, lord, we heard a dragon!' shouted a voice that he recognized as that of the chief priest. 'Do you require help, sir?'

'No! I am dealing with the dragon . . . Stay away!'

Denki-bō returned to the shipwrecked mariner and saw that he was weakening fast. Death had already planted his hand on his face. The man raised his hand and took hold of his sleeve, pointing to the tube in the yamabushi's hand. He gestured that it was his as a gift. He tried to pull the wallet closer but his strength was ebbing fast and he slumped weakly back . . . a few minutes passed while Denki-bō intoned the Heart Sutra more or less to himself as he sat beside the stricken man . . . with a faint sigh, the sailor's soul parted from the body and the stranger was dead.

The following day promised to be as dry and warm as the five that had gone before. The fisherman and the yamabushi, the latter held in some awe over the incident with the supposed dragon, left the shrine on the promise that the priests would bury the stranger's corpse, and trudged down the path to the sea strand.

'There's one thing more that the stranger left, sir. It's in my boat.'

'I thought we put everything of his behind the rocks?'

'It's just a box, sir. I hid it under some spare nets. Look, I'll show you.'

Sure enough, he pulled out a smallish iron-strapped round cask and the yamabushi saw at once it would be too heavy to carry with everything else he had inherited. He heaved a sigh and shook his head.

The fisherman wasn't sure what he should do now but decided he ought to go home. His catch was already ruined and he would have to start again. On the other hand, perhaps the yamabushi wouldn't let him go seeing as he had all the mariner's gear.

'I'll help you launch your boat,' offered Denki-bō.

The poor man was surprised since he instinctively realized that he was talking to a former samurai and one of high rank, at that.

'I need a servant. Do you know of a young man who might do?'

'A servant, lord?'

Denki-bō breathed deeply but didn't reprove the fisherman. These poor people had servility and ignorance bred into their very bones.

'Is it possible?'

'Maybe it is; then maybe it isn't.'

'Whoever comes with me will be fed and clothed!'

'Please deign to jump on board, master; if your lordship will be pleased to help me to launch.'

'Of course I will; you cannot do it alone with that shoulder, can you?'

Three hours later, as the evening sun was sinking behind the mountains, they came ashore at a little fishing hamlet that sheltered in a tiny rock-girt cove.

There was much tending to the needs of the fishermen and their familes and it was two months before Denki-bō felt he had done what he could for these poor folk and was ready to move on. Already the early summer heat was becoming oppressive and the rains were imminent. The fisherman had found him the son of a local farmer who had gladly volunteered to become his servant and maybe, later, a *shingyō-sha*, a novice yamabushi. After they left the village behind them, they trudged by a circuitous route through the interior mountains and eventually crossed the border to Higo province and entered the Kikuchi domain. By now, the rains had come and gone and they were in the middle of the stormy season just before the calmer days of autumn.

Almost at once as they descended from the wilds of volcanic Aso-san, they found that the countyside was in upheaval caused by a war between the Kikuchi and the Ryōzōji. The latter had just two days before crossed the northern border from Saga. There was no warning of any trouble as the pair slowly walked down from the mountains, no refugees going the other way, no burning villages, no unburied corpses; just a sudden blare of horagai and they were surrounded by a troop of Ryōzōji horsemen. For a moment matters looked bleak but it may have been fortunate that the leader was a samurai of rank who realized that the yamabushi and his follower were of little import and ordered his men to ride on at once. There were those in many armies in that war-torn period who would think little of robbing a poor peasant for a mouldy rice-cake but here starvation had not yet appeared with pestilence and death in its wake.

The lad, whose name was Aki, was apprehensive as they eventually reached a large village.

'Have no fear, young Aki,' Denki-bō reassured him. 'No one will touch us. Go over to that temple and seek out the priest, then request lodging for your master for a day or so.'

'Yes, master.'

'Oh, and ask him to give us food, too.'

'Yes!'

Denki-bō sauntered slowly along the main street, standing aside when some soldiers hurried past, and eventually reached the Outer Gateway of the temple. There he was met by a crestfallen Aki who had failed in his errand. The yamabushi laughed.

'Follow me!'

He marched purposely through the gate, passing through its centre and not its more humble side wicket, and down the avenue to the Prayer Hall. Once inside, they put down their belongings and Aki was commanded forcefully to look after them. Denki-bō produced his hora and blew a long blast before the statue of Fudō Myō-ō and a smaller one of Marishi-ten. Out from the side offices tumbled three shaven monks followed in short order by several more, but Denki-bō ignored them and in a loud voice began to chant part of the Peacock Sutra.

'You cannot do that . . .' ventured one of the monks, but the yamabushi only strengthened his voice, all the time interspersing the words with the ritual seals of empowerment with his hands.

'Sir Yamabushi; you . . .'

Three of the monk were becoming angry and Aki was sure they were about to lay hands on this wild priest and throw him out, when Denki-bō suddenly whipped out his slung sword and uttered a great shout. The monks took one look at the glinting blade and prudently leapt back to the walls whilst the priest ritually cut twice in each of the Four Directions before executing a last flashing cut to his right side. Returning the longsword with a snap, he bowed low to the figure of the War Goddess and turned to glare at the uncertain crowd.

'You refused my request,' he bellowed, taking a step forwards as he did so.

The crowding monks fell back a step, too.

'Who is your head?' He glared at them, beard bristling. 'Well? Answer me at once!'

'He's Master Goshun, sir,' one of the older monks quavered.

'And where is this Master Goshun, eh?'

'He has travelled to Kikuchi town, sir.'

'Doubtless to save his skin! Who was left in charge?'

The monks looked one to the other before one ventured: 'No one, master.'

'Then you will not refuse guests against the Law of the Buddha – and these guests almost starving!'

'Master . . .'

Denki-bō ground his teeth.

'Don't "Master" me! Food . . . at once!'

His fierce look sent them all scurrying but the senior of them requested that they follow him to the guest quarters. Soon, a brimming rice container was brought and another containing cooked vegetables and steamed fish. All were duly set out so that both master and servant could eat in some style.

'Where is the war being fought?' Denki-bō asked when the older monk returned. 'What are the merits of each side?'

'There are Ryōzōji soldiers everywhere, sir . . . er . . . master . . .' The monk wrung his hands in despair. 'Just beyond the mountain they have burnt a village and . . . done terrible things!'

'How do you know this?'

'Someone trying to escape from there said it was so; that's how we heard . . !'

'Then you will know if the Kikuchi are active, won't you?'

'We haven't heard from our lord, sir.'

'Didn't Kikuchi-dono order the border barriers closed?'

'I cannot answer that, master.'

'Well, we simply walked through. There was no one there!'

Just then there was a confused shouting outside and two young novices ran precipitately through the *shōji*.

'They are here, master; many soldiers are here . . !'

'Oh, may the Buddha have mercy on us!' wailed the old monk.

There was a shrieking and another monk flung himself onto the step, blood streaming from a deep cut to his right shoulder.

Denki-bō calmly finished the last of his rice then motioned to Aki to gather up their belongings; the yamabushi, himself, carried the iron tube in its bag.

'Where are the kitchens,' he asked the monk, but the fellow was in a state of abject fear and couldn't utter a single coherent word in reply.

Aki sniffed the air.

'This way, master.'

Denki-bō stretched with a yawn, then calmly walked after the young man.

'Please hurry, master; those soldiers are very close!'

'Oh, I don't think they will be any trouble!'

'But, master; they seem very angry . . .'

'Such people often are! They bawl loudly to cover their own cowardice!'

They came to the temple kitchens built, as expected, close by the Guest Quarters. The yamabushi crossed over to the hearth and, drawing out a small length of thin braided cord from his kimono, he stooped and set one end to the fire embers before pointing to the store-room corridor.

'That way, Aki.'

At the back of one of the near empty storerooms was an outer door.

'Bar that one, Aki-san, while I do the same here.'

As he expected, there was a trapdoor flap in the floor which he lifted.

'Down there, Aki-san, and smartly.'

He pulled a chest across and carefully propped it against the open flap, then climbed down after his servant. When he jerked the flap shut, the chest fell across it, hopefully masking their exit. Now they were under the building amongst the forest of heavy support timbers. On the far left they could see the legs of armoured men milling about and could hear confused shouting.

'Sit still, Aki, and remain calm!'

'Master, have you been in a war before?'

'Me? Just one or two; nothing much, but don't you worry; just do as I tell you.'

'I am fearful, sir . . . I have seen what footsoldiers can do!'

'And what was that, eh?'

'They once came to our village and . . . and . . . It's why I'm not married, sir.'

'They did things to the women, did they?'

'I couldn't tell you, master; it was so bad.'

'I quite understand.'

They smelt woodsmoke quite clearly. The soldiers had set fire to some of the temple buildings.

'Follow me, and keep close.'

The yamabushi crawled swiftly on all fours through the timbers. Occasionally they could see thick eddies of white smoke hiding the more distant uprights but hardly affecting them. The soldiers were still milling about but evidently now under greater discipline to judge from the shouted orders. Muttering some invocations, Denki-bō set about some cabalistic moves with his long tube and its paraphernalia, unperturbed by the threatened nearness of death in a variety of unpleasant forms. Eventually, he declared himself satisfied leaving Aki to wonder how it was possible that his master should be so unconcerned at this fearful time.

'And now, Aki, we must look for the Ryōzōji general!'

Aki swallowed hard. 'The general?' he ventured in disbelief.

'Yes; an army is really composed of very many parts but has only one head. Come now, we find the *taishō* and we shall nearly have won the war!'

Brushing himself down, Denki-bō took out from his own bag a number of the more usual items worn by the yamabushi including the badger pelt apron and the stole with six white 'rosettes'. He placed a small black *tokin* 'pill-box' hat on Aki's head and secured it in place.

'Now we're ready!' he pronounced, picking up the long iron tube as though it were a staff. 'Aki, leave everything else here; follow me out and keep at a respectful distance so that you act the part of my acolyte. Carry my *bonden* and take no notice of anyone or anything except my orders . . . Oh, and stand straight!'

They came out from under the side verandah, made sure everything was as it should be, then marched round the corner of the building into the crowded temple concourse. At once they were faced with samurai and ashigaru, all fierce and armoured, but because Denki-bō showed not the slightest hesitation or fear and strolled along as if he owned the place, not a word was said to them.

'Who is your general?' demanded the yamabushi, accosting a pair of senior *yari-mochi* footsoldiers.

'Why, 'tis Hiyoshi Sugamoto-dono, master.'

'Excellent! Hiyoshi Sugamoto-*taishō*! Conduct me to him at once!'

'We have to get permission first!'

'Not necessary! Any delay will be serious!'

'But, master . . .'

Seeing the severe look on Denki-bō's face, the two yari-mochi exchanged glances and obeyed.

The general, resplendent in his brightly laced armour, sat on his camp stool surrounded by five officers. He eyed the yamabushi somewhat balefully.

'What do you want, then?'

'Sir, I have come to give you victory!'

For a moment there was silence, then Sugamoto and his entourage roared with laughter.

'We are already doing quite well!'

'That is debatable, general.'

'Why so? We are here, aren't we?'

'That is true, my lord; but these are not your lands but those of the Kikuchi who have held them for more than seven hundred years.'

'Get to your point, monk!'

'I have a weapon that by itself can win great wars!'

'A weapon? I see no weapon! Where is it hidden, fool?'

'It is right in front of you, my lord; it is this staff that I hold in my hand.'

Sugamoto's eyes opened wide.

'It was given you by Marishi-ten, you are going to tell me next?' he grinned.

'It comes from no other, indeed.'

'Pah! You claim to be a tactician?'

'No, not a tactician; better than that! A master of strategy, no less.'

'Who have you served?'

'I serve no master, my lord.'

'What, no master, and you would claim to be a master strategist . . ! You waste my time, charlatan!'

'No, my lord; test me and you can judge for yourself.'

'With that misshapen tube thing . . ! I think not!' Sugamoto, despite his very evident scepticism, looked at his grinning officers. 'At least we are entertained while we await developments! You, Ishida-sama! What would you have this master of strategy explain?'

General Ishida was a hard-looking man who wore an all black lacquered *dō-maru* armour.

'That's easy! Tell me, fellow, what would you do if you thought Lord Kikuchi was out to attack right now? How would you make your plans?'

'I would already know, my lord,' replied Denki-bō.

'Know? How would you know?'

'I would have sent out clouds of spies.'

'Why?'

'Because, my lord, this is not my territory, therefore I need to know everything; every scrap of information that I can.'

'That much is obvious!'

'But, my lord, it is often overlooked by many men of high rank and expectation.'

Ishida cocked his head a little to one side. Was this yamabushi being insolent, he wondered.

'So, by receiving information from your spies you would then make your depositions?'

'I would already have done so. To be prepared would give me the advantage.'

'And you have a secret vouchsafed to you by Marishi-ten?'

'That is so.'

Ishida snorted. He went along with all of this because it pleased his lord, but now his patience was wearing thin.

'Many claims are made but most come to nothing!'

'In such a case one should always enquire deeply.'

'Yamabushi! You are impertinent!'

'No, my lords; as Master Sonshi taught: "*War is of vital importance to the state; it must be studied thoroughly. To overlook even a slight matter may affect the outcome of the whole.*"'

Sugamoto smote his thigh with his fist. 'I can waste no more time here . . . Ishida-sama, gather our men, we shall drive west at once!'

'That is your decision, my lord?' said Denki-bō, looking solemn.

Poor Aki felt cold sweat run down between his shoulder blades. Now he was certain the end had come.

'You are no strategist, yamabushi! Go before I have you beaten!'

'In that case, my lord, I shall have to await Lord Kikuchi who is about to appear.'

'Impossible! How can you know that?'

'In one minute he will appear around that corner!'

The Ryōzōji officers looked at each other in amazment. They began to laugh but some of them were not comfortable. In the meantime, Denki-bō took up his iron tube and carefully set the glowing woven cord in the serpentine as he had practised.

'Pass the ball, Aki-san, please, and the little flask.'

In the meantime, Sugamoto-*taishō* rose from his stool, flourishing his war-fan.

'Where the devil are they?' he demanded of Ishida, but it was Denki-bō who answered.

'They will be here, my lord; and when they come I shall demonstrate my secret weapon of immediate victory!'

'Pah! This will be interesting! You say it will win the war?'

'Assuredly it will, sir.'

A conch's mournful call sounded some way off and was answered by another much closer by.

'Those are not ours, Ishida-sama . . .'

The black-armoured general was on his feet bawling out orders.

'It is too late, sir. Your spies have failed you!' remarked Denki-bō softly.

About twenty Kikuchi bowmen rushed into view and knelt down, bows ready. An officer raised his arm.

'A moment, sir!' called out the yamabushi. He turned to Hiyoshi Sugamoto. 'You wanted to know how I would win the war, I believe? Because you are a fool I would do it thus!'

He pulled the little trigger and there was a huge report. The Ryōzōji commander fell back onto his stool which collapsed under his weight. He was stone dead! His men, literally thunderstruck, simply ran away.

Never before, in the annals of Japan, had a matchlock been used and in this case it did indeed win the war!

10

LI-TEN-DONO

There is a curious story contained in the ancient records of the Torii-ke that is reputed to date from the middle years of the Nanbokuchō upheavals, a time when the Torii remained faithful to the Imperial Prince of the Pagoda, part of those true *buke* known to many as the Southern Faction. The story concerns a scion of the family, one Torii Tomoharu, who by all accounts was a formidably skilful kenshi and spent many years wandering the land as a masterless rōnin in order to follow the *Ken-no-michi*, the 'Sword's Path' as the *Bugei* arts of the battlefield were known.

It was said later that Tomoharu eventually practised in south-eastern Hitachi, the domain of Kashima Motonari, and was, in the years of the fifth Shōgun, buried close to the great shrine

For many years, though at intervals, a rich flotilla of vessels gathered at one or other of the seaports of the Inland Sea and, when ready, set sail to the port of Ningpō, an island just south of the great Yangtse River in the land of Mu. These particular fleets carried with them part of a token or tally that was given to the previous commander by a high Chinese official before the vessels returned to Japan. The following admiral must take the Japanese half of the tally back with him to China where it would be matched against the Chinese half and if it fitted perfectly the ensuing commerce was sanctioned by the Imperial government. The provincial lords vied with each other to despatch their agents and goods in these fleets and certain favoured merchants stood to make great fortunes from the profits of their ventures. Once the fleet reached the safety of Chinese waters and anchored in the shelter of Ningpō, a small number of favoured merchants and the representatives of powerful lords were able to travel to the capital as guests of the Imperial Court in order to exchange extravagant gifts and conclude their important business deals; the rest of those accompanying the fleet comprising minor merchants, warriors, private individuals, priests, and the numerous escort, remained at Ningpō until the small party of important personages returned. This period was sometimes several months in duration.

All this would not have concerned Tomoharu but for an accident of time and place in the sixth year of the *Embum* era.[8] At that time, when he was already a mature bugeisha aged forty, he had wandered in his usual leisurely manner down the northern coast of the Inland Sea and arrived early one evening at the tiny fishing port of Tada-no-ura in the Aki domain where he hoped to find a fisherman who would ferry him across the water to the Murakami domain and specifically the large island of Omishima, clearly in sight just across the tranquil blue waters. There, he intended to pray at the Ō-yama-zumi shrine for success in a match that was being arranged with a strong swordsman of the Mihara clan, one Sakingo Uchibei. The match would probably take place on the day of the next new moon in the fourth month, some fifteen days from now, that is if his representative in Mihara was successful. This man, Uchibei, was reputed to be a master with the naginata but Tomoharu knew of the reputation of certain Murakami warriors using the long-bladed nagamaki that he, himself, favoured.

However, unbeknown to him, the Murakami had agreed with the Aki lords to supply guard ships and men to escort the tally fleet now gathered around the harbour of Kure and ready to venture across the broad ocean billows to Mu. This year the official flotilla would be a large one and many swift escort vessels were needed. The Murakami were notorious in the Inland Sea, preserving what they saw as their right to control all merchant shipping plying these sheltered waters from their fortified bases amongst the cluster of islands that constricted the Geiyō Straits. Their main strength lay on the islands of In-no-shima and Omishima and from here they

---

[8] *Embum 6*: 1361

exacted tolls on every vessel sailing through the narrows both to the east and the west.

On this night and under the mantle of darkness so that they were not observed by potential enemies, the Murakami *suigun,* sea warriors, left their many fortified jetties and were rowing in small convoys towards Kure. It was Tomoharu's misfortune to fall in with one such small group from In-no-shima, his fisherman heaving-to without demur at the first hail.

A samurai boarded his craft and looked at Torii Tomoharu closely in the light of a closed lantern.

'You are a rōnin, sir?' he asked.

'That is so.'

'What clan?'

'I am Torii Tomoharu. My family served the Nitta-ke. They are of hatamoto rank, sir.'

'Why are you here this night?'

'It is my intention to pray to Lord Ō-yama-zumi at his great shrine.'

'Is that so? Praying for skill in battle?'

'Praying for assistance in understanding the *Sonshi.* You are familiar with those writings?'

'Pardon me, Torii-sama, but yes, I do have a little knowledge in that direction; but just now, it is unfortunate that I cannot permit you to fulfil this ambition on Omishima. However, before you protest I have an alternative offer to put to you that you may find of interest and not a little value.'

'May I know your name, sir?'

'Your pardon . . . I am Murakami Yasu-ie, the grandson of Murakami Iemitsu-dono, brother of the lord of this domain.'

'Tell me your offer, Murakami-sama; I hope that I can agree.'

'An important event happens every few years, although the recent troubles have proved a hindrance.'

'And that event is?' prompted Tomoharu.

'Tomorrow, about noon, the Aki lord will despatch his official ships to China and my clan is providing part of the escort.'

'Indeed? But your offer?'

'Why do you not travel with us, Torii-sama; you may meet men of like mind as yourself in the great country?'

'Ah, yes! So I might! Unfortunately, sir, I have arranged a match with a *kenshi* in Mihara, some fifteen days from now, and cannot, for my honour's sake, fail to be on hand.'

Yasu-ie raised the lantern closer to his face and Tomoharu saw that he was smiling.

'Your match is with a certain Sakingo Uchibei, is it not?'

'It is!' He felt some surprise that the news had spread so soon. 'But, sir, how did you know?'

'You may be surprised to learn that your opponent has decided to sail with us, too, and is even now on one of my father's boats just ahead of us where the moonlight falls by that island.'

Tomoharu considered what Yasu-ie had just said and thought the news odd. He came to a decision.

'That being the case, I will travel with you as you suggest, Murakami-sama. Will you accept me amongst your *kerai*?'

'With much pleasure, sir.'

And so matters were settled.

The weather of that year had been unusually clement and the voyage of the tally fleet uneventful and fast, making landfall on the coast of the Celestial Empire not sixty miles south of Ningpō. It was also unusual that no attempt had been made to harry the fleet on the part of the fierce *wakō* pirates who infested the southern coasts of Chōsen or the inlets off western Kyūshū. They dropped anchor in Ningpō Bay and were at once surrounded by clouds of small Chinese boats offering to bring supplies of every kind, but it was noticeable that the Governor of that province was so wary of the barbarian fighting men that he had anchored five towering junks, all flying enormous decorated banners, to guard the approaches to the harbour bund until such time as the voyagers were ratified by the Imperial officials expected shortly from the Capital.

At last, after several weary days, the Imperial papers were issued and the travellers permitted to land to take up the accommodation arranged by the authorities through their Chinese agents. Torii Tomoharu found himself in the privileged position of lodging in a large mansion allocated to Murakami Yasu-ie and his entourage. The fact that he was a rōnin was of no import and he was treated with the respect due to his rank. It was now the first time that he was able to enquire about Sakingo Uchibei, who was to have been his opponent in the match about this date; however, Yasu-ie-dono had not forgotten and made enquiries from the Aki fleet commander on what should be done in the circumstances. It was decided that with the Chinese governor's approval the match should go ahead two days after the official delegation departed for the capital. The Chinese view was that it was a matter of little consequence to them what these barbarians did, provided no untoward disturbance ensued.

Naturally, amongst the samurai word of the impending match spread like wildfire and even the ashigaru felt their spirits rise at the prospect. The population of the port had swelled significantly with the fleet's arrival and, for the first time in their lives, most of the Japanese had seen 'foreigners' in the crowded streets. In the wasteland adjacent to the harbour, a vast number of booths had been constructed to accommodate both the Chinese traders and these 'barbarians' who had brought rich goods to Ningpō in the hope of excellent trade and profit.

The day of the match arrived and it was to be held at the tenth hour in a field hard by the Governor's residence. It was announced that this was not a fight, as such, but a demonstration in the use of two different weapons by masters intent on attracting future business. Triangular flags with cut fringes fluttered gaily in the off-shore breeze and other banners, gaudily coloured in vermillion and gold, proclaimed the purpose for all to see. It was, of course, to be a demonstration of warfare technique but in no way a serious fight. No one could ever point to any impropriety or blameworthiness, whatever the actual outcome. But of all this Tomoharu was unaware as he privately prepared inside the Murakami mansion; only Sakingo Uchibei understood and basked in the limelight.

Torii Tomoharu had dressed meticulously for the match shunning any of the colourful silks that men of his rank might have worn, instead having a plain indigo hakama of cotton and a grey kimono over which he donned a sleeveless plain *haori*. Sekingo, on the other hand, wore a striped red *sashinuki-bakama* with the bottoms pulled in and secured beneath red and gold decorated *kyahan*. His kimono had a bold printed design in red on a golden bistre background and drawstring sleeves tied back by a black *tasuke*. Both men, wary of the Chinese ground, wore woven string sandals but it was noted by some that only Tomoharu had taken the trouble to moisten the strings and pass a strong thread through the knot so that they wouldn't loosen in the conflict.

Sakingo announced to the chief judge that, in accordance with his right as the challenged party he had decided to use a live-bladed naginata about eight *shaku* in length, its blade strongly curved and measuring just two-and-a-half *shaku*. Tomoharu, on the other hand, came to the match armed only with his swords and the relatively short-shafted wooden nagamaki, the length of which was a mere six *shaku*. A cord handgrip round the shaft meant that his 'blade' was only just over two *shaku* in length.

Both men sat on their folding stools on opposite sides of the match area and on the north side stood a large war drum ferried specially from one of the larger Murakami galleys to give the signals for the event. The forward judge was Murakami Saburō, second son of Lord Iemitsu. This bushi was also acting as *bugyō* governing law and order in the fleet.

Although Tomoharu hardly gave any attention to the crowd he did notice a plainly dressed Chinese who he recognized to be a 'mandarin' from the white ball on the crown of his hat and the long pheasant's tail feather alongside. This man was accompanied by a strange-looking foreigner who wore a fur-trimmed cloak but who regarded the adversaries intently past his long hooked nose. The drummer raised his baton as Murakami Saburō nodded his head. He struck the taut skin with three strong measured beats then followed with a series of quicker strikes, at first low but becoming faster and louder, finally giving way to three more measured beats, but Sakingo, with a fierce yell, had already leapt to his feet and was flourishing his halberd over his head with great menace, advancing four of five feet before the drumming was completed.

While the rules of the match had been clearly laid down by Murakami-dono, he ignored the infringement as no harm had been done and Tomoharu remained calm, but nonetheless, Sakingo had sought an advantage.

'That was an unwise move, Sakingo-sama,' remarked Tomoharu as he brought his nagamaki down to his front. 'You may regret that!'

A frown crossed the other's brow.

'Impertinent upstart!' he growled, and rushed forward whirling his naginata like a dragon in great sweeping windmill strokes, but, as in all such exertions, Sakingo was forced to retire to regain his breath when his attack failed to connect, and at this moment Tomoharu shortened his grip and struck the naginata blade with his own wooden one, causing the weapon to snag the rammed earth ground. Sakingo missed his step and almost fell.

The Torii spearman stood back.

'Please recover, sir. It wouldn't be proper if I took advantage of such an unexpected accident.'

His opponent became angry and again rushed fiercely to the attack but this time his second cut was received by Tomoharu's oaken blade on his right forearm and the spearman twisted causing Sakingo to stumble forwards and to his left.

Again, Tomoharu stepped back and calmly waited for his adversary to recover.

Sakingo, his face suffused red with rage, snorted and prepared to deliver a third attack but Tomoharu sharply knocked down his quivering blade and instantly placed the tip of his own weapon against Sakingo's left neck below his chin.

Murakami-dono raised his war fan and the drum beat out to signal the conclusion of the match, but it was evident that Sakingo Uchibei would not accept the decision.

'I won,' he blared. 'That man only made two cuts, neither very effective, whereas mine would have cut him in half!'

'No. Master Sakingo; you were clearly defeated and had Torii-dono wished, you would now be dead with your throat gaping wide!'

Torii Tomoharu bowed to the bugyō.

'I am willing to continue to settle the matter if you will permit?'

Murakami Saburō looked at him with pursed lips and nodded.

'As you wish. Are you agreed, Sakingo-sama?'

Giving a perfunctory nod, Tomoharu's opponent squared his shoulders and again rushed in making a rapid low cut to the right knee, but the Torii spearman simply stepped over the attack, again engaging the naginata and flipped it upwards with an increased degree of force which spun Sakingo round like a child's top. Instantly, the butt of the nagamaki struck the halberdier behind one of his knees and he fell sprawling to the ground.

'Do you consider that you are defeated now, Sakingo Uchibei?'

The man glared up balefully; there was nothing he could do but concede.

Later that evening, Murakami Yasu-ie invited his guest to dine in his private quarters and Tomoharu found himself seated opposite the rather striking foreigner who he had noticed in the crowd prior to the match. Also present was the man he had surmised to be a mandarin as well as Yasu-ie's two chief followers.

'This is Lord Shu Huang, cousin of the High Governor of this province, and this gentleman is Master Li-ten who has travelled here from the lands far beyond the setting sun.'

Tomoharu bowed respectfully, wondering why this strange looking man should be treated with such obvious dignity.

As if in answer to his thoughts, Yasu-ie, waiting until some rather pleasant Chinese wine was poured by the delightful serving girls, added: 'Master Li-ten is a kenshi from the far West.'

'A kenshi? In the same way as we understand the term?'

'Yes; he is a master of the *bugei*.'

'Can that be so, my lord?' Tomoharu regarded the man with renewed interest. 'May I ask if he can speak Chinese or our language?'

'He is polite in Mandarin but lacks command of our language as yet.'

'How shall we communicate, my lord; surely it will be difficult?'

Murakami Yasu-ie laughed.

'Torii-sama, you are both swordsmen! Communication between you will not be difficult; in fact, it will be far easier than you think!'

As the delicate rice-wine began to flow so tongues became less constrained and soon Tomoharu found out that Li-ten was about forty-five years of age and had travelled through many countries in order to reach here. By sign language and the showing of minor scars, he also discovered that the stranger had taken part in a number of wars in his own country. The talk turned inevitably to the morning's match and Master Li-ten shook his head, indicating that in his opinion, Sakingo was a very bad person. But he also conveyed with little difficulty that he admired the manner in which Tomoharu had dealt with him.

When the dinner party broke up it was agreed that the two would meet the following day at the Phoenix Temple and matters were left like that. Tomoharu found, to his surprise, that he and the long-nosed stranger with the Chinese-sounding name, had many things in common.

Over the following two weeks, the two very different swordsmen met and practised together each day; first in the grounds of the Phoenix Temple and then outside the town adjacent to a small single-roomed summerhouse on Lord Shu Huang's estate a mile or so west in the hills. This was the time for the two to relax and get to know each other, chiefly through taking it in turns to demonstrate and explain their respective techniques. Shu Huang was a highly educated man who had achieved a good post through his abilities in the public examination system but now lived as a wealthy gentleman-of-leisure, merely acting on occasion as a magistrate. To make matters easier he had employed two far-travelled men as interpreters; one had lived for many years in Japan, serving the lord of Karatsu and was fluent in Japanese, the other was a former caravan master who had, in his long life, travelled as far as Constantinople and even to Vienna, thus gaining a working knowledge of many languages. It was he who found out that Li-ten was familiar with Hungarian and understood other Slavic and Turkic dialects. All this took time but the results were spectacular.

No one could say for sure just how long this contact could continue until the main delegation returned from the capital but in the past their business had usually taken two to four months. In the mornings, now that any lingering doubts had been dispelled, the two men examined the sword and spear techniques of Torii Tomoharu, while each afternoon, they changed so that Li-ten demonstrated his methods with the same weapon groups. Long hours were devoted to practice and even longer hours to writing notes at every available free moment. In the meantime, Shu Huang sent his agents out to visit the many temples that had long been established on this holy island in order to search for scrolls and books discoursing on these warrior arts and especially to find a master familiar with the use of the straight spear . . . and in this part of the quest they were successful. Such a man was discovered sitting in a quayside tavern gazing daily at the anchored Japanese vessels.

His name was Fa-hai and had served in the Imperial armies in the western interior provinces but had left when his value as a military expert was seriously overlooked through the arrant nepotism of the commanding general. He had been attracted to Ningpō by reports that many fine swords had been brought to the Empire by merchants who knew that they had a ready market for such Japanese-made Chinese-style weapons; he was not to be disappointed. He, too, had witnessed the defeat of Sakingo but had been unable to follow this up later. Now, fifteen days on, his luck had changed when he was approached by Lord Shu Huang's factor having made not a single move to be noticed.

Introductions concluded and the niceties over, Fa-hai asked: 'Why did you agree to fight that bigotted man, Master Torii?'

'I had arranged to do so on the basis of a report about his prowess.'

Tomoharu shook his head wryly.

'You should have killed him; the world would have been greatly improved without his presence!'

Torii Tomoharu wondered if or how he could explain his feelings on the subject.

'I don't like to advance my personal opinion but since what I did in that match is part of this discussion I have to say that while we live in violent times, I do not feel that my weapons are given to me in order to take life. Can you understand my reasoning?'

'Why have them, then?' asked Fa-hai directly when this had been interpreted.

'Perhaps I was given them together with my slight skill in order to teach me to observe correctness. You know, in my country many of us try to follow the teachings of Jukyō; those precepts that here you recognize as the words of Confucius.'

Fa-hai bowed deeply. 'I meant no offence, Master Torii; but I felt that between us fighting men, or gentlemen by birth, we should understand the root causes of our actions. It is an era of war and strife, master, I agree, but I can see your point very well. You played with that worthless fellow in your match, that much was very clear to me from where I observed everything. Did you hope that by turning his brutal attacks back onto him he might learn?'

'Possibly, quite possibly. It was always a hope.'

'That kind never learn! They are eaten up by their own arrogance. It is as the sage once said: "a little knowledge is a dangerous thing!" I think, master, that you played with him and thus brought him to his defeat.'

'That is praise, Master Fa-hai. You think that my skill was enough, eh?'

All this was translated into Li-ten's attentive ear and he held up his hands and stood up, ruefully rubbing his knees.

'Achh! How do you manage to kneel on the ground for so long, tell me? I'm as stiff as a board!' He pointed at Fa-hai. 'Let us see, Master Spearman! Let us see!'

He caught up a couple of long staves, each of which were padded at one end, and passed one to Fa-hai.

'Now, we will find out the truth! Do you strike at my knee!'

A grim smile spread over Fa-hai's chubby cheeks. Without blinking an eye, he stabbed forward with his shaft tip . . . and found himself lying flat on his back looking up at Li-ten whose lined face also wore a smile. The Chinese spearman was still grasping his staff and without warning swept it back at the foreigner's feet but had his wrist pressed down by a foot and the tip of his opponent's shaft just feathering his neck below his Adam's apple.

'Interesting, is it not?' Li-ten looked across at Tomoharu.

The latter pursed his lips and nodded. Oh, yes, it was interesting alright, but . . . He took up his wooden nagamaki and bowed. Pointing to Li-ten, he indicated for him to thrust as Fa-hai had done.

With the slightest movement of his leading wrist he engaged the thrusting spear, deflected it fractionally from its course . . . and stood to one side.

'Eh? But you . . .'

This time the staff was brought down with a thwack across Li-ten's palm and the thrust delivered with the butt. Again, the lightest of deflections and the foreigner, an undoubted master of his weapon as they all well knew, was totally defenceless . . . and was well-aware that it was so!

Both Fa-hai and Li-ten were astonished. Such skill was a revelation to them such as they have never before encountered.

Later, Tomoharu was asked who had taught him in the use of the spear.

'I learnt So-jutsu from one of our leading hatamoto,' he answered, shaking his head slightly, 'but he was instructed by a Chinese servant captured after the great storm that destroyed the Emperor's fleet seventy years ago. I remember watching them practise in a field beside the yashiki when I was a child and often tried to do the same . . . Ah, that was an interesting time and I was frequently chided by my *ama* for the dirt that covered my clothes . . . I lost count of the number of times I sprawled headlong to the ground!'

Fa-hai wrinkled his nose.

'But you used your nagamaki just now. Surely the curved blade is different from the straight spear?'

'Not at all! Look, my friends, I will tell you the secret soon, but not just yet.'

The heat of the Chinese summer had well and truly arrived by the seventh month but the three men were too deeply immersed in their studies to feel the discomfort. They simply rose earlier before dawn in order to practise ere the sun heated the morning air.

Fa-hai, far leaner and stronger that when he had been recruited, was interested in Tomoharu's bugei ancestry.

'All the war arts in my country can be traced back to the principles set out by the Sonshi . . . ah . . . Sun Tzu here, of course. Many masters follow the precept that all warfare is based on deception and it is this teaching that made me accept Murakami-dono's invitation to travel here in Lord Ako's fleet. If Sun Tzu taught these principles nearly two thousand years ago, what better place to come to study!' Tomoharu scratched his chin as he looked at the others as they all took their rest under a shady tree. 'As I told you some weeks ago, Master Li-ten, I watched the practice of our *Ō-karō*, that means "chief-councillor", and he, in his turn, had studied hard to master the So-jutsu from Mo-ye, the servant captured in Hakata bay . . .'

'Mo-ye, you say,' exclaimed Fa-hai, 'but that's a woman's name here?'

'Correct! She was indeed a woman, but what a one! One who was, I am told, an expert with the sword, spear, halberd, and the bow. She was found by Araki Heishirō soon after the great fleet had foundered in the storm and was hidden by him and his men in case she was killed. Her value soon became evident and she became Araki-*taishō*'s trusted servant though never his concubine

'As the years passed, Araki became almost as skilful as she, but was unfortunately killed in battle in Mikawa some thirty years ago when in his seventieth year. Mo-ye passed away eight years later but not before she had taught me many things.'

'You must have been only a child?' said Fa-hai.

'True enough! I was barely eighteen but already my feet were set on the Path when I was just three years old!'

Li-ten grunted and nodded his head.

'It is a year and seven months only since I crossed into the Celestial Empire but I can see similarities in you both. Am I right, Tomoharu-sama, that the movements taught you by the woman, Mo-ye, when you were very young, formed the basis of your understanding?'

'Yes; you have understood perfectly.'

'But you, Master Fa-hai, have studied the "Chinese Way" directly from experts living here?'

'I have, indeed, but our friend here has had the advantage of learning when he was unable to understand the teaching except by "doing". His understanding has come from within and is based on the premise that "to know and to act are one and the same thing".'

'Ach, so! That is really interesting!'

'I can show you something, my friend,' said Tomoharu. 'I wouldn't normally do this but in your case I make a special exception.' He undid the long braid *himo* that was looped through the pierced toggle on his sword sheath where it was secured to his hakama, removing the longsword from his hip. 'Take a look at my *tsuba*, Master Li-ten, and tell me what you see?'

'Tsuba? Achh, you mean the "guard", hein?'

Torii Tomoharu's sword was mounted with a very plain russet iron tsuba; one that, at first glance, one would have dismissed as crudely forged and ill-formed. Closer inspection, however, revealed that it was pierced with a stylized version of a shrine *torii*, the emblem of his clan, and that cunningly engraved into the background were a number of cursively 'written' characters.

'So, I have seen your device and some characters that it would be impossible for me to read.'

'Correct! Those characters are a famous maxim amongst the bugeisha in my country. They read thus:

In quietness, there is movement;
In movement, there is quietness.'

'This is the teaching that I do my best to follow.'

A little later after they had enjoyed a cooling drink brought to them by one of the female servants, Li-ten asked: 'Have either of you gentlemen practised with a hooked spear?'

'A hooked spear?' Fa-hai pricked his ears. 'You mean one shaped like the sickle used by farmers for harvesting?'

'No, Master Fa-hai; I rather think that our friend means a *kagi-yari* such as I heard one of our best swordsmiths, Bizen Masahide, made recently.' Tomoharu asked their interpreter for a small piece of paper and with a brush quickly drew the blade he had in mind,

'Ja!' shouted out Li-ten and, catching up the ink brush with a flourish, he sketched a rather larger weapon where the crowbill side blade was opposed on the opposite side of the head with a sort of hammer.

Both the others became enthusiastic and passed the drawings and some added measurements to the secretary scribe requesting that three practice weapons should be fashioned without delay. . . Two days later these spears, or 'war-hammers' as they were termed by Li-ten, were delivered into their hands by Shu Huang's master carpenter. He had questioned Li-ten closely as to his precise needs and carved from a branched joint of deep red rosewood to produce spears that he hoped would stand up to these masters' practice needs.

'This is beautiful wood,' remarked Tomoharu, admiringly. 'Where did it originally grow?'

'Usually I would keep that a secret, master,' smiled the carpenter, 'but in this case Lord Shu Huang insisted that I must speak . . . if I was asked! The tree grew far off in the north, near the Sungari river. There it was felled more than thirty years ago and properly seasoned within the same forest. My honoured master despatched me to select and purchase two wagons of such wonderful wood just five years since.'

'Would you fashion me two wooden bokken from the same rosewood, with permission from our host? I would dearly love to take them back to my country when I finally return.'

'That I will gladly do, my lord.' The carpenter picked up one of the 'war-hammers' and remarked: 'While I followed your instructions, did you know that in some ways these halberds are very like our ancient "*ge*" such as our armies used from long before the "Warring States" times to only three or four-hundred years ago?'

Shu Huang, seated in his ornately carved chair and shaded further from any shafts of sunlight by a large tasselled parasol borne by a slave, waved a languid hand.

'My carpenter is a rarity, my friends, for he is an educated man. In what he says he is perfectly correct for this is a matter of felicitous ancient record. Were you aware, Torii-dono, that the plains where grow this fine rosewood, were also the place of origin of those barbarous tribes who moved east and south before at last crossing to your land . . . and finally establishing your Imperial line?'

Li-ten bowed deeply.

'These "war-hammers" have only recently been fashioned for battle in my country, my lord; but I, too, have seen ancient bronze blades like the ones you describe that have been dug up by treasure seekers in the course of searching for buried gold.'

The mandarin nodded his head, brushing away a fly with his whisk.

'I take it that you know how such a weapon should be used?'

'It is the reason that I requested Master T'ang to fashion them, my lord.'

'Fa-hai; I wish to see what you would do with your spear against Li-ten's . . . er . . . "war-hammer".'

'Without any practice, lord?'

'There are no such luxuries on the battlefield!'

Fa-hai tucked his spear under his right arm, point lowered, and casually wandered around in a circle, eying Li-ten who had assumed a static upright stance in the centre of the practice area. As Fa-hai moved so Li-ten rotated first his head and then his feet so that he never let his opponent reach more than a quarter turn from his front. It was almost exactly as a cat might play with a mouse except the 'mouse', in this case, was also a skilful predator. It must be held in mind that warfare is never a game and we should recall the ancient doggerel verse quoted to their raw recruits for as long as fighting men have taken to the field:

One thing only we must
Keep in our minds:
Against our enemy, one thing;
The spear is to cut
or to thrust.

In the course of his slow circling steps, Tomoharu noted that Fa-hai allowed his 'blade' to stray more and more to his right side and to rise so that the butt was no longer beneath his right arm. After nearly a full minute of the preliminary circumambulation, he suddenly judged his moment and swept the spear back, down, and round to deliver a wheeling upwards cut at Li-ten, absolutely 'without colour', as our forbears used to say. Li-ten thrust down using his branch blade first to engage then deflect the spear, but Fa-hai was ready and, at first fractionally resisting, jerked the shaft back before thrusting high at his long-nosed opponent's exposed armpit. But Li-ten twisted his halberd and just managed to deflect the attack before he was struck. Fa-hai circled his blade in a tight arc and struck down lightly on the halbarder's leading wrist.

'Very good!' exclaimed Shu Huang.

'Sound tactics,' Tomoharu approved, 'but what do you think, Master Li-ten?'

'Fa-hai is indeed a strong spearman, perhaps the strongest I have encountered in all my travels. His circling created some confusion in my mind so that when his attack came I was slow to act.'

The mandarin nodded. 'You were well and truly trapped, you'll agree?'

'I was deceived in both my moves and paid the penalty; ja, that is so!'

'Torii-sama, would you deign to practise now?' asked Li-ten.

Tomoharu bowed and drew back his deep sleeves with his *tasuke* sash.

'I'm ready, my friend, and leave it to you which weapons should be used.'

'Ah! Do I detect a shade of deception in that, sir?' smiled Fa-hai.

'Do you think I would do that, eh?'

'The Sonshi advocated such traps and strategms.'

'So he did! But here I offer you the whole choice; something over which I have no possible influence. Is that not the truth?'

Li-ten scratched his chin and shrewdly eyed his Japanese friend. At last he said: 'In that case I suggest we both use the war-hammers.'

'These are fine weapons, Master T'ang; perfect weight and balance,' observed Tomoharu appreciatively. 'You have certainly done well!' He turned to the foreigner to ask 'In your country, Master Li-ten, do these hammers fall into a special category or rank like you were saying about some other weapons?'

'Ja, that is so, Torii-sama! These halberds are used by men of high rank or their "champions" in personal combat such as when affairs are settled by a judicial contest "in the ring", as we call it. Much the same as your fight with that wretch, Uchibei.'

Tomoharu hefted one of the rosewood halberds and said: 'This one will do for me. There can be little in it; you have this one, if you are happy?'

When they took their places there were at least two more hours light left even though the sun was sinking towards the horizon. The mandarin invited Fa-hai to act as judge and the spearman bowed then drew a folding fan from his sash.

Without further ceremony other than a bow, Li-ten swept up his hammer blade from his right, aiming at Tomoharu's head, but the kenshi shortened his grip and blocked the strike. Without pausing, Li-ten stepped away, threatening to rake his opponent's leading ankle, his retreat covered by this dangerous attack since it forced

Tomoharu to deflect the rake by dropping the butt end of his shaft. Both drew back a few steps . . .

This time, the kenshi struck at Li-ten's groin forcing the 'foreigner' to jump back, hammer raised to deal a counter stroke if there was a chance . . . He thought he saw a gap and struck down but it was a trap . . . His blow was caught and thrown violently aside and Li-ten came down heavily on one knee.

'It is enough!' shouted Fa-hai, his fan raised.

'That being the case,' said Torii Tomoharu, giving a hand to Li-ten to bring him to his feet, 'we must devote the remainder of our time to severe practice!'

His opponent brushed the dust from his trousers and seemed about to embrace the samurai but remembered proper custom just in time.

'Did you know that you used my favourite technique on me?' he asked.

Tomoharu was about to reply when Shu Huang rose from his carved chair and stepped down to the rammed earth practice area, closely followed by his bearer.

'I received word a little earlier that the official delegation prepares to leave the Imperial Presence on the second day of the ninth month. This allows us to devote just thirty more days to our activities at an informed guess.'

Refreshments were brought and they seated themselves beneath the spreading chestnut tree to rest from their exertions. The discussion naturally centred on the day's encounters.

Fa-hai was adamant. 'Master Torii has received his talent from the gods', he declared. 'No one could fault you, Master Li-ten, but today it was impossible that you could win . . . You fought a veritable god of war!'

'If such a deity exists, he certainly was present,' replied the long-nosed foreigner, ruefully.

Tomoharu held up his hand.

'No, my good friends! Please don't embarrass me because of some slight hint of advantage. The art of war was set out by such enlightened philosophers as Sonshi seventeen-hundred years ago. They explained the principles with which we are all familiar; but it is the application of these principles that we need to recognize. It is "to know and to act" that comes from within and such revelation derives from Marishi-ten, Master Li-ten.' He smiled at the older man. 'I know and respect your belief in only one god, my friend, and have no wish to give any offence, but since you have travelled vast distances and undergone great dangers in order to reach here to study these arts I cannot believe that you would be upset or stopper-up your ears by encountering our beliefs, would you? It is these beliefs that profoundly underpin our view of these arts and their application in battle.'

'I follow you, Master Torii. It was not just the techniques of making war that I left my country in order to study, it was what lies beneath. During my travels I have seen and done my best to remember many such techniques, but now, here in Ningpō, I have at last met genius! Where does this inner teaching come from?'

Fa-hai looked across at Shu Huang who imperceptably nodded.

'In that case, Master Li-ten, it is our honourable host's will that you shall find out.'

Mystified, the foreign swordsman bowed, but the mandarin raised his hand. 'We do not intend your discomfort, my friend; we only intend to help you towards deeper understanding since that is your wish. The night after tomorrow will be that of the full moon; you shall accordingly dress as ordinary people and go to Lao-shan on which mountain stands a small temple.'

'Is it far, my lord?' Li-ten was anxious in case the journey would lose him precious time from practice.

'Nay, 'tis that peak behind the town. You see it each time you leave this courtyard.'

Around noon the next day, the three masters separately left the town by different gates, unrecognizable in their plain simple apparel and only carrying a sword or stave. Two hours later, at the heat of the day, they gathered at their pre-arranged rendezvous at a wayside shrine where they found the magistrate awaiting them with horses. He gave them some instructions and introduced a mute servant who was to act as their guide.

'You will not accompany us, my lord?' asked Tomoharu in surprise.

'No; these two or three nights are for you three only. You have provisions and everything you may need. The gods of good fortune smile on you!'

Their guide moved off the moment they were ready and Torii Tomoharu was relieved to find their weapons neatly wrapped in sheeting on the back of the spare horse.

Once they had left the rice fields, the mute took them by a circuitous path apparently to skirt the seaward side of the mountain promontary yet soon the track became choked with underbrush and even thickets of bamboo as well as significantly steepening. It was heavy going under the hot afternoon sun.

'Few people come to this temple,' remarked Fa-hai, wiping his streaming brow and neck.

Tomoharu took a deep breath, almost glad to rest his mount, hardened as he was to such privations. 'There might be another route, of course.'

'Oi, you!' called Fa-hai to the mute. 'Do you know where you are going?'

'He can't answer you,' remarked Li-ten, 'He's lost his tongue!'

Fa-hai shrugged and took a short swig from his waterbag.

An hour later, as the sun reached the line of the distant hills on the far side of the plain, they reached a shoulder apparently quite near to the summit and in a deep declivity saw the almost roofless temple.

'Surely that can't be where Lord Shu Huang intended, can it?' grunted the Chinese spearman. 'It is a ruin!'

As they led the horses up a final series of steep pitched stairs and through what had once been a handsome outer gateway, now reduced to just two decayed ivy-clad uprights, Tomoharu shook his head.

'It wouldn't surprise me to know that no one had visited this place for a hundred years or more! Just look at it . . .'

After coaxing the ponies up and through to the temple yard, to graze the luxuriant grass that grew thick through the broken paving, the three warriors cautiously took a look around but everywhere they found only advanced decay. Yet this wasn't an abandoned shrine, it simply reminded them of the conditions of wartime where they might, each in his own country, stumble on a deserted church or temple whose priests had long fled for fear of the invading enemy.

Time and termites had taken their inevitable toll; the floorboarding was rotten and broken, leaving dangerous gaps for unwary feet, stairways were deathtraps, balustrades rickety, and roof tiles dislodged, oftimes balanced on the very edge, threatening to fall at the slightest disturbance. But now, worst of all as the evening thickened, a roll of thunder presaged a rainstorm. In fact, with the mute's help, they were barely able to rig up an oiled sheet between the gaunt uprights of the once beautiful gateway before the storm burst about their ears.

'It would be here,' sniffed Li-ten. 'It had to gather about this mountain, of course!'

Fa-hai stared at the two disintegrating rice balls handed him by the servant, and muttered: 'Summer heat soon turns to rain hereabouts!'

Only Tomoharu was cheerful.

'For whatever reason we have been sent up here by our host, we are hardly likely to be disturbed.'

'That's true enough! Only phantoms would want to come to this ruin!'

'Come now, Fa-hai; surely a master spearman like you would not be worried by a goblin or two?'

'Not I!' declared the Chinese warrior. 'I was worried about you, Master Li-ten, after you have wandered through the ghost-wailing wastes of the Tien-shan and the vast Gobi deserts!'

They all laughed and pulled such cover as they had closer about them.

The storm raged for about two hours and stopped as suddenly as it had begun. An eerie silence ensued that was all the stranger when Fa-hai remarked that this must be the first place he had ever been in on a warm and damp night where there was no sound of crickets; not one lone voice . . . nothing!

It was well after midnight, so they judged, when they settled down as best they could to sleep. The skies had now cleared and a half moon cast a strange brilliance onto the wraiths of mist that were beginning to rise.

Torii Tomoharu, who had slept many nights in ruined shrines as the wars first against the Hōjō usurpers and then between the Two Courts ravaged his own country, woke up without a movement, to see the foreigner, Li-ten rise from his place and walk slowly to the centre of the courtyard. He carried with him his favourite polearm with its wicked side blade and hammerhead. The bushi noted, too, that he had carefully slung his strange 'hand-and-a-half' longsword by its leather belt across his shoulders. The Fa-hai and the mute still slept peacefully.

There was a movement at the gaping half-fallen doors of the former prayer hall; at least, he thought he saw something there, but it was only after a couple of minutes that his mind was set at rest as first a priest appeared, shortly followed by a second. The first proved to be a tall man in contrast to the second who was powerfully built but squat. The taller man, clearly to be seen in the moonlight, supported himself on a long staff whilst his companion carried what looked like a wooden sword; but that was hardly priestly gear, thought the warrior.

Without warning, the shorter of the pair brandished his cudgel and rushed headlong at Li-ten. The latter, who had clearly seen his danger, met the attack with a sweeping cross defence that should have bowled the priest off his feet . . . if, of course, he had been struck!

Feeling the warm flank of one of the packhorses at his neck, Tomoharu eased himself up to a more comfortable position to observe. For a moment he felt like rubbing his eyes, hardly believing what he saw, for instead of having his legs swept from under him, the monk appeared to fly over the halberd and whilst doing so dealt Li-ten a crack across his shoulders. The kenshi heard the audible grunt given as the blow connected, but Li-ten, used to hard blows, deftly struck upwards with the lower end of his war-hammer, seeking to catch his opponent as his feet reached the ground . . . but to no avail.

A loud peal of laughter rang out from the taller priest and Li-ten realized that he now faced two adversaries, one to either side. For the first time in these three months, Torii Tomoharu saw the real strength of this mature foreigner. He moved like greased lightning first one way and then another, seemingly at random, but the warrior realized that his intention was always to keep good distance and to work his enemies so that both were within his line of vision . . . Cut followed slice, attack and defence flowing into one movement in the moonlight. Li-ten rocked down and across, but his attack was turned by what must be the squat priest's wooden sword, only to find that the taller monk was threatening a cut to his legs which, perforce, he must block. With an unintelligible roar in some barbarous tongue, Li-ten flailed with his war-hammer in great ferocious arcs, driving back first one then the other. It was only then, as the shorter priest came closer to where he lay, that Tomoharu had the impression that the fellow had a beaked nose. His loose robes, secured back to his shoulders, flew and flapped as he moved and tumbled . . . surely not like those mythical tengu of his home province of distant Kōzuke . . ?

His mind must have wandered briefly. There was absolute silence . . . The couryard was empty; no priests, no Li-ten! Seconds passed into minutes . . . nothing!

A hollow whisper called out: 'Torii-dono . . .'

Tomoharu rose to his feet, every nerve alert, his slung sword silently unsheathed in his hand. A wild laugh almost made him start but instead of turning to look, he ducked down, spinning in the faintest zephyr of air like a wraith of smoke from a small pile of burning leaves, and cut horizontally to his former rear which was now his front. The razor sharp blade flashed round and just missed the hips of an assailant . . . he 'knew' there were three . . . Dropping to a deep squatting position he cut to his rear and again to his front with unbelievable speed . . .

'Good! That is better, Torii-dono! Now deal with this . . !'

A arrow flew past his ear as Tomoharu saw a tumbling bouncing attacker coming in from his left and, sensing a second arrow, he slashed upwards with his tachi, cutting a shaft in two and, ducking low, closed and grasped the new opponent by his loose garment, swinging him in front of him just as a third arrow sank into his victim. In a blur he blocked a strike from a long hafted weapon, deflecting it downwards and, shouting out a high-pitched yell, stamped down on the shaft before the priestly owner could withdraw . . .

'Enough! You have learnt well, Lord Torii . . . Our sacred Mistress will indeed be pleased . . . deign to allow my pupil to retire!'

'Pupil? You put an arrow through him!'

'You thought I did!'

The little man with the hawk-like face, grinned in the moonlight, eyes glittering, cartwheeled away, and vanished! Tomoharu looked around, certain that his swordblade had done its deadly work on at least one more attacker, but there was no one.

'Where is my friend,' he demanded softly.

'Ah, Master Li-ten, eh? He is well . . . But go and seek your rest, Lord Torii; tomorrow's dawn will soon be here . . . Do you pray then to our Mistress . . . Do not omit a prayer . . .

The kenshi's body was soaked with sweat; he felt much as he did long years before when a small party of warriors he was with were ambushed in a narrow defile close to the upper waters of the Tamagawa and fought their way clear almost without loss. Surely all this had taken place in just a few minutes . . . A mere blink of the eyes. Or was it all a dream brought on by their recent daily exercises and the strangeness of this ruin? And yet the trampled grass lay all around him; that much he could see by the light of the setting moon . . . His breathing was disordered although he fought to regulate it by force of his will, just in case he was suddenly assailed again. It must have been a dream-vision, he closed his eyes and shook his head, hair flying unbound. Already to the east the horizon had begun to streak dull red presaging the coming day. He fell to his knees, sword placed before him, and formally placed his palms together before his face to offer his gratitude to Marishi-ten.

Fa-hai was astonished at their reports of the battles they imagined they had fought. He swore that he hadn't slept a wink all night but even if he had slipped into a short doze, he would have awakened at the noise of combat. The mute servant, too, shook his head vigorously when asked and was clearly telling the truth. Strangest of all, Li-ten was found asleep beneath his cover and could remember nothing other than a vague dream about some fight he had been in years before. Only Tomoharu appeared to have experienced something and it was all a puzzling mystery.

It remained the subject of conversation all that day, going over the kenshi's account of the two battles but without stirring fresh memories. When night drew on, as on the previous evenings, the storm clouds gathered over the plains and they remarked on an extraordinary brittleness charged with energy that filled the air. When the storm broke it was truly the start of the Autumn rains and made those of the previous two nights seem like mere showers. As before, they sought cover from the downpour and, at first, the almost continuous lightning and thunder that enveloped the Lao-shan. Deafened by the stentorian detonations, no one could hope to speak without shouting and then not be heard.

In the midst of all this the tall priest stood before them and beckoned all three to cross to the prayer hall. When they entered they found the interior lit by several large lanterns and three priests kneeling in a line to one side of a large gilt figure of Dainichi Nyōrai. This was no ruin, thought Tomoharu, but he couldn't understand . . . The three soaking warriors knelt before the statue, even Li-ten unquestioning.

The faint tinkling of a bell was heard and the tall priest, his robe completely dry, appeared to the right of the altar platform. He struck the floor with the end of his *shaku-jo* staff making the iron rings jangle loudly.

'I have but one question to put to each of you, O fighting men. By the Nine Successors, tell me, Master Fa-hai, what you would do if you were attacked at this moment?' His voice was penetrating and clear, despite the storm that raged outside.

'I would examine the situation, then decide, master!'

'You would be dead!' came the dry comment. 'Your answer, please, Master Li-ten!'

'I would roar like a lion and attack!'

'You would diffuse your strength and soon die!'

It was clearly Torii Tomoharu's turn. The priest gave him a piercing look.

'If I were attacked right now, Lord Priest, I would dissemble and move. I would cloak every action and thought in invisibility, thus forcing my enemies to think whilst I simply acted! Does that satisfy you, apparition?'

'Lord Torii, you understand the teaching and your mind is already free. From this time you will become stronger and stronger! For you, O Spearman Fa-hai, you now understand the task ahead of you but still have some distance to go! It is decreed that you must cross the ocean waves in the company of your master and practise daily in the mountain called Hide-hiko! That is all I have for you . . . Success and fame are vouchsafed to you only if you follow this Path, but it shall not be in your own country!

'Master Li-ten, you have journeyed far in a long quest. Your eyes are now opened and you understand that success does not necessarily go with power. It is by subtlety and the unexpected that you may achieve the victory that no man can define or understand. Remember, oppose power with apparent weakness, the obvious with deception. You said you would defend yourself like a roaring lion but why not like a tiger? Go back to your land and whilst travelling consider this matter carefully. If you can find the correct answer then your skills will be remembered even to the fortieth generation but then, I say, they will still not be understood!'

Outside, the great storm rose to a fury, the lashing rain driven before a furious wind. The sliding shōji fell inwards and instantly the wind extinguished the lanterns, plunging the hall into inky darkness.

'We must leave!' bawled Tomoharu, clutching at his companions' clothing. 'Come on!'

Somehow or other, they fought their way to the opening, carefully picking their way down the decayed stairway to the courtyard and dashed to shelter by the gate where their mute stood calming the horses. With a last thunderous clap the storm blew over and was soon gone. As the moon came out into the clearing night sky they could see that it would have been impossible for them to have sheltered in the ruin since at least half its roof appeared to have collapsed inwards . . .

At first light, the small column of men and horses made its way down the mountain tracks and reached Lord Shu Huang's mansion early in the afternoon.

Strike the enemy where he does not expect you.

Probe his right, attack his left; withdraw when he is in disarray, then destroy him.

Make this your simple truth and in battle you will never suffer defeat!

Postscript

This story is based on the strong hints found in the Japanese bugei that a number of kenshi may very well have travelled to China either with the Tally fleets or privately between the mid-fourteenth century and the third decade of the sixteenth century with the express purpose of studying the philosophical and practical roots of the Arts of War. They were well aware at that time that it was the female war-deity, Mārīcī (Jap. Marishi-ten), whose cult spread from the Danube to Korea, from the northern Russian steppe south to Persia and India, and even in a slightly more primitive form to the extremes of Western Europe and Scandinavia, that covertly underpinned the understanding of warfare throughout this vast region. In Japan, Marishi-ten was frequently invoked as the source of the most original and inspired understanding. Her 'messengers' (Jap. 'otsukai') were the semi-legendary tengu, often depicted as bird-like beings endowed with phenomenal skill with hand weapons and long-equated with a number of aspects of the Shugendō yamabushi.

Johann Liechtenauer, here fictionalized as Li-ten, was a south-German fechtmeister who lived, it is thought, sometime between the thirteenth and early fourteenth century, and became so interested in studying the use of weapons that 'he travelled the world' in pursuit of these techniques. His developed style was transmitted through the following century, to be illustrated in detail, in the 'Fechtbuch' of another German fechtmeister, Hans Talhoffer, in his manuscripts of 1443, 1451, and 1467. (See Martin Wierschin, *Meister Johann Liechtenauers Kunst des Fechtens*, München, 1965.) Analysis of some of the more 'advanced' forms of the use of the spear and the longsword in the Talhoffer tradition (always ascribed by the early German writers to Johann Liechtenauer) have identified an extraordinarily close similarity, not to be found anywhere else, with a surprising number of early Japanese bugei transmissions. That these German/Japanese techniques should have appeared at all in this narrow 'window' of time is surprising, but that they should have so many precise points in common, can hardly be explained as 'accidental' since these are some of the most advanced battlefield forms that can only have been developed by men who possessed profound understanding in this field.

The inference is some common source or that some expert masters were able to study undisturbed at a place of cultural exchange such as the periods when the Tally Fleets remained at Ningpō. If Liechtenauer did in fact reach eastern China, and many western travellers certainly did visit Cathay in those centuries, and did benefit from such direct contact with the far-eastern kenshi, then it is quite reasonable to argue that his fuller and more mature studies led him to develop his teachings more quickly on his return to Bavaria. The Japanese transmissions, also lacking full written evidence, seem to date from the early-fifteenth century and 'flowered' into some of the surviving traditions from the end of that century and the early decades of the next.

It is probable that mastery of the straight-bladed spear and the single side-projection spear (hōkō) first came to Japan from experience gained by the Japanese bushi in opposing the abortive Mongol invasions in the late-thirteenth century; however, it is also suspected that many spear techniques (as opposed to those of Naginata-jutsu) were either taught by Chinese masters or that kenshi did, in fact, travel to China in order to study. One of the foundations of this theory is that the Chinese arts of the spear contain many wide-spaced foot and leg postures and a certain athleticism that is characteristic of the continent rather than the Japanese archipelago. These special movements are not acquired easily, taking many years to ingrain into the subconscious, and they are not easily transmitted down the generations; this can only be done by constant returning 'to the well-springs' or a succession of native masters ensuring that the forms remain pure.

In every surviving tradition rooted in the late-fifteenth to the mid-sixteenth century in Japan that contain what are known as 'tengu-shō' upper (or secret) levels, the teaching is held to have been transmitted from Marishi-ten through her otsukai, or 'messengers', the tengu. (Author)

11

THE MOON UNDER WATER

Although the records tell us that warfare between the contending lords and the many ambitious vassals spread everywhere during the strife-torn years after the Great Ōnin War until late in the following century, there was in many parts of the provinces relative tranquillity and peace. At least, this was the case at the time of the ninth Shogun, Ashikaga Yoshihisa. All this came to an end with the rising by Sasaki Takeyori in Omi province and the ambitions of Hōjō Sōun in the Kantō.

The increasingly violent conditions in the provinces, brought about through the decline of the Ashikaga Bakufu, did not at this stage really concern those who recorded the annals of the Torii-ke. For them, the shift towards political weakness brought more immediate problems so that we find these chronicles at times relatively terse whilst at others remarkably detailed. Slipped in amongst the official genealogies and accounts of warfare are the occasional, though rare, scrolls that often provide odd glimpses of warrior life. One such concerns a nephew of Torii Toranosuke, the brother of the Kōzuke Deputy-Constable, Torii Munemori. This nephew was, at the time, a young man named Kusatsu Kotarō.

This account, written down just after these events by a cultured Shintō priest, tells us that this Kotarō was directly descended from the main Torii-ke through a branch of the family who were also hatamoto. From an early age he had been prepared for adult life with increasingly severe training in the Bujutsu, readying him for command on the field of battle as he matured. Thus, by the age of twenty-two, he was already a strong swordsman and showed excellence with the spear, but his heart was not yet committed to this Path and he inclined, in his personal aspirations, towards the arts of peace.

In his grandfather's day, some of the higher-ranked warriors occupied an important position in society, maintaining the cultural life as well as providing stability for their peasant farmers. While not moving by any means in the refined atmosphere of the indolent aristocrats, many nonetheless encouraged within their domains arts like painting, poetry and dance, not only amongst many of their retainers but even at the lower level of the better-off farmers. This was due to the fact that with some of these very old families, they still felt a benevolent sense of responsibility towards those dependent upon them.

Kotarō spent long hours daily at his military training and had earned the approval of his father and the senior retainers with his prowess, but for every hour spent out in the sun, wind, rain or snow, sword or spear in hand, he devoted what remained to improving his dexterity with the brush, in carving, in iron-smithing, and in the composition of what some believed to be elegant verse. At length, he decided that he needed proper instruction in calligraphy and painting which he felt could not be found in a poor mountain backwater in the Kantō. He resolved that he must travel to Miyakō and seek out some teacher amongst the remaining aristocrats who must still retain the old high culture.

Accordingly, he went one day to his father and, bowing low, requested his permission to travel to the capital, this purpose in mind. His father was somewhat taken aback by the request but said that the decision must rest with his brother as it affected the immediate family.

'It will be a waste of the young man's time,' was Tarōemon's opinion. 'Most of the remaining aristocratic families in Miyakō live in near penury, their lands long confiscated or sequestered by the Yamana or the Hosokawa during the Ōnin War. He'll find most of those who are left are charlatans and will do almost anything to part such a youngster from his gold!'

Kusatsu Mune'emon, Kotarō's father, recalled his own impetuous youthful wanderings.

'Don't you think it would be no bad thing for your nephew to broaden his experience by travelling?'

'Hmmm! I know what you mean but we did it by hunting on foot or undergoing *musha-shugyō* with bokutō or staff. He wants to write poetry!'

'Ah, but, honoured brother, suppose he were given permission to travel as a musha-shugyōsha? We could require that his purpose was to visit a hundred shrines and that he must practise his bugei before the deities at each one!'

Tarōemon accepted some rice wine from his brother and for a while they sipped the delicious ō-sake in silence.

'If Kotarō experiences a little more at first hand the state of the Tokaidō as he travels out, or of the Nakasendō on his return, that would stand him in good stead, wouldn't it?'

Mune-emon savoured his wine.

'Perhaps I should regret that my eldest son hankers after the culture of bygone days. Many now see the rôle of the samurai to be purely that of fighting.' He shook his head and sighed.

'Young Kotarō needs his eyes opened. He is no fool! Send him on his way, brother, but let him do it the hard way with little spare coin and on foot! He will return the better!'

Furnished with the necessary papers giving the young samurai permission to leave his duties and become a temporary rōnin so that he could pass through the many barriers along the main highways, and to the unspoken fears of his mother as he bowed respectfully before leaving the outer gate of the yashiki. It was a fine spring morning on the first day of the cherry blossom; a small pack on his back, staff in hand, and a blithe heart. He had sufficient silver to permit him to eat frugally and lodge each night in the cheaper establishments that abounded along the way for the comfort of respectable travellers, particularly poor samurai, and thus he made his slow way south through the domain of the Shin-Hōjō and along the famous Tokaidō as far as Mikawa.

On the border with Owari, he found that an uprising by one of the local gentry against his suzerain, Shiba Yoshitoshi, was in full swing. He was forced to employ his time in Kiyosu seeking out some swordsmen who gave instruction in the town. He found them to have little talent and it was certainly fortunate that the rebellion suddenly resolved itself, Shiba Yoshitoshi-dono escaping north to Echizen, allowing him to evade the anger of the defeated pretenders' students at their master's humiliation by an unknown young kenshi. Without delay, he passed across the border into Mino province intending to stay a few days in the small town of Ogaki before continuing to Omi and Miyakō, itself.

In Ogaki he was told that the situation in Omi province around the great lake of Biwa was very fluid since two or three lords from the north of the province had been thwarted in their ambitions to seize Miyakō by the large force of warrior 'monks' attached to the Miidera and the temples clustered on Hiei-zan. Accordingly, he determined to lodge a few days in a small posting inn that he discovered just off the main thoroughfare.

The innmaster was a dour fellow who said little and drank much; his wife more than compensated for her husband's taciturn nature by her bustling and talkative nature. To her, all the world was a friend yet, at the same time, she managed to combine her geniality with a shrewd mind and an ability to keep strict order without being in the least overbearing. Almost as Kotarō presented himself she decided, through instinct, that he wasn't one of the usual riff-raff of rōnin who frequented these cheaper inns and gave him a small four mat room on the upper floor next to her family quarters. The inn seemed to be the focal point for a number of the ladies of the night since the town lay astride a busy main highway. Lucrative business was always to be had both from strong wine and other vices. None of this bothered the aspiring young poet who spent his time sipping green tea and composing quite good verse to record his impressions of his journey and its sights. Not for him the wiles of the colourful bevy of girls or the pitfalls of strong drink.

By the third night, such is the nature of these 'butterflies', they had already accepted him and even included him in their gay banter. The softer side of his nature prompted him to brush a rather elegant *uta* (poem) praising the flowers that often brightened the grey and uncertain world, but when he presented this shyly to the innkeeper's wife he wondered if he hadn't made a serious mistake and would be offered one of the girls as his paramour for the duration of his stay!

'Oh, sir; you write wonderful things,' she enthused. 'Many gentlemen who stop here are so . . . er . . .' She paused, thinking that perhaps she shouldn't complete the sentence.

'Ah, Oka-san, we must remember times are hard and many samurai lack the means to give their children a proper education'

While he said this gently, he thought at once that the words sounded unctious.

'Do you study . . . er . . . literature, sir?' she asked, indicating that she would serve him a cup of *ō-sake*. When he pointed to the *ō-cha*, she smiled and held back the deep sleeve of her kimono with one hand as she poured. 'No wine? I am sorry, I forgot, master.'

He smiled and shook his head.

'I don't think a samurai should drink as it confuses the mind; that's just my feeling so I resolved to keep to that principle for as long as I serve my lord . . . You ask about my studies? Well, I don't have any real skill which is the reason that I am travelling to Miyakō. It is my hope that once there I can persuade some person of culture to kindly instruct me in these arts.'

The woman sat upright, covering her mouth with the fingers of one hand.

'Why, have I said something amusing?' he enquired.

'No, master . . . but no one is left in . . .' She paused. 'You should speak with that girl who sits over there, the one a little apart from the rest.'

'But why should that be, Oka-san?' He glanced across and saw a melancholic-looking young woman who may have been around eighteen. He fervently hoped that he would not be expected to behave as most young samurai did.

'Yuki-san; Oi! Yuki-san!'

The girl looked up at the innmaster's wife's shout and slowly but gracefully came across carrying a wine bottle. Kotarō saw that one strand of her raven hair fell across her forehead rather attractively.

'Mistress?'

'You're from Miyakō, ain't you, Yuki-san? This gentleman intends to go there soon. 'E's a poet and wants to learn how to write better . . . You won't need that *sake* 'cos he don't drink!' She rose to her feet seeing two samurai enter the outer door, straightening her kimono. 'Must be off! Look after Master Kotarō here, there's a good girl . . .'

The young man gave an embarrassed cough.

'Don't worry, master; I know you don't want me,' she said, almost flatly.

'Look, Miss . . . er . . . Yuki-san; why don't we sit over there out of the way? I'm not sure why Mama-san called you across but she probably thought that as I'm going to Miyakō, maybe you can give me some advice?'

When they sat down on the mat, they were partly obscured from the rest of the noisy patrons by a large upright.

'You are from the capital, aren't you?'

'Yes, master; I lived there until I was thirteen.'

When he looked her in the face something told him that she was deeply unhappy.

'Why did you leave, Yuki-san?' he asked.

She hid her face in her gaudy kimono sleeve.

'You can tell me; I won't talk about it to anyone else,' he said encouragingly.

'Master, I . . . I was stolen . . .'

'Stolen? At such a tender age?'

'Some men came to the inn my parents lived in and simply took me away, sir.'

'What did your parents do? Didn't they protest?'

Yuki whispered. 'My mother wept pitifully, but I think my father took something from one of them and turned away.'

Kotarō hadn't realized that such dreadful things really went on.

'Who were your parents, Yuki-san?'

The girl spilt some wine into the cup and swallowed it down.

'I'm sorry, master . . . My father was once a courtier but . . . but had no money left . . . My mother came of a better family but had to sell everything in order to feed us . . . She taught calligraphy because she had a very fine hand but could find no one who wanted to learn, I . . . I was the last thing of value that they had . . . that's why I was taken.'

A large tear hung on a eyelid but she dabbed it away with the corner of her kimono sleeve.

Kotarō thought about what she had told him. Sold into inevitable prostitution by her destitute and desperate parents, themselves minor *kuge*. How shameful! But what did this really mean?

The girl rose quickly and almost ran back to join the boisterous group carousing in the centre of the large room. Drinking some water to slake a sudden dryness, Kotarō caught up his sword ready to go up to his room. Glancing back, he noticed that Yuki was no longer there and shrugged his shoulders. Probably most of these girls could tell similar stories. Still, she was very unhappy, he thought, and that was hardly surprising.

He didn't see the girl again until on the fifth morning he decided to continue his journey. In fact, he was just tying his second waraji sitting on the inner step when someone rushed past him shouting out that a woman's body had been found amongst the reeds at the side of the river. Curious, he finished securing his sandal and hurried down with the rest from the inn to the scene.

It was poor Yuki, of course. He knew at once. Kotarō saw that there was no sign of a struggle but that in her desperation she had knelt amongst the reed stems and stabbed her soft throat with a small knife. It was the classic death of women of the kuge and samurai classes. With a heavy heart he was about to rise when he noticed that in the loosened fingers of her left hand she still held a small figure of Our Lady of Mercy. There was a sad irony since when he held the figure he saw that it was finely crafted in pure gold. It must have belonged to her family when they still held position in Miyakō.

Weighing it in his hand he knew that it was worth many times the price that those men had paid her father.

A few days later he passed through the hamlet of Seki and trudged along the road that wound between the field to cross the moorland of Sekigahara beneath the cloud shrouded bulk of Ibuki-san. Ahead he could now see right across the small province of Omi and Biwa-ko to the blue-grey mountains of Tamba, indistinct under a threatening sky. He gave an involuntary shudder at a feeling almost of foreboding but, shrugging his shoulders, stepped out more purposefully towards the great lake. The land-locked province barely surrounded the lake at its centre, what land there was lay mostly on the eastern and northern side, skirted by rugged mountain ranges, but threaded by a number of routes used by merchants and predatory armies focussed on the great city of Miyakō which lay only twenty miles west of the lake's southern tip; Miyakō, the fancied source of both wealth and its product, power, now á bare three or four days walk away.

The Nakasendō highway took him close to the southern end of Biwa-ko but he found the hostelries dramatically fewer and, correspondingly, more expensive. The threat of rain seemed to have passed on the second day and as the afternoon wore on he decided that it wouldn't hurt to sleep in the open if he could find a suitable place where he wouldn't be discovered by brigands. A lone man, even a determined samurai, needed to be prudent.

Now he was glad that he had elected to travel in the rôle of a wandering rōnin, clearly not walking the highway with any clear purpose, so when he turned away to take a side track any others on the road would merely think he was looking for a shaded place where he might sit and eat. At length he took another branch track that led down towards the lake shore, vaguely thinking that he might gaze across at the towering mountains and compose some few lines on the beauty of the scene. Before him were the ridges of Hiei-zan and in the near distance to the south, the little town of Otsu just beyond which lay the famous Miidera monastery. His heart was lifted by the knowledge that he might achieve the first part of his ambition and reach Miyakō in just two days from now.

The shore was fringed by dense thickets of bamboo and trees. It was noticeable that most of the farmlands just here were untilled and derelict. Many of the rice fields had their banks broken down and were choked with weeds, others were partially flooded, home to wading birds and wildfowl. He passed through two fishing hamlets that lay in ruins, burnt to the ground and without any sign of human life, just a starving dog or two. A mile or so beyond this wasteland the trees started again and as he walked, he thought he glimpsed the thatched roof of a small shrine. With some difficulty he picked his way through the marshy underbrush and found that he was right.

It was a rustic shrine and he judged that it had been built three or four-hundred years before, somehow escaping the depredations of marauding armies, probably because it was too small to accommodate a priest. It had an unpretentious lacquered torii, a small shinden and just to one side an even smaller house for a lesser deity. It struck him as odd that there was an offering table in front of the main structure and despite its firmly closed doors, this table bore some fresh vegetables and a small pile of rice cakes showing that the unnamed deity resided there was still venerated.

With the evening fast drawing on, the spectacular red and crimson skies over Hieizan had lost all their colour and were taking on a uniform grey with a huge bank of cloud building to the north-west over what he thought might be the Wakasa-wan. Kotarō sniffed the air and considered that his decision to sleep out may have been the wrong one; just his luck he supposed, but there was nothing he could do about it now.

He walked over to the smaller structure, a diminutive shinden raised to the honour of some minor deity or the consort of the main god, just who he could not tell as there was no painted name board and the roof *chigi* were lost, their shape at least would have told him whether the god was male or female. The upper timbers of this shrine were rotted away and the structure canted drunkenly to the right, but its broad platform appeared sound and promised an adequate roof shelter if it did rain. Despite the gloom, he found the ground beneath dry although there were signs that someone else had slept there in the past few days. Well, it would do for him and the previous occupier may have frightened away any snakes or mishievious badgers! Making himself reasonably comfortable, he munched half his last rice ball then, with a yawn, settled himself to go to sleep.

Kotarō's mind was too alert to permit him to drop off straightaway; the prospect of achieving his ambition by somehow finding a refined teacher willing to instruct him in the arts of the brush and composing elegant verse, for the two went together, set his brain to turning over this and that. He couldn't rid himself of the memory of that poor young girl, Yuki, forced into the awful degradation and misery of prostitution. While he had only spoken briefly to her at the inn, he was touched by the sadness in her face and the shock of learning that she had afterwards taken her own life. He hoped that this decision wasn't partly his fault for bringing back memories of her childhood? And why was it that the innmaster's wife seemed so amused that he should want to go to Miyakō to study . . ?

Gradually these crowding thoughts settled down and he dozed to the occasional sound of some *inoshishi* foraging for roots in the derelict fields just beyond the trees. He recalled hearing a dog-fox bark a couple of times and the answering howls from some scavenging pack of curs . . .

Hardly had his eyes closed when he was awakened to see the light of a lantern over to the right in front of the main shinden. Had he fallen in with bandits, he asked himself, and was comforted as he felt the hilt of his katana clasped close to his side.

'Rest here, my husband . . .' came a lady's voice.

'Our daughter will meet us in this barbarous place? How strange . . .'

'She has done so many times before, husband. See, such a rustic shrine has a simple beauty such as we have always admired.'

Kotarō, wide awake now, was about to shift his position when he thought that any movement might be discovered. For the moment he had better remain still.

'Ah! Here she comes!' exclaimed the lady in a carefully modulated voice. 'How beautiful she looks!'

Coming up the path came a young lady dressed in a pale kimono and wearing a veiled broad-brimmed hat such as high-ranking women donned when they ventured abroad. She was accompanied by another person who carried a lantern on a long pole and when they came closer, Kotarō saw that this person was a yamabushi.

'Welcome, daughter,' her father greeted. 'Your journey was well-merited?'

That was an odd turn of phrase, thought Kotarō.

'It was an easy one, honoured father, guided by this good yamabushi who yesterday left Echizen to go to Yoshino but paused to order my steps. To him I am indeed grateful!'

Kotarō saw the girl hold up her veil and gracefully acknowledge the caped yamabushi. Just then a sudden flash of lightning lit up the nearby lake shore and heavy drops of rain began to patter to the ground. Kotarō, through habit, counted the seconds before the thunder crashed out and reckoned the storm to be a mile or so away. Oddly, the small party made not the slightest effort to find shelter from the coming storm.

A third lantern came swaying along the track.

'Not much chance of sleep for me this night,' thought the samurai. 'Far too busy!'

The newcomer was an elderly Shintō priest, complete with his distinctive lacquered *eboshi*. He said nothing to the others but positioned himself before the shinden and began, without delay, to intone some long invokation to the unknown deity.

The lightning flared again, much closer this time. The girl was addressing her parents, still holding her veil back on either side with her delicate hands. In the sudden brilliant light, Kotarō thought that her pale face seemed elongated, almost . . . and this was not possible . . . like that of a beautiful white fox. What was that she had said about the yamabushi? That he had just left Echizen province yesterday . . ? He must have misheard; such a journey was impossible!

The rain started to come down with avengeance . . . Like an arrow-storm, the drops bouncing up from the ground and off the wooden balustrades in a foaming spray. Still the group sought no shelter; in fact, they had set out a fine picnic and were now seating themselves after the refined manner of the wealthy to enjoy the rustic repast.

'Did you meet anyone of merit on your journey, my daughter?' asked the maiden's mother.

'Oh, how can our daughter answer such a question, my lady consort, when no one of merit resides in these uncouth wastes?'

'Husband, please deign to allow her to reply. One is always mindful of one's family.'

'Only one such person did I meet, respected parent. Just the one in the five days that I have been absent.'

'That is a rarity, indeed,' hissed her father, carefully rearranging his fine robes. 'Do tell us more that we can be entertained.'

Just then, the yamabushi held out his *bonden* staff and pointed it towards Kotarō.

'We have a guest, a companion who we should respect!'

'Then he must join us and enjoy sharing our supper repast . . . Honoured priest, do you invite our guest to sit with us.'

The priest, who had been sheltering from the rain as best he could under the swept eaves, splashed through the puddles and was almost at once completely soaked. He invited Kotarō to do as he was requested.

Resigned to whatever fate held in store, Kotarō bowed low.

'My name is Kusatsu Kotarō, my lord.'

'A samurai of the Torii-ke!' barked the yamabushi, much to the young man's surprise.

'Why, yes; but how did you know that, sir?'

It was the priest who replied, gently, shielding his mouth behind his raised palm.

'A talented man like Gompiro-bō knows many things.'

'So, daughter, you met this young gentleman?' asked the girl's father.

'That is so, honoured father.'

Another flash of lightning that lit up the rainstorm for a full second clearly confirmed to a confused young man that the maiden was indeed a white fox.

'Please partake of some of our delightful refreshments, respected guest,' urged the maiden's mother, fastidiously offering a lacquered tray of small ō-mochi cakes and sushi, but while Kotarō accepted one he didn't place it between his lips.

They sat about a spread cloth exactly as people did when they ventured out as a happy party to view the new-flowering cherry trees, their lanterns casting a warm glow over the picnic. All about them raged the violent thunderstorm and yet although only the old Shintō priest and the young samurai were soaked through; not a single drop fell on the spread cloth or their four companions.

'Do you travel to Miyakō, Kusatsu-sama?' enquired the lady.

'It is my intention, madam.'

Kotarō hoped his voice sounded polite as he felt a runnel of rainwater pour down his neck from his wet hair queue, All the time he pondered why this lady thought he had met the maiden? How could that possibly be?

Her husband had produced a fan and elegantly cooled his brow. It was odd to look at the couple, the man was beautifully dressed in a white robe with sharply pressed deep sleeves, the long cuffs of which were threaded with purple *himo* knotted elaborately at their lower ends, the breast of the robe secured to the right of his throat but showing his delicate green silk under kimono. On his head he wore a tall gauze eboshi of the type often seen on formal occasions in the Torii yashiki and which he had been told were the fashion in the aristocratic families. One of the lanterns hung a little behind the man and its light shone through the gauze showing how fine was the lacquer-stiffened material. His wife wore her hair immaculately dressed in a long thick tress down her back, secured in place with two silken bows. Her face was whitened and her teeth blackened according to the fashion of a lady of her evident rank. Kotarō observed that she wore exactly nine fine kimono, each layered and of a selected contrasting colour to set off the one before and the one that followed . . .

'Shall you serve in the Shōgun's guard, Kusatsu-sama?' she asked.

'It was not my intention, madam; it is my hope to find a teacher who will be prepared to instruct my poor hand in calligraphy and to permit me to develop my understanding of the poetic arts.'

'So fine an ambition, is it not, husband?' exclaimed the lady. 'So cultured a young man is rarely to be found these days . . .'

The yamabushi snorted.

'Those days are long past! You would be better prepared in your desires by entering a monastery, Kusatsu-sama . . !'

'Or following the "Tengu-road",' murmured the priest.

The girl lightly touched his sleeve. Her veil had slipped down but it seemed to Kotarō, as he ventured a sideways glance, that she didn't have a fox's face. It must have been a trick of the light? No, she certainly wasn't a fox . . . but there was something about her, though, that stirred his memory although he couldn't for the life of him place it . . . he knew no beautiful maids of her tender years . . .

'You will find it extremely difficult to find such a teacher in Miyakō,' the priest was saying, but the samurai wasn't paying proper attention. He was wondering why the girl pulled lightly at his sleeve and inclined his head a little and asked if she wished to say something.

'Sir, was your journey here safely accomplished?' She had covered her small mouth demurely with her extended fingers, her other hand lightly holding back the folds of her veil.

'I travelled far, honoured mistress; only one incident marred my journey, but it is not something I would mention here.'

'If it was unpleasant, please do not recount it, sir.'

'If that is your wish,' he bowed his head. Suddenly, he felt a desperate lassitude sweep over him, reaching into his very bones. He took up his square wooden cup that was full of ō-sake and, with trembling fingers, lifted it to his lips.

Quite suddenly he heard the Shintō priest say, as though through a tunnel:

'Remember, Kusatsu Kotarō, the *Five Commandments* of the Lord Buddha!'

Just in time the words registered and the cup fell from his nerveless fingers onto the wet ground. The wine mingled with the raindrops and was soon lost. Raising his face to the heavens he felt suddenly refreshed. When he opened his eyes, he saw that the maiden had opened a fan and had begun to dance gracefully on the further side of the picnic spread.

The Shintō priest leant over and whispered in his ear.

'All this is illusion, Kusatsu-sama; all life is an illusion. I came to the priesthood from a lifetime of service to the Lord Buddha in a temple within the confines of my shrine and I am well-versed in the scriptures. This strange yamabushi, for example; have you thought how he could have journeyed so far in one day? See, he carries a feathered fan that hasn't become bedraggled by a drop of this heavy rain! His fan represents invisibility and he, by carrying it, is certainly a *dai-tengu* . . . yet he appears to be exactly as all other yamabushi . . . I advise you to listen carefully to what the Courtier says, my friend.'

The aristocrat delicately raised his folded fan, pointing at Kotarō as he began to speak: 'Kusatsu-dono, you have expressed a wish to be instructed in Miyakō, have you not?' Somehow or other, the man's voice had a certain hollowness about it, as if it came from some distance. 'There is no finer teacher in all that city than my wife here . . . To her came many great lords with their wives and daughters, all imploring to learn how to use the brush in a refined manner, to compose sublime poems that would be the envy of their circle, to execute paintings with consummate ease on subjects that would rival the works of the sage-poets of Mu . . . Drink of our wine, young man, and assuredly this lady will listen favourably to your request to become her pupil. If you do this your future fame is assured . . .'

The bedraggled old priest again leant close to Kotarō's ear.

'These people do not exist as you know the meaning of the term. Their mansion, once a fine place where many cultured people flocked, lies with roofs gaping open to the skies, weeds springing from the ruins of the fallen thatch, saplings thirty feet high growing through what remains of the painted screens and the grooved cedar floorboards, now all crumbling and decayed. Where the feet of princes once so elegantly paced, the verandahs are splintered and the balustrades worm-eaten and leaning . . . All they had is now gone after the cruel ravages of Ōnin these twenty years since . . .'

Kotarō frowned.

'How can this be, priest? They are both here before us to see and to touch!'

'Five years ago, my friend, this lord and his wife were as destitute as the meanest beggar; their fortune robbed away or dissipated . . . all gone! They survived with only the barest possessions and their daughter . . . This is what that sage disciple of the Lord Buddha said when he brought the Lotus Sutra from India to China long centuries ago: *"Reality exists only in the mind; nothing is but thinking makes it so."* Creep away now, my young friend; slip away while the fox-maiden dances. Gather your things and take the path that you will find behind this shrine . . . Go back to your home!'

Kotarō did as he was bid and his parting was not remarked. A few minutes later he found the narrow track that the priest had described and silently picked his way through the downpour towards the edge of the thickets.

During the following five or six days as he retraced his steps along the Nakasendō highway, he considered what he had seen and heard during the storm. At least all the advice given him directly or indirectly was against his continuing to Miyakō. Of that he was clear. They couldn't all have been wrong, could they? But who were that family, he wondered? There was something about the maiden that seemed to conjure up the memory of Yuki-san, that poor suicide, but he dismissed that as impossible. And the tengu-yamabushi? He laughed at the thought and recalled the pleasant fiction about such a tengu who had helped raise an army for Lord Nitta Yoshisada before the Kamakura battles a hundred-and-fifty years ago! Simple people were gullible enough to believe anything if they were told it by priests . . ! The old *gūji* was real enough! By the time he had crept away, the poor man was shaking with the soaking he had received, and not surprising when he appeared to have not one ounce of fat on his meagre frame!

He trudged down to Ogaki and out of a sense of polite obligation rather than lack of funds, presented himself about mid-morning at the same hostelry that he had stayed at before; his return greeted with the familiar surly scowls from the innmaster and delight from his ebullient wife.

'What a surprise that you are back so soon, master,' she called out, bustling across the near empty room since it was a little too early for the wastrels who liked to imbibe there, 'but we did have word that you were returning, you know. You took my advice about Miyakō, eh? Did you find it a poor place full of impudent whores and ne'er-do-wells? No nice clean girls like those that live here!'

As she busied herself preparing some fresh noodles for her samurai guest – nay, almost protégé – he enquired, out of curiosity, how she could possibly have known he was coming.

'That's easy, master . . . why he's just left but an hour ago. Stayed two nights, he did.'

'But who, Oka-san; who was it?'

'Oh, just a brown-robed yamabushi . . . You know, they all look alike, they do . . . We don't see too many just like him about here but 'e said 'e was on his way back to Kōzuke or some such place. Muttered something about the threat of war brewing around the *on-sen*.' She busied herself wiping some tiny grains of rice from the mats then scurried off to fetch a tray for her guest. 'There, eat this up, good master; 'twill refresh you and make you feel like new!'

'Thank you, Oka-san! It looks very good and I must confess that I didn't have anything to break my fast this morning. When I've finished, I think I shall visit the grave of that girl who used to work here. Yuki, wasn't that her name? Can you direct me to it, madam?'

The woman looked at him blankly so, thinking that she hadn't heard because of the laughter of the four girls who had just come in, he repeated his request.

'Yuki? Yes, I understand that is a girl's name but, master, what about her? We haven't had a girl with that name here for a number of years, not that I recall.' She turned her head and shouted out: 'Oi! You lot; did you know a "Yuki" who used to work here?'

The girls stopped their merriment and looked one to the other, shaking their heads.

One of the older women frowned slightly in an effort to remember.

'Wasn't that the name of that lass who stabbed herself, madam? But that was some years back.' She shook her head sadly. 'She was named Yuki, I think.'

'But,' Kotarō said, frowning, 'she took her own life down by the river not two weeks since . . .'

He fell silent and slowly ate his *ō-soba* without another word. Shaking her head, the innkeeper's wife moved off though she wondered if the young man had fallen sick or something. Poetry may have turned his brain or he had had his head knocked in a match? Those heavy staves that some swordsmen carried were dangerous things and her samurai's remarks made her fear the worst!

Two weeks later, as he slowly paced the dusty Nakasendō, young Kotarō felt relief that he would follow the warrior's path once more. It was as both his parents wished and he was grateful for their teaching. He wondered about the strange yamabushi, but then, they were an odd breed and he had seen quite a number who came through the clan domain from Hagurō-san . . . That was a timely reminder from the old Shintō *gūji* that he shouldn't let a drop of strong drink pass his lips that night at the picnic . . . and resolved that it would be his iron rule to take no alchohol from this day forth . . . If he wrote poetry he would set his own goals and the ancient bonze at the local temple would be happy to guide his hand towards the elegance he wanted to find. So why did he want to go to Miyakō in the first place . . ? Later, he turned over in his mind with a feeling of regret the memory of that sad girl named so delicately after the deep white snow that lay on the high Shinano peaks . . . Was it really all a cruel illusion as the old man had said?

12

THE RECLUSE

When all had settled down across the provinces after the violent clashes between the Genji and the Heike, some warriors and aristocrats became so disillusioned with those recent events that they took holy orders and retired from their previous life to the quietness of a monastery. One such was a wealthy estate owner, a man whose support for the Genji brought lustre to his name but who found no peace for his soul when he recalled the incidents attending on war. Eventually, he followed his conscience, settled his affairs, and withdrew to the Shingon monastery of Hōraiji in Mikawa where he shaved his head, took the name Shinsei, and studied the scriptures. After ten years, divorced from a world now dominated by the warriors, he felt that he must retire even further from his fellow men in order to absorb the teachings of the Buddha; accordingly, he took up his simple scrip and a small bowl, girding himself to take the dusty roads towards the mountains of Yoshino. In those fastnesses he knew that others long before him had sought and found the peace and solitude that his soul craved.

Throughout the long Era of Peace that had so recently come to an end, Yoshino had enjoyed an increasing prestige as a focal locality for holy men and those who would, by their devout pilgrimages and support, also find a measure of peace; but although Shinsei found Yoshino a haven of tranquillity, nonetheless it was often thronged by these pilgrims, frequently of high court rank, and the increasing numbers of adherents to the Shugen faith. He decided that after only a few months, if he couldn't come to terms with interruptions from these nobles and their fussy retinues, he would have to withdraw further; not to cut himself off from his fellow man, mind you, but to find a somewhat less accessible residence.

In the spring following his arrival, he gathered his simple belongings, less now than when he first sought a secluded lodging at the foot of the steep steps leading up to the rustic Yoshimizu shrine, and tramped up the narrow street lined with many small taverns whose owners vied with each other to attract the patronage of the pilgrims. It must have been thus every spring, summer and autumn season since Yoshino first gained its reputation as an exceptionally holy place replete with beautiful cherry trees.

With a characteristic shrug of his shoulders, Shinsei took a firmer grip on his simple staff and turned uphill to the right to follow the increasingly steep track that would take him past the tiny Kizō temple and a little further on, the recently built and imposing Chikurin-in. The path was steep and, despite his warrior's rude health, he was glad to accept some water offered him by two rough-looking yamabushi sitting in the shade of a gateway.

'Where are you bound, honoured priest?' enquired one.

'Anywhere where I may find shelter for my poor body and peace to tell my beads, my friends.'

The yamabushi looked at each other, shaking their heads. The one who had offered Shinsei the water scratched his bushy mop of hair.

'There's little peace to be had down there . . . and not a lot up there,' jerking his thumb up the mountain track, the well-trodden route to Kinpu-sen.

'I shall pray that my steps are guided by the grace of the Buddha.'

'Uhh! That might work, priest, but then again, it might not.'

'Archh! Don't discourage him, In-ei! If you would care to hear my opinion, master priest, go on up this track then, at the Water-kami's shrine, branch off slightly north. Do that, and at the top of the next ridge you will look down into the Kawakami valley. No pilgrims or busybodies there, I can assure you. Just the occasional woodcutter and hunter, none else!'

Shinsei thanked them for their kindness in guiding his steps and continued on his way up the increasingly steep paths that were unimaginably different from the broad well-beaten tracks taken by the devout today. It took him all that morning to reach the gushing waters that sprang inexplicably from the bare rocky cliff which a woodsman he encountered nearby told him was the home of the rain god. After a short rest, he followed the directions of the yamabushi and with the sun sinking low over the distant serried heights behind him, sought for some place to shelter for the night. The quietness of this untouched wilderness already soothed his spirit and he knew that he would soon find that which he sought.

Shinsei had little difficulty finding the perfect place to build his little grass thatched hut on a terrace that provided him with a wonderful view of the winding Kawakami valley and the mountains inhabited solely by the wild beasts of the virgin forest and songbirds. A short distance down the hillside, a mere hour's walk away, lay a tiny hamlet where three or four families of hunters lived and welcomed the holy recluse, even helping him clear some ground so that he could grow radishes. After the following four or five years, his little cherry saplings bore their first fruit and his tiny abode had just enough substance to keep out the winter snows and cold. The forest and his little plot of soil provided him with all he needed and, with a tiny tumbling stream nearby for fresh pure water, his happiness was complete. He was content.

It is the way of the world that word of such contentment should eventually reach the ears of the curious; where the first one treads for his own peace, others must inevitably follow to try to savour that which he has discovered but which they will soon sully for ever.

Although the priest lived with the utmost simplicity, there were still a few items that he needed such as millet and the occasional small sack of rice and for these items he traded the nuts that he had collected in the forest and, because his little field produced such an abundance of radishes he pickled many as *takuan-zuke* and gave them to the poor peasants in the valley. He also applied his skills in curing various maladies for their general welfare and they soon came to regard him as their mentor and protector; perhaps, too, with some awe that such a clearly refined man could exist in such a remote place on less than they had themselves.

Thus, very gradually, stories of his piety and goodness spread beyond the rustic purlieu of the Kawakami valleys and eventually reached the ears of the steward who served one of the Fujiwara courtiers. This steward, knowing how eagerly his master attended to matters of his immortal soul and desired to do good works, particularly those that sponsored the building of temples that, incidentally, enhanced his growing reputation and name, repeated the rumours that he had heard to his lord. At once, this powerful man knew that he had a very good chance to advance his reputation with the Court Chamberlain, though first he must make the pilgrimage to find this hitherto unknown holy man and evaluate for himself his worthiness.

At the first opportunity, just as the forests began to take on the spectacular beauty of their autumn hues, this dignitary announced that he was to take leave of absence in order to fulfil a solemn vow and travel, with his entourage, to pay reverence in the temples in Yoshino; duly reaching this region towards the end of the tenth month. Further enquiries by his servants, under the direction of the steward, elicited information from one of the wandering yamabushi at the Zao-dō that he had heard from another ascetic, one who rarely left the wilds of Kumano, that he had once directed a solitary priest to seek the peace of the Kawakami valley. Three of the entourage were promptly ordered to forsake the comforts of their temple accommodation and make the hazardous journey into the wastes of forest and turbulent streams to locate this recluse and ascertain if he was indeed the one their master was seeking.

The little Kawakami hamlet was hardly large enough to warrant having a headman; indeed, woodcutters, foresters, and those who existed through their skills in hunting, rarely paid any taxes and while this valley and its forests was doubtless considered to be part of some lord's domain, a claim that was probably traceable back to Yamato times, the steward at last located the residence of Shinsei and informed his master of the fact.

Out of the reverence due to so secluded a hermit and the glowing reputation that was accorded him by the villagers, who were naturally overawed to be in the presence of so exalted a personage, a priest attached to the retinue was guided up the mountain track one fine late-autumn day to humbly request Shinsei to receive his master, a man of great piety and humility.

This priest was somewhat alarmed to find that Shinsei existed in such austerity, particularly as Shinsei did not seem inclined to invite him inside his broken-down hovel. (He was unable to find another description for the abode, though by the time he returned to report he diplomatically decided to omit this point, hoping for the best.) The visit was to take place on the day after the morrow, he reported, and the exalted personage agreed.

Shinsei, by this time, had been removed from fashionable society for as much as fifteen or so years, and even before that had lived the frugal life of a warrior-noble, despite his wealth eschewing most of the things that the wealthy enjoy. He spent the intervening day in the company of an elderly widow whose departed husband, a rough forester, had helped the recluse erect his simple, two roomed abode, and between them they had set everything to order and tidied up the vegetable plot and tiny orchard. Not that this was an arduous task, there was so little to put straight.

The great personage struggled up the steep hill and, ordering his attendants to wait his return, went on alone to be greeted by Shinsei under the cover of what passed for the outjutting eaves that sheltered the split log that provided a step to the raised floor. The rather corpulent Augustness was sweating profusely after his exertions mounting the track and sat there for several minutes puffing and blowing. Shinsei waited politely for his guest to recover, then ushered him inside and seated him in the 'upper' place, his own favourite spot since it commanded a wonderfully harmonious prospect of the now colourful sunlit mountainsides through the open *shōji*. He had, through his sympathetic relationship with the many wild birds who lived around him, brought several of them to a high degree of trust so that they often regaled him with their melodious singing while he sat and read his copies of the holy sutras. On this glorious afternoon they flew down to their perches in the cherry and magnolia trees and did the same, though it was possibly a distraction for the sybaritic courtier whose wish was to probe Shinsei's profound understanding of the Buddha's teachings and so evaluate his worth in terms of generous future patronage.

At length, Shinsei remembered that he should offer his guest some refreshment; after all, he had travelled a long way and suffered a significant measure of discomfort to reach here. Accordingly, he excused himself and brought in a bowl of simple rice cakes, fresh-grilled fish taken only that morning from the rushing waters of the Kawakami river, and some of his own yellow takuan-zuke. He had also managed to obtain a small jar of the finest *ō-sake*, possibly the first he had possessed for nigh on fifteen years. At the same time, and with apologies for giving her the trouble, he requested that the elderly widow take similar sustenance to His Highness's attendants sitting uncomfortably beyond his tiny orchard.

He served his guest as best he could, and poured out the wine, apologizing the while that he had vowed only to permit food to pass his lips when the sun had gone to its rest. Of course, the courtier understood . . .

After two hours of edifying conversation on the deepest of philosophical subjects, the August Personage politely and courteously took his leave, having devoted precisely the correct space of time to this interview, and Shinsei, in his clean (but only) threadbare robe and woven *hanten*, escorted him down his path to the waiting steward and servants. He stood in a respectful posture until the party had descended the hillside and disappeared, bowing politely whenever the great man glanced back, which was only twice as the breeze caught the shading umbrella that protected him from the slanting afternoon sunlight. As they filed down the stony descent, the steward coughed discreetly and ventured to ask his master if he was satisfied in his expectations for the meeting with the holy Shinsei.

'To tell the truth,' replied the Courtier, 'I found him a remarkable priest, filled with evident sanctity and deep understanding of the Lotus Sutra . . . He lived up to my expectations in all respects but one, and it is this single matter that perplexes me.'

The steward felt that he may, without being presumptuous, ask what this defect might be.

'I had expected and was prepared for the obvious poverty of this recluse. He clearly had almost nothing to keep his body and soul together, and he claimed, though I will admit, not in so many words, that it was poverty and solitude that bestowed quietness and tranquillity on his soul. And yet, while he declined to partake of any of the repast he served me, prefering to wait for the sunset according to a vow, he was able to give me some of the finest wine I have had the pleasure of tasting, even, and dare I say this to you in every confidence, my steward, even at Imperial banquet feasts!'

'But, my lord, was he in every way the devout priest you had hoped to find?'

'That is true, steward, but for that one nagging doubt.'

They descended another difficult steep pitch and rested to take in the mountain prospect.

'My lord, if I may make so bold . . .'

'Feel free to speak for this is an important matter!'

'The Holy Shinsei is a humble priest who has almost totally rejected the material in his search for the spiritual . . . I found out, my lord, that before he became a priest and shaved his head, he lived the life of a very wealthy man . . . a man with countless servants and every civilized amenity such as only those of the highest rank in the Capital enjoy. My lord, he gave up every single aspect of his former life in order to follow the teachings of the Lord Buddha. Would you begrudge him one small luxury to honour you, his only guest in many years of profound austerity?'

13

THE PUPPETEERS

Magobei and his brother settled themselves as unobtrusively as possible in a corner of the tavern. In these disturbed times one needed to keep one's wits alert and all the senses sharpened, and to do this both day and night. The brothers were puppeteers, forced to eke a living from giving entertainments at every festival they could find in order to keep body and soul together; although they had once been warriors serving a small clan in northern Hitachi they were now wandering rōnin after war destroyed their masters and deprived them of their meagre remuneration. They knew that they were fortunate to have some slight skills manipulating marionettes, dexterity inherited from their mother who had always loved to surround herself with children, but concealed the fact that they were samurai since wearing a long sword would alienate them from the common people. Samurai were men apart and nearly always created fear . . .

Their mother had bequeathed to the brothers her love for children and a number of childish playlets, stories they acted out with their four or five simple puppets, that appealed just as much to the poor peasants as to their offspring. From her own childhood in Echigo came the rather charming story of the fisherman who, one night, climbed on a large rock in the Chikuma river and cast his lines out with some success - but perhaps we might learn more about this later . . . then they had the ever-popular story of the hero Benkei at the Barrier . . .

Two priests entered, the one looking careworn and grey and the other little more than a youth and clearly his acolyte. They, too, settled in a quiet corner which happened to be close to the brothers, hard against the stable partition. Magobei was discussing with his brother, Heibei, where they would go next, it being the time of the spring rice planting and any number of local festivals held to welcome the mountain kami to come down to the land. Deep in conversation, they took no more than a passing interest in the priests or, just beyond the low partition from the main tavern room, the boisterous roistering of several rōnin and townsfolk who were dicing and drinking without a thought for the morrow. A great shout went up when, at the end of a game, someone had evidently won quite a sum of cash, and two of the rōnin detached themselves from the rest, probably in disgust at their losses. Loudly calling for more ō-sake, they, too, moved round the partition and sat at the one remaining low table to drown their sorrows in wine.

Magobei heard the older priest whisper to the *shingyaku* to push his wallet round between them, out of sight of the rōnin; one could never be too safe. For some reason, the puppet master noted in his memory that the older of the men had a badly scarred knee, though why he noted that he couldn't say.

'What have you there, monk,' said one of the wavemen, seeing the movement.

'Nothing, master; I just asked my companion to move our bundle to give you more space.'

'I bet you're carrying gold for your temple!' joked the warrior.

'Oh, no, sir; do we look as if we would be doing that?'

Magobei, with a sideways glance, thought the older monk's brow was glistening with perspiration and he spoke a little too quickly.

'Just my humour, old man,' laughed the samurai. 'No one would risk something valuable with the likes of you two, now would they?'

'No, master; that would be foolish . . . wouldn't it, Kyu'emon?'

The lad looked gormless, judging by his slack chin

'Er, master; I don't know rightly what you mean . . . We have . . .'

'Nothing of any worth,' butted in his senior, hastily.

The two rōnin grinned and turned to their drink and not another word was said for quite a while. Their attention was diverted by a sudden quarrel near the sliding doors and a woman screeched out that if there was going to be an argument, it had best be conducted outside! Anyway, nothing came of it, and the usual babble of crowded drinkers prevailed.

The next day dawned and soon the village was filled with peasants from the whole neighbourhood who flocked in to attend the Yokota shrine Inoshishi-no-matsuri where large images of the wild boars were carried about in honour of Hachiman, the deity of war. Magobei and his brother set up their little theatre booth in readiness for their first performance after the initial parade of the day had passed, for until then they were unlikely to find any spectators. Just after the six drummers were carried past, riding on seats each mounted on two poles and carried, shoulder high, by eight near-naked young men, the puppeteers noticed the young novice, Kyu'emon, wandering aimlessly in the crowd. He looked so confused that Magobei sent his brother to fetch him across.

'We saw you at the tavern last night, Kyu'emon-san; do you remember?'

The acolyte shook his head.

'Never mind,' said Magobei, 'but where is your master?'

'My master . . . Tankei-sama . . ?'

'That's right, lad; the priest you were with.'

'Tankei . . ?'

The novice clutched and pulled at his robe front, his mouth opening and closing as though he was trying to say something.

'Is there something wrong, lad? Maybe we can help you?'

'Do I need help, master?'

'We all need help from time to time . . .'

Magobei was surprised by a sudden smile that lit up the youth's face. A look of understanding appeared in his eyes.

'That's the same words that Master Tankei uses . . . He often says them to me . . . but . . .'

The boy's face began to work and tears flowed down his cheeks.

Heibei got the lad to sit down at the corner of their flimsy stage; he put his arm about his shoulders.

'Has something happened to the priest, to Tankei? Please tell us if you can.'

'I won't hear his voice ever again, masters. He's gone to sleep and doesn't want to wake up.'

Magobei looked at his brother with a frown.

'Stay here, Heibei, while I slip back to the tavern. You know what I am thinking, don't you?'

The priest's corpse was soon discovered indifferently hidden under some soiled straw in the stable. Magobei saw at once that the poor man had been strangled some hours before and half-stripped by his attacker who was clearly looking for valuables, as if an old priest would have anything worth taking. Shaking his head sadly, he made his way back towards his brother and their little theatre.

'I'm afraid it's true, young Kyu'emon; your friend has indeed gone to sleep. It is something that must be reported to the Constables' office . . .' A thought came into his mind. 'You almost said something last night about what was in Master Tankei's wallet. Can you tell me what it was?'

'Oh, yes; master. That's easy! We were taking some gold to the Hongu-ji . . . that's our temple, master, and . . .'

The youth's eyes became vacant again and he looked about him as confused by his surroundings as before. It was clear that they would find out nothing more for the present.

'I shall have to make that report, Heibei. The killer must still be in the village, you know.'

'They'll never find him, brother.'

'Maybe you are right but it's the least I can do.'

Heibei was right, of course; the samurai at the domain constables' office couldn't care less about some vagrant priest who was killed and robbed of gold. They completely dismissed the idea as absurd and said some offensive things about the young half-witted acolyte.

'Gold! Don't be stupid! Where does a priest and a half-wit like that get gold, huh?'

'But, sirs, Master Tankei has been strangled . . . His body's in the inn stable . . .'

'So what! How, in the name of the King of Hell, do you think we could find the killer amongst a crowd like there is today? You find the evidence and then we might act!'

'But the killer might be one of those rōnin, masters?'

'Oh, go away! If you don't we will arrest you!'

A crestfallen Magobei walked back to Heibei and Kyu'emon, defeated. It was clear to him that the Suzuki-ke would take no further interest in something so insignificant as the death of a humble priest. With a heavy heart, he went through the motions of their puppet play and they collected just about enough that day to pay for their lodging and a small meal, but he knew that his act of kindness in calling the lad over when he could just as easily ignored him, had bestowed on him the obligation to take care of poor Kyu'emon until such time as they could deliver him to the safety to the Hongu temple.

The two rōnin had not moved on, despite Magobei's fears, but they showed not the slightest sign of any guilt and, in fact, kept clear of the dicing table and even too much strong ō-sake ... Not that they were likely to get that in this tavern, anyway, and Magobei was certain that the landlord watered the brew as well as serving short measure in the jars. His suspicions now aroused, Magobei alerted his brother so that both kept a surreptitious watch on the two rōnin. When, finally, the two men left the inn, both Magobei and Heibei were certain that the gold hadn't gone with them, which meant that they must have hidden it somewhere intending to return at a later date.

With the addition of the young simpleton, Kyu'emon, to their troupe, the brothers enlisted his aid to beat a drum around the streets to attract interest, largely children, of course, and soon their daily performances became very popular, not only in this village but with the peasants of the other hamlets dotted nearby. Warfare had, thus far, not touched the southern part of Kumano, and the good harvests of the previous few years had left the peasant families relatively well-to-do and easily able to meet the demands of the domain tax collectors. This, in turn, meant that the puppeteers profited and at the very least were able to remain lodged at the same tavern. In fact, Magobei devised two more playlets for their puppets to act, but one of these he kept in reserve.

Gradually the memory of the unfortunate Tankei's murder faded together with any clear image of those rōnin. They were much like any other arrogant samurai, nondescript and anonymous; similar to just about every other masterless men who wandered the highways all over the islands ... Even if they turned up to retrieve the stolen gold, Magobei seriously doubted if either he or his brother would recognize them! He had tried to find out more from Kyu'emon but the novice seemed to have effaced every vestige of memory even of Tankei, his mentor, and was now single-mindedly focussed on playing their flat drum.

Reports of conflicts flaring to the west in Wakayama, at Tanabe, and in Ise province, were a good incentive to remain in the Suzuki domain, unless, of course, they were to choose to leave by boat to some more distant region, but that would risk capture by the clouds of pirate *kaizoku* who infested all these coasts. While times remained good there was no reason to look for change.

Just a year after the murder, in fact at the same annual Inoshishi-no-matsuri, the three were staging, by popular request, their play about the fisherman who went out one night to try his luck in the rippling shallows of the wide Chikuma-gawa, although for the sake of their audience, they changed the river's name to the Kumano-gawa. Seeing in the gloom of the cloudy night a large flattish rock in midstream ... and the children were easily able to imagine the scene ... the fisherman cast his lines and waited for a bite. He saw near his feet a strange sight ... two slightly glowing balls that reminded him of crystal, only much bigger ... but he went on fishing until, at that moment the full moon popped out from behind a cloud he saw, to his horror, that he wasn't standing on a rock at all ... but on the back of a huge frog and the glowing balls were its eyes! With a great splash he leapt off into the river and ran for his very life!

Their audience, as always, split their sides with laughter, and soon called for more. It was at this moment that Magobei caught sight of two rōnin in the midst of the crowd, his memory was jogged but the image in his mind wasn't at all clear. The spring day was exceptionally mild, not to say hot, and nearly everyone had abandoned their heavy clothing in favour of what amounted to light summer wear. Now, Magobei warned his brother that they would perform '*Benkei at the Barrier*' and called on the two rōnin and one or two other adults to come closer and seat themselves comfortably at the front so that the children behind could have a better view. Good naturedly, they all complied and he saw that one of the 'wavemen' had a scarred knee ... but for the life of him he couldn't recall whether it should be the left or the right one ...

Everyone loved this exciting story about the resourceful yamabushi and his master, the ill-starred Yoshitsune, but when it was finished, Magobei announced that he and Heibei had between them composed a completely new play but that they were reluctant to perform it in case their audience wouldn't approve. Naturally, the crowd clamoured to see it and grew all the larger in anticipation.

The story was based on the robbery and killing of Tankei, of course, but Magobei had added the hiding of the gold in a secret place which he thought to be under the supports of the tavern floor. While he and his brother manipulated the strings and intoned the words, he watched the two rōnin closely through the slits in his black hood ... for puppeteers always dressed all in black so as to be 'invisible' to their audience ... and saw that both men were becoming uncomfortable and could hardly wait for the play to end.

Almost as he spoke the final words where samurai came and arrested the murderers, Kyu'emon, standing a little to one side, beat a great tattoo on the drum and shouted out that he saw Tankei's killers . . . Magobei dropped his puppet, tore off his black hood, and challenged the surprised rōnin, yelling out to three watching Suzuki-ke retainers to arrest the pair.

The two rōnin leapt to their feet, becoming very angry, and drew out their swords; at first unsure of what to do. They turned and made a dash across the village street to the narrow alley behind the tavern, one of them snatching up a child clinging to its mother's kimono as he rushed past. Magobei's shout to the Suzuki samurai had gone unheeded in the general confusion and because at that very moment the 'Wild Boar' procession restarted with a great outburst of cheering from the nearby dancers . . .

'Heibei; follow those men round the back but stay well away from them!' ordered Magobei. 'I shall go inside to fetch out our swords!'

Somehow, the brothers had always known that they must return to their former status one day.

'Those are the men, Master Magobei . . .'

Kyu'emon ran by his side, his face alert and understanding.

'Lad, I want you to run to the *Bugyō's* guardroom . . . Do you understand?'

'Yes, master . . .'

'Tell them what has happened and request men to be sent to the tavern. Go; don't delay!'

Magobei watched the novice, robe skirts flying, dash away up the street . . . just as the crowd around the bobbing images of the boars rounded the corner the other way.

'Now what?' he thought.

Shrugging his shoulders, Magobei knew that for the present what happened next would depend on Heibei and himself.

It was the work of a few moments to extricate their katana from their oiled covers; he quickly thrust his dirk into his obi and, long swords in hand, ran back outside and round to where Heibei and a handful of villagers stood watching the stables.

Handing his brother his katana, Magobei asked if the rōnin were inside.

'Master, they have my son,' cried the tearful young mother. 'Please, sir, please get him back . . .'

'You will have him; I promise!' He turned to his brother. 'This is what I want you to do . . . I shall go back inside. Count to fifteen then most of you, not all mind, run suddenly to the left of the stable; count to five and run back again. That's all. It will be just enough to provide me with a diversion.'

'Will the child be alright, brother?'

'Heibei, the boy is as good as dead already . . . I shall do my best! Now, wait until I am out of sight then count. Make plenty of noise, remember!'

Magobei entered the tavern as silently as he could and crept along the wall. The afternoon sunshine slanted through the slatted windows dappling the floor. He was counting up to fifteen slowly, hoping that he was doing so at about the same speed as his brother. Suddenly, he heard a roar go up as Heibei and the rest ran across the yard and gathering himself, he made a dash to the side of the stable partitions where they had sat drinking a whole year before. He could hear no noises, only the distant throb of the festival drums and some shouting, but then Heibei and his mob ran back. Setting his eye to a small crack, he peered into the byre . . . It was empty.

Muttering an imprecation, he realized that the two rōnin had taken their hostage and immediately escaped before he was able to get here! What now? They could only have crossed the street under the cover of the festival confusion, but where . . ? The river . . ? There was only the river . . . He was off again out the shōji. Glimpsing his brother, he shouted to him to start searching under the shop platforms and, seeing him wave in assent, dashed across the street and down a narrow alley towards the river banks.

But he had forgotten that the images of the wild boars were carried to the water at the conclusion of the festival procession and ceremonially set on fire before being turned loose to float away. It was believed that this would ward off the depredations of these destructive animals during the coming growing season . . .

As luck would have it, he was just in time to glimpse the rōnin vanish amongst the excited crowds of nearly naked young men and brightly dressed matrons and girls, all gyrating round the bobbing images of the boars. Over everything floated many banners and paper streamers. As he ran, he tucked up the skirts of his kimono, praying that he hadn't forgotten how to use his sword in the years that he and Heibei had made their living as wandering puppeteers. It was no time to contemplate; it was time for action!

He reached the dancing throng just as the images of the boars were being lifted up high amidst a great roar. Twice more they were hoisted before the flames were applied and they were carried into the torrent. Maybe there was just a chance to get through . . . Some in that crowd saw their puppetmaster as an armed samurai for the first time and drew back out of his way in haste, even fear, but others he was forced to shoulder aside. Already the revellers were turning to rush to the water's edge when he broke through, and he saw the fugitives trying to cross a shingle spit to the main channel that separated them from their pursuer and escape. Further downstream, drawn up on another bank, lay an empty fishing boat. The younger of the two held the child beneath his left arm and Magobei could see that the senior of the rōnin carried a heavy bag corded across his shoulders. The gold, maybe?

The puppet-master eyed the main stream and knew that the two ciminals might have great difficulty in fording the current. He also realized that they had made a mistake and chosen the wrong shingle bank! He slowed his pace to a walk in order to regain his breath, then paddled through the knee-deep waters to the same spit. By now, he was just fifty or so paces from the rōnin and it was time to decide on the best course of action. The rōnin clearly couldn't cross, at least not here, and now realized that in their hurry they had made the wrong decision. Now, their only course was either to wade back through the shallows or to stand and make a fight of it . . . They still had their infant hostage . . .

Magobei glanced back the way he had come but no help was yet to be seen and the revellers, intent on hurling the four flaming inoshishi into the river, hadn't realized the drama that was unfolding so close by. He sat down on the trunk of a fallen tree stranded on the spit and looked at the two murderers.

'Are you the stinking puppeteer from the village?'

'That I am, sir!'

'Who gave you the right to wear the two swords, wretched peasant?'

Magobei smiled at the gibe.

'The same right as you, I suspect,' he replied, but he was hoping that he might be able to anger one or both of these men. An angry enemy was often a danger to himself.

The older man had clearly decided that the pair of them couldn't ford that torrent and turned away to take stock of Magobei's threat.

'We shall kill you, peasant; you know that, don't you?'

Magobei laughed at the remark, seeing the first of the inoshishi floating down towards them.

'That rather depends on who Marishi-ten favours, doesn't it, sir?' he called. 'See, here comes the first of her "messengers"!'

He could see that the following three 'boars' had somehow floated together and would pass in a few moments . . . they might even ground if they were caught in the back eddy caused by the end of the shingle spit . . .

'Why don't you put the child down. You have no quarrel with him, have you. Two of you against my poor skill gives you the best advantage, you know. In fact, my blade is even rusted in places and

I might not even be able to draw it out of its sheath . . .' He was playing for time; he only needed a few seconds more, perhaps.'Anyway, I shall do my best to cut you even if I lose my life in doing so for what you did to that poor priest last year!'

The two rōnin almost choked with laughter at that.

'You kill us, eh? For relieving that stupid old man of his gold! Well, at least you are an entertainer, puppeteer!'

A sudden pall of white smoke billowed across the spit as the images grounded with a sudden shock, and Magobei leapt forward from the log, running like a hare towards the left hand man who was just setting the child down as the smoke blotted the trio from view.The puppet-master veered to his left and into the smoke, at the same time hurling a broken stick out to his right. He heard a sudden curse and the sound of a swordcut striking the wood; glimpsed the younger man half-turning at the sound, and cut upwards two-handed from his right, jumped his feet back and cut down again as hard as he could. With a throttled groan his victim fell to the stones, his sword clattering away from his claw-like fingers. The child was safe . . . for the moment. Magobei registered a slight movement to his right and swiftly ducked as the other rōnin's blade swept past his head, thrusting one-handed outwards . . . A slight shock told him that at least the tip had caught the other and he hurled himself to his left, jumping up to his feet on the very brink of the river . . .The smoke eddied, giving him just enough warning of the riposte to enable him to sway aside, but his foot caught on a stone and he stumbled, instinctively raising his sword across his head . . . the rōnin's blade struck and slid aside, Magobei spinning and cutting back at the same time as he crashed onto the shingle . . .Was this the end . . ?

Another eddy of the smoke revealed that he had managed to strike his enemy's right ribs; the rōnin had staggered away, left hand grasping the wound and already a dark stain spreading through his fingers . . .The child stood right behind him!

Scrambling to his feet, Magobei yelled out for the man to stand and fight, and started towards him as the smoke cleared . . . He caught up a rock just as the rōnin saw the child and reached out to grab the boy to him . . . Hurling the stone with all his might, Magobei leapt forward. The stone did his work for him, catching the murderous samurai beside his left ear and stunning him; enough time for the puppet-master to grapple him to the ground and hit him hard with another stone so that he lay senseless on his face.

'Master . . .!' warned the child, just giving Magobei enough time to be aware of the danger from the first rōnin who, sore wounded as he was, threatened to stab him with his short sword.

Twisting sideways, the samurai thrust back into the man's belly, pulled his katana free, and saw his attacker double down into a heap across his partner's legs.

It was all over and Magobei sat up onto his knees, his arms enfolding the child as the relief surged through his body.

Using the rōnin's own sword *himo*, Magobei swiftly tied his wrists high behind his back with the cord around his neck, first relieving him of the bundle containing the gold. In fact, it was this very gold that had preserved his life from Magobei's last cut. Irony, indeed! The younger of the two rōnin was near to death when, at long last, the Suzuki-ke watchmen splashed through the shallows to take charge of the criminals.

Following slowly in their wake, Magobei let the child ride on his shoulders, the boy seemingly little the worse for his experience. The lad's mother rushed down to meet them just below the village, her eyes brimful of tears of relief and gratitude. Magobei's brother bowed deeply out of respect.

The evidence against the two murderers was overwhelming, especially now that poor Kyu'emon had appeared to recover most of his wits. The village headman and the Suzuki bugyō discussed the case later that evening and, on the following morning, both the felons were sent to the clan yashiki to be condemned and executed. Two days later they were summoned by the headman to the Watch office where one of the middle retainers, who had been informed of the incident as he was passing through, had been authorized by letter to make Magobei and his brother a proposition.

'I understand that the Chamberlain may offer you employment as a reward,' he said in a rather patronizing tone, but Magobei and his brother politely refused in the grounds that they intended to escort the shingyaku, Kyu'emon, to his temple and see that he was safe. They owed that help to the lad partly from pity and from a sense of honouring the old priest's soul. In any case, they both knew that the Suzuki-ke offer would probably amount to not more that fifty *koku* of rice each, if it was as much as that, and they would be expected to serve at a level only just above the most menial samurai.

Truly, it is as the poet once wrote:

Life and death,
past and present;
Marionettes on a toy stage,
When the strings are broken
Behold the broken pieces

14

THE SWORDSMAN

Kawada Nobuhide had trudged a long way that day following a narrow roadway that was little better than a cart track, winding its convoluted way past the waving expanse of tall *shiba* grass at the eastern end of the Tega marshes. He was hot and tired and very wet from the incessant rain, scarcely protected by his straw rain cape which, in any case, made him sweat and itch all across his chest and shoulders. The shaft of his yari felt oily and slippery but he had managed to keep his braided sword hilts dry, at least for the present. Now he needed to find somewhere to shelter for the night, if such a place could be found in this forsaken region?

Mile after mile he had walked on this damnable track, seemingly getting nowhere but hopefully travelling west, his horizon restricted by the endless waving heads of the coarse marsh grasses that grew thickly on all sides and always stood taller than his head, and now, as the light thickened and the rain pelted down, he wondered if his poor luck had run out and he was in for a miserable night. The last traveller he had seen had been about noon and not one soul since then! He came round a bend in the track and found the reed beds had opened out slightly to show a rickety jetty where, presumably, a ferryman would come in to land his dispirited passengers . . . it was scarcely likely that they would be happy in such continuous rain. Fortune smiled upon him, raising his spirits once more, for there, next to the muddy open space stood a small shrine that must surely be dedicated to Saruda-Hiko-sama, the deity of the highways and protector of all those who trod them!

Grateful, he bowed respectfully, unable to make an offering, and peered in the gathering gloom underneath the platform framework to find out if there was enough room to give him shelter.

He crawled through and found that if he curled up into a ball he might be dry, at least his body, but the water soaking the little shrine above found a channel to drip steadily onto where his legs lay. With a sigh, he sat up as best he could and took a rice ball out of his wallet and some *takuan*. Even the rice was damp and the ball disintegrated in his hand.

'Pshaahh!' he said, shaking his head. He had hung up his grass cape in the hope that it would dry off and be a little more use on the morrow. His straw jingasa would certainly be alright as it was lined. With legs crossed, he sat and stared out at the teeming rainstorm, thinking about the weeks that he had just spent living alone in the forest of the Kashima shrine.

Four the last seven years he had walked about the length of the Japanese islands as far down as Kikuchi in the south-west and to Towada Lake in the far north of Mutsu, everywhere seeking out the strongest masters of *hei-jutsu* to improve his understanding; sometimes just discussing tactics and strategy, sometimes testing skill with the heavy wooden bokutō or yari. He had built a small hut in the wild shrine forest that was presided over by the Kashima-*daimyōjin*, Takemika-zouchi-no-kami, bringing together in his mind and body all that he thought valuable from his hard-won experiences, and praying to the god to bestow on him a divinely-inspired understanding that would give him great power for the future. His name would be remembered down the generations with lasting honour . . . Alas, it seemed it was not to be! Nearly a whole year had passed where he trained with yari, nagamaki, and sword every single day, often for as much as eight or nine exhausting hours, rising in the cold dawn light and finishing only when the evening darkness drew in. Only the sacred deer were witness of his self-imposed hardships, although many local people connected with the shrine and warriors of the Kashima-han knew that he was there and what he hoped to achieve. He realized that other warriors had undergone similar self-imposed regimes before him; some even, it was said, achieving their *reimu*, or 'divine revelation' from the great god, himself, but in the end he began to question if this was indeed the case as it certainly didn't seem so for him.

On the other hand, he recalled enduring memories of the great shrine of the warrior deity with considerable pleasure. It was, perhaps, the surprising feeling of calm that pervaded the place and all who went there; the balm of stripping to just his *fundoshi* and entering the chill waters of the *mitarashi* pool in the first light of dawn in order to call on Marishi-ten and the Kashima-daimyōjin to heed his appeals for inner understanding. Cooling on a summer's daybreak; chilling to the bone in the hard frosts of winter . . . or the satisfying sight of thin spirals of blue smoke curling up into the dappling sunlight from the little heaps of swept autumn leaves smouldering along the great avenue of cypress trees . . . How pleasant did that aromatic scent play in his nostrils . . . He recalled how once he had been practising a difficult series of cuts that he had devised, striking with his bokutō at a couple of stout trees that he used as targets, when two messengers, unusually dressed in the most formal manner, bowed before him and request that he ceased his training 'as it disturbed their master'. Disturbed? Resentful at this intrusion, he had strode after the pair and emerged from the thick undergrowth to find that the important personage was praying before the shrine of the 'Earthquake' deity . It was no less a dignitary than the fourth Shōgun, himself, Ashikaga Yoshimochi!

His wild appearance must have come as a great surprise to the high-ranking and self-important officials surrounding the shōgun who was, in this case, paying a private visit to the great shrine. Perhaps they thought that the deity had actually appeared to him in person . . . Afterwards he felt uneasy that he had come face to face with the man who, only two years before, had murdered his own brother, Ashikaga Yoshitsugu, in the Sōkoku-ji on the trumped up charge of conspiracy to seize control of the shōgunate!

Nobuhide smiled to himself, despite the dripping discomfort of the rain, at the picture in his mind's eye of those half-kneeling retainers caught completely unawares by his materialization out of the dark forest! He had demanded to know why his practice had been interupted so rudely, then, realizing who this lord was, simply bowed and vanished back into the bushes . . . No one had said a word! He heard a day or so later from one of the gūji that one of the senior people in the retinue had expressed his master's apologies for causing some disruption to a *kenshi* in the woods!

The swordsman awoke with a start; he must have dozed off, uncomfortable as he was. He rolled his head from side to side to ease the stiffness in his neck and realized that the rain had temporarily eased off but he had no idea of the hour although it may have been towards dawn. It was difficult to be sure with the rising mist which gave the night a slightly luminous quality. The question was whether he should try and curl down or simply give up any thought of further sleep?

Feeling a call of nature, he stirred himself and slid out from under the shrine's timbers, his training ensuring that he thrust his dirk into his obi and picked up his longsword. Stepping a yard or so to the nearest clump of reeds, he passed a stream of water and sighed with the animal relief that simple act brought. Yawning silently, he rubbed his palm vigorously across his bushy hair, and sniffed the air a couple of times. He would rest a little longer, he thought, with a shake of his head.

'Must be getting old . . . and lazy,' he said to himself.

Something made him feel uneasy. He heard no sound but felt the hairs prickle at the nape of his neck . . . Now his senses were completely alert . . . With a swift couple of steps he was crouching down behind the tiny shrine, his sword now firmly settled at his hip, thumb easing forwards the *tsuba* so that the blade lay loosened in its scabbard . . .

A minute or two passed and he began to question his judgement. By Saruda-hiko, he was imagining things . . . Slowly he tightened his left thumb so that it pulled back on the iron swordguard, again silently borne of long experience, and felt the deadly katana begin to seat itself firmly into the mouth of its sheath . . . No, there was a sound and instantly he knew that at least two men were nearby . . .

There came a grunt and a shadowy shape emerged into the open space by the tiny jetty. Another figure followed, evidently having some difficulty with a third, but smaller, person.

'Oi! Don't bite, you slut!' said one sharply, and Nobuhide thought that the speaker must be the second of the straw-caped figures.

There came a grunt as something fell in a heap in a puddle of rainwater.

'Shut your noise!' hissed the first figure, and delivered a hefty kick at what must have been their prisoner

The 'captive' gave a muffled yelp.

'It'll be dawn soon an' the ferryman'll be across to see about 'is first earnin's o' the day.'

'You'll not sell me . . . I'll not let you . . .'

'Shut yer mouth! You ain't got no choice an' yer knows it!'

'Yeah; you are goin' to Tsuchiura an' that's where you're goin' to stay . . .'

' 'Til you rots away wiv the pox!'

Both the men laughed uproariously until the first one warned: 'Shut yer merriment, Jubei; we ain't bin paid yet.'

'In that case, you stop kickin' of 'er! Ev'ry time yer does that you costs us siller!'

'You picking a fight wiv me? Yer jus' wait 'til this bitch's delivered an I'll beat yer stupid . . .'

'Not as stupid as you are . . . That's impossible . . !'

The woman lay on the ground apparently sobbing silently; Nobuhide could see in the slightly better light of dawn her back rising and falling spasmodically. Often women were snatched to be sold into distant brothels, sometimes they were so desperate that they sold themselves to such verminous pimps, if that's what these two were? It certainly seemed so from what he had heard.

He could now see that both men carried swords and one of them had a staff that might, of course, be a yari.

'That bloody rain; I'm soaked to the skin.'

'Aw, stop mouthin' off about everythin'! Moanin' about nuffin' all the blasted time, you are . . .'

'I'll bloody kill yer one day soon, 'shouted the one named Jubei.

'You will? Wiv who's 'elp, eh? You're jus' a wimp, yer miserable little bastard!'

Nobuhide thought it time he appeared on the scene. He carefully drew out from under his night shelter his thick bokutō and thrust it through his obi next to his katana. The two pimps had actually exchanged a couple of blows, not that any harm was done as these punches were little better than wild swings accompanied with hissing and gutteral mouthings. One of the two stamped on the prostrate woman who again gave a sharp cry.

'You have disturbed my night's rest!' said Nobuhide in a calm voice.

The pair stood staring at each other, chest's heaving and took no notice of his appearance. They started shouting again.

'I said: "you disturbed my rest",' he repeated. 'Please stop this shouting!'

This time the bigger of the two glared at him.

'This is our quarrel; keep your nose out of it, rōnin!'

He started squaring up to the other and shouting at the top of his voice.

'I requested that you stop this! Also, release that woman!'

The burly man turned his head and spat insolently at Nobuhide's feet.

'I'll break your head if you interfere again,' he threatened.

'I don't think you will,' Nobuhide said in a low clear voice.

The fellow jerked out his sword and pointed it at the samurai. His companion wasn't sure what to do but picked up his fallen staff which Nobuhide could now see was a short-bladed yari and levelled it, too.

'Release that woman!'

'You make me! We're two to one and'll thrash yer!'

Nobuhide began to turn away then suddenly drew out his bokutō and, with a sharp upwards strike, broke in half the blade of the pimps' longsword, leaving the fellow gaping at the useless stump. His companion, Jubei, tried to thrust half-heartedly with the yari but ended up tossed unceremoniously into the marsh as Nobuhide dropped his hardwood sword, caught hold of the shaft below the head, and with a double-hand twist sent Jubei flying.

'Now release the woman . . . and I shall not ask this again!'

Jubei managed to regain the bank and hastily scuttled across and tugged at the knotted rope that tied the woman's arms to her waist. The rope dropped down and the pair took to their heels into the mist.

'Are you alright?' asked Nobuhide. 'It's safe now, that pair have gone but just to be sure I'll get rid of this yari.' He picked it up, stamped down hard on the shaft which snapped at once, and hurled it out into the reedbeds. He walked across to the shrine and pulled out his satchel and his own yari then came back.

The woman rubbed her side then wiped her tear-stained face, pushing back her dishevelled hair.

'Thank you, master; I think I'm alright. . .'

She tried to set her kimono to order but that was difficult in the state those two miscreants had left her.

'I will turn away if you would like to adjust your clothing, mistress.'

He walked across to where he could now see some way in both directions. The dawn light was stronger now and a pale opalescent brightness showed where the sun would eventually rise above the mist. There was no sign of the straw-caped pimps but he didn't relax his vigilance just in case. Glancing over his shoulder he saw that the woman had managed to regain her modesty,

'I think we shall see the ferryman as the sun rises,' he remarked, then he realized that now that the kidnapped woman had returned more to normality and in the increasing light, she was far from mature; in fact, this was a young girl.

'You must excuse my appearance, sir . . .' she began to say, but Nobuhide held up his hand to stop her.

'Please tell me your name, girl?'

She held her palm before her face, looking slightly aside.

'I am called Masuko, sir.'

'How old are you?'

'I am sixteen.'

Now he saw that she was indeed young . . . and fine featured, too.

'You are not a . . ?'

She inclined her head slightly, lifting her chin.

'Do I look like a servant girl, master? Am I like an "entertainer"?'

While he was talking he secured his bokutō and wallet behind his left shoulder, then adjusted his dirk and katana.

'I am sorry, Masuko-san, but I cannot offer you any food. All I had was ruined in last night's rain. Perhaps, when the ferryman comes, we can find something across the marshes?

She smiled wanly. 'As you say, master. I can wait and it is for you to decide.'

'Where are you from, girl? Where are your parents?'

She looked down but he thought that he saw a shadow cross her face.

'I lived until recently in a village near to Kashiwa, sir. I have no parents, they . . . they are now . . .' She swallowed and raised her head. 'They are passed from this life, sir.'

There was something in her choice of words, or was it her speech, that prompted Nobuhide to bow politely.

'I haven't told you who I am,' he said. 'My name is Kawada Nobuhide. As you can see, I am a wanderer. But you, Masuko-san, are also of samurai birth, are you not?' He leant his weight against his yari. 'How did you come to get involved with those two?'

She told him that a few weeks before her village found itself between two contending neighbouring lords and their troops attacked each other one night, which resulted in the village destroyed and her parents' house burnt to the ground. In the confusion, she and two servants had escaped and hidden themselves but later, when it was safe to do so, they found that everything had gone except one or two peasants who had hidden as they had done. Later, as they wandered the roads looking for her parents, a seemingly helpful merchant had befriended her, passed her into the care of a yamabushi, who then, without warning, sold her on to those two men. That's how she came to be here.

'Your father is a samurai? He serves which lord?'

'You are correct, master; my father is, if he is alive still, named Osumi Masanari, He is a retainer of Satomi Nori'e-dono.'

'Did he farm his own lands?'

'He was one of the fortunate ones, Kawada-sama; our family served the Ashikaga and were rewarded just after the Nanbokuchō wars began. We enjoyed almost five-hundred *koku*.'

'Is that so?' That was a sizeable income by any standards.

Nobuhide was beginning to realize that he would be unable to settle this young woman anywhere in the hope that she would be safe and later find her missing parents. He had, by rescuing her, taken on a considerable obligation to return her in person since hers was evidently a middle-ranking warrior family. For the present he would be unable to wander the country as chaff before the wind. She would have to come, too!

There was a pause in their conversation as a wandering yamabushi, muttering to himself and telling his rosary beads, passed by along the track, walking in the direction that Nobuhide had come the evening before. How odd, thought the swordsman, how all these strange priests looked alike with their pillbox *tokin* on their heads and *oi* boxes on their backs . . . The yamabushi appeared not even to notice the ill-assorted couple by the jetty.

They watched him until he was out of sight then a little later the girl asked him about his family.

'You must excuse my directness, Kawada-sama, but shouldn't I know your rank since we must travel together?'

He smiled wryly to himself.

'I understand, of course, Masuko-san; I have two sisters . . . er . . . as direct as you! I am, at the present time, a rōnin so that I can wander the "Sword's Path" in order to study the military arts . . .'

'And your family?' She detected a reluctance on his part to elaborate.

'My family? My ancestors have always served the Torii-ke in Kōzuke . . .'

'The Torii-ke? They are vassals of the Nagao-ke, are they not?'

'Correct!'

'Then, I think that your family is of senior retainer rank!'

'How do you know that, eh? Maybe we are just lower ranking retainers?'

'You wouldn't be studying the *Sonshi*, sir.' She made this statement flatly without a trace of coquettishness. 'You are a man of rank!'

He kept his council. Did she need to know that his family enjoyed four times the Osumi-ke income and commanded two fortified *yashiki*? Many warriors trained in the *bugei* arts, yet this mere girl used the name '*Sonshi*' which implied a considerably deeper level of understanding? Better for the present to let the questions stop.

The sun was just showing over the mist banks when the ferryman, heralded by the creaking of his leather tholestrap, poled his flat-bottomed boat into sight. Nobuhide felt some relief as he was sure that those two mean-looking pimps would not give up their investment so easily and he thought it more than likely that they would recruit some strong-armed half-starved rōnin to take him on and drag Masuko back into their clutches.

The ferryman came into the jetty and as Nobuhide put his hand out to help the girl step aboard she hitched up her bedraggled kimono and made her way amidships without the slightest trace of being afraid of losing her balance.

'So far, so good!' he thought, with some admiration. He sat down alongside her and the boatman shoved off without delay.

'I only go to my village which is a hour's walk from Sawara, master,' the boatman called.

'Wherever; we don't mind. Can we find something to eat where you live?'

'Plenty of places, master. The road to Tsuchiura passes through but I'd best warn you that the border's closed just now. Them lords is always bickering!'

'That's not good news,' said the samurai, scratching his neck.

'You could go to Itako, master. Only take a day, an' then go up between the lakes or by boat . . . that's if you want Tsuchiura, of course!'

'We'll think about it when we've filled our stomachs!'

The boatman poled on, their passage sending up many wildfowl as they passed the reed clumps. All the while the mist was thinning and the sun getting warmer. As they neared the further shore their wet clothes had almost completely dried but both were famished.

Nobuhide paid the ferryman and was directed towards a small establishment where, he was assured, they would be given a fine repast and shortly afterwards they were sitting at the back of the wine shop whilst the owner and his wife prepared them a meal of *ō-soba*. The only other person in the shop was a swarthy skinned rōnin whose clothes were so threadbare as to almost be in tatters but at least he didn't bother them whilst they swallowed the ō-soba gratefully.

'Oka-san,' Nobuhide called out.

'*Hai!*'

'This lady has had a difficult few days. If I give you this piece of silver, can you help her to tidy up before we continue on our way? We are heading for Kashima, you know.' He added, necessarily suspicious of the frequent glances that the rōnin made in their direction.

'Of course, master.' She beckoned to Masuko. 'Please come with me, miss.'

'Not outside the building, Oka-san,' he murmured The woman nodded.

A few minutes later the rōnin came to his feet and ambled across to squat down on the raised bench opposite the swordsman.

'Excuse me for asking, sir, but did I hear you are travelling to Kashima?' he asked.

Nobuhide grunted in assent.

'I'm going that way, too . . . Uchiemon's my name! Going to pray for better times in front of the shinden.'

'Is that so?'

'Good looking girl you have with you, sir. Is she from these parts, eh?'

Nobuhide replied with a noncommital 'Not really.' He didn't feel inclined to let this conversation go on any longer than necessary.

'No offence meant, sir; just curious, that's all . . . From the look of you, you're a swordsman . . . Ah, don't reply if you don't want to, 'cause I can see I'm right . . . I have some skill myself. Perhaps one day soon . . . at the shrine . . . we might try a bout? What d'you say to that.'

'That may not be possible, sir,' said Nobuhide firmly.

For a moment he thought the rōnin would take offence at his reticence but the fellow merely muttered something about their meeting one day and retired back to his original place, calling for another jar of rice wine.

A few minutes later Masuko returned with the inn-keeper's wife, looking much fresher and wearing a plain kimono.

'No payment needed, good sir,' said the woman. 'You gave me more than enough and, in any case, this is a old kimono of my daughter's when she was this lady's age.' She leant across and smoothed out a fold, then apologized for her rudeness. Masuko smiled, saying that she was very kind. The woman turned her head and whispered that the rōnin was a dangerous fellow that they suspected of being employed by a local gangmaster. He'd visited the inn before a month or two back.

The girl covered up this remark by uttering a quick laugh as if they had been told a joke and Nobuhide slapped his thigh and tried to look completely relaxed. He nodded, his face wreathed in an affable smile, then gathered up his things telling the girl that it was time to be on their way.

The innkeeper and his wife accompanied them into the street, bowing and pointing the direction to take for Sawara there to seek a passage across the smaller lake, Kita-ura, to Kashima.

For the first hour or two they appeared to be alone on that narrow highway, but at length, Masu-ko touched his sleeve lightly and told Nobuhide that the rōnin, Uchiemon, was following on behind them.

'He said he was going to Kashima but I suspect he may be up to no good,' he replied.

A little further on, he asked the girl if she had been taught by her parents how to use a dirk, to which she replied that she had.

'Take this, Masuko-san. It may come in useful. Can you use a yari, too?'

'I have only been instructed with the naginata, Kawada-sama. Maybe the two are much the same?'

He smiled. 'It is lighter, that's true, but thrusting is sharper. Keep that in mind if I toss you my spear.'

'You're teasing me, master. It's just as if you were expecting trouble!'

'Who knows? Best to be aware and therefore ready . . .'

They continued along the dusty track through the desolate flat landscape until, at length the reeds gave way to the open banks of the wide Tone river. All about lay the detritus from the previous spring's flooding and not far away to the west reared the sacred double peaks of Tsukuba mountain, seemingly floating above the waving crests of the sea of reeds. The odd pair trudged on and came to another ferry landing and had the good fortune to be within hailing distance of the boatman.

'If you're go to Itako, master, it's no use crossing 'ere. Best go on along of the road!'

'No, we wish to cross over. We're on our way to Ushibori.'

'It's a longer way round!'

'Never mind . . . That's our decision.'

'Settle yerselves down, then, master . . . er . . . miss. Off we go!'

Hardly had they floated twenty or thirty yards from the strand when the rōnin, Uchiemon, ran down to the weed-covered landing stage, shouting and bawling for them to come back to pick him up, too. The boatman, thinking of another fare, at once began to turn the prow of his narrow boat and scull back to the shore. Hitching up his short kimono, the rōnin shouted his thanks and splashed out to meet them as they returned to the shallows. Soon he was aboard and, with an expansive grin spread over his unshaven face, greeted Nobuhide and the girl as if he were their long-lost brother.

'You see, honoured sam'rai, we should have travelled together! It's safer, you know . . . There's bandits everywhere these days. Many of them hide out in these marshes, don't they, boatman?'

'That they do, good master; that they do!'

After the spring and early summer rains the river had overflowed its banks so that in some parts it was difficult to tell it apart from the surrounding marshes, but the ferryman seemed to know his way between the great clumps of reeds and the location of the main channel as he pushed and pulled at his double sculling oar which creaked and groaned as it swayed to and fro on its rope tether.

The rōnin scooped water in his cupped hand and vigorously cleaned away the mud from both feet and his leg wrappings.

'That's better,' he pronounced at last. 'I must stink like a farmyard!'

'I thought you said you were going to Kashima?' said Nobuhide.

'You announced the same, sam'rai . . . An' I didn't catch your name? You already know mine . . . Uchiemon, lately a *yumi-ashigaru*, first class, to the Satomi clan! Leastways, I reached those heights before they lost out and their forts were destroyed!'

'So, you were a bow carrier, were you?' Nobuhide thought it best to humour the fellow rather than wholly alienate him. Since you ask, my name is Kawada Nobuhide and this lady is . . .'

'Osumi Masuko,' she interposed before he could finish.

'I ain't properly spoken to people of sam'rai families before, so you must forgive me if I'm a little rough an' ready.'

Nobuhide smiled.

'I quite understand, Ichiemon-san . . .'

'It's Uchiemon, sir, not Ichiemon. Folks is always making that mistake. No matter, it will all be diff'rent soon when I gets to be a sam'rai, won't it. An' as I told you, I've skill with me sword. That's why I wanted to have a bout with your honour . . . Really, Kawada-sama, it's true.'

The man had a sort of rough spirit; untamed but, in Nobuhide's judgement, honest enough. As a yumi-carrier footsoldier . . . and 'first-class' at that . . . he was at least on the first rung of the ladder and might well have been retained after any emergency but for the misfortune of being on the losing side.

'Well, Master Uchiemon, in an unguarded moment back at the inn I may have given you some hope of a practice; maybe I will honour that, though not quite yet. If you wish, you may come along with this young lady and myself, but only on condition. Do you want to hear what I shall say?'

Uchiemon wasn't sure how he should react as he instinctively knew that this samurai was used to command. He leant down and picked a flake of drying mud from his frayed kimono hem, and sniffed hard.

'I'm listening . . . er . . . master . . .'

'Good! My conditions are simple; you will remember that at all times you are an ashigaru and not a samurai. At the first chance we have we shall purchase some cleaner clothes for you and you will have a bath! Do you agree?'

Uchiemon wrinkled his nose up and looked sheepish. 'What your honour really means is that I talk far too much! Right? As I see it, either I shall have to take up robbery to live . . . and that can be quite a short career . . . or I get to smell a bit sweeter and serve a fine gentleman like you?'

Even the ferryman smirked when he heard the rōnin's words.

'That's just about the long and the short of it, my friend.'

'In that case, I ain't got no real choice, have I? But you will look at 'ow good I am with my sword, eh?'

'I promise nothing, but I'm sure there will be an opportunity! Good! Is it settled then?'

Nobuhide turned to the girl.

'Do you agree with my decision, Masuko-san?'

She dropped her eyes slightly.

'In my family, my father made the decisions; why should it be different now in the present circumstances?'

'Ushibori, eh?' grunted Uchiemon. 'Well, there are worse places I suppose!'

'You said that these marshes are infested with bandits, Master Uchiemon; is this true?'

'True enough, master. They can hide out here with ease and have the use of boats to move quickly from place to place. It's only back there near to Sawara and beyond that the domain lords are able to keep them in check.'

The winding track took them in and out of great swathes of rank tufted grass and reeds with occasional glimpses of Tsukuba-san's peaks and the great expanse of Kasumi-ga-ura's broad surface shimmering in the heat.

'When will we make Ushibori, I wonder,' Masuko wondered.

'About sundown, miss; not before.'

They paused for a breather at a ramshakle lean-to shelter and sat down on two benches. At once, a peasant woman appeared from nowhere and served then a cold cordial to freshen their parched throats.

'The lady was askin' 'ow far 'tis to Ushibori, Oka-san,' said Uchiemon.

'Another four or so miles, master; could be further . . . I ain't rightly sure 'cos that's furrin' parts, that is! My 'usband's been there but he said he ain't goin' again. No point, really.'

'That's real countryfolk for you, Kawada-sama,' Masuko smiled.

Uchiemon pulled a long face but said nothing.

'Many other folk passed this way today, Mistress?' Nobuhide enquired.

'Not many, master.'

The samurai was just securing his straw jingasa when she added: 'There was a gang 'o five went on through a couple of hours off noon . . . Rough lookin' lot, too. Reckoned they was lookin' fer a girl an' a sam'rai who owed them siller!'

'That's alright, then, Oka-san, 'cos we're three an' not two like what they said,' Uchiemon said, obliquely.

'Suppose it is, but, then, yer can't be too careful, not these days, can you?'

The swordsman pursed his lips.

'Five of them, eh? Oka-san, I don't suppose one could have been rather well-built and had a loud mouth, while one of the others was named "Jubei"?'

'Oi wouldn't rightly like to say about that, master, but you could be right.'

When they left the wayside shelter, a few yards along the track, Nobuhide turned and faced the former ashigaru.

'Are you prepared for a rough journey, my friend? We can rely on you, can we?'

Uchiemon looked at him and grinned.

'I've made me decision an' I've given you me word, ain't I? If it's a fight that's comin' you'll find me right alongside of you, master; never you fear!'

'I'm not doubting you, Uchiemon-san; I'm just making sure.' At a nod from the girl, he went on to describe what had happened only the previous dawn. 'It was one of the reasons that I was a trifle cool towards you back at that inn.'

'Can't say as I rightly noticed, master. A bit too full 'o me'self, of course!'

With the sun setting fast, the three crossed through the barrier that guarded the far side of the bridge between Shimosa and Hitachi. Only four ashigaru lounged by the gate and the two languid samurai in charge cast a cursory eye over Nobuhide's passport when he told them that all three were together and were travelling to the Kashima shrine. A short time later they had found what appeared to be a fairly respectable inn where they would stop overnight.

Ushibori was just a mean backwater settlement built on a slightly raised spit of land that saved it from the devastating innundations that drowned all the floodplain of the Tone-gawa nearly every other year. It stood close to the waterways that connected the broad Kasumi-ga-ura with the Tone river in a series of convoluted and ever-changing streams, lakes, and marshes, and the waters flowing down to join them from the smaller Kita-ga-ura, beyond which lay the mysterious strip of land, the domain of the Kashima clan, ancient guardians of the great shrine. With all this water, the region teemed with wildlife in general, and many local estate owners could foresee its potential were it to be tamed and partially drained. This was truly the 'Land of Reed Plains'. Ushibori's only claim for attention was its rôle as both a landing place for the men who garnered the rich fishing on the lake, and a staging post for travellers taking the narrow highway that hugged the north-eastern shore of the great lake to Ogawa, a distance of about twenty miles. A short way to the south-east lay the little town of Itako, praised by the poets for its splendid waterlilies, long a favoured symbol of the samurai . . . Ah, Itako, made beautiful by its many waterways . . .

The inn boasted three rooms, one of which was much smaller than the rest and could be partitioned. This one he paid for so that Masuko was able to settle down after they had eaten with a degree of privacy, the men having their mats just outside her shōji and between her and the rest of the inn. The only other travellers making use of the place were two yamabushi of *sendatsu* rank who kept themselves to themselves all evening but began to snore loudly just as soon as they put their heads down.

Following his usual habit, despite his tiring day, Nobuhide washed himself down but lay under the thin cover to his mat, his long sword hilt close to his hand where it was concealed. He had positioned himself to the left of the shōji next to the outer wall, a precaution borne of hard-won experience. Uchiemon lay just to the right. After they had settled themselves, they heard some boisterous men enter the front of the inn and call for ō-sake. Perhaps they were a band of fishermen or wildfowlers returning late from a hard day's work, but they were noisy and disturbed the yamabushi, one of whom called out for them to keep quiet! At length they did quieten down but more than an hour had passed. Nobuhide could hear the girl's regular breathing for his ears were keen, Uchiemon was out like a light as soon as he lay down, of course, and that was to be expected of his simple uncomplicated kind!

The swordsman always slept with one eye open, as it were; never to be taken unawares at a moment of apparent weakness; his training saw to that . . . it was known amongst those who were adepts of the heihō as '*zanshin-no-ri*', or 'intuitive awareness', and this ability may well have saved many a master's life. About an hour after all had quietened down and peace descended on the little settlement; the moon in its third quarter shedding a weak light over the surrounding marshes, Nobuhide heard the faint sound of a sliding shōji being carefully opened in the room where the yamabushi lay snoring. A deep silence followed before he was sure that it wasn't one of the pair answering a call of nature . . . it was certainly careful steps across the floorboards by someone in bare feet . . .

Silently he rose to his feet, folding his bedding back so that it might appear that he was still beneath the cover, his drawn sword in hand . . . Whoever was there just behind the shōji breathed out through their nose, feeling for the edge of the door and slowly drawing it back . . . a little too carefully because they must have been slightly lifting and it jambed in the lower runnel. With a muttered imprecation, hardly aspirated, the intruder managed to open the frame completely and crept into their room on all fours . . . The kenshi could see in the faint light that the man was unarmed, except for a short sword, that is, and was intent on stealing whatever he could lay his hands on.

First, he felt over the swordsman's clothes but found nothing, then he moved on to his wallet and sat himself cross-legged to open it up. Nobuhide stepped behind the thief and brushed his fingers lightly down the man's back . . .

The fellow froze before opening his mouth to shout out in alarm but Nobuhide's left hand clamped hard across his mouth and the man saw the gleam of the swordblade in front of his chest.

'One syllable and I shall cut your dirty little throat!' whispered the samurai.

The thief remained motionless.

'Who sent you here?' breathed Nobuhide into the man's ear.

The fellow tried to shake his head but the sword's edge came closer.

'My . . . friend . . . er . . . Jubei says I should come, master . . . Take care, sir; . . . please . . !'

The faint speech was enough to disturb Uchiemon who woke with a start, his hand trying to find his sword.

'What the . . ?'

'Shhssh!' cautioned Nobuhide. 'We don't want to awaken Miss Masuko, do we?'

'But, master . . ?'

'I'll do the talking, Uchiemon-san. Do you just sit behind this man and if he makes a sound other than whispering in reply to my questions, break his filthy neck!'

Uchiemon was fully awake by now and enthusiastically did as he was bid. The samurai sheathed his katana and sat down cross-legged in front of their captive.

'Who is this Jubei, eh? Whisper or Uchiemon will twist you head right off!'

The rōnin grinned in the faint moonlight filtering through the window slats, and took hold of the miserable thief's ears.

'Ju . . . Jubei hangs around here, good master: I owes 'im money . . .'

'You owe money? Why?'

'It's the dice games, master . . . He'll kill me, 'e will . . .'

'And he sent you here to rob us, eh?'

Uchiemon gave a sudden little jerk and the wretch almost fell in terror.

' 'E says I was to take what I could find an' . . . er . . .'

'And what?'

Nobuhide lifted his sheathed katana, his left thumb twitching menacingly.

'Oooh, master, . . . careful, please! I'll tell you everythin' but . . please . . . my family's poor . . . and . . .'

'What did Jubei want as well?'

'Ma . . . Master, 'e wanted to find out if you was 'ere, just you an' the woman, but I ain't seen 'er, 'ave I?'

'Where is Jubei at the moment, then?'

Their captive was shaking as if with ague.

'I . . . I was to give 'im what I found at the Dōsō-jin shrine where 'e . . . If I tells you, 'e'll kill me . . .'

'Maybe not him!' murmured Nobuhide grimly.

Uchiemon 'encouraged' the thief a little more.

'The gang 'angs out there, master.'

'How many are there?'

'I'm a dead man . . . Have some mercy, my lord . . !'

'Come on, I need to know the numbers . . . Five . . ? Six . . ?'

The man swallowed hard.

'Seven of them, sir; the leader is . . . er . . . Magazō. 'E's a hard 'un. Once 'e was an *umatori* fer the Kashima over the lake, but they chucked 'im out 'cos 'e only knew 'ow to be cruel to 'orses! An' there's Tsuhei . . . 'e's just a miserable drunkard . . . Oh, I 'ates all of them . . .'

'Hmm! How far is this shrine, the Dōsō-jin, eh?'

'Less than a mile, sir . . .'

Nobuhide sat for a moment considering what he had learnt. Was the fellow telling the truth or was this a trap to lure them away from Osumi Masu-ko?

'What you say is the truth?' he hissed, and Uchiemon took a firmer grip with both his hands, beginning to twist.

'By the Buddha, master, an' my life . . .'

'You will come with us to guide. One sound out of you, the slightest hint of a warning, and you will be a dead man . . . Understand?'

Uchiemon deftly dropped a noose over the man's head and knotted the tail end so that it wouldn't escape his grip.

'Now, tell us your name?'

'Shin'emon, my lord . . .'

Nobuhide decided he had to take the risk. Better to attack rather that wait for Matazō and Jubei to seek the place of their choosing to get the girl back!

The Dōsō-jin shrine was a neglected couple of buildings, so far as either Nobuhide or Uchiemon could see, lying in an overgrown tangle of woodland and bamboo just a short distance up one of the shallow valleys that led into the neck of low hills between the two lakes. That much they could see in the pale moonlight as they crept forward. They had left Shin'emon bound and gagged out of the way behind the broken down torii and would release him later, provided matters didn't go awry!

After a few minutes reconnoitring in which Nobuhide discovered that only two of the gang sat awake throwing dice and the rest appeared to be lying asleep further back in the depths, to judge from the snoring, he decided on a course of action. Retiring back to the shelter of the smaller building, he whispered to Uchiemon to make his way round to the rear of the shinden and set fire to the ruin. As soon as he had done so he was to rejoin the swordsman at the front and between them they would deal with the criminals. Simple enough . . .

Uchiemon soon gathered an armful of tinder and spread it carefully under the broken boards of the verandah apron. In no time at all the flames caught as the fire took hold and spread . . . He rejoined the samurai and they stood on either side of the delapidated outer shōji; nor did they have to wait long! They could hear the crackle of flames before the first shout of alarm went up, then men scrabbling to find their weapons and escape their danger . . .

The first of the gang, shouting like a maniac, emerged backwards, practically naked, with his arms full of clothing and his swords, only to be speared by Uchiemon and thrust back into the fog of smoke eddying out from the gaping doorway. A second man appeared and was promtly cut down by Nobuhide . . . The men inside, dazed by sleep and too much strong drink, began to realize that they were attacked but by now they were caught between a wall of hungry flames spreading fast in both directions along the rear wall and the flashing blades awaiting them if they tried to rush out the front . . .

Shouts turned to screams of rage, then to fear as they saw they were trapped. One more, braver than the rest, shot through the door, totally naked but for a kimono fluttering about his head, his sword flailing to ward off their unseen attackers, was speared in his side and sprawled headlong down the outer steps. His sword flew off into the darkness of the open yard while the wretch howled at the searing pain in his side, twisting and writhing . . . A few seconds later a fourth man rushed out, beating at the hungry flames that had caught his unbound hair, spinning round and slashing out with his sword in terror and pain . . . Nobuhide's blade swept up and took his raised arm off at the shoulder, sending him reeling into the balustrade where he sat, open-mouthed, staring at the blood spurting from his terrible wound . . .

'That will do, Uchiemon; we'll return to the *ryokan*. The fire will do the rest of our work!'

As they left, part of the roof at the rear collapsed downwards with a crash, sending a great surge of sparks and flames up into the night sky. If any of the remaining members of the gang escaped, they could count themselves very fortunate and would hardly be likely to be of further danger to anyone . . . Back at the torii, they soon released Shin'emon but took him with them, just in case; the former ashigaru whispering dire threats of instant retribution should he try to escape. They needn't have worried for the sight of the burning shrine was enough to show the terrified man that these two men meant every word they said!

Silently, they hurried back into the inn and, sitting down on the inner step, began to take off their straw *waraji* when the innkeeper and his wife appeared with a lantern and evidently in a very disturbed state. As soon as they saw the samurai they fell to their knees, the woman in tears and her husband almost speechless.

'Master . . .', the innkeeper managed to blurt out. 'Master . . .'

Nobuhide frowned.

'What is it? Out with it!'

'The . . . those two . . . er . . . priests, They . . .'

'You are talking about the two yamabushi through there?'

'Yes, master; but they've gone . . !'

'Gone? It's the middle of the night . . ?'

'They've taken the young lady with them, master!'

Nobuhide's mind raced; he had been guilty of an error of judgement. It was now he remembered that lone yamabushi who had passed Masuko and he while they waited for the ferryman on the other side of the marshes. Of course, why should one of these strange priests be abroad and going in the same direction as the two pimps at that early time of day? And then two more *shugenja* turn up at this inn? One of them was probably the same as the man that he had seen . . .

'How long have they been gone, eh?' he asked.

'We . . . er . . . we heard you go out about an hour since, master, an' they two left a few minutes later . . . Oka-san here, saw 'em go with the girl . . . lady. They were talkin' to 'er an' she seemed . . . er . . . worried by somethin''.

'Which direction did they take?'

The innkeeper's wife dabbed her tearful face and pointed.

'They took the track there up into the hills, master . . .'

'What's up there?'

'It leads to Kita-ura, master, but if they turns off before, they might go to the "Three Kami" shrine a little way to the south o' the lake . . ."

'Is there a branch track on the way they've taken?'

The couple looked blankly at each other, but Shin'emon coughed.

'If they turn off east jus' after the bridge over the brook, it would bring 'em onto the way direct to that there shrine . . . I . . . I could be yer guide, master . . .'

Nobuhide gave the innkeeper and his wife some broken silver for their trouble and the three set off in pursuit. The glare from the burning Dōsō-jin shrine lit up the forest to their right and they could just hear some people shouting at the southern end of the village as news of the fire became known. Shin'emon took them east of the Kita-ura track and they soon found themselves climbing up to the low plateau, the stony path barely lit by the setting moon. Through the swordsman's mind went the question as to why Masuko had apparently gone freely with these yamabushi. When he had looked in her room, he hadn't found his dirk so she must have taken it with her. That was something, at least. He hoped, too, that he hadn't made the wrong assumption that these yamabushi had taken the side track to the 'Three Kami' shrine instead of continuing northwards. Perhaps they had tricked Masuko into believing that he, Nobuhide, had arranged to meet them after dealing with the gang at the Dōsō-jin shrine . . . but how would either they or she know that was what they were about?

The moon had practically disappeared which meant that there would be an hour or so of darkness before the first paling in the eastern sky at dawn; would they miss their quarry, that was the question? Surely the girl had the commonsense to realize by now that she had been duped . . ? There was just enough light to know that the track had swung northwards and after a while they came to the edge of this particular area of plateau. Difficult country, this, and very easy to get lost, he supposed, now glad that Shin-emon had volunteered to act as their guide . . . if he was to be trusted.

The eastern horizon was well-defined as they breasted the next height and for a space the scrub and bamboo thickets petered out and they could see the faint gleam of the lake.

'The shrine lies straight ahead, master,' Shin'emon whispered.

Nobuhide merely grunted in reply, then, with the dawn light driving back the darkness, he thought he glimpsed a faint moving patch at the foot of the hill, and a flood of relief filled his spirit.

'I see them . . ! Look!'

Uchiemon peered down the hill.

'Can't say as I can, master . . . no . . . hold on! Yes, you mean that pale shape . . . You're right!'

Shin'emon stood and wiped his brow.

'I thought this was the right road, master.'

'We don't know yet, my friend; but if it is indeed them, you can go back to your home happy!'

Their quarry disappeared amongst the dark mass of some woods and Nobuhide quickened his pace causing the others to almost trot to keep up with him. To his mind, experience told him that speed was of the essence. The yamabushi may have thought that they had two or three hours advantage, even if the swordsman had selected the correct road, but with their twists to the east they may have got clean away. If he could close on them before they became aware of the nearness of his pursuit, the advantage would lie with him. They must reach the woodland before the increasing daylight gave them away . . .

'Shin'emon, do you know this shoreline well?' whispered Nobuhide, looking at the still waters of the lake now taking on a brassy hue with the appraching dawn.

'Aye, master; I share a boat down near that shrine with me friend, Hanbei. We often fishes Kita lake.'

'Where would those two head, do you think?'

'Well, master, if I were them, I'd want a short rest after this walk, then I'd take the ferry over t'other shore.'

'What do you think, Uchiemon-san?'

'The girl'll need a rest, master; that's for sure. Reckon e's right.'

'Is there a short cut to the shrine, Shin'emon?'

The fisherman scratched his cheek, thinking hard.

'I thinks there is a path down through to the narrow paddy, but las' time I took it, I remember it was choked with grasses, sir . . .'

'Take us down that way . . . but with as little noise as possible, both of you!'

The turn was only a hundred or so paces further on but just before they reached it, Nobuhide saw a tiny piece of material on the ground. He stooped and picked it up and recognized it for a strip torn from Masuko's kimono.

'Good girl!' he murmured to himself.

Shin'emon's memory was right in that once they reached the valley floor the path along the field banks was difficult because of the rank grass and rushes choking the drainage ditches. The descent from the crumbling sandy cliff top wasn't so bad. In between the unkempt fields the path was often covered in the invading marsh and the encroaching scrub; the farmer evidently had given up clearing this marginal land, but at last as the first sign that the sun was about to appear over the flat-topped Kashima hills, they saw the roof of the 'Three Kami' shrine amongst the pine trees.

With great care, all three men crept forward but could detect no sign of their quarry. It looked as if by taking the steep path they had indeed got ahead of the yamabushi and their captive.

'Where's the ferry landing?' hissed Nobuhide.

Shin'emon pointed away to the right.

'About quarter of a mile, master,' he whispered.

Nobuhide turned his head aside from the man's sour breath.

'What's at the front of the shrine, by that torii?'

'Ahhh! The track crosses over a little bridge, master. It ain't got any . . .'

He was going to finish with 'rails' but the samurai had signed to Uchiemon to follow him and was off at a crouching run.

'You stay put, or else . . .' warned the rōnin as he followed on.

'Don't you worry, master; I'm not likely to move, no how!' Shin'emon whispered to himself.

Just beyond the rustic torii, once painted vermillion but now sadly decayed with much of the paint flaked away, a bridge spanned a deep drainage ditch cut across the track to allow water to make its sluggish way down to the lake. The bridge was about five or six feet wide and, in the cold light of dawn, the timbers were clearly well-worn and splintered.

'Check your waraji ties, Uchiemon . . Make sure they are secure . . . This is what I want you to do. Cross over and get down beneath the timbers so that you can't be seen. Wait until whoever comes is on the bridge and I have challenged them, then come up behind them. Clear?'

This done, the kenshi squatted down against the gateway uprights and Uchiemon took up his concealed position amongst a thick clump of tall shiba grass, nor was it long before their patience was rewarded.

First appeared the bigger of the two yamabushi, striding boldly along with his bonden stave under his right arm. Nobuhide noted that the man wore a slung sword at his left hip. Behind him came three more figures; two more mountain warriors and the girl being forced on ahead by one of the others. One carried a large naginata over his shoulder.

They hadn't yet noticed the swordsman sitting on the further side of the bridge and one of the group called out that his waraji cord had just broken and he needed to stop.

'You'll stop when I tell you, and not before!' the leader called back.

'You're a hard bastard!'

'You'll pay for that remark, shortly!' snarled the first yamabushi, pausing to look back. 'Come on, close up!'

When he turned back, Nobuhide stood there at the end of the bridge barring his way.

'Release the girl!' he ordered.

'She's ours!' growled the sendatsu. 'You will have to take her and three to one are large odds especially when we are also well-trained!'

He brought his *bonden* staff across his chest, thumping it into his left hand with a loud 'thwack', and strode towards Nobuhide who stood facing him with his bokuto.

'Stop, priest. That is not a common girl you may think to sell! You know that?'

The yamabushi paused halfway across the planking.

'Master samurai, I am well-aware of that! She is the daughter of Osumi Masanari who has thwarted my temple on more than one occasion! Now he has fallen along with his Satomi lord and we have burnt down his yashiki and retaken our temple lands on which it was built! I shall do what I want with any of his kin to bring disgrace on his name!'

'That's as may be, priest! But first you will have to deal with me!'

The yamabushi snorted, circling his thick staff round and aiming a heavy blow at Nobuhide's head but the swordsman ducked beneath the attack and deflected the bonden down to the side, almost sending it flying from the priest's grasp. With a grunt, his attacker regained his grip and tried to jab back with the other end. The swordsman again struck down and this time did disarm the mountain priest, who jumped back and drew out his long sword . . . Meantime, his associate with the long curved halberd, roared out a battle shout and whirled the vicious weapon like a waterwheel, but couldn't join the fight because of the narrowness of the bridge.

It was at this point that Uchiemon came to his feet and without warning thrust upwards with his yari, the keen blade goring deep into the halbardier's left thigh just below his buttocks. With a lurid oath, the yamabushi turned and struck down at his tormentor, the wicked trenchant blade easily severing the yari head from its shaft and narrowly missing Uchiemon's leading hand. The rōnin, now at a disadvantage, scrambled back past the shiba grass clump and up onto the bank . . . He was in the greatest danger from the third of the yamabushi who, by now, had drawn out his slung sword and was preparing to join the fray. Now, Masuko took a hand. From inside the breast of her kimono she deftly pulled Nobuhide's dagger and without the slightest hesitation grasped the third priest's upper sleeve, dragging him round, and thrust the point deep into the man's armpit. He staggered to one side, clawing at the wound with his left hand, but managing, at the same time, to slash across at Masuko with his long blade. The edge came so close that it cut through her loose right sleeve.

Nobuhide shouted loudly, hurling his bokutō up into the air above the sendatsu's head, distracting him for half a second . . . and, dropping to his left knee, drew his katana upwards, his keen blade striking the man just above his right elbow, whirled it round and cut back deep into his victim's left hip. With a howl of anger and the searing pain, the sendatsu collapsed onto the splintered planking and rolled over the side into the water below . . .

Swinging his long-bladed naginata in great scything arcs, the wounded yamabushi stood defiant in the centre of the bridge, watched like a hawk by Nobuhide, now back on his feet. Behind the man stood the third priest, blood glistening in the strong slanting rays of the rising sun as it poured from his wounded side. He glared at Uchiemon, calling down dire threats on his immortal soul, but it was Masuko who settled the matter by hurling the dagger with all her might and deadly accuracy into his throat. Almost before he fell to the ground, she had leapt in to pull the blade out from the frothing blood that oozed out of the death wound, and turned to face the man on the bridge.

'Have a care, Masuko-san!' warned Nobuhide. 'He will be a wounded tiger . . .'

Uchiemon was unsure what he should do but nonetheless advanced to join her. He shouted a great *kiai*, chiefly as a distraction, and feinted as if he would run at the side of the bridge, Masuko moving the other way. The yamabushi's right leg was pouring with blood from the deep spear thrust and he was weakening fast.

'Throw down your halberd, priest! Our quarrel is not with you!' called out Nobuhide.

'Never!' came the reply, but the loss of blood was too much and the yamabushi sank to his haunches, his halberd falling with a clatter onto the timbers and then point first into the stream.

'What temple are you from?' asked Nobuhide.

'A branch of the Dewa-sanzan!'

'We can staunch your wound if you give up now!'

'You will turn me over to this domain; I know your type, samurai!'

Uchiemon sniffed.

'If he lives, my lord, he will only continue the vendetta. Let me finish him off!'

'Too much blood has been spilt already in this matter,' said Nobuhide, shaking his head sadly. 'Such affairs only drag on often getting worse as time passes and the original cause is forgotten.'

Quite suddenly, the yamabushi drew out his dirk and drew back his arm intending to hurl it at Nobuhide but Uchiemon, fully alert, thrust down with his sword, the point deeply piercing the man's chest. With a final gasp the yamabushi keeled over onto his side and it was finished.

'That was quick action, Uchiemon, for which I thank you.' The kenshi looked about him. 'Gather up what weapons you can. If they are rubbish we shall throw them into the lake.'

'Shall we bury the bodies, master?'

'Only if you can find mattocks and spades; usually there are some kept behind the main shrine building . . .'

Uchiemon called to Shin'emon and the two set about carrying out the swordsman's orders. In the meantime, Nobuhide sat down near Masuko on the verandah steps and carefully began to examine and clean his swordblade and the yari, removing the cut off broken remnant of the shaft.

He looked across at the girl who was setting about the same task with his dagger.

'You were extremely fortunate to escape that last cut from the man you thrust, Masuko-san,' he said, quietly. 'It was a brave action to deal with him, though!'

'I was taught well enough, Kawada-sama.'

'You weren't wounded by that yamabushi's sword tip, were you?'

'He cut off part of this sleeve; I gained the merest nick . . . It is nothing.'

'Any wound is something, Masuko-san,' he said, gravely, 'and I can see blood staining your side.'

'It is nothing, sir . . . please.'

'I wish to see for myself, though I regret you have no female attendant so you must let me decide the issue. I am sorry.'

She shook her head half-heartedly but let him take her up into the front of the shinden. There, she pulled aside her kimono and he saw that the blade had cut through her under shift. The cotton garment had soaked up a lot of the bleeding but there was enough blood to give cause for concern.

'I must ask you to pull aside the shift, Masuko-san . . . It is necessary.'

The blade had neatly sliced across her side just below her left rib cage leaving a wound about five inches in length but luckily, so far as he could see, not carrying material into the gash. She was very lucky that it hadn't cut her breast . . . Quickly he rumaged in his wallet and found a clean fundoshi and a hachimaki. The former he folded lengthwise and got her to pass it round her body so that he could secure it as tightly as possible. Over the top she did the same for the hachimaki cloth, which fortunately was generously long.

'We must get that properly cleaned and dressed as soon as we cross the lake, I will be happier when we are in the Kashima domain and, therefore, safe!'

She rearranged her shift and kimono and they returned to sit outside the shōji.

Shortly after noon they landed on the Kashima shore of Kita-ura and took shelter in the only tavern that Tsukahara village boasted. At once Nobuhide brushed a letter to Tsukahara Heihachirō, lord of the yashiki that guarded the northern approach to Kashima, setting out his rank, that of Masuko, and, briefly, the events of the past three days. He added the fact that the young woman required urgent attention for a sword cut received in that morning's fight.

Not an hour after he despatched the letter with the innmaster, three samurai arrived at the tavern on horseback with an invitation from the commander of the yashiki for Nobuhide and his party to accompany the escort back. They were received with every kindness, including the rōnin, Uchiemon, and the fisherman. At once, Masuko was taken to the women's quarters where she was bathed and her wound properly dressed. She was also given clothes suited to her rank. After he had bathed, Kawada Nobuhide, also freshly attired, was ushered before Tsukahara Heihachirō, who knew, of course, that he had been the kenshi seeking his reimu in the shrine precincts for more than nine months of the past year. After hearing his account in more detail, Tsukahara-dono requested that the swordsman should remain as his guest whilst enquiries were made in Shimosa and Musashi provinces regarding the fate of the Osumi-ke and particularly of Osumi Masanari.

'You know, Kawada-sama, my family have some skill in the arts of hei-jutsu?' asked Tsukahara-dono.

'I had heard, my lord, that many ancient secrets are preserved by the Kashima-han.'

'And you, Master Kawada? Did you succeed in finding your secrets?'

'Perhaps, my lord; but not immediately from the Kashima-daimyōjin, or so I thought. If you had asked me that question yesterday night I would have replied in the negative; now, after the events this morning, I am inclined to think differently.'

'Interesting! Perhaps one day you will inform me of your teaching, Kawada-sama?'

In his inner being, Nobuhide was now convinced that he had been permitted insight into the blend of the 'expected' with the 'unexpected'. The truth was illustrated at the moment he had tossed his bokutō into the air above the yamabushi sendatsu's head, instantly dropping very low as he drew out his sword to make his initial cut . . . He now realized just how powerful such a move might be in a number of circumstances . . . This was indeed inspired by his devotion to Marishi-ten and honouring the Great Kami of Kashima. As for the fate of Masuko's family and the young girl, herself, that is another story buried somewhere in the records, perhaps to be found one day in the future? For the time being, they were all safe.

15

KOMUSŌ

Stories abound concerning robbers and of spies endowed with immense secret skills, those wild and lawless men who seem to have attracted the admiration and curiosity of shallow-minded people since ancient times. Mind you, of the former, most of these supposed legendary heroes lived in times now long past and romantically posed no threat to the living; they were naturally very different from those outlaws who bully and terrorize whole districts to-day. There were many sorts of these notorious men; some were warriors forced into brigandage in order to raise arrow-tax so that they could gain strength in order to recover lost lands; others were cast-off samurai following the *seppuku* of their erstwhile lord on some lost battle ground; still others were cowardly fellows, former foot-soldiers and lazy peasants who sought an easier living by theft rather than starve when the crops failed, taxes bcame oppressive, or wanton armies destroyed their villages and murdered their kin. Still others were indigent flotsam, sunk so low that begging and extortion became their sole means of eking out their worthless lives.

Gōsuke Heibei was something of an exception, though; once a middle-ranking warrior whose holdings afforded him a modest one-hundred-and-fifty *koku* income and whose former lord, a vassal of the Nagao-ke long since dead when his yashiki was attacked and burned during the Yūki War, had left him masterless, bereft of his fields and with an aged mother to nurse and sustain. Such an unfortunate series of circumstances had forced him to build a secret hut deep in the forest above the temple where he made his parent as comfortable as was possible – she was crippled with swollen and aching joints – whilst he tried to make some sort of living cutting wood for sale to the Daitoku priests or the well-to-do merchants who resided in the township hoping for the protection of the local lord whose fortress commanded the highway just down the broad valley to the east. But few wanted kindling, especially now the rainy season was here and the dog-days of summer were just around the corner. With starvation facing both his helpless mother and himself, Gōsuke Heibei was forced to take to robbery in order that they might survive. He soon established his base in the shelter of a little used narrow track that passed one of the temple's small side wicket gateways just where one of the main highways began to descend the hill to the town below, and it was here that he carried out his occasional crimes.

One result of the recent upsurge of confused violence in this area around Shibukawa and the petty wars that had drawn so many vassals and their followers south into the Kantō had led to Torii Kōzuke-no-kami Masashige despatching his brother, Shinzaemon Tora-no-suke, with a detachment of some hundred riders to strengthen the remaining garrison and help maintain order in this small town until their overlord, Takasaki Rokuemon, returned. Torii Shinzaemon arrived on the fifth day of the sixth month and set up quarters for himself and his men in the vacant Ōta yashiki, a fortified mansion that stood on an elevated spot some few hundred yards west of the main gateway tower of the Daitoku temple.

On the second day after he moved into the yashiki, three of the servants despatched down to the township late in the afternoon in order to bring up some fresh vegetables packed onto the back of a stout pony were waylaid by a gang of ruffians, severely belaboured when they attempted resistance, and deprived of their goods. All three eventually dragged themselves to the outer gate of the yashiki through the drenching rain and reported the robbery. The guard commander, a member of Asari Kuro'emon's provost unit – this hard-bitten officer had been appointed *ō-metsuke* by Torii Shinzaemon – immediately placed all three under arrest and sent a messenger to his master briefly outling the circumstances of the theft.

The three bruised men told how they had been accosted by no less than seven or eight fierce fellows who had simply appeared out of the dusk and rain, beaten them ferociously before any of them could draw their swords, and run off with the packhorse into the gloom. Stable-Overseer Katō, the guard commander, frankly didn't believe a word of what they said and found out under separate questioning that they had, in fact, been attacked by only one man, albeit a large fellow, and simply run away because they thought that he 'was an *ōni*'! They had then, out of fear of punishment, beaten each other to make it look as if they had been really attacked.

At that point, just as Asari Kuro'emon came in person to the guardroom, the two sentries posted outside the closed gateway, reported the arrival of the packhorse still with its load! It was when the animal was led into the courtyard that it was noted that a small bag of root vegetables, *daikan*, and about two *kan* of grain was missing. A negligible loss it would seem. The Ō-metsuke ordered that the three should be confined until the morrow and he returned to the main yashiki quite mystified at this curious incident. As his duties required, he recounted this entertaining little story to his lord and while the senior retainers enjoyed the fable, no one attached much importance to the incident.

The rains dried up at the beginning of the following week and the days and nights became significantly warmer. On the night of the full moon, the fourteenth or fifteenth day of the month, another robbery took place and it transpired that it happened at about the same place on the roadway just past the temple. Again, it was eventide and the enormous moon was just rising over the mountain spur to the east. This time the robbers were alleged to have leapt out of the darkness and attacked like veritable demons sending the lackeys scattering in terror down the hill towards the yashiki, their three pack animals left as booty with their assailants. As it happened, Overseer Katō was again on guard duty and at once sent three armed riders back up the hill to seek out the brigand gang with orders to capture and bind them fast. They reached the spot, now bathed in the clear moonlight, merely finding a wandering flautist sitting at the temple corner with his *shakuhachi*. They judged by his woven basket headgear that this was clearly a mendicant *komusō*.

Reining in his mount, the leader of the detachment said:

'Sir priest, have you seen any armed men nearby?'

The wanderer rose to his feet and bowed respectfully, his bamboo flute held in his left hand.

'No, master samurai; I haven't seen anyone but one fellow walking that way,' he said, pointing towards the corner of the temple wall, 'he was leading three laden horses.'

'He had horses, you say?'

'Three of them, sir. Back down the hill some men were running headlong in the direction your honour has just come from.'

The samurai grunted. 'The man took the horses that way, sirrah? We had better get on!'

'No necessity to hurry, sir; the animals are just around that corner where the fellow tethered them. You'll find them there easily enough!'

'Just one man, you say? Not a gang of armed fellows?'

The komusō laughed.

'There was but one man, master. It is as I have said; only one, none else.'

The leader shook his head doubtfully but motioned two of his men to dismount and take a look. The mendicant bowed again then resumed his squatting, putting his shakuhachi to his lips resumed his playing.

In a few moments the two lackeys reappeared leading the packhorses by their halters.

'It was as this priest said, master. They were tethered to a post just round there and pulling at the grass tufts.'

The detachment commander grunted, ordering his men to examine the ponies' loads.

'All seems correct, master,' reported the senior lackey, but one of the men pointed out a loose binding rope at the rear of the animal loaded with rice sacks.

'It looks as if this sack has been tampered with, master,' one of the men called out.

'What's missing?'

'Nothing that we can see, sir!'

The mounted officer shrugged his shoulders. 'If all is still secure then we had best return to the yashiki and I'll put in my report! Remount!'

The komusō shook his head and came to his feet.

'One moment, sir; I feel the need to apologize to your commander for not being in a position to help more. Should anything be found to be missing I somehow feel responsibility.'

'These wandering mendicants were all odd people', thought the leader but he nodded his head to acknowledge what was said.

Just as they were about to ride off the komusō recited some lines of what appeared to be a poem.

Notice of this second incident had already reached the ears of Asari Kuro'emon who was at the gateway tower when the packhorses and their escort returned. When all was duly reported Kuro'emon remained seated on the folding stool that his aide had placed for his comfort. The detachment commander remained kneeling before him.

'So you say that the only person you saw was this mendicant?'

'He witnessed most if not all the incident, my lord.'

'And nothing was taken?'

'Not so far as we could ascertain, my lord!'

'But one pack was unsecured?'

'Partly, sir. I have ordered that the particular sack should be weighed just in case the rice merchant had tried to give my lord short measure.'

'Hmm!'

'And you saw nothing else suspicious?'

'Nothing, master.'

Kuro'emon shrugged his shoulders slightly and gazed balefully towards the guardroom where the three lackeys were being held.

'I suppose I shall have to detail some foot soldiers to guard future supplies . . .' he mused, more to himself than the senior ashigaru still kneeling before him.

'Sir, there was just one other thing that I thought odd, if I may speak again?'

'Well?'

'The komusō made a point of apologizing for the trouble caused; I have no idea at all why.'

'He did? Nothing else?'

'He recited some lines of a poem, too . . .'

'Can you remember them?'

The soldier scratched his head with the effort of recalling the words. 'Yes, my lord; it was a simple verse:

> *The blossoms have fallen;*
> *I stare without seeing at a world*
> *Bereft of colour.*'

'"*The blossoms have fallen . . .*"? Those were the words, eh?'

The lackey-samurai bowed again and agreed.

Kuro'emon thought deeply before he said: 'I would like to meet this mendicant and hear the account from his lips. See if you can find him!'

'Now, sir? It grows late and he may have gone to wherever he lives . . .'

'Not now! Go to the temple at the Hour of the Dragon tomorrow morning . . . Make enquiries . . . Thorough ones, you understand!'

By wearing the dress of a wandering mendicant, some men, for their own private reasons, remain invisible to the world. Such komusō were often to be seen playing mournful melodies on their deep-throated shakuhachi with their faces forever hidden. Who could distinguish one from another in those troubled times? The senior lackey could glean nothing from the temple nor down in the small town, although he did accost three such persons whose clothing was varied but not one seemed to be the fellow he was seeking. Returning to the temple, he ventured up the side track past the mud plastered eastern wall, but went no further than the edge of the thick overmantling forest. He had been told than no one lived up there but a poor woodcutter and his aged mother, but during these wet early summer days none of the monks saw this forester and supposed he was far up the mountain slopes preparing wood to sell in the autumn and winter.

At last he returned to report to his master that there was nothing to learn and the matter was dismissed from their minds. The miserable servants who had run from their supposed attackers were lightly punished and that was that. Subsequent supply teams were given an armed escort and nothing untoward happened for a full month.

It was on the evening of the twentieth day of the seventh month after an unusually hot day that the next incident occurred. Clouds had been building up over the high mountains to the west but there was no rain to relieve the cloying late afternoon heat. A group of ashigaru escorting some supplies, in accordance with the clan orders, had passed through the township having left the Torii fort at Onogami that morning. As they climbed up the track towards the Daitoku temple, the main troop of *yari-mochi* riders detached themselves and sped onwards over the crest to descend to the yashiki. They were soon out of sight leaving the rest to follow on. Little did they realize that malevolent eyes were watching them from concealment near that same place where those earlier incidents had occured.

None of the leaders of the escort had been on duty a month earlier so none took the slightest heed of the komusō sitting in the shadows beneath the wide eaves of the temple gateway. It was as they breasted the hilltop that the heavens opened in a freak and violent summer storm heralded by two or three blinding bolts and a deafening crash of thunder over the forested mountainside just above.

The packhorses, frightened by the earsplitting noise, milled about and it was all the ostlers could do to hold them in check. The eight or nine ashigaru hastily ran to shelter against the tile capped temple walls, attempting to cover their weapons from the teeming rain.

It was at this moment that several armed men rushed out from concealment, swords drawn, and threw themselves at the astonished and, it must regrettably be said, totally surprised men. In the space of a few moments a few of the escort were lying dead, some without even drawing their swords in defence, the rest suffering severe wounds. With the lightning flashing and the beating rain hissing down like an arrow storm, the brigands soon held the field with the dead and wounded on all sides at their feet. It was then that the mendicant came to his feet and sauntered towards the leader, a giant of a man who apparently wore an armour over his near-naked body. So far as could be made out in the stormy gloom he had just five or six companions.

'You have done very well, my friend,' said the komusō mildly, his fingers undoing the chin cords of his woven headgear.

'Who the blazes are you?' demanded the bandit chief.

'This incident of yours has taken place on my patch! It displeases me!'

The bandit's jaw dropped open incredulously.

'What did you say? Your "patch"! Who are you?' he blared.

'I carry out my crimes here, small as they are, sir! Now I shall lose my livelihood because of your thoughtless action! This cannot be permitted!'

The thunder crashed again followed by a blinding flash. In the moment of intense darkness that followed the komusō threw off his hat and drew out his longsword that he wore tachi-style slung at his left hip. With his body swaying and moving in a blur, his blade rose and fell, slashed sideways and upwards in terrifying glinting arcs, each cut slicing effortlessly through the crowding bodies of the bandit gang until, in the space of less than five heartbeats only the chieftain remained, backing away with his trenchant naginata held across his chest. A further crackle of lightning lit up the hellish scene but the demonic komusō had disappeared; vanished as if he had never been . . .

One of the maimed bandits, his forearm nearly severed in two so that his useless wrist and hand hung bloodily at his sides, screamed out loud as he staggered towards his leader waving his katana wildly in the air.

'You said we would have no trouble . . .' he yelled.

The chieftain's trenchant blade slashed upwards deeply gashing the wounded man's side.

'Where is he . . ?' roared the brigand.

A peal of laughter made him whirl round.

At that moment the komusō drove his dagger blade into the flank of the nearest packhorse and the galling pain set the creature rearing and plunging straight at the half-naked armoured man. In a trice, the fellow was bowled over under the flailing hooves and it was the work of a moment for the mendicant to secure him with a thin length of rope.

One of the ashigaru had escaped the first attack and ran headlong down the track to raise the alarm at the yashiki. Not ten minutes later, some mounted samurai and footsoldiers reached the scene and stared aghast at the bloody wounded and the corpses of those who had met their deaths. One of the last to arrive was Asari Kuro'emon accompanying his lord, Kōzuke-no-kami Shinzaemon.

'We need torches despite the rain!'

'Torches are being brought, lord,' replied the Ō-metsuke. 'In the meanwhile, my lord, we might shelter under the Outer Gate.'

'You have set guards?'

'All is done, sir!'

'Strange business, isn't it?'

Just then a slight movent to their right caused the Provost to level his naginata and demand who was there. With the storm abating and rolling further off down the valley, the evening skies became brighter, two fearful monks ventured through the puddles of rain-water bearing a couple of flaring spluttering torches which they set in the iron braziers that stood on the lower course of the stone steps. In the flickering light the two warriors saw that they had perhaps disturbed a mendicant priest, or so he seemed.

'What is your name, priest?' demanded the Provost.

'I was once known as Gōsuke, sir,' replied the komusō.

'Did you see what happened out there/'

'I saw it all, sir, insofar as the storm permitted, of course.'

The armoured Provost's brows knitted.

'Were you the man who witnessed the incident around here last month?' he demanded.

Gōsuke bowed but didn't reply.

'Incident?' Kōzuke-no-kami-sama remarked.

The Ō-metsuke bowed and explained what had occured. He then said: 'It seems odd to me that in such a storm you should be here when a second attack took place . . .'

Just then one of the retainers ran across to the gateway and, kneeling, reported what had been found. Most of the small escort had evidently been surprised by the sudden attack and hacked down. They were all dead. The mystery was that all but one of the bandits had also been despatched and that, more strangely, they had each died from a single sword cut.

'A single cut; no other wounds?'

'One or two had been gashed earlier in the struggle, sir, but it was just one heavy cut that sent each to Emma-ō.

'And one man survived, you say?'

'He was trussed up with a long *koshi-no-o*,[9] my lord.'

'I suppose he tied himself up on his own, eh?' Asari Kuro'emon breathed deeply. 'Someone must have secured him?'

The prisoner was marched across and forced to his knees in front of the lord and his Provost.

'You were responsible for this outrage, fellow? You can't deny it!'

The brigand chieftain merely spat saliva insultingly onto the stone steps at their feet.

'Who bound you captive, eh?'

'It was a demon and his henchmen . . .'

'It is odd, but whenever something has happened near this gate, all those involved claim they were attacked by a whole gang of goblins or evilly disposed ghosts! I will ask you just once again, who or what was responsible for your men's deaths and your capture?'

Either the bandit was too ashamed or too mortified that his planned theft had gone so disastrously wrong that he made no answer. The Provost turned to Gōsuke. 'You, sir priest, were here when our servants ran off terrified from their duties early last month and again when the escort had their pack animals taken . . . And you are here again when this far more serious incident occured. Are you attached to this temple? Besides which, I see that you carry a long sword and wear a heavy dirk? You are a former warrior?'

Gōsuke Heibei bowed respectfully.

'I am a rōnin, honoured sirs, caring for my ancient parent in a small hut on the mountainside. Usually I cut wood for those that need it hereabouts but in the summertime I must needs play my flute and trust in the Lord Buddha that passers-by will give me alms. All I have left of my former estate are these two weapons.'

'It is odd, but in those previous incidents all we found missing after the claimed "attacks" by "demons" was two or three *kin* of rice and a handful of root vegetables . . You would know nothing of that, I suppose?'

'I am the guilty party, my lord,' admitted the komusō with another bow.

'But you were – are – a samurai?'

---

[9] *Koshi-no-o*: An armour braid cord.

Kōzuke-no-kami coughed.

'Hearing this, Master Gōsuke,' he said, 'I believe that you took the grain to feed your parent? Is this so?'

The mendicant rōnin bowed deeply once more. 'My respected mother is frail and cannot now walk, my lord. I am guilty of the theft, I admit it.'

'How did these lawless fellows come to die, I wonder? Did you take a hand in that?'

'My lord, if they had carried out their crime and successfully stolen your goods at this place, how would I have been able to live? I would have had to take my mother's life rather than permit her the agony of starving to death and at once followed her spirit to explain such a crime to the Examiners set by Lord Emma-ō. The deaths of these evil men was determined before their birth.'

'Yet you spared their leader?'

'He was needed as testimony for your enquiries.'

The Provost gave orders for his men to clear the highway. A little later he turned to Gōsuke. 'It was reported to me that you are a poet?'

'No, my lord; I am not a poet as such though I have a good memory for things I have read.'

'You recited some syllables to my follower, as I recall: "*The blossoms have fallen. I stare blankly at a world bereft of colour. . .*"' Lord Kōzuke-no-kami laughed. ' "*In the wide vacant sky the spring rains have fallen.*" These were lines composed by the Princess Shikushi more than two-hundred years ago, if I am not mistaken?'

'Living alone in this space between the rocks, far from the city . . .' said Gōsuke Heibei softly.

' "*Here, where no one can see me, I shall give myself to grief.*" Why, these are the words of the Priest Saigyō,' Kōzuke-no-kami tilted his head slightly as he observed the komusō through the fading light. 'Tell me, master rōnin, why you recite such sad verses?'

'It is because I pity my aged parent, my lord.'

'Who did you serve?'

'My lord served the Nagao-ke before he lost his lands and his life.'

Kōzuke-no-kami looked across at Asari Kuro'emon, saying: 'A few grains of rice and some daikan lost hardly constitute a crime, do they?'

'Not really, my lord.'

'You killed those men single-handedly?'

'The gods sent the storm to assist me. It was nothing, really.'

'You have studied the bugei, I take it?'

'I was honoured by Oda Takamitsu, my lord.'

'What was your stipend, Gōsuke-san?'

'One-hundred-and-eighty *koku*, my lord.'

'Hardly enough for so accomplished a man . . . Asari-sama, I feel we have need for an expert of the bugei, do we not?'

Thus it was that Gōsuke Heibei became one of the renowned commanders of the Torii-ke and fought in several wars during the unrest caused by the great conflict of the Ōnin period and its aftermath. According to the annals, this general was awarded three-hundred koku but after his lands were restored together with other rewards his income rose to a thousand koku or more. His son distinguished himself in the defence of the Yazawa fortress during the course of an incursion into the Uesugi domain in the eighth year of *Eishō*[10] at the time of Ashikaga Yoshitane, committing *seppuku* when the castle fell.

---

[10] *Eishō 8*: 1510

16

INOSHISHI

Twelve years had passed since the Taira heroes sank beneath the waves at the sea battle of Dan-no-ura. Twelve years since the Genji bushi and their men had returned to their homes, knowing that victory had been theirs and that Minamoto-no-Yoritomo had been awarded the high office of Shōgun in Kamakura. Momentous events indeed for those whose interests lay in the affairs of state. Profound were the changes to the lives of those who sought power; those who should have paused to reflect on how these matters would affect the lives of the ordinary folk, the people who laboured daily in the fields or who starved in the towns, for war has many faces but the one turned towards the humble rarely smiles.

For six long years in the struggle against the red emblems of the Heishi, Torii-no-Ason Masachika had ridden the paths with the white banners of the Genji. He had at first joined the small band that formed round Minamoto-no-Yoritomo when he had burst out of Izu and from the first fight at Ishibashiyama's twin hummocks, where he had escaped with his life, he had followed the fortunes of that bloody conflict until it seemed to some that there would be none left alive to fight. Ah, what it was like to land from the boats at Shimonoseki and to see reflected in the tide races behind them the carmine hues of the setting sun. What exhaltation! What sadness for those brave men, the flower of the warrior families, who had given up their blood and souls so dearly in those dark waters . . .

Masachika often reflected on the past as he rode slowly through the forests. He had found but little return for all his years, not that he had served with the thought of reward. At one time he had been with the fallen and long-dead Yoshitsune; perhaps that had counted against him when the great lords deliberated on the rewards for those who had given so much to the Minamoto cause? Who can tell?

His lands were decayed; his small yashiki ruinous; his villages attacked and burnt by bandits as they lay unprotected while he was battling on the beach at Yashima or hunting down the last pitiful survivors to escape to Kyūshū after the seas finally carried away the defeated. Only a handful of his peasants remained together who, with a few of the old retainers, most of whom had found their farms overgrown with weeds, the haunt of badgers and foxes, their families dead from famine or the pest, still struggled to wrest a living from their lands. They had been faithful to their lord who had been given this valley by Hachiman-tarō Yoshi-ie, himself.

Six years service and the loss of more than half his men under the tempered blades of the Taira were rewarded with steep mountain-sides clad in dark forest but hardly any additional flat ground that might eventually yield rice. Despite the 'reward' there was no real certainty that the forest did not really belong to the Jūon-ji temple that was hidden away amongst the thick pine trees high in the western peak. Better not to have been given any recompense for he and his followers had no thought of reward when they had given up all in order to answer the call of the Kamakura-dono. That had been their bounden duty, their obligation in return for countless past favours received long ago . . .

Masachika lifted his head and looked around. He had been lost in his thoughts and that was dangerous. All he saw was the yellow sunlight filtering through the heavy forest and reflecting in a myriad of glittering points from the water pools and the wet leaves of the underbrush . . . It was four years since they had hunted down and executed the last of the brigands who had come down like carrion birds of prey from the rocky fastnesses nearby. What was there for a brave bushi to fear?

Some yards behind rode his faithful follower, Chubei Tarōemon, and on foot two soldiers who acted as servants whenever their master hunted.

There was nothing to cause any apprehension at all.

Chubei gave a shout.

From out of the brush behind Masachika to the right shot a wild sow followed closely by two quite large young. Squealing shrilly, they stopped on the track in the space between the master and his men but before anyone could move the sow wheeled left and all three crashed up the northern slope and were gone.

No time even for a snap bowshot! Too dangerous; any shaft if it missed, would have been directly at one or other of the men.

'Chubei, go left!' shouted Masachika, as he swung out of the saddle.

Holding tight to the striped reincloths, he watched all three men vanish into the fringing bamboo down the trail before he, too, forced his way into the trees. It was not the sow or her offspring he wanted, but the boar that would surely be near. For two hours they harried the inoshishi along the mountainside, sometimes all four men together, sometimes strung out amongst the jumbled rocks, but it was all to no avail.

Somehow they had lost their quarry and the chance to match themselves against the great boar that the warrior knew lived in these woods. Disconsolate, they retraced their steps to find the two horses left foraging on the trail far below.

From afar came the tolling of the temple bell, the sound echoing sonorously around the slopes.

'The bronze must be flawed,' thought Masachika as he listened. 'I never really noticed before . . .'

'Master,' said Chubei; 'that bell makes the Jūon-ji sound a long way off . . . Those monks are not pulling at the log rope very hard.'

'Strange, isn't it? Probably a trick of the wind.'

'Huh, the pigs went this way.'

The temple was forgotten as his retainer pointed to some fresh droppings and the scuff marks of at least two animals descending a soft patch of ground.

Masachika slid an arrow from his quiver with his right hand, just as a precaution, and motioned one of his men forwards to clear away some of the dense young bamboo with his naginata.

The pitch they were descending dipped away and the hunters were obliged to cross the steep slope to their right and they eventually came out onto a fairly level terrace that seemed to be about the height of the tree tops in the bottom of the narrow valley.

They crossed the easier ground and picked up an ill-defined game path.

'This must be the way down,' said Chubei.

'You know, we have hunted this area all these years yet I don't recollect this place.'

'It's where Old Gōrō does his work, I reckon, master.'

'The woodcutter?'

Chubei was probably right. Here and there in the grass lay small strips of old tree bark.

The bell had ceased its mournful tolling; the monks must be at prayer. A quietness fell over the forest broken only by the faint mewing of the red hawks circling high above the canopy as they, too, hunted for their prey.

Without warning, the black boar shot out of a thick cane brake almost at the side of the unfortunate retainer, its sharp tusks raked up and sideways, ripping through the fellow's baggy trousers and across his belly. With a scream of pain he reeled away, throwing his halberd down and clutching at the wound. Even before he fell to the ground the blood was pouring through his fingers. The inoshishi pivoted and dashed at Chubei who dragged at his horse's reins and his beast just managed to shy away leaving the samurai half out of his saddle clinging to its neck.

Masachika saw the danger as the boar burst on them but the action was so fast he had no time to nock his arrow before the great beast reached his own mount and slashed upwards at its soft belly. In terror, the poor animal reared but snagged a hindleg and fell heavily on its side. The fourth man was some distance behind with two spare bows and arrow quivers, too far to do anything useful.

The wild boar spun round, snorting. If it had been a human commander it would have been well satisfied by the results of its ambuscade, so total had been the effect that it had reduced the odds by a quarter and thrown the enemy into complete disarray. With a shrill squeal, hair standing stiffly upright all down its back, tail erect, the animal charged Masachika again, swerving around the thrashing legs of the stricken horse. Half-winded by the fall, the bushi flung himself desperately to the side and the wicked tusks just missed their victim . . . His right hand found the hilt of his long tantō and as the boar whirled again to renew his assault he was half up to his knees. Seeing the fresh danger he hurled himself to the left but this time the deadly tusks raked his flying right leg, ripping his hunting trousers to shreds. He slashed backwards as he fell and heard the boar grunt as it crashed off into the long grass and vanish . . .

'Master . . ? Are you alright?'

It was Chubei who had dismounted from his frightened horse and came bounding down to Torii Masachika. He found the warrior trying to rise with blood pouring from a gaping wound in his thigh.

'That was close!' muttered the bushi who had fought all through the Gempei Wars and taken only three arrow wounds of any severity in those six turbulent years. Close it certainly was, for the white bone had showed for a moment before the welling blood covered it and flooded out.

'Quick, lord: let me secure my *hachimaki* round the leg . . .'

'Chubei, watch closely . . . that boar will return!'

The deft fingers of his kerai looped the narrow cloth round his master's leg and pulled it tight. Almost immediately the flow of blood eased.

'The wound is deep, my lord; it should be sewn.'

'Then do it, Chubei-san. The hunt must continue . . .'

As he prepared some thread and a needle from his wallet, Chubei glanced at the horse and shook his head.

'Your mount is dying, my lord, and Saburō is dead.'

Masachika grimaced as the needle pierced his thigh, but he said nothing until the junior kerai came running up with the spare bows and knelt down

'Find my sword,' ordered Masachika; 'it fell from my scabbard when the horse was gored.'

'Yes, master!'

He watched the man unloop the cord holding the arrows and place them down beside the bows, then he warily circled the thrashing legs of the doomed horse and started looking in the long grass . . . The warrior would concentrate on anything to take his mind off the excruciating pain of Chubei's stout needle . . .

'It's done, master! That's the best I can do until we return to the yashiki.'

Masachika looked ruefully at the long wound and retied the hachimaki, adding a second since the gash still oozed plenty of blood.

'Chubei-san, I'm certain that I cut that inoshishi with my dagger.'

'Master?'

'It was just after he struck me.'

'If he is bleeding I can track him!'

'Dangerous! Too dangerous!'

'My lord?'

'I will kill him myself.'

'But, master; your leg is badly gashed. It will stiffen up . . . you cannot walk!'

The bushi grimaced.

'A warrior cannot give up just because he has a slight cut! I can ride and use my bow!'

It was no use remonstrating; Chubei recalled an incident before the battle of Yashima fourteen years before when, pierced by three arrows and with several more lodged broken in his armour, Torii Masachika had fought with and overcome two Tosa bushi and taken their heads . . . He knew very well that Masachika-dono was determined enough to succeed.

Chubei helped his master to stand and steadied him for a moment or two before getting him onto the remaining pony. He felt a sense of pride that it was his nag that would be of service. The right leg of his lord's *sashinuki-bakama* was soaked in blood but there were no witnesses to be shocked or horrified by the sight. Meanwhile, the junior *kerai* put the injured horse out of its misery by slitting its throat. They started out to follow the boar's trail, easily picked up by the crushed leaves and occasional smears of blood, crossing the main track and soon climbing the opposite slopes in the direction of Sickle Mountain. Eventually Chubei had to admit that despite being an expert tracker he had lost all signs of their wounded quarry.

Masachika, probably weakened by the sudden loss of blood, sat with rounded shoulders whilst his retainer cast about in the hope of picking up more positive signs, but he kept his concentration just in case. He may in theory be the lord of these forests but the great boar was the undoubted ruler. Thus far, the inoshishi had proved the stronger and the more cunning . . .

Chubei returned elated.

'Lord, I think we have found more signs. Shall we go on?'

'Of course!'

By now his blood-soaked trousers had stiffened but at least he knew that Chubei's stitching and crude bandaging had been effective and the gash no longer freely bled. Briefly they descended but were soon climbing again. The boar had chosen a twisting course but somehow it seemed determined to gain height on the rugged shoulders of Kama-san.

'The temple is not far from where we stand, is it not?'

Chubei looked up at his master as he led the pony.

'This is the direct way, straight over Kama-san. The pilgrim path is only just down there,' he pointed down to where they could just see the tops of some mighty cryptomeria trees, 'but few people would use this route, my lord. They would prefer the main track and flights of steps up from the valley.'

At length, they came into a small clearing where much of the underbrush had been cut, passing five neatly stacked piles of staves. Beyond these were some longer lengths of felled and trimmed saplings supported on the steep slope by restraining stakes driven down deep into the forest mould. Something caught Masachika's eye from his vantage point in the saddle.

'Tōroku,' he said to the remaining kerai with the halberd, 'take a look just beyond that woodstack up there . . . I can see something . . ?'

The fellow used the butt of his naginata to help him up the mountainside, his orange printed trousers making a splash of colour as he crossed a patch of sunshine. Chubei continued across the hillside leading the horse but hadn't taken more than a dozen steps when Tōroku turned.

'Master; it's a dead man . . . the old woodcutter!'

Masachika frowned. 'Was this the boar's work,' he wondered?

'Lord, it's old Gorō. He's been killed!'

'By the inoshishi?'

'I only glanced at his body, master, but it's possible.'

Chubei brought the horse's head round and they coaxed the reluctant animal up the needle covered slope. The corpse was indeed that of the woodsman. Masachika didn't dismount but stared down at the pitiful body in sorrow. Gorō had served his family faithfully for more than sixty years . . . now he lay dead covered in blood from a number of savage wounds. How sad to die beneath the tusks of a maddened and vengeful beast when all his long life he had been a friend of the wild secret places and everything that lived there.

For some reason he paused before telling his retainer to continue with their search.

'Chubei-san, there's something wrong here. Please turn Gorō over.'

The kerai frowned, giving the corpse a hard look. He signed to Tōroku to use the end of his naginata shaft to lever over the limp body where it flopped grotesquely against the stacked logs.

Chubei grunted and leant over the wood. The old man's face had almost been torn away; all but one side was ripped loose, eyeball and all, and hung tattered around the lips and nose. His jaw, too, was forced out of its socket. Somehow, whatever had attacked the defenceless old peasant had clawed a huge gaping gash into his upper left arm and right across his chest, carrying away the thin threadbare kimono and breaking out three ribs . . .

'Such wounds all over his body, front and back; these are not the work of a wild boar,' observed Masachika.

'More like a malignant spirit!' growled Chubei.

'Look at those gashes in his arm; they are far too clean edged for any tusks!'

'You know, master, I saw some of the bodies dragged from the waves at Dan-no-ura. They were Taira men who had been clawed from behind their protecting shields by the *kumade* rakes. They were ripped rather like these, only . . .'

'Only what?' said Masachika, absently. He was still gazing down at the dreadful remains.

'Only these are much worse, lord!'

'You are saying that far more force was used?'

'That's right, master,' said Chubei with a shudder.

'So you are of the opinion that this was not the work of our enemy, the boar?'

'No, lord; it was something much more terrible!'

Masachika sighed as he looked about him.

'We have to kill the boar. Perhaps it will change into a demon.'

Tōroku stared about him fearfully at the mention of a 'demon'. While he was brave in battle, now he was fast becoming fearful of his own shadow!

Once again the Jūon-ji bell sang out its doleful sound that echoed through the deep valleys, disturbing a cloud of birds who rose from the trees with a clatter of wings.

'Master, we are close to the temple.'

As if to confirm what Chubei said, they slid down through the underbrush to a broad track sending a veritable landslide of small stones bouncing down to the steep path. There were deep scuffs in the banking and some dark spots of blood. Chubei touched one with his finger and found that it hadn't yet congealed. The boar was only just ahead of its pursuers.

'The beast is headed up the track, my lord,' announced the retainer after some consideration.

They turned and quite soon caught sight of the sweeping corner of a thatched roof high above. So far there was no sign that their quarry had veered off into the forest. The struggle of the pony to mount these steep pitches of track made Masachika's injury ache abominably.

At last he requested Chubei to help him dismount.

'Is that wise, my lord?'

'My leg needs the exercise, Chubei-san. If I sit here much longer it may stiffen and fail me when I need to move quickly, besides this animal threatens me with worse injuries. Your horse would never make the next pitch and that flight of steps up there with me in the saddle, I'll have to walk.'

'Careful, master!' cautioned his retainer as he saw a grimace cross his lord's face. 'Perhaps the boar will have left the path before that, master?'

Masachika smiled wryly.

'You know, I suspect it will have gone all the way to the temple. I cannot say why, but I just think this will be the case!'

Chubei was concerned for his lord.

'Nevertheless . . . Tōroku-san, keep a sharp watch on your side; and your ears open!'

'Master!'

The Jūon-ji made no claim to be a famous temple and although it did belong to the Shingon-shu, it hadn't been constructed or embellished by the ubiquitous Kōbō Daishi and so becoming one of those establishments that enjoyed the traditional visits of white-clad pilgrims. In fact, the merest handful of people travelled especially to pray in its precincts and make offerings for its upkeep. It was the home of a tiny number of elderly monks and the occasional itinerant yamabushi who spent their time in prayer. Its income was derived, some thought, from the piety of a minor noble family in the distant capital, an income now sharply declining following the ferocious destruction and hunting down of the Heike. The result was that the once beautiful and harmonious buildings carried a sad air of advancing decay, although the monks, just managing to keep body and soul together, doubtless felt themselves fortunate that the very remoteness of their temple separated it from the vicissitudes of political upheaval.

After a final struggle up the irregular stone steps leading to the partially ruined gateway, Torii Masachika had to take a rest, his strength sapped by the deep wound. He leant briefly against one of the heavy black uprights while Chubei led the horse through to the paved court beyond; Tōroku stood near his lord with his stained halberd under his arm.

Once Masachika had realized that the wounded animal was making for the temple, a gnawing suspicion had insinuated itself into the back of his mind that there was something odd about all this. Who or what had so savagely killed the old man, and how was it that they had never before been troubled by such a ferocious boar which must surely have lived long years in these mountains to have attained that size? Possibly Chubei had a point when he lightly said it was a demon masquerading in the guise of a wild inoshishi? Such things were possible, he supposed, and they were all familiar with stories of ghostly terrors where foxes or cats possessed human beings.

Beyond the Inner Gate the great bronze bell tolled once more, the sound waves making the heavy upright against which he leant tremble with the reverberations. It rang out again, but not so strongly . . . and again . . . Odd, that . . ? The beats were hardly as regular as one would normally expect from the pious efforts of pilgrims anxious for the Buddha or his Bodhisattvas to note their humble messages . . . but that thought was pushed from his mind when they all heard the sharp squeal and grunting of wild pigs.

'Bar the gate, Chubei-san! If our enemy is within, he shall not escape this time!'

The two kerai strained at the iron-bound black doors and with protesting shrieks they slowly closed. The thick wooden beam that barred their opening was dropped into place and it was done. Masachika reached behind him and drew from his quiver one of the long signal arrows with its tempered forked blade and swelling striped neck. He carefully fitted it to his bowstring and in a line abreast the three men walked slowly across the centre of the outer court. They left their horse loose by the gateway behind them.

The Inner Gate stood at the top of another flight of wide stone steps. It had lost one of its doors and the other hung crazily by only one of the great iron hinge pins. Many of the once handsome rows of blue glazed tiles that roofed the outer eaves beneath the main thatch lay broken on the flagstones, dislodged by the tearing violence of countless storms. Just as they mounted the last steps to cross the threshold another tile fell and smashed into a hundred pieces at Masachika's feet . . .

It was then that the sow dashed at them from the shadows, eyes glinting evilly . . .

Tōroku swung his long naginata blade but missed his stroke for the inoshishi was too nimble. She darted with a mighty snort directly at Masachika . . . He had already drawn back his powerful Kantō bow and loosed the whistling shaft to sink the forked head deep into the sow's thick neck. In mid-stride she stumbled and veered to one side, tumbling down the stone steps and to finish lifeless at their foot.

Scarcely had he nocked a second arrow and turned towards the gate when came a terrible screaming from the compound beyond. Chubei, who was nearest, ran forward with his bow. He stopped in surprise at the far side of the tilted door, then in haste jumped back into the shade. Something black half-appeared and seemed to totter before crumpling to the ground. Even Masachika, war-hardened as he was, felt the hair at the nape of his neck begin to prickle, but as he stepped forward Chubei held up a warning hand. An indescribable sound, low at first, like the murmur of a distant cascade but gradually rising until it rent the air with howls of torment, filled the sun-drenched precincts . . . and ceased in an instant as though it never was . . . except for the jagged memory lingering in the listeners' minds and the echoes thrown back from the distant crags.

'Fudō-sama, protect us,' breathed the warrior; 'what was that . . ?'

All three men had witnessed many an appalling atrocity during the Gempei fighting; children whose brains had been battered out, women ripped open and their unborn infants beheaded in their gaping wombs, men savagely blinded and maimed; but none of these prepared them for the welcome they were to receive in the serene enclosure that lay through that ravaged gateway . . .

'*DOOONNNGGGGG-G-G – G - G!*'

Under its small thatched roof the huge bronze bell rang out as if in warning and the sound seemed to draw their eyes towards the belfry as they stepped over the thick baulk of blackened timber into the blinding sunshine reflecting from the white lime-washed walls. A heavy black bundle appeared to dangle beside the bell, but immediately they were aware of other shapeless heaps scattered around the yard. Disturbed by their arrival a thick cloud of flies swarmed up into the heavy air with a sawing drone.

'*DONNNGGGG –g – g –g –g!*'

Tōroku pushed at the fallen monk in the gateway. His body flopped loosely over. Where the face had been was just a bleeding mess of flesh and exposed bone coated on one side by the greyish-brown dust. A beetle was feebly waving its legs to free itself from the bloody ooze. The man was not quite dead. Nearby, another old priest lay propped unnaturally against the crumbling plaster side wall but when Chubei plucked at his torn sleeve the forearm fell out, jaggedly severed below the elbow . . . The corpse slipped sideways . . . Where the throat had been was just a gaping hole edged by wrinkled skin.

Again there came the half-hearted tolling . . .

The warriors moved carefully out across the open space that was spattered with blood as though emptied from carelessly thrown buckets . . . None of the samurai really wished to find out the nature of that dark bundle that swayed beneath the horizontal log; they were compelled to look by some horrible curiosity that they were unable to resist. In the shade beneath that heavy flaring roof they saw two monks hanging heads downward, lashed together at their waists. In the light breeze that swirled eddies of dust across the open yard, they swung against the log so that the iron-strapped end struck the inside of the bell to give it voice. The platform beneath the patterned bronze was dark and ominous rivulets streamed down the steps and soaked into the gaps between the paving stones . . . It was almost in disbelief that Masachika realized that all the limbs were missing from these two poor men.

Chubei found his voice.

'This has to be the work of bandits or a malevolent ghost, lord,' he croaked.

'More like a madman . . . whoever or whatever dismembered these men was no trained butcher. Look, my friend; their limbs have been torn away . . .'

'My lord, I once witnessed some peasants catch an ashigaru who had violated two of their womenfolk,' said Chubei. 'They tied him between two strong oxen by his arms and legs . . . When one of his legs came off I was amazed to see how long his entrails were . . .'

'Careful, Chubei; this blood is quite fresh. In this heat it would thicken in a few minutes, you know.'

'You mean, lord, that the bandits are still here?'

'If it was bandits . . .'

Masachika raised his bow high and pulled back the hempen string. He had changed the shaft for the second of his turnip-headed signal arrows.

'We shall see what happens. I'm told that evil spirits don't take kindly to this noise!'

He paused a moment before releasing the string. The powerful bow sprang forwards and with a shrill whistle the long arrow flashed across the azure sky and buried itself in the middle of the carved wooden ridge beam of the Lecture Hall on the further side of the yard. The silence that followed was made all the more intense by the bizarre massacre and the brief shrill of the arrowhead . . .

It was just a second or two before the warrior was answered by that awful welling howl that they had heard as they came to the inner gateway.

Masachika knitted his brows, unsure of just where the unearthly sound came. He looked at Chubei but he, too, was perplexed. The howl seemed to come from all three sides of the yard at once. Only Tōroku was more positive. He pointed with his halberd at the inner gateway and started off at a run in that direction.

'Careful, Tōroku-san,' shouted Chubei, 'the boar . . .'

But the servant had already dragged open the sliding door that gave access to the steep stair ladder.

'It came from up here,' they heard him call.

More slowly, master and retainer reached the building and peered up into the dark shadows where Tōroku was clambering to the chamber high above. They could hear the bang and clatter of his naginata against the boarding and thick timbers. He uttered a oath when he found the upper door firmly closed but, managing to reverse his halberd, he braced himself back against the roof sills and began smashing with the metal ferrule to break the woodwork asunder.

'The devils of Hell!' muttered Chubei as a large splinter just missed his upturned face.

A veritable shower followed but at last Tōroku succeeded in forcing a hole large enough for him to peer through.

'Can't see anything, master,' he called down. 'I'll get through in a moment!'

The naginata pounded again and there was a rending sound followed by the servant's growl of satisfaction.

Once more Chubei warned him to take care but they saw him go headfirst through into the darkness. He clearly hadn't heard.

Masachika looked about him.

'I'm not at all convinced that sound came from here; it seemed more like from the nearer side of the Lecture Hall.'

'Master, I thought for a moment as if it came from the hall but at the same time it struck me that it might be as Tōroku said.'

The servant reappeared above.

'There's nothing that I can see, my lord,' he shouted down. 'The place has been shut up for a long time. It just stinks of bat droppings.' He sounded quite crestfallen.

'Come on down,' rasped Chubei. 'Our master wants to look in the main hall across there.'

As Tōroku's legs came into view, they turned to pick their way gingerly across that grim place of death, waiting a moment for him to join them.

'There has to be a reasonable explanation for this carnage,' remarked Masachika, almost to himself.

Chubei grunted.

'We've seen no one alive; even the monk without a face is dead now!'

'That's exactly what I mean, Chubei-san.'

They mounted the broad wooden steps and crossed to the delapidated sliding doors. For a moment they paused and looked back over the awful scene. It was still difficult to take in the full horror. A creak from the heavy *shōji* spun all three round, ready to meet any danger; but it was only a benign old monk who bid them enter with a deep bow.

'What has happened here, priest?' demanded Chubei.

'Happened here, lord samurai?' The monk seemed surprised at the question. 'What should have happened?'

Torii Masachika's wound compelled him to sit down, but not wishing to show his weakness he requested that the others sit as well.

'We have just seen terrible things in the compound . . . Who committed these crimes? Are they still here ?'

The monk's forehead seemed to wrinkle all the more, the ancient seams picked out by the strong daylight that streamed in through the open shōji. He appeared to be listening to the bushi.

'Excuse me, lord samurai, but I have lived here for many long years and I know nothing of any . . . er . . . unpleasantness in this temple.'

Seeing that the hunters did not believe him the monk bowed his shaven head to the floor.

'Forgive me, masters; doubtless you will think me an idiot dotard in denying what you have stated to be the truth. Of course you must have witnessed something as your honours would not have asked me those questions . . . That is true enough . . . Deign to accompany me to my master, the Honourable Abbot, and I am certain that he will be able to reassure you better than my miserable self.'

Masachika and Chubei exchanged glances. Both men came to their feet and drew out their long swords in readiness.

'Oh, my masters; this is a house of peace and tranquillity. In our serene life we have no place for the weapons of strife.' The monk was quite concerned. His manner and reaction to the warriors' warlike caution seemed so normal and sincere that for a moment even Masachika felt unsure.

'Guide us to the Abbot, priest,' he growled. 'I intend to get to the truth of all this! Be warned!'

The old monk shuffled to the half-open outer shōji and tried to open it as a courtesy to the warriors. It was far too heavy and had jammed fast. With apologies, he stood aside to let them go first but Tōroku brusquely caught him by the arm and ordered him to step out before them.

The wide courtyard lay bathed in the brilliant sunshine and was completely devoid of any sign of the massacre whose memory defied description . . . In disbelief the samurai stood at the balustrade and stared about them. It was true that the buildings were still delapidated and decayed; true, also, that some of the dislodged blue tiles lay shattered below the gateway on the stony ground. They looked sharply at the bell log where the two dismembered corpses had so shockingly hung lashed together, but they were nowhere to be seen. Instead a white-robed pilgrim was tugging at the thick braided cable as he prepared to haul the log back to sound out his supplication to the Buddha . . . How was it possible that all could look so normal . . ?

'My son, I can quite understand your deep concerns,' said the Abbot sibilantly. He was a large-framed man with a mature, even hard, lined face, who sat formally on a threadbare brocade cushion. 'But as you have seen, there is nothing here that could possibly give rise to your fears . . . abosolutely nothing at all.'

Masachika still couldn't grasp what had happened and explained to the prelate what they had experienced during the morning's hunt. His wound was real enough and his torn, blood-soaked sashinuki-bakama were proof that the great boar did indeed exist. In addition, he and his men had seen with their own eyes the awful corpses scattered around the temple precincts.

'I agree, my lord Torii, that there must be an explanation. Such things are oftimes the work of evil spirits, of foxes and badgers, designed to lead mankind into madness. It is clear that it is my bounden duty to help you recover from this possession.'

'Possession? You think that we are under a spell laid by some malicious spirit?' Masachika barked. He never had much time for patronizing monks or priests and his experiences over the years gave him many grounds for distrust.

Chubei, like his master, was suspicious of most in holy orders, considering them humbugs. His only exceptions were certain yamabushi he knew who sought special powers in the remoteness of the high mountains and who could demonstrate deep skill in the arts of healing both minds and bodies. His position as a simple warrior allowed him a certain coarseness of action that was, in truth, denied to his lord. He jumped to his feet with an oath, raised his rattan bound bow to full height above him, pulled the empty bowstring back to full stretch, and loosed it with a loud twang.

'If there are any lurking demons here that sound will drive them off!' he shouted. 'Master, this monk does not believe you. Maybe he will change his mind when he sees the dead sow killed by your signal arrow!'

He ran down the outer steps and across the yard to the gateway. Inside the Lecture Hall the monk and the two warriors sat motionless. They all heard Chubei's sudden exclamation uttered almost as he disappeared from sight. Tōroku came to his feet, his naginata firmly grasped in both fists.

'Sit down!' ordered Masachika. 'Sit and await Chubei's return!'

Reluctantly, his faithful kerai sank back to the half-kneeling position favoured by fighting men.

Chubei reappeared and trotted to the foot of the verandah.

'That damned inoshishi has gone . . . and so has your arrow, my lord,' he called up.

Torii Masachika sat quietly, turning matters over in his mind. He shrugged his shoulders and looked searchingly at the Abbot.

'You are quite right, my lord; we should pray to the Buddha,' he said, carefully. 'Chubei-san, please come up here; you must pray as well.'

'Tchah!'

Mildly, Masachika remonstrated with his chief kerai.

'No, the Lord Abbot is quite correct in what he has said. I cannot understand what has happened and all that is left is to offer our supplications to the Kwannon or the Lord Buddha that we shall be delivered.'

'Honourable master, prayers will do no good!'

'Nevertheless, Chubei-san, it is my wish to follow the sage recommendation of the Reverend Abbot.'

The hardy retainer didn't argue further but mounted the steps and knelt down just within the outer shōji. It was enough to satisfy Masachika who turned to face the Abbot and bowed once more. The prelate sat impassive throughout this outburst but all of them could see the occasional glint of his narrowed eyes as they flickered from one man to the other. The old priest who had brought them to his master moved forwards to seat himself beside the hanging bronze gong. The prelate turned to the altar and began to intone what sounded like the Heart Sutra.

Very slowly at first, almost in a murmur the short prayer came out but gradually the warrior was aware that the words were being repeated again and again . . . and there was something else, too.

A suspicion formed in his mind that he had heard this tone somewhere before . . . In any case, why the Heart Sutra? Although the Shingon sect employed this powerful formula in their rituals, it was primarily an invocation to Lord Fudō-myō-ō for *his* protection; the more usual form would be the Lotus Sutra, surely?

He stared at the black-robed priests as they sat clicking their rosaries, his mind very far from being purged of the disturbing 'possession'. Slowly, he turned his head to look across to Chubei who was kneeling staring impassively at the altar. Out of the corner of his eye he somehow seemed to sense that the monk on the right no longer had the thin stooped shoulders of advanced years but was altogether broader, his black robes inexplicably roughened . . .

Concentrating hard, he saw that he was mistaken. It was just a slightly shrunken old man who had raised his short baton to strike the gong. Whatever it was, the illusion, a trick of the light, left him with an uncomfortable feeling of unease.

A third monk silently joined them, first bowing his shaven head right down to the glistening floorboards before adding to the blurred cadences of the chanted formula. Odd how from where Masachika sat, the crouching priest, sharply silhouetted against the brilliant daylight beyond the balustrade, also appeared to have a certain roughness around the curve of his shoulders. It must be the *kesa* hood resting across his back? The chanting welled up in strength, its tempo increasing . . .

The meaningless words of unintelligible Sanskrit were all about them, cloying waves that wrapped and twisted themselves into their heads, stifling all other thoughts . . . Masachika struggled to recall that he had once heard this invocation employed by some wandering mendicants at a village in Shikoku thought infested with fox spirits . . . That had a strange effect on the toughened warriors in his party. Afterwards, not one man had been able to give a coherent account of what they had all witnessed that day . . . There was something menacing in that slowly rising tone . . .

That was it! He knew . . !

He fought against himself to throw off the lethargy that appeared to drain his very being, rising painfully to his feet, his right hand firmly grasping the hilt of his *tachi*. As he stepped forwards to his right the forged blade leapt out like a bright ribbon of light and slashed into the side of the monk at the gong, biting with dreadful ease under his left arm and passing upwards to his right neck before curving back to strike into the falling body a second time even as it began to topple sideways in a spray of dark blood. As if the passage of time had slowed he was aware that Chubei was moving, too, and that the newly arrived monk was glancing up and beginning to come to his feet, a sort of laugh curling at the corners of his mouth. His retainer twisted and sprang into the air, in that instant his sword smoothly swept sideways, at first slowly, then like the wind . . . and the monk's grinning head flew from his bristly shoulders . . .

No, surely that could not be . . ?

Masachika turned to his left as if in a trance, shouting hoarsely to Tōroku to thrust the Abbot through with his halberd; the moment he uttered the order he knew within himself that the priest would vanish into thin air. Like a thunderbolt the servant hurled himself forwards raking the upturned blade at the brocaded cushion . . . but he sprawled heavily to the boards when no body was there. The cushion spun up into the air . . . and fell amongst the candles beside the altar.

A roar of fury filled the hall. Masachika grasped Tōroku's collar and yelled with all his strength: 'Out! Back to the Gateway!'

With dripping blades, Chubei and he dragged Tōroku upright and all three ran from the hall and leapt down the four wide steps. As they did so a gush of flame leapt up from behind the seated Buddha statue, licking hungrily at the dry wormed panelling. They dashed across the uneven precinct while even before their eyes the patches and smears of blood appeared to reform. Masachika paused inside the Gateway, one foot on the thick ground sill.

'Tōroku, hand me your naginata! I left my bow back there! Now get down to the Outer Gate . . . both of you!'

Somehow he knew what was about to happen.

The fire had secured its grip on the ancient structure at an uncanny speed. In the few seconds that it had taken them to cross the open court thick smoke and some hungry tongues of orange flame were gushing from under the heavy eaves. There, on the bloody paving lay the massacred monks just as they had first seen them.

Out of the stricken hall trotted the Abbot and in the heat raised by the fire storm all around his billowing robes he seemed to be without true shape, lacking in real substance. He glared across at the bushi, his mouth opening as if to shout; Masachika realized that he didn't face an angry monk at all but an enormous wild boar which launched itself down to the flagstones and with the stiff gait of its kind, hurled itself at its enemy who stood waiting with the long-bladed naginata held upright at arm's length.

A sudden violent squall of wind drove a thick pall of smoke curling across the open space but like an avenging demon the inoshishi surged at Masachika with a bluish halo of flames clinging to its bristly hide. The warrior dropped to one knee, setting the iron butt firmly against the sill. He could clearly see the boar's maddened eyes, the wicked turned-up tusks, the bloody scored wound made by his dirk . . . the heavy head lowered in preparation for the final deadly ripping rake . . . The furious beast met the swept blade head on and Masachika flung himself to the broken floor as the huge body tore on, driving right down the length of the striped haft. The deadly tusks barely missed his injured leg though one of the forelegs hammered into his thigh with a blow that sent waves of blinding pain through his entire being . . . As he desperately twisted aside to avoid the storming onslaught his dirk's keen point entered the boar's chest just beneath its breastbone and slid effortlessly along its belly . . . Out spilled the stricken animal's guts and a thick flood from the ruptured spleen. The boar somersaulted over the massive sill and with the naginata impaled down its full length vanished from Masachika's sight.

With his wounded leg throbbing and bleeding, Torii Masachika clawed at the ancient timbers and managed to drag himself to his feet. He painfully stepped across the sill and, supported by his drawn sword, gazed searchingly down the steep flight of steps. Only the halberd lay lodged against a boulder. Behind him, the Prayer Hall was a mass of flames, fiery from top to bottom . . . The bronze bell clanged out once . . . twice . . . and again . . . Leaving a bloody footprint with each right step he began the descent but his two retainers ran up to his aid.

'Tōroku-san! Pick up your naginata!'

The two men managed to patch up their master's leg and get him up into the saddle when they at length reached the pathway at the foot of the outer steps. Without a backwards look at the conflagration consuming the Jūon-ji they coaxed the hardy animal to move and slowly retraced their way down the winding mountain track towards the distant yashiki.

There was not the slightest trace of the inoshishi . . .

During that painful descent Masachika contemplated what had transpired that fateful day. With a shake of his head he composed some lines that remained buried in the Torii archives. More than three hundred troubled years later they were read by his descendant, the warrior-turned-monk, the scholarly Enshin, who had often wondered about those overgrown deserted ruins high on the flanks of Kama-san. The poem read:

A soft spring day.
Woodsmoke spirals
over the tranquil
forested heights.
How sad am I
Not to understand

17

DESTRUCTION

Matabei took a deep breath and wiped his perspiring brow on a *tenugui* cloth tied about his left wrist. He carefully coiled up his plumbline and placed it safely on the wide tie beam that he straddled. He was a good carpenter, generally regarded in the whole locality as a true master; in consequence he was rarely without work. Such was his skill that two temples and this important Hachiman shrine, where he busied himself at the moment, took up most of his days. Only the previous year he had overseen a gang of ten men to construct an extra gatetower to add further strength to his lord's new border *shirō*. For this and other meritorious services to the clan he had received a number of kind gifts from Lord Kikkawa Takamasa for which he was deeply grateful.

On this day in the early autumn, he was measuring up and inspecting some old joinery that he believed was put into this corner of the upper shrine roof by none other than his own great-grandfather, possibly seventy or more years before. The Hiru-zan Hachiman jinja had been constructed high up on the flanks of Hiru-zan before the Gempei War and at one time had enjoyed the generous patronage of an important courtier family in Miyakō, but latterly the revenues donated by those estates had more than halved due in part to the terrible upheavals rumoured in the capital and the costs of repairs had to be raised from the farming communities and the Kikkawa lords, themselves . . .

Matabei was reasonably content with his lot. He didn't bother his head about where the revenues came from to make sure of his timber needs; they may be intermittent but then, he could make do with the selection and re-use of old materials that lay sorted and carefully stored beneath the raised floors of the shrine. The last major repairs had been carried out well before his long apprenticeship and overseen by his father. That was as long ago as the thirtieth year of the *O-ei* period,[11] wasn't it?

He reached forward to pick at a couple of the soffits where the complex layering of the outshot timbers distributed the full weight of the upswept corner of the roof. The thickness of the roof itself was upwards of a full *shaku* and that meant that a great deal of strength was required to distribute and reduce the outward stresses in order to bring them back onto the main support structure. It was a complicated system but it successfully resisted the worst weather and the passage of time. Looking closely he knew that he was right . . . two of the short bridged members were decayed. Over many years there must have been a tiny flaw in the roofing that allowed the rainwater to seep in, possibly only once or twice a year when an adverse wind blew, but enough to cause this problem where the air couldn't circulate and dry out the resulting damp. A sure sign was this thin layer of moss and a line of tiny orange fungus.

What should be done, eh? Matabei straightened his aching back. His fifty years was beginning to tell, he supposed. As he did so a cloud covered the sun and the ensuing gloom prevented further examination for the time being. He eased his position, taking a pull at his water skin that was carefully protected by a fine woven sling . . . His gaze strayed idly across the mountainside below. This corner of the corballed roof flared out from the southern side so that his position, if he cared to consider it, was more than fifty or sixty feet above the falling ground. A sizeable drop, putting it mildly.

Down to his left he had a clear view of the central courtyard that fronted the *shinden* which, just a few minutes ago, had been a brilliant vermillion. He heard a regular drumming from the Hall of Ceremony which lay just out of his view further round and frowned as he saw the figure of a yamabushi run into view and scurry towards the entrance to his building immediately below. Nothing really odd about that though most people never scampered as fast as that in such precincts. A few moments later the heavy shōji below slammed

---

[11] *O-ei* 30: 1424.

shut and there came the sound of someone clambering up the steep wooden staircase leading to the upper floor. A second sliding door was opened and then firmly closed. Whoever had come up seemed to be familiar with the layout and had entered the narrow walkway corridor that allowed access to the roof – all in almost complete darkness. Matabei speculated that this was the mountain priest who had attached himself to the shrine.

A distant movement caught his eye far down in the ancient forest where the old path climbed up in stages through the towering cypress trees. He heard the protesting neigh of a horse and knew that the reluctant animal was being coaxed up the steep track beside the uneven flights of stone steps. No beast took kindly to that slope but mount it they must if loaded with timber and roofing straw . . . Of course, it might be the animal ridden by some hardened samurai who considered it beneath his dignity to dismount!

That put his mind to thinking. The goings on amongst the samurai hardly affected him though he had half-a-mind to be grateful for their destructive nature when called on to make good the damage they inflicted through their bickering. Not that war had really touched this small Kikkawa domain, enclosed as it was in the folds of the valleys surrounding the north-eastern mass of Daisen and Hiru Mountain with its centre on the little township of Kawakami. The Kikkawa were by no means wealthy or powerful lords nor did their lands control any great highways. About the only noteworthy feature of this farm and forest fief was that a small part of the trackway from the San'in-dō running southwards into Mimasaka province passed briefly through the Kikkawa barrier at the eastern corner on its way south towards Yubara and on into Bizen. Hardly a strategic or important region at all. Most travellers were priests or yamabushi leaving that roadway – perhaps too grand a name – to make their way more directly to Daisen's holy temples and shrine.

There was a flash of autumn lightning and the inevitable roll of thunder. The beautiful warm morning gave way to a sudden storm over Daisen's towering ridges and Hiru-zan. If only Matabei could see in the gathering gloom he might find where some of the torrential rain now cascading from the great roof trickled into the defect . . ?

There was another flash followed by an earsplitting crash of thunder . . . A discreet cough told Matabei that he wasn't alone. The next brilliant flash revealed the face of the yamabushi who had somehow crept up into the complex of beams and braces to join him in his solitude.

Matabei was unperturbed and opened his mouth to greet his visitor when the mountain priest pressed his forefinger to his lips to signal silence.

'I was . . .' the carpenter began to say.

Again the yamabushi urgently cut him off but this time pointing at the valley below. The only unobstructed view of the path leading to the jinja and temple was immediately outside the modest entrance gate. The rest was hidden by the dense *sugi* forest although a few gaps in the canopy suggested where the course of the lower parts of the track or steps lay. Matabei peered through the hanging skeins of rain and thought that he caught a brief glimpse of at least one horseman and a number of people on foot before the storm's fury blotted everything out.

The mountain priest carefully made himself comfortable with his back firmly against one of the upright posts, sitting crosslegged on the tie beam; with deliberate care he tucked his wide hakama, supposedly once white but now travel-stained and threadbare, beneath his thighs, making sure that no part would be seen by a casual observer from below.

The carpenter eyed his unexpected companion with interest but some shouts floated up to their eyrie through the downpour and the crash of thunder. He leant out slightly and at once saw four or five ashigaru armed with spears running here and there in the compound, clearly searching for anyone concealed in the surrounding buildings. Taking his cue from the yamabushi who was by now fingering his *iritaka-nenju* rosary, he prudently drew himself back deeper into the complexity of the roof timbers and carefully made certain that none of his tools lay anywhere near the edge and were in danger of falling by accident. More men appeared and at once sought shelter from the elements. The rain by now was falling heavily at a shallow angle, driven by a gale of wind.

Moments later, as the storm reached its climax, another knot of figures, indistinct because of the rain, emerged into view and were made to stand in a group in the rain-soaked courtyard. They were clearly under the eyes of two spearmen. Matabei strained his eyes to make them out clearly but the light was too poor. The yamabushi leant forward and tapped his sleeve. For a moment the carpenter wondered what he was about and then realized that the stranger was tracing a line with a spittle-wetted finger. Frowning, he watched carefully before realizing that the man was drawing a *mon*. Two wavy bars contained in a hexagon . . . It dawned on him that it was the Kikkawa mon. but why that? Seeing his furrowed brow, the mountain priest pointed down at the miserable huddle out in the pouring rain . . . Two or three men, a small number of women, and at least three children. Were they peasants, or . . . ? Again the yamabushi plucked at his sleeve. He pointed at the mon and then at the yard.

'Oh, it cannot be!' thought Matabei, fear clutching at his heart.

A slight easing of the downpour confirmed his worst fears. These sodden people were, without any doubt, his lord's kinsfolk, some of whom over the course of the years he had only seen at a suitable distance whilst carrying out his tasks at the main yashiki.

For a few seconds his mind went blank; all he could think about was that he and his forbears had served the Kikkawa faithfully, as farmers, armed supporters in time of war, and as carpenters since the end of the wars of succession in the time of Lord Ashikaga Yoshimitsu. He felt numbed and had to grasp the edges of the wide beam with both hands in case he actually fell. A sudden bolt of lightning lit up the complex joinery and he clearly saw the place where the water trickled in . . . The shock of the flash brought him back to reality. Who had brought these unfortunates here? Surely Kikkawa-dono was fully protected and powerful enough not to fall victim to some unexpected attack? Surely what was happening was unthinkable?

The storm was easing and blue skies showed behind the heavy clouds beyond the next ridge. The rain would soon be gone and the warm autumn sunshine would dry up everything.

Down in the yard where a couple of bedraggled ashigaru armed with long spears guarded the roped Kikkawa prisoners, there could be no escape; in fascinated horror the yamabushi and he were forced to watch the drama that now unfolded.

As the first shafts of sunshine burst from the edge of the retreating tempest, three men wearing full armour emerged from their shelter under the stable roofs. One of them shouted some orders and two of the menials recommenced their interrupted search of the main buildings, finding two cringing priests and a bent fellow that Matabei knew to be employed here as a sweeper. They were herded out into the yard, unnecessarily forced to witness what was about to follow whilst standing ankle deep in a pool of rainwater. Both watchers kept very still as one of the samurai clambered up the staircase to the chamber below, banging open a shōji and even splintering some of the venerable painted panels that had stood here since the middle of the Heian era three or four hundred years ago.

'No one here, my lord,' this miscreant shouted.

'Get down, then! We've work to do!'

Amidst loud wails of lamentation, orders were harshly barked out and the three children roughly torn away from their mothers or nurses and dragged well clear. The ashigaru guards levelled their yari threateningly . . . The children, the youngest one no more than four or five, were forced to kneel in a line facing the adults. One older boy folded his hands in an attitude of prayer . . .

Matabei closed his eyes fast, guessing at what was to follow. The yamabushi was muttering some words calling on the mercy of the Lord Buddha or Fudō-myō-ō, the Protector of the Buddha's Law. It was all over in just a few minutes and coarse laughter floated up from that awful place. Matabei opened his eyes, not daring to look down, his gaze fixed on the mountainsides to where, under the sun's warmth, a curl of mist was already forming amongst the tops of the sugi. He fervently prayed to the Lady Kannon to receive their poor souls.

Hardly daring to glance down, further shouted orders told him that those murderous renegades were preparing to hurl their pitiful victims out into the abyss where the evidence of their crime would soon be consumed by wild beasts. It was then that a wave of anger swept over him. There were none to raise a hand to save those innocent people who were kinsfolk of the Kikkawa-ke; who would know of the cruel fate that had befallen them? So far as he knew, no one cared . . . Such a bloody deed implied that the Kikkawa were no more . . . There had been not the faintest rumour of any trouble, no whispers of a power struggle . . . That very morning, as dawn was breaking over the eastern heights, he had passed by the short road that led up to the imposing gate tower of the Kikkawa border fort and seen the banners proudly flying in the morning breeze. All was perfectly normal, all was in its allotted place just as it should be . . . Even old Jubei, the forester who had just walked past the outer works of the barrier, greeted him affably as he always did . . . Now, in the late afternoon of what had seemed a normal humdrum day, the whole world was turned upside down . . .

More shouting and bellowed orders down in the yard told him that rather than risk the descent through the wet forest, the samurai and their men intended to bivouac in the temple buildings for the night. Why was it that those in command, even of only a few men, found it necessary to bawl at the tops of their voices? From the movements in the gathering dusk Matabei noted that they had selected the Prayer Hall as their night quarters. Probably the best choice as the samurai, themselves, would doubtless commandeer the monk's sleeping cells.

At last, Matabei and the yamabushi could ease their aching and stiffened limbs. It was only a remote possibility that a further search would be made and their presence discovered. While they could not kindle a light and must sit in the thick gloom, at least they could converse provided they remained on the upper floor and spoke in whispers. A germ of an idea insidiously entered the carpenter's head. Maybe he could repay his ancestral debt to his lord's family? Whilst not one of them had ever addressed a single word to him, all orders were transmitted downwards by the *ō-karō* to the steward's master-of-works, nonetheless the Kikkawa-ke had always been good lords and carefully preserved the domain even in years of pestilence and famine that had wrought havoc elsewhere. Their devout support of the spiritual needs of themselves and their people, high and low, had meant that generations of his family had enjoyed their benevolent patronage.

'Master yamabushi,' Matabei directly faced the priest even though he could only just make out his form, 'are you a man who can be trusted?'

He heard an answering grunt in the dark.

'You know, I was wondering the selfsame thing about you!'

'Perhaps I asked that in the wrong words,' sighed the carpenter, 'but I was wondering . . .'

'You were thinking about those unfortunates whose souls are about to speed on their eternal journey. You were going to request my assistance, isn't that so?'

'But . . . but how did you . . . ?'

'How did I know, eh? Am I not a mountain priest who talks with great and small kami and wrestles with evil spirits? My friend, what you are thinking . . . hoping . . . is quite natural. There's no mystery!'

Matabei's native caution compelled him to dissemble, at least for the present. Wasn't it all too quick? It was his fault for starting the conversation.

'I wasn't going to ask anything . . .'

The yamabushi chuckled quietly.

'You are not a warrior, my friend; one trained to give nothing away. I know exactly what you are thinking.'

'You tell me, then!' Matabei ground out the words with some asperity, now beginning to be nettled by the other. Too clever by half, these roving priests. 'What was I a-goin' to say?'

'Keep calm, my friend, and above all remember to keep your voice down.'

The yamabushi began to tell off his string of wooden beads, muttering a short invocation as he did so. In the last of the sunset glow that filtered in from the open shōji, Matabei registered that this man carried both a long slungsword and a staff that bowed just a little in its upper part. This was clear as the man placed the staff on the floor by his side and the carpenter could see down its length.

'I'm sorry, master; I will remember,' he whispered. 'Er, may I be permitted to ask what sort of yamabushi you are?'

'What sort? Tchahh!' snorted the other. 'I am the difficult sort who wanders the most secret paths in order to drive out demons who seek to hurt mankind . . . I walk in the ancient ways, my friend, unattached to any faction or sect . . . Now, out with it! Tell me that idea that has rooted in your brain . . . You plan revenge, don't you?'

The colour had gone from the western skies as the two men silently descended from their hiding place and slipped from the back of the shrine down into the depths of the forest. They carefully circled round and about a hundred or so feet lower down from the gateway they picked up the main track. Exercising great care, not so much of discovery but for fear of pitching down the mountain cliffs to certain injury or worse, they finally reached a sort of flat platform where, spanning the rushing Hiru-gawa as it hurled itself over a series of short rocky falls, a narrow humped wooden bridge spanned the gulf.

'Matabei-san, you have never served the Kikkawa under arms, have you?' asked the yamabushi as they took a rest on the jumbled rocks on the further side of the bridge. 'What I mean is, have you no experience of war?'

The carpenter shook his head. He was still trying to marshal ideas in his mind about what sort of action he could possibly take. His preoccupation had twice endangered his descent, it was only the sharp reaction of his companion that had stopped him slipping down to probable oblivion.

'What you say is true, master,' he reluctantly admitted.

'I thought as much! Well, we must consider the situation seriously . . . Up there are at least eight or ten armed men who will, one guesses, come down here after dawn. It seems to me that you intend violence towards them but I have to point out that you are just one man and without any fighting skill. Possibly you hope for my assistance, eh? Still, even supposing I give this help, these are poor odds, you will doubtless agree?'

Matabei drew a deep breath that sounded more like a sigh. He shook his head ruefully.

'But I . . . we . . . must do something . . !'

'If there were more of us, even three more, all armed with yari or naginata, we might hold such a place,' mused the yamabushi. 'It has been done before as I recall. The famous example was the fight at the bridge over the Uji-gawa during the Gempei War.' He laughed when he saw Matabei perk up. 'But,' he continued, 'we are just two and only one of us knows how to use a halberd!'

With that, he slipped off the slightly curved sheath of what passed for a long staff the yamabushi term a *bonden*, revealing, in the half-light, a wicked-looking slim bladed nagamaki, elegantly formed and about two-and-a-half to three shaku in length. He whirled the weapon around in a series of flashing arcs, executing both 'windmill' and 'butterfly' strokes.

Matabei watched, open mouthed. 'You . . . you . . . you're an expert,' he managed to stutter at last.

'Not an expert, my friend, although I must admit that I have received some teaching from a real master.'

'A great deal of teaching,' thought Matabei. Aloud, he ventured: 'The Uji Bridge, sir; wasn't that where Tajima-sama gained his name, the "Arrow-Cutter"?'

'You've heard the story? Well, well! In that case you doubtless admire Lord Kusunoki Masashige in the defence of Chihaya castle? So now, what is going through your mind, Master Carpenter, eh?'

Matabei stood and rubbed his stubbly chin.

'That fight was at the bridge, master, wasn't it? It took three men to break up the planking . . . We aren't three, as you say, but look down there if you would!'

He pointed down into the depths.

The yamabushi shook his head, muttering something to himself which might just have been about insanity amongst artisans. Dawn was at least an hour away and he could see nothing in the inky depths of that narrow canyon.

'What are you saying?' he asked 'You'll have to tell me as I've not the slightest idea of what you're driving at!'

Matabei grinned to himself secretly.

'Tajima-sama and his companions held back an entire army until driven away by arrows, didn't they?'

'Y-es . . !'

'But their enemies crossed in the end?'

'True . . ?'

'Well, I . . . er . . . I thought just now what you said about needing more fighting men if we were to hold those murderers off, but even then, would we be able to defeat them? Once any of them were across we would be pursued and hunted down, wouldn't we?'

'So what are you saying, carpenter?'

Matabei paused and swallowed. He could now give form to the awesome thought that had entered his mind up there after the death of . . . The thought was hateful to him, one that went directly against his whole nature. He broke out into a cold sweat and shivered despite himself. 'I agree that we are much less strong, master, 'cos I don't know anything about fighting . . . and I know what those samurai would do to me if I made any threat, my being a peasant at that. But I think I can suggest a way that might get rid of all of them without a single blow being struck by either of us!'

The yamabushi sat back and stared at his companion through the night gloom.

'Now that sounds interesting, my good friend. You don't happen to be a tengu disguised to be a carpenter, do you?'

Matabei, feeling rather more confident now that he was explaining a topic that he knew inside out, outlined what he thought could be done. It was fortunate that when they slipped away from the shrine he had the presence of mind to catch up his precious bag of tools. They were far too valuable to be abandoned up there. Dawn was still far off but already clouds were thickening to cover the stars. If it rained, as it often did around daybreak in these high mountains, those violent men up in the temple might just delay their descent at least until full daylight, particularly if they had to bring down horses.

If the murderous samurai and their ashigaru would experience difficulty in coming down, it would be as nothing compared with Matabei and the yamabushi's dangerous climb down into the rocky chasm to reach the foundations of the bridge, all in near total darkness. It was at this point that the shugenja also came into his own. He swiftly uncoiled a long length of strong rope that he carried looped across one shoulder and his chest.

'We use this when we climb the crags in the wildest parts of the mountains,' he explained. 'We yamabushi never look for an easy route around difficult places but go up or down as directly as we can. That's especially so in the Ōmine rites and on Daisen!'

'And that's one reason why many ignorant folk think you have the power of flight!'

In the faint light Matabei saw the yamabushi's lips draw back in a smile.

With the greatest care one at a time they lowered themselves down the treacherous lichen covered rocks and precariously clung to the wet timbers, soon to find a slippery perch wedged against the foundations on the western foot of the bridge, the side that they had crossed over to earlier. Looping his own shorter cord around the upright to give him a degree of greater safety, Matabei set to work, more by feel than anything, to see if his iron awl could locate any rotten joint. He knew that the bridge had last been repaired twice in his father's day but not once in recent years. He'd have known about that for certain.

After a few minutes probing he gave a grunt of satisfaction. His legs ached abominably from his cramped position as did the thighs of the yamabushi, but neither complained.

'Can you work your way to the other side of me, master,' he requested.

'Probably!' came the laconic reply.

About twenty feet below them the boiling torrent spilled over the third successive ledge and on its way hurled itself against a spur of rock, sending up a fine spray when the river was in spate. Everything ran with moisture and it was this constant dampness that Matabei hoped to exploit.

More by touch than anything else, they found some sort of firm lodgement and the carpenter guided the yamabushi's hand to where he was to pick and prize away as much decayed wood as he could. On the other side of that weak junction, practically suspended by his rope and often having to pause in order to breath properly, Matabei hammered away with his heavy maul and chisel. As he suspected, this lowest frame was jointed to a horizontal timber that was itself spiked to the cliff face in order to provide a sill, a base for the main supports. It had been fashioned with a single thick tenon mortised into this sill. Just by feeling, Matabei realized that this would be the weakest point but had survived the years, like the other three similar joints, from the pressure exerted by the weight bearing down from above. If this tusk could be destroyed then, possibly, the whole bridge would become unstable.

It took a full hour's hard labour to prize away the ancient sodden wood but at last Matabei felt a slight movement at the base of the timber leg, a slip that wedged his chisel against the sill. In haste, he warned the yamabushi to move away . . . Suppose the chisel now acted as a wedge? It was quite possible and all their work would have been in vain.

'I'll knock it free,' said the priest.

'But I should do that . . .'

'No, you can't! I have the longer rope so I'll do it. You just pull me up afterwards!'

Gripping the handle of the maul between his teeth, the shugenja lowered himself down and placing his two feet against the rock face, he took a couple of swings at the offending chisel wedge.

'Try to knock it sideways, master . . . sideways,' called down an anxious Matabei, but he knew that he would lose that precious tool forever.

With the third swing, the maul glanced off its target and flew from the yamabushi's hand plummeting down into the foaming waters . . .

'Haul me towards you,' shouted the dangling priest.

As Matabei tugged hard so the yamabushi was able to kick out with one heel and, luckily, hammered the wedged chisel sideways. It fell clear but they both felt the heavy framework of the bridge lurch a little to one side. Desperation and, perhaps, a measure of fear, spurred the yamabushi to scrabble his way up to Matabei who caught his outstretched wrist and soon helped him to safety. Whether their efforts had been enough depended now on the kami. There was nothing else they could do.

High above them in the forested slopes floated the mournful signal call of a horagai and almost at once another replied from further down the river valley.

'Your lord's enemies are closer than we thought, Matabei-san! There's nothing much else we can do but await the decision of the gods!' With a grunt, the yamabushi looked about him before adding: 'We had better not be found idling here if they get across or, of course, if their friends arrive first.' He pointed to a rocky outcrop that dominated the bridgehead. 'If we can get up there we can watch events. We might even manage to get away afterwards if Marishi-ten looks on us kindly!'

The predictable dawn rain began and almost without warning it was coming down like an arrow storm. Both men were already soaked through with sweat from their exertions, the rain hardly made any difference. They reached the top of the outcrop after a stiff climb and concealed themselves beneath a lone bush where they could view the bridge. All Matabei could think of was the loss of his precious maul and chisel, his tired brain refusing to admit anything else, even the horror up in the shrine yard. He thrust aside any lurking fear of what might happen if they were caught.

They didn't have to wait long, either. Some ten or so horsemen appeared from the forest track coming up from the valley. They were accompanied by a number of ashigaru who were clearly glad to get their breath back before crossing and tackling the stiff climb to the temple far above. Most of the new arrivals dismounted and followed the footsoldiers across the rickety bridge and began to file up the steep path on the further side where they soon disappeared into the rain leaving just two menials to guard their mounts.

'Remain here!' whispered the yamabushi to Matabei. 'I have a little work to do!'

Mystified, the carpenter strained to see what this shugenja intended. A couple of minutes passed before he reappeared, supported by his long stave, striding purposefully through the rain towards the bridge. The ashigaru challenged him and he paused a moment in a humble attitude, mumbling as he fumbled with his rosary in the manner of these mysterious forest priests. Matabei watched closely as the yamabushi shuffled towards the guards and, without any warning, pulled off the sheath of his halberd and erupt into violent action resulting in the two unfortunate footsoldiers pitching over the treacherous wet edge to the rocks below. It was all over in a few seconds. The ragged and by now bedraggled priest separated four horses from the rest and drove them individually across the bridge where they at once began to graze as though nothing had happened. The remaining beasts he sent off back down the forest trail and, moments later, reappeared on top of the outcrop, lying down beside the carpenter as if nothing had happened.

While it seemed likely that they wouldn't be observed by anyone descending the mountain, they couldn't be absolutely certain so the yamabushi cannily enjoined Matabei to lie completely motionless despite his cramped limbs. The rain had eased to a steady drizzle and the daylight strengthened when they caught the first sounds from the further hillside. A string of imprecations suggested that someone had fallen on the treacherous slope and these were quickly followed by some unkind laughter until silenced by a peremptory order! Someone exclaimed at noticing the four loose horses and further orders were shouted for the animals to be caught, something the beasts were unwilling to happen. By now the whole party had reached the flat space on the further side.

'Where, in the name of Emma-ō, are those two fools?'

'Oi, Tahei . . . Heibei . .!'

One of the armoured samurai stamped with vexation.

'They've run off 'cos they've lost the other horses, master!'

The yamabushi grinned mischieviously at Matabei.

'I think this will stir them up,' he whispered, catching up his own hora which lay beside him. To Matabei's consternation, the priest rolled over onto his back, placed the mouthpiece to his lips, and produced a mighty blast which had an instant galvanizing effect on the men on the further bank.

Swords were whipped out from their scabbards, spears levelled and orders barked out with the footsoldiers and samurai trying to take up defensive positions in the expectation of an immediate onslaught .... Nothing happened for a few seconds and the excitement began to settle down, but then, from afar, Matabei distinctly heard another horagai. Both men listened intently.

'That's the call "*Gather*",' breathed the yamabushi into Matabei's ear.

'But what did you blow, master?'

'Me? You saw their reaction ... I blew "*Prepare to Attack*"! I'll add to that! There's nothing like confusion at times like this!'

With great care, belly flat to the wet rock, the shugenja wormed himself backwards. Once completely out of sight, he sounded another call; three short blasts and a longer one that ended with an upwards whoop. Again, the results were dramatic. The leading samurai bawled out something and was assisted up onto his saddled horse. Somehow the ashigaru managed to control the loose mounts and these, too, soon had armoured men on their backs.

Another conch sounded, closer this time, followed immediately by another.

'What are they, master?'

'Matabei-san, does it really matter, eh? It's what this lot do now that is important ... Just be content to watch!'

Hardly had the horagai blasts ceased to echo back and forth across the valley, mournful yet menacing, than the samurai leader raised his riding whip and pointed at their rock. He must have glimpsed some slight betraying movement. Shouting out an order, whip raised, all five horsemen surged onto the bridge and were closely followed by their men. Their intention was abundantly clear: they would make short work of any spies they captured. Poor Matabei felt the cold hand of fear clutch his heart and wondered why he had even thought of taking vengeance on these treasonous murderers ... His eyes, tight closed as he heard a sudden shout of alarm, opened wide.

The five horsemen had crossed the humped centre of the bridge in a bunch while all but one straggler behind them dashed to keep up. The sudden shift of weight from one side to the other brought huge pressure on the damaged support and it gave way without warning. With the tenon gone the rotten stump slipped away causing the riders to veer to their right. The safety balustrade gave way and first one man skidded into the abyss then all the rest ... With a tearing and splintering noise, the entire framework disintegrated sending men, and horses to their doom. There was no escape ... just one ashigaru stood helplessly, mouth agape, clinging precariously to the loosened end post, staring disbelievingly into space . . . For a moment all was still before the post gave way pitching him to his death.

With faltering steps, his legs feeling weak, Matabei stood by the last remnants of the bridge, sweating despite the cold drizzle. He felt unable to comprehend what had happened before his very eyes.

'That second call, master . . ?'

' "*Attack*", that's all!'

'But . . . but we heard two more signals blown, didn't we? What . . . what were they?'

The yamabushi laughed mirthlessly.

'I don't know. Perhaps you and your enemies thought you had heard something? Maybe there wasn't any call, my friend, and it or they were only in your mind? Come, we shouldn't stay here. I advise you to go and seek out your lord, if he still lives. Say nothing of all this to anyone you meet, even your kin; only to him.'

Matabei shook his head.

'You are not coming with me, master? No one will believe a poor carpenter.'

'Don't worry on that score, Matabei-san; you can show them plenty of proof.'

The yamabushi had straightened his rainsodden clothing and other belongings. He stood leaning on his nagamaki-bonden.

'You'll find me on Daisen, my friend, if you feel the need to change your life and become a shugenja, but I fancy that you'll soon forget all this and will be given a great deal of work by Kikkawa-dono. Never fear, for some men destiny can be cruel, for others, like yourself, the kami smile.'

In a few moments he had gone, not down the valley track but away into the mountainous wilds.